To dear Dorothy

Lovers Lost in Time:
Delightful tales with a supernatural twist

Deryn Lake

with every good wish in the world,

Deryn Lake

© Deryn Lake 2018

Deryn Lake has asserted her rights under the Copyright, Design and Patents Act, 1988, to be identified as the author of this work.

First published as a collection in 2018 by Endeavour Media Ltd.

The Moonlit Baths was first published in 1987 in three parts by *Women's Realm*.
The Gemini Syndrome was first published in 1990 by *Women's Realm Magazine*.
The Wardrobe was first published in 1990 in two parts by *Women's Realm Magazine*.
The Anklets was first published in 1990 by *Women's Realm Magazine*.
The Staircase was first published in 1990 in two parts by *Women's Realm Magazine*.
The Mermaid's Kiss was first published in 2017 by Endeavour Press Ltd.

Table of Contents

The Moonlit Baths…………………………………….5

The Gemini Syndrome……………………………77

The Wardrobe……………………………………..149

The Anklets………………………………………211

The Staircase……………………………………..291

The Mermaid's Kiss……………………………...379

About the Author…………………………………475

The Moonlit Baths

The evening was like a seashell, pink and clear, and full of strands of rainbow colour which seemed to reflect on the hills and again on the silver coil of the River Avon, suffusing the terraced city of Bath with the tints of a wild rose.

Lady Arabella Wynter, her eyes directed beyond her brother Frederick's shoulder to see better through the coach's inadequate window, gave a delighted gasp, while her elder brother Julian, sitting opposite her and beside their father, exclaimed, "The Devil! What a handsome place!" Their parent, Lord Midhurst, duly smiled at all this, raised his quizzing glass for a peremptory glance about him and said, "Handsome enough. Nothing else would have induced me to build a house here, for you know how easily I tire of ugly surroundings."

Julian and Arabella exchanged a glance and he gave the merest flicker of his eyelid. Their father, the Earl, was a man of fashion and a wit, and made a great show of boredom, though his sleepy eyes masked a strength and determination which he was at pains to disguise. In fact now, in the midst of all their excitement, the Earl pretended to doze as his family coach — the Midhurst coat of arms emblazoned upon the side — started the descent to Bath, that most fashionable of towns, and the house which had been built especially for him that he might enjoy the season in the greatest possible comfort.

A loud peal of bells from the Abbey made him open his eyes again, however, and George, the youngest of the four children, took this opportunity to say, "Why are they doing that, Papa? Is it for us?"

"Oh yes," replied his father calmly. "The bells are always rung to welcome a stranger's arrival. And soon you will hear the voices and music of the city waits greeting us."

"Waits?" said George doubtfully, and Frederick answered, "Singers, silly. Don't you know anything?"

The Earl flapped a languid hand at them, which brought instant silence as the coach drew to a halt before a house set back in its own grounds at the end of a gracious avenue. Arabella saw colonnades and arches and three great windows on the first floor which led out to a balcony.

"Oh Father, how beautiful!" she breathed. "Why, I declare it is even finer than Midhurst Place."

The Earl laughed and gave her an amused pat on the head. "Go to, chatterbox. You haven't been inside yet."

He stood up and a flunkey pulled down the carriage steps, and even as he alighted the waits appeared with their musicians and began a noisy chorus of welcome which brought a flush of pleasure to Arabella's cheeks and made Julian laugh. She wished then that she could have been more like her brother, noisier and less inhibited, but the death of their mother giving birth to George, when Arabella had been only six, had made her withdrawn. The girl sometimes thought that Lady Midhurst had wanted this, had wanted her to be thoughtful and quiet, and unlike the boisterous boys. In this way, or so it seemed to Arabella, her mother could come back to her and they could talk. Of course these conversations were only inside her head, but sometimes they seemed terribly real.

Arabella's attention came abruptly back to the present as the Earl threw a handful of coins to the waits, who fell upon them like starving cats.

"Come on, come on," he was saying and led the way through an army of crimson-coated footmen into the elegant entrance. In an excited whirl the children followed him and Arabella stood in the doorway, open-mouthed, looking to where a delicately curving staircase rose up from the spacious hall to a dome, painted with scenes of Neptune sporting amongst bare-breasted mermaids and muscular mermen, jolly little boys on dolphins swimming in their midst. Arabella thought it rather shocking.

It was at that moment, with her foot on the bottom stair, that she heard the roar of laughter. As if from a great distance there was a guffaw of men's voices, just as though a joke had been told and masculine company had seen the meaning simultaneously. Arabella looked round, startled. There was no one in the hall except Frederick and George and she thought it most unlikely that the servants would dare behave so badly with m'Lord in residence.

"What was that?" she called to Julian who was just disappearing onto the first floor landing.

"What was what?"

"That noise. As if a lot of people laughed together."

"I didn't hear anything," he answered carelessly. "Come on, Arabella. Don't you want to see your bedroom?"

Shaking her head she hurried after him, thinking she had been mistaken. But all other thoughts were driven from her mind as, following the Earl and her brother, she entered a room of such sweet simple elegance that Arabella knew she had never seen anything so perfect. Long windows looked out over emerald lawns and brilliant flowerbeds, a gleaming crystal chandelier caught the evening light, while a marble fireplace in which a welcoming fire was already lit warmed a bed, delicately draped in white, beside which her maid stood unpacking.

In a gesture more typical of Julian, Arabella flung herself at the Earl who held her at arm's length attempting to look indifferent. But a grin cracked his face and he said, "Are you pleased, sweetheart? Is the room to your liking?"

"You know it is," she answered, smothering his cheek with kisses.

"Enough," he said, dusting his waistcoat as if she had made a mark. "Now hurry up. I am not used to dining late and I shall faint from hunger, so I will, if we don't eat within the hour."

Lord Midhurst's words were always a command and exactly thirty minutes later the entire family sat down at table, the Earl at the head and Julian at the foot, the servants hovering about them. Nobody spoke until the first course had been cleared, at which point Julian and his brothers plied their father with questions about their new home. He, however, refused to answer until he had a goodly portion of mutton stuffed with cockles and herrings set before him. Then finally he spoke.

"I found the site by accident, Julian. I liked it because it seemed set apart from the general hurly-burly, yet was still within the confines of the old Roman city."

Arabella, who had been studying the candlelight reflected in her wine glass, found herself listening intently.

"Yes, of course," Julian was answering. "Bath was famous in Roman times. Now what was it called...?"

"It was Aquae Sulis," answered George surprisingly. "We had a lesson on it with one of the tutors. He said that the Romans used to come here to bathe and take the waters just as we do."

The Earl raised his quizzing glass. "Well spoken, child. It is always rewarding to know that at least one of my sons listens to his teachers." The lens flashed briefly over Julian and Frederick and then came to rest on Arabella. "And what about you, my dear? Had you heard of Aquae Sulis?"

"No, Father. But I'd like to."

The Earl adopted the bored expression which he used to conceal the fact he was genuinely interested in a subject.

"They say there was a thriving community here, centred round a temple dedicated to the goddess Minerva. Why this very year a workman digging a sewer trench near Stall Street found a life-sized bronze head of her. And there was a villa on this site too. The builders discovered foundations and artifacts which proved that ours is not the first house to be built here."

The four children were silent, each one wondering what kind of dwelling could have been there before and who had lived within, but it was Julian who leapt to the obvious conclusion and said. "The Devil, Papa! Do you think this place is haunted?"

The Earl looked annoyed and said, "Really, Julian, you should know better. You'll give the little one nightmares," while George protested vigorously that he was twelve and at least as fearless as both his brothers

Arabella said nothing to this, remembering that sudden disembodied burst of laughter when she had stood in the hall.

"I think it is," she put in quietly.

"Oh pooh," answered Frederick rudely. "You're always seeing things, Arabella."

Lord Midhurst's face hardened. "I am excessively tired of this conversation already. Ghosts are figments of the imagination and nothing more. Frederick, you will leave the table and go to bed at once. I will not tolerate bad manners. Rudeness to your sister — to any member of the opposite sex in fact — is neither clever nor permissible."

The boy gulped miserably, muttered, "I'm sorry, Arabella", and went out fighting back tears, only too aware that the servants were studying the floor in an over-obvious manner.

The jovial mood was broken and the rest of the meal was punctuated only with desultory conversation. So much so that Arabella was relieved when her father and Julian ordered their port and she was able to leave the table, claiming fatigue, and make for the privacy of her room. Once there she willingly allowed her maid to assist her to undress and, with the warming pan newly run over the sheets, got swiftly into bed.

With the candle blown out the lovely lines of the room became blurred by firelight, the flames throwing strange leaping shapes onto the walls and curtains. Arabella closed her eyes and then opened them abruptly. Surely she must be mistaken, yet she could have sworn that hidden in the dark recesses of the house, men were singing. Arabella sat up in bewilderment, straining her ears. A total silence enveloped her broken only by the crackle of the fire. She lay down again and the sound came once more; somewhere loud merry voices were raised in raucous song.

Pulling the pillow over her head, Arabella tried to be rational. The noise was obviously coming from outside: it was a party of rakes on their way to a gambling house, it was men of fashion returning home to change before the evening rout. Yet fear still lay along her spine like an icy finger and it was only the fact that she was exhausted by the journey that finally allowed her to drop off to sleep.

How long she was unconscious she never afterwards knew, but it must have been some hours for as she woke, swiftly and completely, she realised that the room was in darkness and the fire had long since died out. Arabella could see nothing, could hear nothing, yet knew with sickening lurch of the heart, that somebody was in the room with her.

"Who's there?" she called, her voice shaking.

There was no answer and with a trembling hand Arabella struck a tinder and lit the candle that stood by her bed. The shapes of the room focused and became clear and it was then that she saw the gleam of a red tunic, a pair of muscular legs, and realised that a man in some outlandish garb was standing by the bed staring at her.

The scream froze in her throat and she leapt out and made for the door, passing within a foot of him as she did so. She received a vivid impression of strong hard features, a pair of brilliant eyes beneath slanting black brows and — overriding all else — the smell of his skin, clean, yet with the scent of leather about it.

Without looking over her shoulder Arabella ran towards Julian's room.

"My God, what's happened?" her brother demanded.

"There's a man in my room! He was standing by the bed and staring at me. It frightened me terribly."

Julian did not even answer, making for the open door of Arabella's chamber and going in with his fists up. She heard him pushing back chairs and opening the balcony windows, calling out "If you're hiding I'll find you, damn you!" but there was no reply.

Nervously, Arabella retraced her steps. The room was empty except for Julian.

"I think it must have been the man of your dreams, little sister," he said, smiling. "There's nobody hiding in here and he couldn't have run out or we would have seen him. Perhaps it was the ghost that Father doesn't believe exists."

"But I could smell him." insisted Arabella. "He was real."

Julian's face cracked into a smile. "Damme, now I've heard everything. A phantom who doesn't wash his feet!"

"There was someone here, I tell you," Arabella said angrily.

Without answering, Julian took her by the elbow and propelled her round the room, opening doors, and making her peer beneath the bed.

"There!" he said. "Are you satisfied? Now go back to sleep."

As the door closed behind her brother, Arabella took a flying leap into bed, pulled the coverlets over her head and shut her eyes. And when, as it seemed to her, she opened them a few minutes later it was morning and everything was normal.

The family took no breakfast at home, this being the day that m'Lord of Midhurst would pay his subscriptions for the season and then, this duty done, break his fast with hot chocolate and Sally Lunn cakes and butter in the Pump Room, both to be seen and to see the passing parade and its fashions.

It being only a short stroll, the Earl — gorgeously attired in scarlet and gold — strode forth with Arabella on his arm, the younger men walking behind. And it was in this formation that they entered the Pump Room to find the Master of Bath, the great Beau Nash himself, waiting to greet them. Arabella thought him comic, a jowl-faced man in a grubby white hat, but she knew his fierce reputation and made a respectful curtsey.

It being too late to bathe, the family took the waters — Frederick and George declaring that it tasted like bad eggs — and then sat for public breakfast.

No sooner had they found a table, however, than Julian leapt to his feet shouting, "The Devil! There's Rufus Abinger. Why, I haven't seen him since Eton," and vanished at great speed amongst the jostling crowd in pursuit of a tall, burly, fair-haired young man.

"Hey, hey," yawned the Earl, "how the *beau monde* gathers here," then started as a voice said in his ear, "Indeed it does, Lord Midhurst. How very pleasant to see you again."

The voice held a soft, purring quality and Arabella found herself staring at a sleek little creature with dark hair and green eyes and more than her fair share of beauty.

The Earl meanwhile had risen and bowed to the newcomer. "Why, Lady Woodruff. How dee do? I haven't seen you for..."

"Three years, my Lord. I have been in mourning for my husband. This is my first season since his sad departure." The cold green eyes swept Arabella. "And this must be Lady Midhurst. Will you present me?"

The Earl laughed. "This is my daughter, madam. I am a widower. Arabella, make your curtsey to Lady Woodruff if you please."

Like the raising of a blind the lovely face before Arabella was suddenly wreathed in smiles. "My dear, how sweet to see you. Why, I declare, Lord Midhurst, your daughter is the prettiest girl in Bath. We must become the greatest friends, Arabella. We can bathe together and go to the ladies' coffee house and chat of this and that without the troublesome company of men."

She slipped her arm through Arabella's.

"My dear Lady Woodruff, how very kind. Since the death of her mother Arabella has sadly lacked female companionship. Speak up my girl. Tell Lady Woodruff how grateful you are."

Arabella opened her mouth but was saved the misery of murmuring hypocritical thanks by the return of her brother bearing in his wake a great windmill of a young man who, at the sight of Arabella, turned the colour of a peony.

"Father," said Julian, all enthusiasm, "this is Lord Rufus Abinger, my old school friend. Oh..." he stopped short on seeing Lady Woodruff who gave him a heart-stopping smile and said, "What a handsome family you have to be sure, my Lord."

The Earl bowed over her hand and said, "Will you join us for breakfast, Lady Woodruff?"

They all sat down, packed very tightly round a small table, and it was only the chatter of the two smaller boys which hid the fact that both Julian and Rufus had been struck dumb, one staring at Lady Woodruff and the other at Arabella, while Lord Midhurst and the beautiful widow had eyes for no-one but each other.

Arabella thought she had never seen such a throng as they left the relative safety of the Pump Room and moved in the general direction of the Queen's Bath. On every side belles of fashion rubbed shoulders with maiden aunts and ladies of midnight, whilst noblemen and rakes could scarcely be differentiated from the charlatans and mountebanks come to Bath to prey upon the gullible and unsuspecting.

In the press, Arabella found herself separated from Lord Rufus and standing alone, her family lost to view. She waited a moment, wondering what to do, and then on impulse she could not explain descended a gloomy flight of steps lying just beyond the Queen's Bath and leading away from the hurly-burly. Instantly she was immersed in a great cloud of white vapour and paused, a little afraid.

The sound of voices and distant splashing puzzled Arabella, unaware that there were more than two baths in this part of the city, and she descended the rest of the flight and hurried along a paved and pillared corridor, thinking that really she ought to go back and join the others. But the noise of water coming from an archway on her right aroused her curiosity and telling herself that she would just take a peep. Arabella paused and looked through.

A large circular bath was the dominant feature of the room into which she found herself staring; a circular bath with four lots of stone steps leading down into it and a fish fountain at the far end spurting out bubbling fresh water. But it was not to the bath that Arabella's horrified gaze was drawn, but to the occupants of the room itself. Naked men were everywhere — diving into the water, swimming, sitting on benches at the side, towelling themselves dry.

Arabella felt a hot flush burn her cheeks and would have looked away at once had not her attention been drawn to one man just climbing out of the bath. She saw slanting black eyebrows and vivid topaz eyes; her visitor of the previous night was swimming that day.

He saw her. At that very moment he looked up and their eyes met where she stood in the archway, the only woman in that crowd of sporting carefree men. Arabella saw a horrified expression cross his face as his hands grabbed for a towel held by a servant. Only when he had covered his nakedness did he look over at her again and Arabella knew that Julian had been wrong. This was no ghost nor figment of her imaginings. This was a living man.

She turned and ran as fast as she could back up the steps, through the strange white cloud, not stopping until she was outside the Abbey where Julian and an anxious Lord Rufus stood awaiting her.

"Where *have* you been?" said her brother. "We were terribly worried. I thought you might have been kidnapped."

Arabella opened her mouth to tell him what she had seen and then thought better of it. She suddenly had the feeling that she should keep her sight of the bath a secret. Instead she answered, "I got lost for a few minutes. I'm very sorry."

"I was anxious," said Lord Rufus heartily. "But as long as no harm has come to you, Lady Arabella."

"None at all." She was silent for a moment then said, "Is this your first visit to Bath, my Lord?"

"No, my second."

"Then perhaps you would know how many baths there actually are in the city?"

"Five." Rufus answered rather promptly. "The King's and the Queen's in this part and over to the south-west the Hot, the Cross and the Leper's, which is not much frequented."

"And the King's Bath. Is it round with a fountain like a fish at one end?"

Rufus stared at her. "No, my Lady. It is square with a small building with seats in its midst."

Arabella looked astonished. "Then where is the circular bath?"

"I don't know unless you mean the Hot Bath."

"I don't think I do, for did you not say that it was some distance from here?"

"Yes," answered Rufus, very puzzled.

Just as she was wondering if she should offer some sort of explanation, Arabella was saved by the appearance of the Earl, a smug-looking Lady Woodruff clinging to his arm.

"Into divine service," he said briskly, "and then we shall all pass the time until the dining hour by reading in the book-sellers' shops before being seen upon the parade." He looked at Arabella closely. "You appear rather pale, my child. Is anything wrong?"

"No, Papa," she answered, dropping a small curtsey.

"Charming," cooed Lydia Woodruff. "She is quite, quite delightful, Charles."

"Oh, it's 'Charles' now, is it?" muttered Frederick to George, only to be silenced by a cold glance from Julian.

"Thank you," answered the Earl. "Well, I hope you will look after her this evening, Lydia, this is her first ball in Bath."

Lady Woodruff smiled. "And she will be the Belle of it."

"Of the young girls, perhaps," answered the Earl with a bow. "But of the women you will shine the fairest, my dear Lydia."

Behind her, Arabella heard George murmur, "Oh, la la and odds my life!" But fortunately nobody heard.

Knowing her young brothers' ideas of fun it was quite a relief to Arabella to see them sent to bed for the night, leaving her not only to prepare herself for the rout but to be alone in the quiet of her room. Memories of last night's visitation came to her at once and she tried to think of a rational explanation.

Having seen him in the mysterious circular bath — Arabella went pink at the very recollection — she was certain that the stranger was real and very far from a phantom. But what was he doing wandering in the Earl of Midhurst's house in fancy dress? It occurred to her then that he might be a servant who had entered her room by mistake. Yet, if that were so, why was it that Julian was unable to find him? With her head still buzzing, Arabella stepped into her father's light coach and set off with the Earl and Julian for the Assembly Rooms.

The ball was to begin at six o'clock promptly, by order of Mr Nash, and to ensure this the Beau himself was there to greet the arriving guests, wearing a very full wig and richly embroidered coat. Nonetheless, Arabella still thought him a comic figure but was made to revise her opinion, when, on the very last chime of the clock, Mr Nash went forward like a king, bowed low to old Lady Daventry and then the Earl, and led them forth in the minuet to begin the dancing. He had paid his respects to the most noble lord and lady present and by doing this encouraged the assembled company to join in.

Arabella became aware that Rufus was bowing before her, asking if she would be his partner. With a grateful smile she accepted, but as he led her onto the floor her thoughts went to the stranger and she looked round the dancers to see if he was amongst them. But there was no sign and firmly putting him from her mind, Arabella concentrated on enjoying her very first ball at Bath.

After his initial dance with Lady Daventry, the Earl at once led out Lydia Woodruff leaving Julian, who had been about to engage her, glowering in a corner.

"Damn," he said, as Arabella and Rufus joined him, "I do declare Father is making an idiot of himself. Why, Lady Woodruff can be little over thirty and Papa is..."

"Only forty-six." Arabella said quietly. "He is hardly an old man, Julian."

"Well, I don't like it. I don't like it at all."

Unexpectedly, Rufus put in. "My mother declares that Lady Woodruff is tired of being a widow of limited means and is after a good match this season. She set her cap at Lord Baltimore last week, not realising that he had a sickly wife who did not join him at the routs."

"Gracious!" said Arabella. "Is she a fortune hunter?"

"It would not surprise me."

The three young people stared at each other gloomily as Lydia Woodruff, looking absolutely splendid in a lilac gown with silver tissue petticoat beneath, her dark hair woven with fresh flowers, danced elegantly past and gave them a seraphic smile.

"Oh dear," said Arabella. "I do hope I can escape her in the morning."

Only just audibly, Julian murmured, "I'd never escape her if I had my way."

Almost to ensure that her wish came true, Arabella rose early after a peaceful and dreamless sleep, and dressed in her bathing clothes — a stiff canvas gown that hid her from neck to foot — was taken in a closed sedan chair to the bath. Relieved to see that there was no sign of Lady Woodruff, Arabella was escorted into the Queen's Bath by an attendant where she sat, up to her neck in water, placing her handkerchief and nosegay on a little floating dish which also had a place for a snuff box. Because this was her first visit a guide helped her to walk across the bath and then, as she stepped out into a side room, Arabella was stripped and immediately wrapped in a flannel nightgown so that she would not take cold after the heat of the bathe.

"Will my Lady be going home at once or would you like to sit by the fire?" asked her guide.

With another sudden impulse, Arabella answered, "I'll rest here for a while."

"Very good, my Lady. I'll make you comfortable."

Thinking of her reward at the end of the season the attendant put a cushion behind Arabella's back and brought a footstool. But no sooner had she gone out than Arabella rose from her chair and left the private room, creeping round the side of the bath to the place where only the day before she had temporarily lost Julian and Rufus.

Today it was too early for the milling throng and passing only one or two other bathers, Arabella made her way to the top of the stone steps. A sign that she had not noticed before, reading "Danger. Do not enter", greeted her as she went to descend. Slightly puzzled, Arabella decided to ignore it and went down four paces — and then the flight ended. It simply was not there. In the place where yesterday Arabella had gone down to the circular bath there was now a filled-in floor. It was as if overnight the flight of steps had been blocked off.

Incredulously she climbed back up, thinking that she must have gone to the wrong place. But, on looking round, Arabella was certain that this was the same spot. There was no logical explanation for such an extraordinary turn of events. She stood helplessly, staring at all that was left of the enigmatical steps and then, not knowing what else to do, wandered back to her slip room like a sleepwalker.

How she got home she could never afterwards recall. It seemed to her that she woke after a troubled sleep — put to bed as bathers always were in order to sweat out impurities — to find that it was only an hour off the time to dine. Slowly Arabella arose and rang for her maid in order to help her dress.

The house was very quiet, her father and brothers still out enjoying the sights, and listlessly Arabella wandered into the library, thinking to while away an hour with a book.

The room was full of afternoon sunshine and the curtains at one of the open windows leading onto the lower terrace blew in the light breeze. Arabella shaded her eyes to look at it and then stiffened in horror. There, standing in the opening and staring straight at her was the stranger, dressed once more in that ridiculous red tunic. She would have turned to run, but before she could do so he stepped into the room and said, "What are you doing here?"

His accent was heavy, difficult to understand, as if his English was recently learned and not very well at that.

Hardly recognising her own voice. Arabella answered, "I live here."

"Are you a slave?"

"Of course not," she answered indignantly. "My father is the Earl of Midhurst and owns this house."

He obviously did not understand a word she was saying, for he answered, "It would be better if you did not stay. The Commandant strictly forbids women on the premises, other than the slaves."

Very suddenly Arabella grew angry. Obviously the man was either insane or playing some not very funny practical joke. She marched up to him and stood staring into his face, seeing for the first time the scar on his cheek and how his dark lashes threw a shadow above the brilliant eyes.

"Listen, you," she said rudely. "If you don't leave here immediately I shall call the servants to throw you out. You are trespassing on my father's property. So go at once."

He frowned and then smiled, his weathered skin creasing around his eyes. "I believe you're mad," he said, "or else very naughty."

"What do you mean?"

"Well, only a scamp would wander through the Baths staring at us all and then be found in the Soldiers' Villa. I believe that you are not only pretty but provocative."

"How dare you!" stormed Arabella, stamping her foot.

The stranger smiled all the more. "You are sparkling with rage. It turns your eyes dark blue."

"Hateful, hateful creature," Arabella answered furiously and ran headlong out of the door and into the entrance hall. The moment could not have been more fortuitous for at that second the footmen were opening the doors to admit the returning family.

"Father, Father," called Arabella, hurrying straight to him.

"Yes, my dear. What is it?"

"There is an intruder in the house. He is in the library at this very moment and refusing to leave. I think he is a madman."

"What!" exclaimed the Earl. "Julian, go and fetch the men. Bell and Davis you come with me. Arabella, wait here."

He went striding off, flanked by his servants and, suddenly weak, Arabella sat down. Distantly she heard the sounds of people in the library, searching, then combing the gardens. Finally came the march of her father's returning footsteps.

"We've lost him," he said angrily. "The villain must have run away before you could raise the alarm."

"Oh," she answered in a small voice which masked the conflict within. For how could she feel such a ridiculous sense of relief?

". . . but don't worry," the Earl was continuing. "I'll find him sooner or later. Tell me what he looked like."

Tremendously aware that Julian had joined them and was gazing at her with the strangest expression on his face, Arabella said, "He had dark hair and lightish eyes. I didn't really get a very good look at him."

"I suppose he didn't resemble the man you saw in your room the other night?" her brother asked flatly.

Arabella could have struck him, feeling a sense almost of betrayal. She longed to say, "Yes, it was the same person. And I know he is real because I have seen him naked," but instead she hung her head in shame, saying nothing.

"What's this?" put in the Earl.

"Arabella dreamt somebody was standing by her bed watching her. I didn't think it necessary to wake you."

The Earl's eyebrows rose and he surveyed Arabella through his quizzing glass. "How very strange. Did you dream *this*, my dear?"

"No, I was wide awake. In the library. How could I have been asleep?"

"Well your visit to the baths seemed to exhaust you somewhat," answered the Earl mildly. "Perhaps you have been dozing all day."

Arabella knew that she should have made a spirited reply, but suddenly she felt too tired and miserable. Turning on her heel she walked rapidly up the curving staircase, her nose in the air, and went into her bedroom in a dignified manner. But once there she crumpled, flinging herself down onto the bed and weeping bitterly, and refusing to come out to dine on the pretext of having a headache.

She could think of nothing but the stranger, reluctantly admitting to herself that though he might be mad he was nonetheless fascinating. She remembered the way his black hair curled about his head, the slant of his dark brows, the vivid eyes, almost golden in shade. She remembered too the glimpse of his body, packed hard with muscle and carrying no spare flesh. Finally Arabella fell asleep wishing that he might perhaps steal into her room again. But there was no sign of him and the next morning all she could recall was waking at midnight, hearing the distant sound of men's laughter and remembering the words. "Soldiers' Villa".

"I think we shall give a ball," said the Earl over breakfast, taken today at home and not in the Pump or

Assembly Rooms. "I was discussing it with Lady Woodruff over cards last night. She has kindly agreed to act as my hostess, if you will assist her, Arabella. Which reminds me, how is your headache, my dear?"

"Quite recovered, thank you, Father," she answered demurely, wondering if he was going to say anything about yesterday's incident.

But he was obviously choosing to ignore the matter for he answered, "Splendid, splendid. Then we shall start to plan it this very day. I have asked Lady Woodruff to dine with us and we can decide what sort of rout it shall be."

"I am afraid I am engaged with Rufus Abinger tonight," answered Julian abruptly. "By the way, Arabella, he asked after you and I told him we would all be in the Pump House later this morning. Was that all right?"

"I shall be pleased to see him if Father has no objection," Arabella answered cautiously, still wondering if the Earl was angry.

But again he decided to overlook her behaviour, merely saying, "I have no objection at all, my dear. I find Lord Rufus a very personable young man."

And personable and helpful indeed he was during the next few days in which Lydia Woodruff, in her element as mistress of m'Lord of Midhurst's grand house, sent armies of servants and cooks scurrying hither and thither to purchase decorations and flowers, fine wines and delicacies, to grace the table for the Earl's grand ball, driving his family almost insane in the meanwhile.

Lydia had decided that the theme of the rout should be Roman and that all invited should come in that dress.

"We shall turn the clock back to the times of Aquae Sulis," she announced joyfully, with her little silver laugh. "What do you say, Charles?"

"Splendid, my dear, splendid," he answered, looking at her fondly.

"Then I shall arrange for some dressmakers to come, so that we might all be suitably arrayed. I think, Charles, that you and I should go as an Emperor and his consort."

"Oh dear," groaned Frederick in the background. "He is weakening."

"Ssh," said Arabella. But her brother had put her fears into words and it was with a very heavy heart that she put on the delicate costume, her maid kneeling on the floor to assist her, and turned to the mirror to see herself transformed. For a Roman girl looked back at her, proud and beautiful in her long diaphanous tunic, her golden hair in a knot upon her head.

"You are lovely, my Lady," said the servant. "Any man would be proud to dance with you tonight."

Arabella smiled wistfully, wishing that she could see the stranger again, and thinking how well he would partner her in the perculiarly Roman clothes he always chose to wear. Yet stare as she might amongst the throngs of guests — it seemed all of Bath was present at the Earl of Midhurst's home that night — there was no sign of him.

"And even if he was here," she thought sadly, "he could hardly speak to me, for Rufus seems to be constantly at my side."

And so he was. The large young man, ill at ease in a vast white toga, paid her constant attention, almost to the point where Arabella felt she could scream. But finally he was whisked away by an eager mother, anxious to find partners for her shy daughter, and Arabella was at last alone. With a sigh of relief she went through the open windows and out into the scented night air.

Somehow she had known he would be there; some secret sixth sense had told her all along that he would come. She could smell his skin, fresh and firm, even before she turned and glimpsed the red tunic. Arabella saw then that the vivid eyes were regarding her in wonderment.

"Is this the Commandant's banquet?" he asked in his halting English. "And are you his daughter? Is that the explanation?"

"I am the Earl's daughter," she answered. "Who are you?"

"Gaius Petronius," he answered. "A legionary with the Twentieth Valeria Victrix, on leave from the Emperor Hadrian's Wall."

Arabella moved close to him, smiling. "Please don't make fun of me again. The game is over. Tell me who you really are."

"I am Gaius Petronius," he answered, with such a look of bewilderment that Arabella realised with dread that he was telling the truth.

"But you cannot be. It is the year 1727. King George rules England and Scotland. There is no-one on Hadrian's Wall."

"But the Emperor Constantine rules Britannia from Rome and I am part of the occupying force," he answered with desperation. "I swear it by the goddess Minerva to whom our temple at Aquae Sulis is dedicated."

The outlines of the garden began to blur and a great spiral of darkness dragged Arabella downwards. She was only saved from falling by Gaius, who caught her to him and held her tightly. And then as his lips sought hers in a kiss, unbearable in its intensity, Arabella Wynter knew that somehow the door of time had opened and she was falling in love with a man who had died centuries before she was even born.

The dream had been so realistic that the soldier woke almost with a sense of wonderment, puzzling where lay truth and where fantasy. In his sleeping mind he had risen from his bed, walking quietly past the slumbering form of Lucius Marcellus, and made his way through a villa full of the quiet of midnight and bathed in silver light so sharp and fine that he had exclaimed aloud with pleasure.

In the dream, the house in which he had found himself had been strange to him, unknown, so that when he had passed through a moonlit door and entered a curving corridor furnished in a fashion he did not know, Gaius Petronius, legionary of Rome, had thought little of it, other than to note that the Soldiers' Villa, as the place in which he was staying on leave was known, was larger than he had at first noticed.

In that mad uncertain light, Gaius had walked on, his feet making no noise and his body throwing no shadow until, on impulse, he had silently opened one of the doors leading off the passageway and gone into the spacious room that lay beyond.

A girl had slept in the white-draped bed near the window, a bed the like of which he had never seen in his life before. A girl whose hair was transformed to a silver cobweb by the colour of the night. Gaius Petronius had drawn near to gaze on her sleeping features and seen a high-boned face, with a mouth whose full lower lip spoke of passion and whose fine small nose showed she did not come from Rome.

As he had watched her, the sleeping eyelids had opened and eyes blue as butterflies had regarded him for a moment. Then Gaius saw them widen, dilate, and an exquisite creature — shy and nervous as a fawn — had run past him and out of the room.

The dream had become jumbled after that. In fact Gaius had had no recollection of going back down that strange curving corridor, nor, indeed, of finding his way to his own room. The next thing he could remember was sitting up in bed and wondering what significance such a strange illusion could possibly have. Had he dreamt it? Or had he walked in his sleep and found himself in quarters that he had not noticed on the previous evening? Shaking his head Gaius had lain down and once more closed his eyes. But sleep would not return and eventually the Roman legionary had given up the struggle and, staring at the ceiling where the moonlight threw ever-lightening shadows, had thought instead of the events that brought him to Aquae Sulis and of the long leave that now awaited him there.

He had not wanted to be posted away from Rome, where he had been born and brought up, joining the army at eighteen years of age. In fact Gaius Petronius had dreaded the prospect of sailing to the sunless isle of Britannia where, so his fellow legionaries assured him, the wind howled and the rain teemed and snow lay upon the land for several months of the year. And, when it came to it, the reality had been even worse than he had imagined, for Gaius had been sent on his first tour of duty straight to the Emperor Hadrian's Wall.

Lying here in the warmth of his bed, his hands folded comfortably beneath his head, he still shivered. Gaius might have left the place more than a week ago, marching down the great road that connected the Wall with Eboracum and then Lindum and finally Londinium itself, but the memory was still all too crystal clear. Mile upon mile of stark plain and hills stretching away as far as the eye could see, and the bleakness of Fort Borcovicum itself, built into the Wall complete with its various dwellings, a frontier to keep out the marauding northern tribes. Gains Petronius had never felt really cold in his life until then, but keeping watch on the Wall, despite his protective leggings and furs, he had thought he would freeze to death.

Thinking about it now must have made him sigh, for Lucius woke and said, "What's the matter?"

Gaius smiled. "I was remembering the fort, that's all."

Lucius shuddered. "Don't remind me. I never knew what bad weather was until I saw that place."

"Well, we're away from it now. A whole month in Aquae Sulis with nothing to do but relax." Lucius stretched lazily. "What a delightful prospect." He swung out of bed and started to dress in the red tunic which denoted him as a soldier in the army of the Emperor Constantine. "Come on, Gaius," he said, over his shoulder, "you may be on leave, but you can't loll in bed all day."

Still remembering his dream, Gaius got up more slowly. "I'm just a bit tired, that's all."

"Didn't you sleep well?"

"Not really. I had a curious dream. I wandered through the Villa and saw a girl asleep. It was very real."

"Oh," answered Lucius, bent over his sandals and obviously not interested. "Well, hurry up. I'm ravenous."

Gaius smiled to himself, knowing his friend to be a simple soul who thought the only important things in life the earthly pleasures, particularly the regular consumption of large amounts of food and drink. But for all that he was a loyal companion, and Gaius dressed quickly so that Lucius would not be kept from his breakfast too long.

It was the custom in the Soldiers' Villa that the men on leave — drawn from all sections of the occupying forces in Britannia — should eat communally. And it was to these dining quarters that Gaius and Lucius now made their way, going down a flight of cool marble steps to reach them.

It was as he neared the bottom that Gaius first noticed a man coming towards him; a man so strangely dressed that the legionary could only stare in amazement. On the stranger's head was a creation of false white hair, tied behind with a black bow; while he wore a long scarlet coat, liberally decorated with braid buttons, and his legs were encased in matching breeches ending at the knee and giving way to fine leggings. On the man's feet were what Gaius could only think of as solid sandals with buckle decorations.

The stranger drew nearer and he and Gaius looked at one another, for a moment holding each other's gaze. Then the man rolled his eyes to heaven, exclaimed, "Oh my Gawd, it's a ghost," and dropped to the floor in a dead faint.

Gaius turned to Lucius. "In the name of the gods, who was that?"

"Who?"

"That extraordinary creature. Walking towards us."

"What extraordinary creature? I saw no one," answered Lucius, looking bewildered.

"Over there. On the floor..." His voice trailed away as Gaius realised he was pointing at nothing, that where the man had lain but a moment before there was now nothing but the bare mosaic tiles.

Lucius looked at him curiously. "I think you're seeing things, Gaius. It strikes me that this leave has come just in time."

"Perhaps you're right. It's said that men suffer visions if they stare over the wild territory long enough."

Lucius nodded, trying to look wise, and Gaius sighed with relief that he had escaped further questioning. But he believed not a word of his own explanation. What he had seen had been too real, almost tangible. He found himself shaking, though neither through cold nor fright but more with an exquisite anticipation of further mysteries to come.

Yet the morning's brightness, as Gaius Petronius stepped forth into the honey-coloured city of Aquae Sulis, dispelled all other thought. For here, set in the hollow of the hills, was a place to raise the spirits of any homesick legionary. Paved streets thronged with people making their way to the focal point of the city; the great temple precinct of Sulis Minerva and the complex of baths that lay beside it.

Gaius and Lucius joined the throng and, passing through an arched and pillared entrance, found themselves in a large rectangular court, the altar and the great temple facing them, the mighty hall which contained the sacred spring where offerings to the goddess were made to their left. Somewhat in awe the two men went through the huge porch and passing through an open passageway, then an arch, came to the place where the sacred spring bubbled up from the very heart of the earth.

At once they entered a dark and mysterious cavern, the only light coming from a window in the eastern wall. The dim hall surrounding the spring vividly reminded Gaius of his dream and a strange sense of unreality came over him as, in company with the jostling crowd, he went forward to one of the three observation places looking directly down upon the water and from which vantage point offerings to the goddess could be thrown in.

It was one of the most unnerving sights he had ever seen. A cloud of vapour rose from the small man-made lake into which the hot spring bubbled, and in that vapour — appearing to float upon the surface of the water — four life-sized statues reared frighteningly. The image directly opposite Gaius was that of a woman and for a moment, in his state of heightened awareness, he thought the girl he had dreamed of must have been the model for it. But when he looked more closely he saw it was only his imagination and that it bore little resemblance to her.

As he watched, a small door in the wall behind the statues opened and a white garbed priest strode through, dramatically raising his arms over his head and then making obeisance to the spring. The crowd gasped, Gaius and Lucius with them, and then as the man began to chant, high and wierdly, offerings were thrown from every side into the water.

All about him, Gaius Petronius could hear whispered prayers, and he added his own.

"Great Goddess Minerva, let me see her again. Let her be reality and not a dream. Let me touch and hold her — and let her no longer be afraid." As he spoke he threw coin upon coin into the water, and all around him others did likewise.

The press of people behind wanting to give their offerings was growing considerably and Gaius and Lucius moved on through a further archway, then stopped, astonished.

"Why, this equals anything I've seen in Rome," said Lucius, enthusiastically.

"I think it might be even finer."

Before them, paved and spacious corridors led to every kind of amenity that a bather could wish. To their left was a great pool in which a dozen men swam vigorously, while off to their right a passageway led to a circular bath — a dolphin fountain gushing in fresh water at one end.

"Where first?" asked Lucius.

"To take some exercise?"

"Certainly."

To the right of the large pool lay a long courtyard in which men, mostly undressed, ran or wrestled, beyond it opened an alcove in which traders sold wine and honey cakes, while leading off from this was the changing room. Having divested themselves of their tunics, Gains and Lucius played a vigorous ball game before being tempted by the refreshments.

A girl served Gaius his wine, and he peered into her face wondering, just for a moment, if she might be the one he had dreamed of. But as she blushed and turned away he saw that she was nothing like the delicate creature who had haunted his midnight.

With his mind turning over the question of whether the dream girl had been flesh and blood or a creature of fantasy, Gaius endured the rigours of, first, the tepidarium and then the fiercely hot caldarium, before being oiled and scraped and massaged, then finally leaping into an ice-cold pool.

With his skin tingling and feeling fitter than he had done for some months, Gaius walked with Lucius, quite unashamed of their nakedness, to the beautiful circular pool and dived in. But even as he swam a curious sensation came over him. He felt that somewhere curious eyes were watching him, that a hidden observer could see not only him but all the occupants of the pool. Not knowing quite why he did so, Gaius swam to one of the two sets of steps and climbed out, his hands outstretched for the towel that an attendant slave held towards him. Then he looked at the square-arched doorway.

It was the girl! Blushing like a summer flower, the exquisite creature of whom he had dreamed stood in the entrance. As they exchanged a long look, the legionary suddenly remembered that he was stark naked and hastily pulled the towel from the servant's hands, wrapping it around himself like a kilt. Only then did he gaze back to see if it was truly she or merely a figment of his imagination.

estedBut the girl was real, there was no doubt about it. No dream or spirit could look so wildly embarrassed, so uncomfortable, at finding herself staring at a crowd of naked men. Just for a second before she turned and ran, something in her glance told Gaius that she recognised him, that she had picked him out from amongst the others.

With a great leap of his heart he realised that last night had been no dream; that she, too, lived in the Soldiers' Villa and that it could not be too long before he ran into her again. Letting out a shout that drew some quizzical glances, Gaius sprinted from the circular pool to look for her, but she had gone and he was left with nothing but the vision of her fine-boned and delicate face.

His good humour bubbled all the rest of that day, so much so that Lucius eventually asked him why he was in such a cheerful mood. But Gaius, on the point of telling him, suddenly changed his mind.

"It must be the effect of the waters. I feel a different person," he said instead.

"You *look* different. Why, I haven't seen you in such high spirits since we left Rome.   Perhaps it is the magic of Aqua Sulis," Gaius suggested jokingly.   "Or maybe it's that girl."

"What girl?"

"The one you dreamed about."

Gaius did not answer and, a little annoyed at being left out, Lucius shrugged his shoulders and went off in the direction of the baths, saying there was a troupe of jugglers he wanted to see. But Gaius, as soon as he was out of sight, doubled back and went straight to his sleeping quarters in the Villa, determined to retrace the steps of his dream.

It was more difficult than he thought. In the bright glow of early daylight everything took on a totally different aspect. Gone were the stark splashes of silver and the ink-black shadows, and now the square and pillared courtyard around which the Soldiers' Villa was built was an oasis of cool green shade.

Gaius felt sure that when he had sleep-walked he had crossed the courtyard, because he could vaguely remember hearing the sounds of trickling water from the fountain. He did so now and found himself entering the quarters where the slaves dwelled. Was that the explanation? Was the girl a servant? But if so, why had she slept in such opulent surroundings?

Very puzzled, Gaius climbed a flight of marble steps and turned a corner, expecting to see the mysterious door through which he had passed during the night. It was not there. In fact there was nothing at all, only a blank outer wall.

Realising he must have been mistaken, Gaius took a different course but, try as he might, the door and the corridor beyond still eluded him. By the time Lucius came back for the early evening meal, his earlier good spirits vanished and he sat moodily, eating little and thinking that, after all, it must have been a dream and he had imagined seeing the girl at the baths. Then a chance piece of conversation from a legionary stationed at Fort Corstopitum suddenly had Gaius riveted, his spine growing cold as he listened.

"I reckon this place is haunted," the soldier was saying.

"Why is that?" asked a companion.

"I was resting after the Baths the other day and heard voices and laughter coming from a part of the Villa that isn't there."

Gaius leant across the table. "Isn't there? What do you mean?"

"Exactly that. I could distinctly hear voices, particularly two boys, but when I went to have a look I found nothing but an external wall. There was nothing beyond."

"Where was this?" Gaius realised that his tone had become a little too anxious, but couldn't help himself.

"In the east wing of the Villa."

"Will you show me?"

The legionary shot him a puzzled glance. "Why, have you heard them too?"

"No, it's not that. It's just that I'm... interested."

The legionary said, "I'll take you now if you like."

They left the table and, crossing the courtyard, entered the slave's quarters.

"I sleep above here," said the legionary. "In the wing adjacent to the Commandant's." He led the way down a corridor, one side of which was an open arched balcony above the quadrangle, then turned left and went into a small single bedroom. They had reached the end of one side of the square.

"Extraordinary," said Gaius. "You say the sounds came from beyond here?"

"Oh yes. From over there." The man waved his arm towards the balcony. "Where, as you can see for yourself, there is nothing but open space."

"Perhaps children were playing below in the courtyard," Gaius suggested.

"I thought of that and actually went down to search. It was the strangest thing, Gaius. I could still hear their voices, shouting and laughing, and yet there was nobody there at all. It frightened me, I can tell you."

On a sudden thought, Gaius asked, "Did you hear a woman's voice as well?"

"Just once, calling out; as if bidding the boys to stop their game. It was very unnerving."

"I still think there must be some rational explanation," Gaius said thoughtfully. "Maybe there is an echo which comes from outside. I think I'll have a look round while it's still daylight."

The legionary turned away. "If you find anything, please let me know. But somehow I don't think you will."

Gaius smiled. "In a way I hope you're right. I rather like your ghost story."

Slowly he made his way to the courtyard, circling the pretty fountain, and then walking round and round until he had looked at every inch of the terrain. Then he proceeded to the back of the Villa, drenched now with the light of the setting sun.

A sudden movement caught Gaius's attention and he saw that something blew in the lazy little breeze that had come up. Shielding his eyes with his hand, he saw that it was drapery, billowing at a window like a sail. Half blinded by the brightness, he went towards it and found that he stood on a huge open terrace, leading into a room beyond. Gaius stared inside.

The girl was there! She stood staring straight at him, her cheeks turning white as chalk. Knowing that she was truly flesh and blood and that he must find out who she was before she ran away, Gaius stepped inside.

His first few words, hampered by the fact that he spoke the language of the natives badly, were not what he really wanted to say at all.

"What are you doing here?" he asked, knowing as he did so that he sounded abrupt.

A little colour come into the drained cheeks and she answered, "I live here."

So she *was* a servant. Yet a privileged one, for Gaius had never seen more luxurious surroundings than the room in which she slept.

"*Are* you a slave?" he asked incredulously.

He saw the small chin tilt up and a flame flicker behind the frightened eyes. Then she answered something that made no sense to him, using words that Gaius did not understand. He heard sounds like "Earl" and "Midhurst" and felt inadequate that his command of the language was so poor. But then surely she added that her father owned the Villa, which was obviously a falsehood?

Thinking how dangerous it was for her to be in the Villa, Gaius said, "It would be better if you did not stay. The Commandant strictly forbids women on the premises, other than the slaves."

Her colour drained away once more, but this time with fury. She marched up so close to Gaius that he could feel the warmth of her body, smell the fragrance of her hair and skin, and see the shadow made on the high curving cheekbone by the sweep of her lashes. He felt then that he wanted to kiss her, wanted to show her that, even if she was a girl who sold her favours indiscriminately, he regarded her differently, saw her as an exquisite and delicate thing.

But she was speaking again, this time in a cross voice. He understood little, except that she seemed to protest that she lived in the Villa, that he was the intruder, and if he did not go at once she'd have him turned out of doors.

Gaius felt a thrill of disappointment that his meeting with the girl he had dreamed of should turn out to be so different from what he had hoped; that all his thoughts of her should culminate in an angry scene. He gave her as disarming a smile as he could muster, but she still regarded him coldly and it was then that he suddenly lost patience.

"I believe you are quite mad," he said, "or else very naughty."

She paused before asking him what he meant and Gaius, despite his irritation, seized the chance of studying her from head to foot. For the first time he realised that she was dressed in the most extraordinary clothes. That instead of a tunic or the gently draped style of a Roman woman of fashion she wore a tightly waisted gown with a wide skirt, above which was a snugly fitted bodice that squeezed her breasts.

She really was quite perfect to look at he thought, though the mystery of her deepened with each passing minute. He decided to challenge her about the incident in the circular bath.

"Well, only a scamp would wander through the Baths staring at us all...

He was hardly aware of the rest of what he said as he watched her eyes, the colour of a summer sky, darken to winter. Gaius would have told her then that for all he cared she could be as wicked as Messalina, wife of the stuttering Claudius, the Emperor who had finally managed to conquer Britannia. But it was too late. The girl looked near to tears and was stamping her foot.

Gaius tried one last-ditch attempt at retrieving the situation. He had once been told that no woman could resist a compliment so now he attempted one, telling the distraught girl how anger became her. He could have not done worse. She ran headlong from the room calling, "Hateful, hateful creature," over her departing shoulder, leaving him to stand forlornly staring after her.

With a thrill of unease another explanation of her identity occurred to Gaius Petronius. In her high light dialect, little of which he had been able to understand, it had seemed to him that she had mentioned her father several times. Surely she could not be the Commandant's daughter? If so, he had made the most terrible error and was likely to be punished. With slow, anxious steps Gaius left the room and made his way back to join his fellow legionaries.

He found Lucius, a look of impatience on his face, saying, "Oh there you are! We've been searching everywhere for you. The soldier from Fort Corstopitum thought you'd been spirited away."

"I wish I had," answered Gaius gloomily. "Do you know, by any chance, if the Commandant has a daughter?"

Lucius stared at him, goggle-eyed. "No. Why? Gaius, what have you been up to?" he added in an accusing tone.

"I'm not sure," came the answer, which made Lucius look more startled than ever. Gaius changed the subject abruptly. "Why were you so anxious to find me."

"Some of us are off to the theatre and wondered if you would come with us." Gaius hesitated and Lucius went on, "Come on, it will do you good. Take your mind off whatever trouble you've got yourself into now."

He smiled broadly, and in a rush of affection for his stolid but faithful companion, Gaius flung his arm round Lucius's shoulders as they left the Villa and went through the dusk to the place north of the temple where, cut into the face of a steep natural slope, a fine crescent shaped amphitheatre, large enough to seat a thousand people, had been built by the Roman settlers.

Afterwards, Gaius found it almost impossible to remember what the play had been about. He sat, shifting a little on the hard stone seat, seeing instead of the actors a pair of great shining eyes opened wide, first in fear then in fury, and mouth that drooped a little as if its owner possessed a languid side to her nature.

Because he was restless the play seemed over-long, and Gaius was glad when the masked actors finally went through the arches behind the acting area and the audience began to stand up.

Not really looking forward to the rest of the night, Gaius crossed the wide street separating the amphitheatre from the temple and went through the pillared and arched entrance, once more finding himself facing the altar and the statue which stood behind it.

For the second time in twenty-four hours he found himself in the mysterious and shadowed hall, built by men around the place where the magic spring bubbled up in clouds of steam from the earth below. At this hour of the night the observation arches were less crowded and Gaius found himself standing almost alone in the central one. He leant forward, staring at the awesome sight of the four statues floating through the cloud of steam which, this evening, seemed almost fog-like in its density. He noticed, too, that the light from the great window at the far end of the hall had faded virtually to nothing as darkness fell on Aquae Sulis.

Reaching into his tunic, Gaius drew out a coin and threw it into the bubbling water below.

"Minerva, let my quarrel with the girl be resolved," he prayed, bowing his head as he did so. The mist swirled about him and for a moment Gaius could see nothing at all, then the dim light returned and he saw that the sacred place was silent, empty; the crowd completely gone.

It was the strangest experience the soldier had ever had. Where but a moment or two before he had been standing with others, throwing their offerings into the spring, now he was alone, only the gleaming water of the deserted shrine telling him that the whole thing had not been a dream. Feeling terribly afraid, Gaius Petronius began to pick his way out over the rough stones that had suddenly taken the place of the paved floor on which he had walked on his way in.

He found himself in the street, to see that the moon had risen, her unearthly light drenching the scene just as it had on the night he had first seen the girl. There were hordes of people everywhere; people dressed in outlandish clothes. Men with waisted coats, strange patches upon their faces, walked with the aid of elegant canes; while the women, their skirts made wide by something they wore beneath, laughed beneath powdered hair or stepped into strange chairs, carried on shafts by perspiring servants.

Gaius leant against a wall, his heart racing in his chest. He knew it was a dream, knew that in a moment he would wake to find himself listening to the snores of Lucius Marcellus, but yet the vision had such terrible clarity. He could see every line and wrinkle on the people's faces, could even smell the fine scents with which they had sprinkled themselves, while snatches of extraordinary conversation drifted past his ears.

"They say that m'Lady Woodruff is setting her cap at Midhurst."

"And he is responding?"

"Apparently so. The death of his wife set him back, but rumour has it he yearns for female companionship again."

"Well, Liddy Woodruff will score a triumph if she manages to haul in that catch."

"Are you going to their rout next week?"

"Indeed I am. To be left off that guest list would mean that one could never raise one's head in polite society again."

The speakers drifted away, leaving Gaius aghast. Surely the girl had mentioned the name Midhurst, though he had not understood what it meant. And it was then, just as he thought of her, that Gaius Petronius saw her, walking along between two young men, one of them very tall and large.

"Please, I must speak to you," he called out.

She did not hear him but went on laughing and chattering, her pretty eyes shining and dancing. A pang of inexplicable jealousy shot through the legionary's heart that she should be so merry in the company of other men and yet so angry when she was with him. He began to hurry towards her, bumping into several people, who, strangely, did not seem to notice him.

"Please stop," he shouted again.

The girl turned her head. "Did you hear anything?" she said. "Did somebody call out?"

"No," answered the large young man, beaming at her fondly.

"Yes, I did," answered Gaius furiously and it was then, hurrying to catch up with her, that he fell, feeling a fool, his tunic riding up and one of his sandals coming untied. Everyone ignored him, in fact the walking throng did not even step over him, merely carrying on about their business as if he wasn't even there.

Cursing, Gaius Petronius struggled to his feet and it was then that a helping hand came towards him and, looking up, he saw the legionary from Fort Corstopitum peering into his face.

"Are you all right? I thought you were having a seizure."

"What do you mean?"

"Well, you were leaning against the wall calling out to no one and staring about you as if you could see something that was not there."

"But there *was* a girl here," Gaius said, "walking along with two men. And that was not all. She was in the midst of a huge crowd. I saw them distinctly."

The legionary smiled. "It is well past midnight. The crowd have all gone. See, we are alone."

He gestured with his hand and Gaius realised that he was right; that they stood in a deserted square with only the solitary figure of a man making his way home for company.

"I must have been dreaming," he said.

"Yes, my friend, I think you must," came the amused reply.

But Gaius knew for sure that could not be the true explanation; that the girl who appeared and disappeared so mysteriously was real. Why, she had stood so close to him that he had smelled the body scent of her; her wild raw perfume, heady as jacinth. Somewhere in this extraordinary city of Aquae Sulis she lay hidden from him, just waiting for the moment when he must eventually find her.

What should have been a time of recuperation, a pleasurable restful leave preparing him for his next tour of duty in the bleak North Lands, began to turn into a nightmare. Wherever Gaius went, both in the Soldiers' Villa and in the city itself, he looked for the girl; staring at strange young women and sometimes getting himself into trouble as a result. Even Lucius Marcellus began to run out of patience and Gaius Petronius decided to make an effort, knowing if he did not pull himself together he would not only ruin his holiday but lose his friend into the bargain. And then came the night when everything changed for ever.

He had gone to bed a little tipsy, the soldiers celebrating the birthday of one of the inmates with a great deal of wine and noisy song. Lucius, in a worse state even than his friend, had fallen asleep at once, but Gaius had lain awake, staring at the moonlight on the ceiling and wondering if he would ever see the girl again.

He must have dozed off without realising it, for he woke abruptly, hearing the sound of many people laughing and talking. Wondering if the birthday revels were still going on he got out of bed but, having done so, Gaius's ears told him that there were too many voices for a simple gathering of soldiers, that he was listening to something like a hundred people chattering and carousing.

Very cautiously, he made his way from his room and across the courtyard, following the direction of the sound. And then he saw it! That strange dark door, silvered by the patterns of the moon, was in the very place that it had been before. Without hesitation, Gaius Petronius opened it and went through, finding himself once more in the curving corridor.

This time he did not turn off, but went straight to the end, down a magnificent staircase, the like of which he had never seen before, and into the thronged hall below. They were there again. All that patched and powdered crowd of people, who had passed him by so uncaringly in the street, were milling about, but this time there was a sinister difference about them. They were all dressed in clothes that he recognised; everyone of them wore a dress that he knew. They were Romans after all.

He realised at once that he must be in the Commandant's quarters, at a banquet given for the Commandant's own particular guests. Knowing that an ordinary legionary staying in the Villa on leave would hardly be welcome at such a gathering, Gaius made rapidly for the garden that he could see beyond the long and unusual windows.

He would have gone then, would have made his escape into the sheltering night had not some instinct made him turn round and look back over his shoulder. Just as he had hoped and prayed, the girl was there, dressed as a young Roman woman should be, her suncloud hair swept to the top of her head and her great eyes looking at him almost fondly.

Gaius knew then that he loved her, that he would not rest until he had held her in his arms and felt all the delicate softness of her pressed finely against him. But first, for once and for all, he must find out her name and who she was.

"Is this the Commandant's banquet? And are you his daughter?"

She laughed and shook her head. "I am the Earl's daughter. Who are you?"

As he told her, he saw her laugh again; as if he had said something amusing. Then she stepped close to him and the smell of wild flowers intoxicated him to the point where he did not trust himself to speak.

"Please don't make fun of me any more. The game is over. Tell me who you really are."

Gaius could not understand her reaction. Why should she not believe that he was who he said?

"I am Gaius Petronius," he repeated, just a little dazed.

She answered him so fearfully that he could not comprehend all she said. But one thing was horribly clear. She was either mad or perpetrating some terrible joke for she was trying to tell him that it was altogether some other time; that somebody called George was the Emperor and that the year was something completely impossible.

Gaius could have wept. He loved her so much and yet she was so strange and, in some ways, frightening. He made one last desperate attempt.

"But the Emperor Constantine rules Britannia from Rome and I am part of the occupying force. I swear it by the goddess Minerva to whom our temple at Aquae Sulis is dedicated."

The girl lost colour so dramatically that he knew she believed him and that something he said had terrified her. She swayed where she stood and his longing for her overwhelmed him. Gaius caught her to him and kissed her as he had never kissed a woman in his life before, all his desperation and desire mingling into one.

"I love you so much," he said. "I don't even know your name, but I am yours to do with what you want."

"This is not possible," she breathed. "None of this can be happening."

"Then if it is a dream I shall wake in paradise," the Roman soldier answered as he held her close to his body and kissed her once more, knowing as he did so that he must never be parted from her again.

Very, very slowly the mist began to clear and Arabella Wynter, looking up, dimly recognised, first, the large and uncompromising shape of Lord Rufus Abinger, then her brother Julian, and just within her line of vision the splendid face of Lydia Woodruff, all leaning forward anxiously and staring down at her. Vaguely, she wondered where she was, then putting out a tentative hand Arabella felt cool slabs of stone and knew that she was outside her father's house, on the terrace leading to the gardens below, and that she was lying flat.

"What am I doing here?" she whispered, and then repeated the words a little louder as Rufus bent down to catch them.

"You fainted, dearest," he answered, his anxiety making him more familiar than he would normally dared to have been.

Arabella tried to sit up, frantically looking round the growing group of people coming from the house to find out what was amiss.

"Where is Gaius?" she murmured.

"Who?" Even though she could not see him Arabella knew by the voice that her father had spoken.

"Gaius Petronius. The man who was here just now."

"She's concussed," said the Earl firmly. "Julian, Lord Rufus, pick her up and carry her into the house. She must be put to bed at once."

"Oh please..." gasped Arabella as she was swung up into Rufus's arms. "I must see him. I don't think he understands."

But the Earl was clearing a path through the onlookers and further conversation was impossible as, pressed into Rufus's chest, she was carried like a doll up the beautiful winding staircase, then along the corridor to the quiet of her bedroom.

"He *was* here," she managed to say as everyone was motioned away and Lady Woodruff herself supervised the invalid being put into bed.

"Yes, yes, my dear," came the reply. "Now just you lie still and rest. Emma shall bring an iced cloth for your head and soon Dr Anstey will be here to see you."

"But I don't need a doctor," Arabella protested, once again struggling to sit up, her cheeks flushed with anxiety. "I am not ill and I most certainly didn't hit my head. I was talking to someone, a man called Gaius Petronius, and then, just for a moment, the shock..."

Her voice died away as Lydia Woodruff's emerald eyes swept over her.

"What shock, Arabella? Come, you may be frank with me. I would like you to regard me as if I were your own dear Mama."

Arabella looked away, knowing that she was defeated. "I could never do that, Lady Woodruff, though I do thank you for your concern. The truth is that I thought I met someone on the terrace, but he was probably not there at all."

Lydia looked thoroughly startled. "I think it best if you have a sleeping draught, Arabella dear. Why, I do vow and declare that you are wandering in your mind."

Arabella lay down again and closed her eyes. "Perhaps I am, my Lady. Yet it all seemed so true — but I expect you are right and it was just my imagination."

Yet behind her closed lids, even while she listened to Lydia and Emma tiptoe out and quietly shut the door, Arabella's thoughts were racing. She *knew* that Gaius was real, could still taste his wild sweet kiss upon her mouth. Somewhere, in a century in which neither he nor she had any true place, they had met and fallen in love.

Arabella sat up in the darkness, suddenly panic stricken. Supposing she could not find him. Supposing that the accident of time which had allowed them to meet had now righted itself. Supposing that she were never to see him again. The very idea was too terrible to bear.

She lay back on the pillow, listening to the noise of the party below and wondering where Gaius Petronius was at that moment, then knew that his mortal remains had long since crumbled to dust, but that in his own time he lived, breathed and loved her. With her head throbbing with the strain of trying to understand, Arabella Wynter finally fell asleep, to dream of a Roman soldier in a red tunic, and a pair of fine dark eyes that had looked at her in a way so excitingly strange and new.

Much to her consternation, Dr Anstey, who called the next morning, insisted that Arabella remain in bed for a week, at the end of which time she could have wept over the delay. So much so that when the Earl, magnificently arrayed in black and gold came on his daily visit to her bedroom, his daughter knew that she must dissemble if she was to get her own way and be allowed to go out and about in Bath immediately.

Composing her features, Arabella gave a smile and said, "Oh Papa, I feel so much better and simply know that taking the waters will restore me to full health."

Lord Midhurst regarded her through his quizzing glass. "Your illness is a strange business, my child. Dr Anstey told me he could find no evidence of damage to your head, yet I personally heard you call out some foreign name and ask where your companion was, when those who were watching you swear that you were alone."

"Oh, I *was* alone when I fainted, Papa," Arabella answered, somehow contriving to make her eyes twinkle. "But just before then some merry young scamp — I do believe he might have been a distant connection of Lord Caernarvon — pretended he was the ghost of a Roman soldier and scared me half witless."

"Hmm," answered the Earl, taking a seat on her bed. "And was it he who frightened you the day you swore there was an intruder in the house? And also on the night you thought you saw someone in your bedroom?"

Feeling out-manoeuvered, Arabella hung her head. "No, Papa. I believe those were just girlish fancies."

The Earl pondered for a moment, his lazy eyes sharp and bright for once. "I think it would be as well if you *did* get up, Arabella. I also think it would be as well if we set about the serious business of finding a husband for you. You have been too much alone since the death of your mother."

"But, Sir..."

"No buts, my girl. My mind is made up. You have a year to find someone whom you feel you could love. Provided he comes from the same background as yourself and his father and I may speak together as men of the world, you have freedom of choice."

Arabella knew that to argue was impossible, so she simply lowered her eyes demurely and whispered, "Yes, Papa."

"Then you shall rise from your sickbed and return to the season, Miss Mouse. You certainly won't meet the man of your dreams lying here."

As the door closed behind him, Arabella could not help but smile at what her father had inadvertently said. "No, indeed I won't," she murmured under her breath, before calling Emma to help her to put on her clothes.

The weather outside the sickroom was quite amazingly warm and Arabella emerged into the sunshine to find that the fine ladies had adopted light muslins and straw hats. By far the coolest and most elegant of them all, Lydia Woodruff — a vision in lace — bore down on Arabella.

"Dearest, you have returned to us," she cried, pressing her soft cheek to Arabella's face for so long that it was a relief to see Lord Rufus, hurrying up. He offered his arm which Arabella took gladly, determinedly ignoring the calculating look which had appeared around Lord Midhurst's mouth.

"Arabella, are you really better? Please say that you are."

"Oh Rufus, I am."

"Is it true that some connection of Caernarvon's played a practical joke on you? Because, by God, if so, I'll thrash the upstart to within an inch of his life."

Arabella laid a hand on his arm. "Something did happen, yes. But I don't know who the culprit was. I can honestly say that it was no one you have met — or are ever likely to. It would make me happier if you forgot the whole thing."

Rufus looked reluctant. "Can't I seek him out?"

"I don't think you would be able to find him," answered Arabella softly.

Rufus seemed content to let the matter drop and changed the subject by asking, "Will I see you at the ball tonight?"

"No, but I shall probably go tomorrow. Papa feels that I should spend my first night at home."

"Then may I call?"

"I would rather you didn't, Rufus. Though I do thank you for the thought. I intend to go to bed very early."

But, in truth, this was not Arabella's plan at all. In fact, she had already decided that as soon as the house was empty of Julian and the Earl, she would creep quietly out and search Bath — all night long if necessary — praying with every ounce of her strength that the extraordinary flaw in the fabric of time would tear open and she could once more find herself in the arms of Gaius Petronius.

It appeared at first that her scheme was working perfectly, for her father and brother announced their intention of dining with Lady Woodruff before the rout, Julian wearing an expression of such agonised enchantment on his face, that Arabella could not help but notice. But then the one thing over which the girl had no control seemed suddenly to turn against her. As evening fell over the city of Bath, the heat of the day met the cool vapours rising from the River Avon, and a thick impenetrable mist rose up and enveloped everything: a mist so thick that it was impossible to see the lights of the chair men or the watch.

As silence settled over the house, Arabella rose from her bed and hurried to the windows to look out. Even the gardens were invisible and she felt as if her room was an island, floating in a sea of timelessness. Arabella thought then, with a thrill of shock, that this was the very night on which time might indeed turn in on itself.

Pulling on her riding habit, she left her room silently and descending the stairs, went out of the house without being seen. Did she dare ride out? she wondered. She decided that having made her escape it would be better simply to melt into the mist without raising any kind of alarm, and with a beating heart Arabella headed north and away from the city's centre, still bustling with activity despite the extraordinary weather.

She had walked some way, feeling herself gathered into the silence of the fog, for her feet gave out no noise and no cry rang out in that curiously disembodied night, before she heard the sound of a large crowd of people making their way through the haze. Arabella paused, having no wish to run into a group some of whom might know and recognise her.

She heard the mob draw nearer and go right by and her spine seethed with the eeriness of the sensation. Though she was aware that a great many people had passed within a few feet of her, she could see nobody, nothing. It was just as if she was witnessing the march of a ghostly army.

The hand at her elbow made her jump and when she wheeled round it was to see a sinister cloaked figure, barely recognisable in that dimmest of lights. But when it spoke, Arabella knew all her prayers had been answered. "My darling, you've come to me," said Gaius Petronius.

She could not help herself, she flung straight into his arms without another word. And it was only there, pressed against that familiar red tunic and feeling safe at last, that she finally dared to speak.

"Gaius, my love — dare I call you that? — what I said was true. We are alive at different times. Only some strange twist of fate has allowed us to meet at all."

"I know," he answered softly. "I stayed with you after you fainted, held you in my arms and tended you, but those who came to help you could not see me. They simply did not know I was there!"

"What did you do?"

"I left you. I went through the garden and found myself back in the Soldiers' Villa. I have made offerings to the goddesses every day since then that I would see you again."

"Oh, Gaius..."

But Arabella could say no more as they continued the kiss that had started in another century.

When finally they drew apart, she said, "Am I in your time?"

"Yes, I think so. I am leaving the theatre with the rest of the audience. The play has been cancelled because of the fog."

"But there is fog in my world too."

"Then who knows where we are — and who cares? We are together for this night at least."

He drew her into the shelter of his cloak, fastened on one shoulder with a buckle, and they walked, arms about each other, into the denseness.

"Where shall we go?" asked Arabella, not frightened but simply curious.

"To where we can be completely alone."

They walked on, climbing up into the hills that surrounded the city, and finding as they reached higher ground that the moon was out and a trillion stars gleamed down on them.

"I think the gods are smiling," said Gaius.

"Gods, God?" answered Arabella. "Who knows?"

He did not answer as, once again, they exchanged the same long embrace that seemed to be a mere extension of the kiss that had gone before. After that the yielding of Arabella's body to his was, she supposed, an inevitable thing. Yet, as he laid his cloak upon the ground for her and she, sitting down, paused to look up into his beautiful brilliant eyes, she drew a frightened breath.

"What is going to happen?"

"I, who am already dead, will take you, who are not yet born, through the gate that only lovers know."

"And will it be a difficult journey?"

"Difficult, dangerous — and ecstatic."

It was as he said. There was wild raw pain; followed by a fear which finally changed to wanting: then, ultimately, came a supreme sensation that Arabella had never dreamed even to exist. They were lovers born to be together; beyond guilt or shame as they lay entwined in each other's arms beneath the unseeing moon; a pair who could never be separated despite time's most wicked trick of all.

"What will happen now?" asked Arabella eventually. "Will we stay together always?"

"I don't believe we can. The door is bound to close again. Perhaps we are doomed to wait for those fleeting moments when it comes ajar."

Arabella wept then, silently and bitterly, leaning her cheek against Gaius's chest and savouring the warm clean smell of his skin.

"Don't, don't, my darling," he said. "Maybe if I pray to the goddesses hard enough they will show me the way."

"There *is* no way for us," she answered with despair.

Neither had noticed that while they had been lost in love, the fog had started to creep up the hills, but now both looked upward, as the face of the moon was suddenly blotted out by the mass of cloud.

"We must go back," said Gaius.

"But to where, to what? Who knows what lies at the foot of those hills — Aquae Sulis or Bath?"

"Nevertheless, we cannot stay here getting colder and colder. We must face what is to come, Arabella."

"Somehow I don't think I can," she answered miserably, as once more he wrapped his cloak about them and they started downward.

As they neared the city they seemed to enter a tunnel of vapour, the walls so white and frightening, that Arabella drew back in alarm. As she did so she stumbled and temporarily let go of Gaius's hand, and when she went to take it again, it had gone. She turned, reaching out for him and calling his name. There was nothing, only the emptiness of the mist and herself alone. Just for a moment, Arabella Wynter put her head back and cried aloud before she regained control of herself and made her stumbling way back.

Much as she had guessed it would the town of Bath lay before her and — oh joy of joys! — an unemployed chair man stood beside his sedan, forlornly waiting for custom on such an inclement night.

"Hey, good fellow," called Arabella. "Take me to my Lord of Midhurst's house and deliver me to the back entrance." Deciding to defy conjecture by being direct, she added, "I've been about mischief and want no one to know it. There's a golden guinea in this for you if you keep a still tongue in your head."

The man leered a little but nonetheless called his assistant and the two of them carried Arabella to her destination.

"I'd clean meself up before me father saw me, if I was you," said the chair man, as Arabella got out.

Arabella gazed down at herself, horrified. The hem of her skirt was hanging in strips and there was a tear in her bodice. Remembering how it got there, colour bloomed in Arabella's cheeks. Afterwards, lying in bed she wondered if, after all, she had dreamt everything. But even as she turned to sleep, she knew that she had not. There was an awareness of her body, that had not been there before. Arabella clung to her pillow at the memory, full of love for Gaius Petronius yet filled at the same time with a feeling of dread.

It seemed to her then that no sooner had she closed her eyes than Emma said by her ear, "You must wake up, my Lady. His Lordship wants to see you as soon as you're dressed."

Arabella sat upright. "Oh? Do you know what for?"

"No, my Lady. He didn't say."

Arabella's mind turned like a mouse in a cage. Did her father know that she had been out nearly all night long? And if he did, what explanation could she possibly give? But as she entered the Earl's study, Arabella saw that her father was smiling.

"Well, my child," he said, his quizzing glass swinging on its ribbon before he raised it to look at her. "I hope you were not too bored and lonely last night."

Arabella lowered her eyes. "No, Papa. I went straight to sleep."

"And did you dream?"

She looked up swiftly in sudden shock. "Why do you ask that?"

"I see that you did, Arabella. And tell me, was it pleasant?"

Did the teasing tone conceal something else or was the Earl genuinely interested?

"I cannot remember, Sir."

"I just wondered if it could have been about weddings?"

Arabella looked at him sharply. "Weddings?" she repeated.

The Earl motioned her to a seat. "Yes, my dear. For they were very much on my mind last evening."

"Oh?"

"Indeed. For no sooner had I had the honour of having my hand in marriage accepted by Lady Woodruff..." Arabella's heart sank to her feet and she could only hope that her consternation did not show. ". . . than Lord Rufus Abinger took me on one side and asked my permission to court you with a view to entering into an engagement to be married."

Arabella feared that her expression must be bleak for her father added hastily, "I told him that I would speak to you. Obviously, my dear, my earlier promise to you holds good." He leant forward, taking Arabella's hand in his. "But though you may choose whomsoever you will, I want you to know that Lord Rufus stands high in my estimation and that such a union would meet with a great deal of favour in my eyes."

Arabella nodded silently and the Earl leant back in his chair, something of his old expression returning to his face.

"And now, my child, aren't you going to congratulate me on my forthcoming marriage? You are to have a stepmamma."

"I wish you every happiness," mumbled Arabella dully.

"And what of Lord Rufus? May I tell him he may call?"

Arabella shot her father a desperate look. "Father, I do not mind him calling, but please give me time to consider any further commitment."

"Have you no fondness for him?"

"I regard him in the same way that I regard Julian. To me he is just another brother."

And with that disappointing reply the Earl of Midhurst had to be content as his daughter left the room.

*

"Come on, Gaius," said Lucius Marcellus. "You've been asleep for hours. The fog has cleared and it's a beautiful day."

Very very slowly, his friend opened his eyes, only too painfully aware that he had, in fact, slept for only one short hour, having spent most of that tormented night looking for Arabella.

"I think I'll stay in bed for a while," he answered slowly. "Actually I had little sleep last night."

Lucius looked at him narrowly. "I don't know what's the matter with you these days. It's almost as if you've forgotten how to enjoy yourself."

"I know, and I'm sorry. To be quite honest with you, I've had something on my mind."

Lucius sat down on his bed, earnestly leaning forward. "Is it anything I can help with? Or has it something to do with that mysterious girl you saw when we first came here?"

"In a way it has. But if I explained it to you, you wouldn't understand." Lucius stood up, obviously annoyed, and Gaius added hastily, "I didn't mean that rudely. It's just that it's a complicated story."

"She's married, I suppose."

"No, she's not — but she is still not available."

"What do you mean?"

"I can't say more, Lucius."

His friend went to the doorway. "Well, you've only another week to resolve the situation. It's back to the Wall after that."

"I know," answered Gaius wretchedly. "You don't have to remind me." He closed his eyes again. "You go on to the Baths, Lucius, and I'll join you there later. I'll just have another hour's sleep."

But the relief of unconsciousness would not come and the legionary lay, turning from one uncomfortable position to another, with his mind in a turmoil. Now that he had held her close to him and made her his own, how could he live without Arabella? How could he march away from Aquae Sulis heading for the North Lands and lose the only chance he had of once more experiencing that mysterious warp of time?

Even now in the bright daylight the thought that the door might just be where it sometimes appeared had Gaius wearily rising from his bed and dressing. But, as he had half suspected, there was nothing in its place but the blank wall and, disconsolately, he made his way from the villa and towards the temple precinct.

It seemed that the sunshine had brought out the entire population and the crowd on its way to make offering at the sacred spring had formed into a slow-moving line. Gaius joined on the end, feeling that his only hope was to seek inspiration from the deities Sulis and Minerva, and to ask them to intercede on his part. In fact he felt so desperate that, when he finally gained the observation arch, he almost threw his mother's wedding ring — worn on his little finger — into the steaming waters beneath, but at the last moment changed his mind and offered instead the bronze brooch set with red enamel that his father had given him when he joined the army. Then, in great humility, Gaius closed his eyes and waited.

Strangely enough, a revelation did come. Rather as if a voice had spoken in his ear, Gaius had the sudden conviction that the key to seeing Arabella again lay in the Baths, and he remembered the day when she had peeped nervously into the circular bath area and seen him naked. With a sense almost of relief, the legionary left the spring and made his way into the bathing complex.

*

"But Arabella dear," Lady Woodruff was saying, "you really must not mope like this. Why, I cannot think what is the matter with you of late."

Her perfect face, rather cross-looking, was so close to Arabella's that the girl had an overwhelming urge to smack it and then shout, "*You* are most of the matter. I simply could not live with you in the same house so I have decided to marry Lord Rufus Abinger just to get away.

And all the time all I want is to be with Gaius Petronius for ever."

But aloud Arabella said, "It is just that I have so much on my mind, Lady Woodruff. Firstly trying to adjust to the fact that Papa is to marry again..." She allowed herself the luxury of a malicious little smile at Lydia. ". . . and then wondering whether or not to accept Lord Rufus. I have been quite preoccupied and you will have to excuse me."

Lydia returned the smile with her lips while maintaining an ice-cold expression. "My dear, I *do* understand. It is not an easy time for we women when marriage is in the air." She changed the subject as if she no longer had any interest in Arabella. "Have you heard that the Prince of Wales is due in Bath? I do believe he will be at Mr Nash's ball tomorrow night. We must make a point of being present."

"Yes, I certainly shall," answered Arabella defiantly. "I have promised Lord Rufus that I will give him an answer then."

"Oh la la!" fluttered Lydia. "How exciting it will be. Handsome princes and betrothals. Why, I declare my head is in a positive whirl."

"I wonder if Mr Nash will wear his grubby white hat or if he will leave it off for the occasion," said Arabella, half smiling.

"Even Beau Nash," answered Lydia Woodruff grandly, "must show respect for the Prince of Wales."

But there she was wrong. The extraordinary character, whose dictates the highest in the land obeyed as if they were rustics, made a bow to the young prince and then calmly informed him of the rules of the Assembly Rooms and requested that he comply with them. Very solemnly, Prince Frederick assured the Master of Ceremonies that nothing would give him greater pleasure, and the evening was set fair for success.

Arabella could not help but notice that of the senior ladies presented to the Prince, Lady Woodruff — glittering in a dress as emerald as her eyes — was the one who caught his attention, and that after politeness had bidden him first to lead out the Duchess of Queensbury, it was Lydia's hand that he sought for the next dance.

But Rufus was suddenly at Arabella's side and she could no longer observe her future stepmother as the young man led her out to dance. Almost at once he blurted out what he obviously longed to say.

"Arabella, have you considered? Oh my darling, say that you agree and you will make me the happiest creature in the world."

"Rufus, I..." she began — but the words stuck in her throat. How could she tell this sweet, affectionate young man that though she would marry him it was for all the wrong reasons? How could she say that he merely offered a means of escape from Lydia Woodruff; that as far as love was concerned she had given herself totally to a ghost from the past and could never love again?

"Rufus..." she tried once more, then gasped, "It is very hot in here. Would you excuse me for a moment?"

"Where are you going?"

"Just to step outside."

And before he could protest any further, Arabella had spun round and hurried from the ballroom, leaving her partner staring mournfully after her.

Not knowing quite why they did so, Arabella found her feet turning towards the stone steps down which she had descended on the day she had seen Gaius Petronius bathing. She prayed that tonight they would have reappeared and she could once more use them and find him waiting for her at the bottom, ready to catch her in his arms and tell her everything would be all right. Holding her breath, Arabella went to the top step beside the notice announcing that they were dangerous, and looked below. The flight had reappeared as mysteriously as it had previously vanished and she could clearly see it winding down to the darkness beneath. Without stopping for a second, Arabella picked up her skirts and started to hurry down the stairs.

*

He could stay no longer in the circular bath, staring at the archway and hoping that she might come. With a movement almost of despair, Gaius Petronius took a towel from an attendant slave and, sitting on one of the wooden seats set at intervals along the walls, started to dry himself while he thought about Arabella.

It was hopeless! He would never see Arabella again. Tomorrow he would start the march back along the great road that led directly from Aquae Sulis, via the fortress town of Eboracum, to the North Lands and the Emperor's Wall. The extraordinary love affair was over; there was no future left.

Pretending to wipe water from his face, Gaius, in fact, brushed away tears. Then, suddenly aware of a shadow looming over him, he looked up.

"*There* you are," said the ever-patient Lucius Marcellus, with only a hint of weariness in his voice. "Gaius, this is our last day. Do try not to ruin it."

Somehow his friend forced a smile. "You're right. I'm not being fair to anyone, particularly you. What would you like to do?"

"First of all, have a race in the Great Bath. Thirty lengths and see who is the fastest."

"But I've been swimming all morning."

"Nonsense, you've just been splashing. Come on — or are you afraid I'll win?"

Gaius stood up. "No. Your challenge is on."

As they walked side by side along the paved passageway, Gaius put his arms round Lucius's shoulders. "Thank you for your patience. I know I've been difficult. I hope I haven't spoiled your leave for you."

"Of course you haven't," answered Lucius gallantly. He paused, then added, "Did you ever resolve your difficulty with that girl?"

"No," said Gaius. "No, I didn't. To be honest with you I never saw her again — and now I know I never will."

*

"Frankly I'm worried," said Lord Rufus to a perspiring Julian Wynter, still out of breath from dancing too fast. "She said she'd only be a minute, but she's been gone half an hour."

Julian lowered his over-worked handkerchief. "My God, why didn't you tell me before?"

"You were too busy enjoying yourself."

"Then what about Father?"

"He looked as if he did not wish to be disturbed," answered Rufus, with just the merest hint of an undertone.

They both stared across to where the elegant figure of my Lord of Midhurst stood on the edge of the ballroom, occasionally raising his quizzing glass and looking with apparent unconcern to where Lydia Woodruff and Frederick, Prince of Wales, paced through a minuet, with eyes for no one but each other.

"So she *is* a vixen," muttered Julian, under his breath. "I came to that conclusion only last week and have put her from my mind ever since."

"Yes, she's a fortune hunter and you should have seen it sooner," answered Rufus brusquely. "But this isn't helping Arabella. I've been to look for her once. Are you coming with me this time?"

"Of course I am. I only hope no ill has befallen her."

*

The flight of steps was getting more difficult to traverse. Now the way was so dark that Arabella had resorted to putting one foot forward and over the edge of the step to carefully feel for the one beneath. And, to add to her difficulty, the fabric of the steps themselves had deteriorated so that she was continually treading on crumbling stonework. If she had not been so desperate to find Gaius she would have turned back to safety.

Yet her ears told her that he was down there somewhere for, as if from a great distance, she was certain she could hear the faint splash of water and the dull murmur of voices. Arabella stopped for a moment to listen, hardly daring to breathe. Then she heard it again. There could be no doubt; down there, living in his own time, Gaius Petronius definitely awaited her.

With a happy little cry, Arabella stepped forward into nothing. There was no step awaiting her and as her feet missed their hold completely, she plunged forward into blackness, screaming Gaius's name over and over again until all sound was stopped by the sensation of water closing over her head.

*

As Rufus and Julian raced up the street they heard the sound of footsteps and, turning, saw the Earl of Midhurst behind them.

"Where are you going?" he called. "What's amiss?"

"It's Arabella, Sir," gasped Rufus. "She was overcome with heat and left the ballroom. I waited for her awhile and then went looking but there is no sign of her. She's been gone almost an hour."

"Has she returned home?"

Rufus and Julian stopped short. "We hadn't thought of that."

"Then I'll go back to the ballroom and ask Lydia to leave in my carriage. She can organise the search of the house while I come with you."

Knowing it was impossible to argue with his father, Julian merely nodded his head while Lord Rufus looked more and more anxious, but ignoring them the Earl turned on his heel and hurried away in the direction of the Assembly Rooms. But even as he approached, the sound of wheels made him draw to one side as a carriage — the Prince of Wales' feathers emblazoned on the door — went past him at speed heading for the north road.

Lord Midhurst had one glimpse of a pair of green eyes and a perfect little face regarding him in a startled manner, before their owner hastily bobbed out of sight and there was nothing to be seen but the bewigged head and Hanoverian profile of the young Prince.

"Grand pox to them both," swore the Earl colourfully — and went rapidly on his way.

*

Beneath the high vaulted roof of the Great Bath, where the sun slanted in through lofty windows, steam collected and convoluted in spirals, giving the shadows of the arched bathing hall a mystical quality. And as Gaius Petronius stepped to the water's edge, dropping his towel onto the square-paved floor, he was reminded vividly of the night when he and Arabella had found and loved one another in the mist above the twin cities of Aquae Sulis and Bath.

"Oh, Minerva," he prayed silently, "I would give anything, even my life, if I could see her once more."

"Ready?" called Lucius, shocking him back to reality.

"Ready."

"Then one, two, three —"

They dived simultaneously, two fine strong young men, dappled by the tilted sunshine.

Gaius, his hair streaming and his eyes open, went straight to the bottom of the greenish pool, preparing to emerge some lengths further on — but, as he did so, a shadow in the water caught his eye. He swam towards it and his heart almost stopped in his chest. Clearly visible beneath the glassy surface, her hair a cloud and her terrified face telling him that she was in mortal danger, Arabella was fighting for her life.

He could not speak to her, he could not even call out, as Gaius broke water once more to draw in a mighty breath, before he dived to where his beloved lay drowning. As he put his arms round her to bring her up, Gaius knew that he must save her if it was the last thing he did.

But, strangely, Arabella did not try to resist. Instead, there in that sparkling green kingdom, where every movement was softened, Gaius saw her turn her great shining eyes on him and then, very gently, pull him into her embrace.

He understood at last what had been intended all along, what the inevitable outcome for them both must be, and as he slipped his mother's wedding ring from his finger to hers, Gaius smiled before he slowly bent his head to kiss her.

*

What brought the search party to the ruined steps they never afterwards could tell. Perhaps it was some instinct of Lord Rufus Abinger's or possibly the Earl of Midhurst's insistence that every inch of Bath should be searched for his missing daughter. But, whatever reason, they did arrive there and sent down one of m'Lord's footmen, well roped for safety. He came up whey faced.

"She's there, my Lord, but I'll need help to bring her up. She's lying in some great pool of water."

"Is she...?"

"Yes, my Lord, I fear so."

Nobody had thought big Lord Rufus to be so sensitive, but he sank down like some gentle giant on hearing those words, and wept as though his heart was breaking. But he was more in control of himself when, an hour later, Julian himself carried her up and laid her on the blanket which somebody had thrown over the pavement.

Arabella looked as if she were asleep, her hair silvered by the moonshine, her face half smiling as if at some happy dream.

"She was so beautiful." said Lord Rufus, and he knelt beside her to kiss her small dead hand. As he did so, something glinted in the moonlight and all of them wondered at the fact that Arabella Wynter, a high-born lady of the eighteenth century, wore on her marriage finger a delicately moulded Roman wedding ring.

The Gemini Syndrome

It was March outside, cold and blowing, blustering at the tremulous crocuses putting up their gallant heads in the squares and parks of London. But inside there was no time, no season, only the enormous blackness of the darkroom before Elizabeth Lacey stretched out her hand and pulled a switch, and the place was instantly transformed to a demonic cavern, red as a dragon's glowing eye.

"The moment of truth," she thought. The film had been removed from her camera and the developing process could now begin but, as always, Elizabeth paused and for a moment stood uncertainly, almost as if she had changed her mind about what she was to do next.

"Oh, come on," she said under her breath. "Even if they *are* there, it doesn't matter. They can't hurt you."

But still she made no move towards the developing sink, instead sitting down on a stool and staring at her hands which had begun to shake.

"Damn!" she said loudly. "This is no use. I thought I had got over all that years ago."

There was no answer from the dense and empty room, and no sound except for the quickening of Elizabeth's heart. Yet it seemed, as she gazed blindly about her, that she could hear a childish voice, her own, and that she relived, yet again, the time when all the inexplicable and terrifying events had started.

It had always been a family legend that Elizabeth had been born at the precise moment when the crown was placed on the Queen's young head. The other story had been that she had come into the world carrying a camera. The first part of the romance had been true; the second, a joke. But nonetheless, the child's love of photography had been extraordinary and she had finally graduated from toy cameras to the real thing when, on her tenth birthday, a bulky parcel had revealed a neat black box in which glistened the magic eye.

Sitting here now in the shadows of her darkroom, Elizabeth felt again all the rushing sensations of that birthday twenty-five long years ago. Brown sandals, blue dress, flying hair the colour of mahogany, lips pursed to blow out candles on a bright pink cake.

For a moment Elizabeth smiled in the glow of the safe light, then her face changed as she remembered all that had followed from that day. As soon as her friends had gone she had rushed into the garden and by the light of a sun just beginning its evening descent had photographed everything in sight: her grandfather asleep in a deck-chair, a newspaper over his face rising and falling; the cat dozing, idly watching a saffron-beaked bird; the apples crowding together on the tree. Afterwards she had fallen into bed happy and innocent, the precious camera on her bedside table, nestling against the light shaped like an owl. A week later she had fetched the prints from the chemist and then everything had changed.

As her thoughts reached this stage, Elizabeth found herself reaching for a cigarette, regardless of the fact that she had given them up ten years ago.

"Fool!" she said, but still her fingers rummaged in her bag for her keys and, having selected one, unlocked a drawer in the bottom of her equipment cupboard. A packet of cigarettes lay there, untouched and ever-tempting, but after a moment's contemplation, Elizabeth ignored them, going instead to a sealed and bulky envelope.

"Why am I doing this?" she muttered, then stood – as if fighting with herself – before she finally withdrew the packet and threw it onto the bench, then switched on the kettle that waited, ever-ready, on a tray. Its homely groaning seemed to counterpoint her mood, in some respects bringing her back to reality, so that when she finally returned to the bench, a steaming mug of black coffee in her hand, she picked up the envelope determinedly, ripped it open and withdrew the top photograph from the small collection within.

Even holding it in her fingers recalled childhood once more. She had rushed home from the chemist, and proudly handed the packet of prints to her mother. How safe it had all seemed, standing in the kitchen and watching Hilda Lacey turning the photographs over.

"Oh dear!" her mother had said, stopping at one of them. "What a shame. That one would have been so nice. But I expect some light got into the camera."

"Let me see." Elizabeth had taken it from her and gone over to the window. The black and white print was of Grandpa snoring, but in the sky behind him was a black blob with two smaller blobs within its compass.

"Doesn't it look strange!" Elizabeth had exclaimed. "Is it really light on the film?"

"Yes, I expect so. We can ask Daddy tonight."

And Elizabeth's father had confirmed that indeed that was the cause of the fault and the whole incident had been forgotten – for a while, anyway.

Now, for the millionth time, Elizabeth looked at the photograph again through a magnifying glass, seeing the extraordinary fault; the outer blob oval and slightly transparent, within it two pale shapes distinctly visible. It resembled nothing in particular and yet had a certain familiar quality about it.

Taking a long pull at her coffee, Elizabeth turned to the second photograph. It had been taken a year later on the same camera and was the first one to bring consternation to the Lacey family and trouble to Elizabeth. The subject this time had been the cat asleep under the apple tree, and sure enough there it was, large and somnolent in the foreground. But beside it, and totally out of proportion to it, were parked two prams, neatly standing side by side.

Mr Lacey had accused Elizabeth of tampering with the negative and of trying to be clever. There had been tears and protestations and Grandpa had refused to eat his supper and finally, in a moment of fury that had given her extra courage, Elizabeth had challenged her father to take the negative to an expert. He had done so. In fact he sent the whole film to the Kodak laboratory and asked for their comments. They had come back succinctly. Kodak could find no evidence of the film having been tampered with and were prepared to swear that it was perfect when it had left them. The mystery had gone unsolved but Elizabeth knew that her father suspected her, for afterwards he often dragged into the conversation the two little girls who claimed to have taken photographs of fairies and had actually deceived the great Conan Doyle.

Now Elizabeth shook her head. If only he had known the horror she had experienced, the sheer unabated bewilderment. For a while it had even put off her beloved hobby – though not for long, nothing could. Somehow, even as a child, she had not felt right without a camera nearby.

Resisting the cigarettes, Elizabeth looked at the third print from the hidden collection. Her own face gazed back at her, twelve years old and already showing the fineness of bone structure that would make her beautiful in her teens.

This time the print was in colour and round the suntanned shoulders her hair glinted redly. But it was not to the beach and the brilliant sea that the eye was drawn but to what was beside Elizabeth on her towel. Two shadowy babies lay there, bare legs kicking, sun bonnets concealing their faces. They would have been, Elizabeth imagined, just over a year old.

This time her father's fury had reached mammoth proportions. Hilda had taken the photograph herself and had sworn that there had been nothing in the viewfinder except Elizabeth. But they had all known that anyway, and Hugh Lacey had personally taken the film and the camera for thorough investigation by an expert. The scientist had gone over every inch of the equipment and negative but had been able to find nothing. Elizabeth had overheard her father say, "The Professor believes that if the child is faking she will go far! He said that only a genius would be able to deceive him."

It had taken Elizabeth a year to recover from it all, a year in which she had shot no photographs, a year in which she had been thoroughly miserable and depressed. But then she had gone on holiday with her parents and the sight of the setting sun behind Tintagel had been too much for her; she had snatched her mother's camera, taken a shot, and won her first photography contest as a result. The prize had been a much better camera and Elizabeth had known when she had held it in her hands for the first time that she could never give up taking pictures, that that was what she wanted to do always and that one day she would study the subject and pursue it professionally.

Now sitting in the dimness of her darkroom, Elizabeth looked to where the camera still hung on the wall, used occasionally for the sake of old times. It was through that camera that she had struck up a friendship with a local photographer, asking if she could use his darkroom to develop the films it took. And just as well! Looking through more of the old snaps, Elizabeth saw herself at sports day, the blurred image of two toddlers somehow muddled up with the sack race; next a group of school children on holiday in France, standing at the foot of the Eiffel Tower, two little boys vaguely visible, also peering at the lens.

Elizabeth laid the photographs down on the bench. "Always the same thing" she thought. "Always vague, always misty – but there! And getting bigger."

She riffled through the pile and picked out three glossy black and white prints blown up to a large size. She had taken these within the last two years but they had never been put on public display. Shaking her head over them, Elizabeth impulsively switched off the safe light and, feeling her way to the door, went out into the daylight of her studio.

It was with a sense of relief that she looked about her, seeing all the familiar tools of her trade, and relishing each one for its normality, for this particular journey into the past had left her shaken.

Not caring that it was only just six o'clock, she went down the stairs to her flat and poured herself a gin and tonic. She sat down, hoping that television would stop her thinking. But it was hopeless; an inane quiz show merely served to irritate and, with an angry movement, Elizabeth jabbed at the remote control. Beside her, omnipresent, were the big prints, lying face down.

"Damn you," she said out loud and picked them up.

The first one showed models, slinky, black, beautiful, leaping down a cat walk; beside them two blurred schoolboys, jumping, having fun. The next was a Royal Ballet dancer taking time off from Covent Garden and appearing in a West End musical; just visible in the wings two boys imitating his movements. The third was of a stately home, still in private hands and leased out by the owners to be used for background shots in an advertising campaign for which Elizabeth had been engaged. From an upstairs window peered two horribly familiar little faces.

Putting the prints down again, Elizabeth crossed to the window and stared out into the evening. The wind had dropped and the view was gentle, placid, the river winding like a snake, silvery and slow, and the sky a lavender bowl, full of pink rosebud clouds.

She had been lucky to buy the top two floors of a Victorian house in Richmond and obtain the necessary permission to use the upper floor as both a studio and darkroom. For from every window she could see the Thames, and the beautiful parkland was only a stone's throw away. A perfect setting in which to live and work and take photographs.

"Without all of Nigel's help, I know I could never have managed it," she thought now, and the very mention of his name, even to herself, made Elizabeth feel a rush of heady emotion.

Nigel had been in charge of the Crystal advertising campaign; Crystal being a smart new drink, hopefully to be drunk by smart new people. Bryant Park, the stately home, had seemed to him the ideal setting for the pictures and Elizabeth Lacey, the most talented woman photographer of the day, had seemed the ideal choice to take them. That was how they met.

Elizabeth poured herself another gin, a little less strong than the first, and once more crossed to the window. It had been eighteen months now since the day she had first set eyes on him, disliking him on sight, thinking him too handsome by half – and knowing it.

She had determined on that glorious autumn morning with the trees on fire and the sky as blue as butterflies, that she wasn't going to like him; that she was going to resist any glances from his particularly vivid eyes, no matter how hard he tried.

Her resolve had lasted all of a week. Nigel seemed to have the knack of reading women's thoughts or, at least, being more than usually sensitive to their moods. He had sensed that Elizabeth did not like him and, as a result, had adopted a business-like approach.

"Everything all right, Miss Lacey? Not having any trouble with Francesca?" A model known for her temperament.

Or, "I think we may have to do an extra day's shooting before the film crew move in, Miss Lacey. If you could kindly negotiate the fee through your agent."

Or, "Good morning, Miss Lacey. Weather getting rather brisk, I fear. Hope you don't mind working in the wind."

In the end, Elizabeth had snapped, "I do wish you could call me Elizabeth, Mr Hart. I'm not used to quite so much formality."

The brilliant blue eyes had darkened, and he had said, "My mother's name. She was known by everyone as Lizbeth."

Elizabeth had wanted to appear disinterested, but he was looking at her so pleasantly that she had just said, "Oh, how charming. So much nicer than Liz."

Nigel had smiled and looked pleased and said, "Thank you," and Elizabeth had promptly felt wicked for entertaining such nasty thoughts about him.

Now, standing at the window, glass in hand, she said, "You clever little devil. You always did that to me – and I still don't know quite how to take you."

On the day when the final photographic session had ended, Nigel and his client had thrown a small party for Viscount Moreton and his wife – the owners of Bryant Park. To it were invited all the models and Elizabeth Lacey.

"So wonderful," gushed Lady Moreton. "I think you're wonderful, Miss Lacey. I would be so pleased if you would do some portraits of my children."

Elizabeth had spun round. She had just developed the print showing the two strange little faces peering from an upper window.

"You have children, you say?" she had said, almost with relief. "Two little boys?"

The Viscountess had stared at her strangely. "No, two girls. But I do have a baby boy. Why?"

Elizabeth had suddenly felt an overwhelming need to confide in someone, to tell someone.

"May I show you something?" she had said.

The print was still in her case in the restaurant's cloakroom. Lady Moreton had stared at it with astonishment.

"Who ever can they be?" she had said, and then added. "They look so faint that I suspect they must be ghosts."

"Why? *Is* Bryant Park haunted?" Elizabeth asked.

"Yes. But only by a Red Lady and a Blue Nun. Sounds like a drink doesn't it?" She had pealed with laughter. "I've never heard of little dead boys."

Standing at the window now, Elizabeth saw the lights appear along the river bank. The silver snake had become a purple thread, speckled with dandelions; the sky was wine for drinking, but changing even as she watched it to a black crystal glistening with quartz. When it was completely dark, Nigel would ring and then she could be happy.

How had she allowed herself to become so vulnerable, Elizabeth wondered? How had dislike been changed to so intense a love? How could a woman of thirty-five imagine that this was the first time that she had ever tasted passion?

She had not seen him after the party in the restaurant but her agent had telephoned within a few weeks to say that Nigel Hart had booked Elizabeth Lacey to photograph another of his campaigns.

"How well do you know him?" the agent had asked curiously.

"Hardly at all. Why?"

"He called you Lizbeth, as if it were a nickname."

"Probably a slip of the tongue."

But inside she had been touched that he should affectionately call her by his mother's name.

They met again in a dripping wet Rue de Rivoli, Nigel surrounded by a crowd of grumpy models preparing to be photographed outside the Paris Opera House. Everybody was thoroughly soaked and snapping at everybody else, except for Nigel himself who appeared to be speaking to no one.

Elizabeth later decided that it was the motherly streak in her that caused all her problems. For as soon as the session was over she had whipped him into a smart restaurant and insisted on buying him dinner.

"The least I could do to thank you for getting me this assignment – and at such an enormous fee."

"It will help pay the mortgage," he had answered lightly. And it had. Elizabeth had put down a deposit on the Richmond flat. But then she had not even considered it, instead wondering at the colour of his eyes, deep as violets in the flickering candlelight.

"Your hair is the colour of damson wine," he had said suddenly, adding, "I should know. My mother used to make it.|"

The coincidence that they were both noting each other's colouring was not lost on her, but Elizabeth merely answered. "You must be very fond of her."

"She's dead, I'm afraid. It was cancer. I was fifteen at the time. It sent me off the rails for a while."

Elizabeth put her hand over his. "I'm so sorry," she said.

Nigel had looked at her very straightly. "You're like her," he had answered. "And I love you for it. And for your talent and beauty and a million other things..."

She hadn't been able to answer but had just sat there, staring into those spectacular eyes and considering how she could have ever thought him insincere.

When Elizabeth finally experienced the revelation of his lovemaking, in a small and unfashionable hotel near the Place de la Concorde, she wondered how she could have wasted so much of her life. For Nigel was everything that she had hoped a man would be. Beautiful to look at, lean, taut, passionate yet kind. He loved without restraint yet there was not that frightening element in him that Elizabeth had encountered before. The threat that when he possessed her body he would also try to possess her spirit; that he would eventually want her to stop being what she was and turn into something of his own creation.

There was nothing of that and the few days in Paris passed so splendidly that Elizabeth feared, as with all beautiful and delicate things, that somehow the dream would shatter and then be gone for ever. And in a way she was right.

As they had left Gatwick Airport and gone to fetch their cars, Nigel had caught her to him.

"Lizbeth, there's something I've got to tell you."

She knew what it was before he had even said it.

"I'm married. No, don't speak. It was a mistake when we were both too young. We go our own ways now, lead separate lives."

"An open marriage," Elizabeth had answered dully.

"Please, don't say it like that. We're not right for each other, she and I, and that's the truth of it. I love you, Lizbeth."

"Thanks very much," Elizabeth had answered harshly and, turning round quickly, had strode off to her car.

Even to remember that conversation was painful and the fact that she now owned her own flat and that he visited her there and they were still lovers, did nothing to ease the recollection.

"Nor how I feel!" Elizabeth thought angrily.

How she hated being a mistress, detested the secrecy of it all, longed for him to get his much spoken of divorce and end the hole-in-the-corner meetings, the snatched weekends, the lies and cheating and deceit.

"I'm not cut out for it," Elizabeth said now, gazing down to where the river flowed like ink, dark as the feelings she often had in her heart. "But I love him too much. I can't live without him."

She spoke aloud and her voice echoed round the empty flat. How many other women, she wondered, had said those very words? How many other women had seen the precious years slip away while they waited for their lover to telephone, to call, or put in an appearance?

It was too dark to see out now and with a sigh, Elizabeth drew the curtains and turned back to her drinks cupboard.

Was she drinking too much, she wondered? Had waiting for Nigel driven her to alcohol?

As a compromise she went to the fridge and poured out a glass of wine and topped it up with soda and it was as she came back into the living room that she saw that one of the big prints had fallen off the sofa and was lying on the floor. Elizabeth stooped to pick it up and recognised it as Bryant Park, the two ghostly children still staring from the upper window.

She sat down thoughtfully, thinking of Lady Moreton's words. Were the boys ghosts and was she, Elizabeth, in some way their unconscious medium? Was that why they came at intervals and deposited themselves in her photographs? But if that was so, what was it they were trying to tell her? Was there any theme linking the places in which they had appeared? Was that the clue?

Elizabeth thought carefully but could see no connection between her childhood back garden, the Eiffel Tower, a West End theatre and a stately home.

"Then what?" she murmured. "What is it you want me to know?"

The pictures stared back enigmatically and with sudden impatience, Elizabeth thrust them into a drawer in her bureau.

"Another day," she said. "I'll solve your puzzle another day."

As she passed the phone on her way to the bedroom, she glared at it. "You're late. You should have rung at six o'clock."

But to her reflection, staring back at her with those fine-drawn features that could be gaunt if she were not careful, she could only whisper, "What a fool."

She undid her hair from the topknot scraped to the crown of her head and watched it fall like water about her shoulders. And it was in this state, slightly dishevelled and more than a little depressed, that Elizabeth herd the front doorbell ring.

"Thought I'd call," Nigel said, when she got there, producing flowers from behind his back. "The phone is so impersonal, don't you think, darling?"

"Oh hell! I look a sight."

"No you don't, you're in your hair, as they say. Well, are you going to let me in?"

"Of course," she said and, as he walked through the entrance, hurled herself into his arms and hugged him till he winced.

"Why didn't you warn me? I could have got some food in, cooked a meal. It would have been wonderful, the wind blowing outside and us cosily indoors."

"Well, so it can be," he replied adding, "for an hour."

"An hour? Is that all?"

Nigel took her face between his hands. "I'm sorry, darling, really I am, but that's all the time I've got. Felicity has gone to some friend or other, but I'm afraid she's not going to be *that* late back."

Elizabeth moved away from him. "But what about you going your way and letting her go hers? An open marriage, you told me. Well, it's seemed rather closed recently."

Nigel laughed, slipping his arm round her waist. "Very witty. Now come on, Lizbeth. Don't spoil the time we've got. There's a bottle of champagne in the car and I rather thought we might open it in bed."

Fury welled inside her like cold poison. "I see. Go round to Lizbeth for a quick coupling, then back home looking like a dutiful husband. Well not with me, Nigel. You've chosen the wrong person."

He didn't answer her at once, busying himself with pouring out a drink. Then he said, "This is new, isn't it? You haven't been averse to that arrangement in the past."

Because he was telling the truth, Elizabeth was angrier than ever.

"Perhaps, but not any more. Either you want to be with me all the time or you can forget the whole thing."

Nigel put his drink down. "But darling, we've just been away for the weekend. Why are you so furious with me?"

Fighting off tears, she answered, "Because those two days together showed me how wonderful it was to share our time Nigel, why can't you ask Felicity for a divorce?"

There was an expression in his eyes that Elizabeth had never seen before and he paused for a moment before he said. "The truth is she's not very well at the moment."

Elizabeth stared at him suspiciously, "What do you mean? What's wrong with her?"

"I don't know. She's been complaining of headaches. The doctor's sent her to a consultant."

"She's probably doing it to attract attention."

The blue eyes were cold. "That wasn't worthy of you, Lizbeth, and you know it."

"Why is it always me that's in the wrong? Why can't it be *her* for a change?" she answered furiously and, whirling round, ran into her bedroom and plunged onto the bed, punching the pillow.

There was a long silence from the other room, punctuated only by the sound of the television being turned on, the splash of the soda syphon and the opening and closing of a bureau drawer. Nigel was obviously in no mood to apologise and it would have to be she that came crawling round.

"I hate you," she said to her reflection as she wiped away the tears and put on make-up. "Why are you always so weak as far as he's concerned? You manage every other part of your life fairly well."

Her reflection grimaced as Elizabeth got up and slowly went back into the living room.

Nigel was not watching television, nor did he have his drink in his hand. Instead he had picked up a magnifying glass and was looking very intently at the photograph of Bryant Place.

"I say, Lizbeth," he said as she came in, "is this genuine?"

"What do you mean?"

"Those misty little creatures at one of the windows. Did you fake the shot or is this an actual ghost photograph?"

Every instinct Elizabeth possessed warned against telling Nigel the story of the years of haunted photographs. Instead she smiled casually and said, "Yes, strange, isn't it? I certainly didn't fake it, and Lady Moreton hasn't got any sons of that age."

"You don't mean it could be the real thing?"

"If you mean... phantoms of some kind, yes, I suppose so. There's no other explanation that I can think of."

Nigel looked up, his face sparkling. "Good God, this is amazing. Lizbeth, can I have this?"

The "No" was out before she could control it, and Nigel stared at her puzzled. "But darling, why not? This is a shot in a million. Don't you think other people should be allowed to see it?"

Elizabeth shook her head. "No, I don't. I can't explain why but somehow that photograph is very personal to me. I don't want people gawping at it."

Nigel laid down the print, shaking his head. "I shall never understand you, Lizbeth. You must have had this a long time and yet you never told me about it. Sometimes I just don't understand your motives."

She looked at him blankly. "I don't have motives, Nigel. Unless, of course, loving you and wanting to spend my life with you can be described as one."

"That's not what I meant," he said, standing up.

"Then what did you mean?"

"The secretive part of you. The part of you that could take a photograph like this one and then keep it utterly to yourself."

Stung, Elizabeth answered. "I didn't. I told Lady Moreton."

"And what did she say?"

"That they were ghosts."

"Well, there you are then!" answered Nigel triumphantly.

"We're going round in circles," Elizabeth said, impatiently. "Let's drop the subject, can we."

Nigel looked reluctant, then smiled. "Very well – but only for the time being. One day I'll feature that picture in an exhibition."

Putting his arm round her shoulders, Nigel kissed Elizabeth on the end of her nose. "Come on, nuisance. I'll take you out on the town for a drink."

It was not till nine o'clock in the evening that Elizabeth finally let herself back into the flat, and, realising that she was hungry, made a snack to eat in front of the television. Without consulting a newspaper, she turned it on.

Even before the TV picture had appeared she knew by the music that the film was creepy and she prepared to switch off, but as the image came through, found her attention caught. An American woman photographer, played by Faye Dunaway, was receiving inexplicable visions of murders yet to come. Elizabeth sat on the edge of her chair, occasionally hiding her eyes when the action grew too frightening. It was almost a relief to hear the distant ringing on her studio telephone and to have to run up the stairs to answer it.

"Darling?"

It was Nigel, speaking softly and obviously telephoning from home. Felicity, no doubt, already tucked up in bed.

"Yes. What is it?"

"Nothing at all, you unromantic baggage. I just called to say I love you, I just called to say how much I care." He was singing very quietly, expecting her to laugh.

"Thank you."

"What's the matter? You sound very formal."

"You know I don't like all this. The thought of Felicity almost in earshot. It depresses me."

"Very well, then I'll go. But I'll see you soon."

"When?"

"Soon."

Before she could say anything further, Elizabeth distinctly heard a woman's voice call out, "Are you *still* in the bathroom?" and Nigel answer, 'Won't be a minute."

Very quietly Elizabeth put down the receiver.

She would have gone downstairs then, but a scream from the television set put her off. She felt that she had run through almost every possible emotion in the last few hours and terror was not one that she wished to add to them. Impulsively, Elizabeth opened the door and stepped into the blackness of her darkroom.

It was terribly quiet, unnervingly so, and she was glad to switch on the safe light and see the red flow light up all but the furthest corners. Almost as if she were looking for something to do, Elizabeth removed the film that she had put into the spiral earlier that day, and took it to the developing sink.

She had shot it during the weekend that she and Nigel had snatched away in the Cotswolds, almost empty of tourists in March. She had loved him with the lens, picking up the colour of his hair and eyes, photographing him against landscapes, contrasting his exuberance against stark trees.

The images began to appear and Elizabeth leant forward to see them more clearly. They were as good as she had hoped, and Nigel looked marvellous.

And then she stopped. Swimming beneath the developing agent she could vaguely see something appearing on one of her best compositions: in the foreground a sundial, in the background Nigel, carved like a chess piece against a fierce but dying sun, in the far distance a broken and derelict windmill. The photograph had dimensions that even Elizabeth had not envisaged, a powerful statement on the ravages of time, the futility of creation. That is, it would have been powerful if it hadn't been for the fault on the negative. But there was no fault on the negative. Elizabeth knew that even before she picked up the darkroom magnifier.

It was them of course. The two little boys, etched as black as Nigel, pawns to his rook, stood one on either side of the sundial, their backs turned to the camera, silently observing. A thrill of fear grasped Elizabeth's spine and she felt her hair crawl. There was something altogether menacing about the way they watched him. Though the faces of all three were invisible, yet there was a terrible atmosphere about the photograph.

"Oh God," she said and turned away from the sink.

When she looked again it was even clearer. The strange ghosts, the mist that usually hung about them supplanted by the sun's aura, were quite definitely staring Nigel out.

On an impulse, Elizabeth rushed to the studio phone, her one thought to warn him.

But her hand stopped even as it reached for the receiver. He would be in bed by now, lying next to Felicity and relishing her warmth on this chilly night. With a great sigh, Elizabeth turned away and slowly walked back into the darkroom, her heart pounding with every step she took at the anticipation of all that was to come.

All night long she had been dreaming; they were wild and frightening dreams in which two little boys ran down an endless corridor while she, tripping and stumbling, tried to catch up with them.

In the nightmare, doors opened off the passage and Elizabeth would peer into the rooms that lay beyond to see if the children were hiding there.

As Elizabeth hastened back into the corridor she saw the children in the distance but though she called to them to stop, they ran into another room, pretending they had not heard. Angrily, Elizabeth swept in after them but then came abruptly to a halt, for there stood Nigel, in a black leather coat, grinning at her.

"We want our daddy," said one of the boys. "Where is he?"

"Hello, nuisances," said Nigel, winking at Elizabeth over the child's head. "Will I do?"

"No you most certainly will not," answered the little boy somewhat precociously.

"Then in that case," answered Nigel, his features changing dramatically, "I'll have to tear you up. Both of you. Because you are nothing but silly little photographs after all."

And with that he picked up the boy who had just spoken and tore him to pieces.

"I'm going to faint," Elizabeth said to herself. "He's killing that helpless child."

She flung herself headlong at Nigel, kicking and punching and screaming at him to stop, but when she looked down at the boy's severed limbs they were, after all, just parts of a photograph.

"Help me!" Elizabeth called out. "Help me, help me, help me!"

She woke, still shouting, to hear her radio alarm going full blast and to see the clock pointing to seven.

"Oh Lord!" she said, and struggled to sit upright, wishing that she had a cup of coffee ready made. But even as she got out of bed and headed for the kitchen, the phone in the living room started to ring.

With the curtains still drawn the place was a cavern, rays of light coming through every crack, full of speckles and twirling motes. Elizabeth realised that outside the sun must be brilliant. Feeling slovenly, she slumped into an armchair and picked up the receiver.

"Good morning, my darling, and do I find you well?" said a voice, and Elizabeth recognised her agent in a bright and breezy mood.

"Max," she groaned, "it's seven o'clock in the morning. I've only just woken up and I've had a terrible night, so for heaven's sake don't be cheerful. I can't take it, not today, anyway."

There was a slight pause at the other end and then, in retaliation, Max started his old Jewish uncle routine. "Oi, my life! That I should find you like this, already. If you vant to make money, you vork like I do. Me, I never, ever sleep. I am much too busy making deals for all my clients..."

"Max, will you shut up!" said Elizabeth, though she was laughing despite herself. "You'd better have a very good reason for getting me out of bed."

An American voice answered back. "Say, sister, this can't be for real! Why, I've already been out and watered the hogs and chopped up my Mammy... I mean my logs. But seriously, folks, I've landed you an assignment that would bring tears to your eyes."

"Yeah?" said Elizabeth, joining in with him.

"Yes, sirree! Ever been to Venice?" The accent changed abruptly to Italian. "Hay, *bella signorina*, you come with me in my gondola. We have a little wine, a little spaghetti, and a little–"

"For God's sake, Max," Elizabeth put in impatiently. "Do come to the point."

"Assignment in Venice. Taking special photographs on the set of a new mega film about Leonardo da Vinci. You know, the painter chappy? You've heard of him, I suppose?" he teased.

"Max, do you mean it?"

At last he spoke normally. "Liz, love, I do. It's a real goody. Apparently the director wants some prestigious photographs of his leading man, none other than the Welsh wonder boy, the Richard Burton clone himself."

"You mean Roderick Rhys?"

"The very man."

"Well, well." Liz stopped slumping and straightened up. "What's the pay and when is it?"

"We're talking grands, darling, and the assignment begins in ten days. I've already booked you in."

"It sounds wonderful."

"And no giving it up because lover boy wants you for something else. You'll lose your other contracts if you work exclusively for Nigel Hart."

Elizabeth held the receiver away from her ear while Max nagged on. He had decided some months ago that he didn't approve of the affair.

"Liz," he'd said, looking serious for once, "that Nigel guy is using you. And you're the only one who can't see it. The sooner you drop him the better off you'll be."

Now Elizabeth said, "Have you quite finished?"

And Max answered, "Yes. Listen, baby, come to my office today and I'll give you a briefing. This is a real plum job."

"I hope the great man will cooperate. I've heard that he can be rather difficult."

The Jewish uncle answered. "Roderick Rhys, difficult? They're all difficult! Whyfore do I put up with all this temperament? The ten per cent, that is why!"

Elizabeth laughed. "I'll come round about noon. Then you can buy me a lettuce leaf."

"You're on."

He hung up and so did Elizabeth. By now she was thoroughly awake and able to think, and lying in a foaming bath she let her mind wander over recent events.

Her premonition that some awful occurrence would overtake Nigel had, of course, been quite unfounded. Six weeks had passed since that moment of panic when she'd seen the boys gazing at him with that curious air of menace. Nothing had happened to him, unless of course Felicity's continuing malaise could be counted. Elizabeth often puzzled over that, sometimes wondering whether Nigel's wife had found out about their affair and was fighting back, using poor health as a weapon.

Then she would go over every single move that she and Nigel had made, wondering if they had slipped up in any way. It was at times like this that Elizabeth cried bitterly; the lies and deceit were becoming more and more of a difficult burden to bear.

Yet though nothing sinister had befallen Nigel, there had been a turn of events that had, at first, terrified Elizabeth and then had intrigued her – so greatly that the fear had been sublimated and in its place, had sprung up an extremely healthy curiosity. And now, with every batch of photographs she took, the ghostly boys appeared and moreover, they were growing up by leaps and bounds.

Elizabeth felt quite sure she was seeing their lives reenacted through the medium of her camera and that one day it would be revealed to her exactly who they were and what had happened to them. Then, she felt, she could right the wrong done them; get them buried in consecrated ground or exorcised from where they had lived. Only with that final act, she felt sure, would the series of ghostly photographs come to an end and stop haunting her.

The boys had passed rapidly through various stages of development and it was only now, from the set of photographs which she had developed the night before, that Elizabeth had realised they were twins, being not only of identical height and build, but also with the same childish good looks.

Now, she went into her studio as soon as she was dressed, and looked again at the latest prints. The boys, dressed in cricket gear, seemed to be aged about twelve. Their identical faces looked solemnly at her from behind the plump form of a City magnate's daughter, photographed for her engagement picture in a billowing organza gown which did not suit her. The misty outline that always surrounded the boys blended beautifully with the floating skirt, creating an incredibly surreal effect, but not one which would be appreciated by the sitter and her father, Elizabeth thought wryly. Fortunately she had several other shots, one in particular making the chubby young lady look ravishing.

"You are very naughty to keep appearing like this," she said to the photograph. "But if you manifest in every shot I take I'll get the psychic research people on to you. I have to make a living!"

The lads stared solemnly back at her as Elizabeth added this latest print to the rapidly increasing hoard that still remained her secret. As she turned the key on the drawer where it was kept, she wondered how full it must become before the mystery of the twins was finally solved. But before she could begin even to think about it, the studio telephone rang and disturbed her concentration.

"Hello, sweetheart." It was Nigel's voice.

"Hello. Where have you been?"

"Busy. Worked to death in fact."

For once, Elizabeth did not feel sympathetic. "I've been pretty frantic as well."

"I'm sorry. Listen darling, I haven't got long so I'll get to the point. Flick–"

"Who?"

" –Felicity hasn't been well again, I'm afraid."

"More headaches?"

"I don't know. I'm getting a bit fed up with it. Anyway she's going to her mother for a few days to rest. Sweetheart, I could come and stay. Wouldn't that be bliss?"

Bliss. And yet Elizabeth could not feel quite the right amount of enthusiasm. To cover up her odd mood, she said in a bright voice. "When are you arriving?"

"Tonight. But, love, I have a favour to ask."

"What is it?"

"My car is in the garage for a service and won't be ready till tomorrow. Could you come and fetch me about six? I'll be home by then and the coast will be well and truly clear."

What a ghastly phrase, Elizabeth thought. As if they were school children planning a wheeze. But she said aloud, "All right I've got to go and see Max but I won't be back late. Expect me at six."

She put the phone down, wondering why she was not buzzing all over with anticipation as once she would have been, and realising that in a way she was almost dreading Nigel's visit.

"But why?" she asked herself. I love him just the same and I still want him. Is it because I'm feeling guilty about Felicity? Making hay while she's ill.

And she must have remained thoughtful, for Max stared at her quizzically over lunch.

"What's the matter with you, Liz? You've hardly smiled. I think you need this Venice trip."

She pulled a face. "Yes. Yes, I think perhaps I do."

"Have you been there before?"

"Once, when I was in my teens. I think I was still too young to really appreciate it."

"It's a photographer's paradise. You can't fail."

"As long as the Great Man doesn't play up."

"Is he such a hell raiser?" asked Max, interested. "What do you know about him?"

"His reputation with women and booze is pretty fierce. A bit like Burton himself."

"I'm sure I've read that he went on the wagon and is a reformed character, and I believe he's only been married and divorced once."

"How boring," said Elizabeth, laughing. "I hope he hasn't become ordinary."   And gave a little shiver of anticipation.

*

As Max put flesh on the bones of her assignment, Elizabeth felt another heartbeat of excitement.

"It's going to be marvellous," she said as she kissed him goodbye. "Thanks for getting me the job. I'll do my best."

"That's why I chose you," answered Max and bounded into a taxi before she could reply.

It was already three o'clock and Elizabeth decided to go round the shops, wondering whether she would be inspired to buy anything for Venice. As it was she got carried away and it was with a boot full of parcels that she finally arrived outside Nigel's expensive mews house, realising that she had never actually set eyes on it before.

Suddenly nervous, Elizabeth sat for a few minutes in the car, not wanting to get out. This wasn't her territory, she was a mistress not a wife and had no right to be here. Yet Nigel was expecting her and finally she had no choice but to walk slowly to the front door. It stood open and with the greatest reluctance, Elizabeth crossed the threshold and stood in the hall.

"Nigel?" she called uncertainly. "It's Liz. I'm here."

There was a muffled shout from above. "I'm in my study, right at the top. Have a look round and then come up."

Feeling just like a Peeping Tom, Elizabeth walked a step or two, then found herself looking into a cosy sitting room, the wallpaper busting with floribunda pink roses, the fabrics carefully matching. Plants were everywhere and though a magnificent fern hid the open fireplace, it was obvious that this was well-used in the winter months. It looked like a photograph from a magazine, bursting with the talent of the woman who had created such a beautiful place. Elizabeth wandered on into a delightful dining room, all Victoriana, mahogany and dark plush chairs, and then finally into the kitchen. It was beautiful, elegant yet simple and on two levels; a lower level housed the working area, and the higher accommodated an antique dresser and interesting bric-a-brac which were from a kitchen of another era.

Yet it was to the dresser that Elizabeth was instantly drawn, for there stood a small framed photograph of Nigel, a blonde woman with a face reminiscent of her namesake, Felicity Kendal, snuggling close to him. An open marriage thought Elizabeth bitterly, and for reasons she didn't stop to analyse took her flash camera from her handbag and photographed the entire room.

"Where are you?" came Nigel's distant voice. "Hurry up!"

Elizabeth went up the stairs, deliberately averting her eyes from the open bedroom door but being forced to visit the bathroom, which was superbly done in white and blue, an original old bath with claw feet standing on its own amidst a mass of plants. Shaking her head in surprise she continued up to the next floor to see a delightful spare bedroom that contained a small double bed draped as a four-poster, situated opposite Nigel's business-like study.

"Well, well," she said, standing in the doorway. "What a delightful home you have. Felicity? Or did you have an interior designer?"

Nigel looked up, and Elizabeth thought she had never seen his eyes look so blue.

"Darling, how *are* you? God, I've missed you. Come over here and kiss me."

Almost as if she were sleepwalking, Elizabeth went to his desk, noticing that it was Georgian and beautifully restored. She bent to kiss his cheek but could manage no warmth in her embrace.

"Here Lizbeth, what's the matter? Has something upset you?" he said sharply.

"No, I'm just recovering from the shock of your house, that's all. It's absolutely beautiful. I had no idea Felicity was so clever. It *was* Felicity, wasn't it?"

Nigel turned his attention to the pile of papers in front of him. "Yes," he said carelessly. "She studied interior design."

"You didn't tell me."

"Why should I? I didn't think you would be interested." He stood up and put his hands on Elizabeth's shoulders. "Listen darling, this house is simply a showplace for my clients. I asked Felicity to design it as part of our marriage agreement."

"What do you mean by that?"

"Well, she wanted to marry me and I needed a good hostess. Don't look so shocked. I told you we should never have got married in the first place."

"Then why did you?" said Elizabeth fiercely. "Did she have plenty of money?"

Nigel's eyes darkened. "That's not worthy of you, Lizbeth."

"You said that before when I accused her of malingering. It's my firm belief, Nigel, that you are in love with her – perfectly content with her anyway."

She turned on her heel and fled down the stairs, Nigel right behind her. As she reached the bedroom, he finally caught her up and pushed her down onto the bed.

"I've a good mind to make love to you," he said. "You won't believe I love you any other way."

"How could you even think about it?" she answered furiously. "In here, full of her things."

"It might be exciting," he said.

"Oh, for God's sake! This is too much." Elizabeth could never remember being more furious. "I'm getting out of here," and with that she heaved her elbow hard into Nigel's stomach and, as he bent double, raced past him and down the stairs, crashing the front door behind her.

Afterwards she never remembered driving home, the tears running down her face echoing the rain splashing on the windscreen. All she could later recollect was putting the key in her own front door, mixing herself a strong drink and sitting in the chair by the window so that she could gaze at the river. With the earlier sunshine gone and the weather cloudy, it crawled like an oil slick, sludgy and unpleasant, the gulls grey and tattered. Nonetheless, it was movement of a sort and Elizabeth sat there until dark when, with a lurch of her heart, she suddenly remembered the photograph she'd taken.

Almost against her will she climbed to the darkroom, removed the film in the blackness and took it to the developing sink. Up came the image of that beautiful kitchen and with it two familiar shapes.

"Not you again," groaned Elizabeth. "Not in this one."

But the boys were there, and as the picture grew ever more distinct, she saw that they were seated at the antique pine table, one on either side, and that now they wore school uniform. In fact on one breast pocket, Elizabeth could even glimpse a badge.

She stood riveted. Here was the very first clue to the twin's identity. If she could just find out which school it was she could go back through their archives and discover whether identical twin boys had ever attended, and what had subsequently happened to them.

The picture grew clearer and instead of looking at Felicity's photograph as she had intended, Elizabeth found herself gazing at the expression on the boy's faces. She had never seen them look more miserable.

"You funny creatures," she said under her breath. "You hate the house as much as I do."

She loved them for it. Strange, touching, loyal little ghosts.

The telephone started to ring and Elizabeth went into the studio, standing by the instrument uncertainly, positive that it was Nigel but wavering in case it wasn't him. Eventually she picked up the receiver but did not speak.

"Hello," said a voice at the other end. "I know that's you, Lizbeth. I'm coming round. I love you, darling. For God's sake, don't leave me like this." Elizabeth said nothing and Nigel went on, "Oh Lizbeth, forgive me, forgive me." Then he hung up.

She replaced the receiver and stood quite still, wondering what to do. She had two options, either to go out and let him find the place empty, or to face him and tell him she could no longer go on with such an unsatisfactory and hollow relationship. Eventually she took the easy way out and drove to a nearby cinema where she sat through a depressing American film about a mistress who killed herself at Christmas time while her lover was celebrating with his family. Feeling thoroughly dispirited, Elizabeth drove home.

As always she had left some lights on in the house, so it was not until she had actually turned the key and opened the front door that Elizabeth sensed a change in the atmosphere of the place. She could see at a glance that everything was exactly as she left it and yet there was a certain quality in the silence, a sensation of being listened to, that was both unnerving and terrifying. For a moment she stood panic-stricken and then logic began to take over.

There had been no forced entry so whoever was in the house had come in with a key.

"Nigel," she called accusingly. "I know you're in here so you'd better come out before I phone the police and report a break-in."

There was no sound for a second or two, then Elizabeth heard the door of her studio open and saw Nigel come down the stairs, his face not conciliatory and sheepish as she had expected, but instead rather angry.

"Darling," he said without any form of apology for entering her house uninvited, "why are you still faking photographs?"

The remark was so unexpected that Elizabeth just stared at him.

"I'm talking about this," he continued and waved beneath her nose the photograph that she had taken in his kitchen. "What is the explanation?"

"They're ghosts," she said flatly. "I expect your house is haunted."

Nigel's face was flushed and Elizabeth caught herself thinking that this was the first time she had ever seen him look unattractive.

"Don't be ridiculous," he said. "I know damned well it isn't. And I also know that you've done this sort of thing before. I saw the picture you took at Bryant Park, don't you remember?"

Elizabeth was suddenly furious. "How dare you come here uninvited, and accuse me of faking! I can assure you that that photograph is genuine, Nigel. Something happened in your bijou residence."

His tone changed to a more placatory level. "Darling, I don't believe you. But what does it matter? If you're into trick photography, so be it. I love you and that's the most important thing."

He made to take her in his arms, but Elizabeth moved away. "If that was true – really true – you wouldn't accuse me of lying."

"I'm not, sweetheart. It's just that I don't go along with your joke. But don't let's talk about it, please. I want to spend the night with you, show you how much I love you. Lizbeth, please. Say you still love me.

She stood staring at him, looking at every detail of that spectacular face, and wondering why she was seeing him suddenly as a nothing man, a walking cliché invented for television: the successful advertising executive with accomplished wife and talented mistress.

"I think you're a bit of a bore, Nigel," she said suddenly, the words seeming to come out of their own volition.

Nigel looked mortified. "Lizbeth, really! What is the matter with you?"

She didn't answer, seeing again that extraordinary photograph of the boys and Nigel, black as night against the crimson sunset. Had this been the disaster she had sensed? Was her breaking up with him the calamity she had envisaged? For if that was so, then those two menacing children had, in a chilling way, played their part in his downfall.

She snatched the photograph of Nigel's kitchen from his hand and gazed at it wide-eyed.

There could be no doubting the expression on the faces of the twins. They disapproved of their beautiful surroundings.

"I know it's what they want," she murmured.

Nigel gazed at her in astonishment. "Lizbeth, darling, what on earth are you talking about? What does who want?"

She looked at him coldly. "Nigel, I think you had better go. I truly think our relationship has fallen under an unlucky star."

"For God's sake!" he shouted. "This is lunacy. I have never needed you more than I do now."

"And why is that?"

He turned away, hunching his shoulders. "Because Felicity is ill."

"Her headaches? Is it serious? Is there something you haven't told me about, Nigel?"

Nigel shuffled his feet. "In a way. You see the truth is she's pregnant. It was a mistake and she was going to get rid of it. But then she changed her mind. Lizbeth, I just don't know how I'll cope."

"Oh, shut up and go away," Elizabeth said, putting her hands over her ears. "I don't want to hear any more from you."

He pulled her arms down roughly. "Oh, don't you? Well, I've got something to say and you'll listen. I'll go now to avoid a scene, but don't think that this is the end of me. I'm not going to give you up."

She turned away from him, the photograph falling from her fingers to the floor. "Goodbye, Nigel," she said flatly.

"Au revoir, Elizabeth. I'll ring you tomorrow."

When he'd gone, she laughed a little and then she cried and finally she rang Max and told him what had happened. Then she drank gin and stared at the inky river until her agent, in striped pyjamas and a raincoat, arrived with his girlfriend, a tall model girl wearing a babydoll nightie and a fur.

Elizabeth became giggly, and the rest of that terrible twenty-four hours turned into a bizarre party which ended with the three of them playing Trivial Pursuit as the dawn came up, beautifully pink and misty, turning the river into a glistening red ribbon.

"Are you all right now?" said Max. "Have you recovered your senses yet?"

"Just about," said Elizabeth and wiped the tears of grief and laughter and sheer weariness from her cheeks.

"We'll help you tidy up," said Beulah the model.

"There's no need."

"Oh, I'd like to really. I hate messy places." She put an apron on over the baby doll and headed into the kitchen.

Max picked up the abandoned photograph. "Who are these?" he said with interest.

"Oh, two young people I know," answered Elizabeth guardedly. "Why do you want to know?"

"They go to my old school, Marlborough College. I recognise the badge on their blazers."

"So that's where they went?" Elizabeth murmured to herself.

"What did you say?"

"I said I thought you were a Cockney, Max. I never knew you went to a good school."

He looked apologetic. "It's better for my image to pretend I worked my way up. But the truth is my father was a highly successful tailor who believed that there was no better investment than his children's education. My sister went to Roedean."

Elizabeth smiled. "Max, you are so wonderfully unpredictable."

He laughed, said, "Thank you," then looked serious. "How are you going to avoid the creep?"

"I shall have the locks changed today and I shall go away for a few days before I leave for Venice."

"Where will you go?"

"How about Marlborough, Max?" Elizabeth said with a laugh. "I'd love to see your old school."

"Great, the very place," Max answered. "But Liz, Beulah and I are staying here until you go. I feel Nigel might make trouble."

"I don't know why he won't just let me go."

"Because he can't bear to lose a girlfriend. People like Nigel just have to win every round."

"It's a little bit pathetic."

"There's nothing pathetic about Nigel Hart," Max answered firmly.

At about nine o'clock the phone rang and Max quickly answered it.

"Ah yes, I was expecting to hear from you, I am remaining at Elizabeth's flat until the locksmith has gone and then I shall be locking it up myself. You see, my client has already left for Italy. No, I have no idea when she is coming back. She told me when she had finished the assignment she intended to take a holiday. Try ringing at Christmas. Goodbye." He put the phone down. "Well, that's the end of him – for the moment," he said.

Elizabeth gave a half-hearted smile. "It's a mess, isn't it?"

"Sweetheart," said Max, "it will all be different when you get back from Italy."

"Why do you say that?"

He winked at her. "Because I'm psychic, of course!"

*

Driving along the motorway, Elizabeth thought of his words and a stir of excitement jumped at her heart. She had a sudden feeling that Max was right, that the situation would now improve. She patted her handbag in which lay the packet containing her photographs of the twins.

"I suppose you're pleased," she said to it. "But it won't be very long before I find out exactly who you are, then I can get rid of you. Not that you haven't been a diversion, of course."

Her mood of elation intensified at the thought that at long last the identity of the ghosts might be revealed. But her hopes were somewhat dashed by the discovery that the school was closed for the Easter holiday and there seemed to be no members of staff about. However, a cleaner directed her to the Bursar's office and a tentative knock on the door produced a response. Elizabeth went in.

"Hello," said a hearty man, "and what can I do for you?"

"Do forgive me barging in like this. Are you the Bursar?"

"No, I'm not. I teach here actually, but I've just come into the office to use the computer. Can I help you with anything?"

"I think perhaps you can," Elizabeth answered, realising that she had not prepared a lie and thinking of one off the top of her head. "I'm an author and I'm doing some research on two boys who once attended this school."

"Oh, really? Tell me, what were their names?"

"That's the difficulty. I'm afraid I don't know."

The man's eyebrows rose, but he made no comment.

"The only clue I have is that they were identical twins."

"Twins?" The man frowned. "I can't recall any in my time. When were they here?"

"Again, I don't know. All I have is this." Elizabeth produced the most recent photograph.

"Um. Could be anyone really. Rum photograph though."

"Why do you say that?"

"They don't look quite real, do they? Rather blurred, like one of those fake ghost photos."

Elizabeth came to a swift decision and said. "Well, you may not believe it, but that's precisely what it is. Only it's not fake. I took it. And I want to find out who they are – or were."

The man's brows rose even higher. "Really? How amazing. Well, well." He studied it more carefully. "That's certainly a Marlborough badge. I wonder how we can trace them without a name."

"We could try old school photos," Elizabeth suggested. "We might recognise the faces."

"Brilliant," answered her helper. "I'm Mike by the way. And who might you be…?"

"Elizabeth."

They shook hands rather formally. "This is intriguing," he said. "If you stay here just a moment I'll get the photos and a couple of magnifying glasses."

Elizabeth thought to herself how lucky she had been to find such an enthusiastic assistant but, for all his good will, when he returned and they saw the enormity of the task that lay before them, both of them were daunted. There was literally hundreds of photographs, divided amongst the various school houses and going back in time to before the turn of the century.

It was like glimpsing another age. Stiff-necked headmasters sporting pince-nez sat amongst their academically-gowned staff, while sturdy matrons of mammoth proportions gazed suspiciously at the lens from beneath their goffered caps. Under their combined basilisk control, boys, uncomfortable in their rigid collars, looked restrained and cautious.

"And now the flannelled fools," said Mike.

Elizabeth could have wept at the well-scrubbed faces of the youths who, within months of the taking of the photograph, would be dying in the trenches of France, the innocent sacrifices to politicians' war-mongering. It was among this series of photographs she felt certain she would find the twins.

But by the end of that day and with a great many more pictures still to look at, Elizabeth began to lose heart.

"I'll have to get back now," Mike said, reluctantly looking at his watch. "Can we continue this tomorrow, Elizabeth?"

"I'd like to, having got this far. But isn't it a nuisance for you?"

He rubbed his hands gleefully. "Not at all. It gives me a good excuse to get out of the house."

As they parted company and evening fell over the school and the intriguing hillock in its grounds known as Merlin's Mound, Elizabeth took some dramatic sunset shots, endeavouring to make the tree-covered hill look as mystic and sinister as its larger counterpart, Silbury. Then on her smaller camera she took some of the school chapel and the swimming pool, the sinking sun reflected in its waters, before she finally turned back towards the hotel.

Rather as she had feared, the next day's search proved fruitless, despite giggling over some photographs of Max looking just the same. There had never been a boy at Marlborough College who even resembled the twins. In fact she and Mike only picked out ten pairs of twins amongst all the hundreds of pupils they looked at.

"I can't understand it," he said scratching his head. "They are definitely in school uniform so they must have come here. But where the hell are they?"

Elizabeth pulled a face. "God knows. Well, no one can say we didn't try, can they?"

Mike stood up. "I've enjoyed it, even though it was a wild goose chase. If you ever do find out about them, be sure to let me know, won't you?"

"I most certainly will."

"When are you off to Italy?"

"Tomorrow. I'll drive direct to Gatwick from here."

"Splendid. Well, good luck. I do hope you manage to track the twins down."

"Thanks so much, Mike. I'll send you a postcard."

"Jolly good. Bye."

He was off with a cheery wave leaving Elizabeth, suddenly deflated and downcast, forced to while away the time until the next morning's departure. She took some more photographs, then handed them into a photographer's studio for urgent developing.

"They'll be ready tomorrow," said a young female assistant.

"Early I hope. You see I have to leave Marlborough by nine-thirty at the latest."

"Call at nine."

"On the dot."

But as luck would have it, Elizabeth overslept and hurled herself into the photographer's at ten o'clock, before skimming down the motorway towards the airport and checking in for her flight with a minute to spare.

It seemed after that that she did not draw breath again until they were in the air, the hostess coming round with the drinks trolley, and Elizabeth daringly ordering some champagne. Only then did she remember the Marlborough photographs and take them out of her briefcase, her heart already thudding with the thought of what might be on them.

They were superb! Merlin's Mound rearing dark and strange, the grotto at its foot full of an odd silver light, while standing inside the grotto looking out at her from behind its iron gate were two familiar shapes.

"You little devils," said Elizabeth under her breath. "What are you playing at?"

But they were no longer so little, for two teenage boys stood in the grotto's confines; two teenage boys who were partially hidden in the light, yet two boys who quite definitely were smiling at the camera.

Elizabeth's flesh crawled with fear. Why had they so suddenly grown and why were they so obviously pleased that she had been unable to find any trace of them? What extraordinary message could these photographs be trying to convey to her?

"God help me," she whispered as the plane roared on relentlessly towards Italy. "I must find out the truth. Before long I must begin to understand."

There was a certain light even in the darkness of Venice that Elizabeth found extraordinary. It was as if the water of the canals reflected the night sky with a radiance that glowed round the entire city so that it was never truly unlit. She thought it breathtaking, exciting, and found it no hardship to rise before dawn in order to arrive on location with the rest of the film crew. In fact she enjoyed being out in the night's freshness, photographing both the people on the set and the glorious buildings, all heightened and made stark by the moon's deceptive shadows.

To avoid tourists it was necessary to start filming at daybreak and though a great many of the exterior shots had already been taken, it was today that Roderick Rhys joined the unit, having flown in from France the night before.

"Good morning, Miss Lacey," said a voice at her elbow, and she turned to see Ned Hacker, the film's director.

"Good morning," Elizabeth answered. "I'm so glad to meet you at last, Mr Hacker. Naturally I've been briefed by my agent, but I just wondered if there was anything in particular about Roderick Rhys that you want me to bring out in my photographs."

Ned smiled. "Try and find the real man and kill the hell-raiser image if you can."

"Why, isn't it true?"

"You'll have to wait and see for yourself. I'll be interested to know your reaction."

"Not half as interested as I'm going to be," Elizabeth muttered almost inaudibly.

"Here he is, Mr Hacker," came a shout, and every eye turned to look at the Grand Canal.

Elizabeth raised her camera and then lowered it again in complete astonishment.

If Roderick Rhys was late he was certainly ready to start working. He stood in the prow of a black gondola, and was already dressed as Leonardo, a belted coat trimmed and lined with fur over a short blue doublet and tights. On his head, over dark hair grown long for the part, he wore a soft fabric hat shaped like a beret. The illusion was tremendous.

The gondola pulled in to the side and the actor stepped ashore, apologising to the director, and the assembled company, for the lateness of his arrival and then, hearing the click of Elizabeth's camera, turned to see what it was. He stared straight into the lens and she realised that her preconceived idea of him was entirely wrong. Not only was he younger than she had imagined, but he was so incredibly alive that he could never be considered to be even remotely tedious. Elizabeth took two rapid shots and lowered the camera.

She was looking into a face that was difficult to describe, for Roderick Rhys had the actor's gift of seeming to change his features to suit his role. Today he was Leonardo, a mystic, a visionary, a seer into men's thoughts, but the black hair was the actor's own and the emerald-bright eyes that surveyed Elizabeth with interest were certainly of the twentieth century.

"You're Elizabeth Lacey," he said, holding out his hand. "I went along to your last exhibition. In my considered opinion, the finest photograph that you ever took was the one of the mermaid."

She stared at him. "The mermaid?"

The Welshman's face altered subtly. "Yes. Don't tell me you didn't notice. I saw her distinctly, swimming in that rough sea, just beyond St David's head. The photograph was called Wind song. Do you remember?"

Elizabeth smiled. "Yes, but there was no mermaid."

Roderick looked at her very seriously. "Oh, there are always mermaids," he said. His voice changed. "They're waiting for me. We will talk later, Elizabeth."

He moved on, leaving her quite breathless with surprise.

And as she watched and photographed him that morning, Elizabeth became more and more impressed with the man. He worked economically and without grumbling, trying to get as much filming as possible done before hordes of sightseers meant that they would have to stop, that the illusion of Venice in 1499 would be utterly ruined.

She watched as Roderick strode through St Mark's Square, pigeons wheeling about his head and, half closing her eyes, Elizabeth could almost imagine that time had moved backwards. A crowd of milling extras, all appropriately costumed, walked the piazza with him and tradesmen of the fifteenth century offered him their wares.

By seven o'clock they had filmed Roderick in an antique gondola, with a gondolier to match, talking earnestly to a fellow painter; Roderick going into the Doge's Palace; Roderick caught up in a street fight. Then the party of unsmiling Japanese, each with three cameras about their neck, who had come on to the edge of the set at daybreak and had been taking photographs ever since, finally grew restless.

"That's it, everyone," said Ned Hacker. "After breakfast we'll go to the recording studio and do the sound. Thank you very much."

The film crew removed the temporary barriers and humped their cameras on to specially chartered water buses, while the actors went off to their hotels. Within a quarter of an hour, Venice had returned to the present time and, as usual, swarmed with tourists of all nationalities.

Suddenly alone, Elizabeth stood for a moment disconsolately. In the general rush to get away she had been passed unnoticed and now she had a few hours to kill before meeting the others. But what better place in which to have time to oneself? Lifting her camera on to her shoulder, Elizabeth set off to explore Venice.

It was on the shop-lined Rialto Bridge that she ran into Roderick Rhys again. This time he wore lightweight trousers and a casual shirt and if it hadn't been for his shoulder-length sweep of hair he might have passed for an ordinary tourist. He even had a camera slung around his neck.

"What's your secret, Elizabeth?" he said, as if they had never stopped speaking. "I can't take a good photograph. The most I can ever do is be lucky."

"I can't act," she answered, falling into step beside him. "We're all given different gifts."

The green eyes looked at her in amusement. "Well, well, you sound like my old Welsh grandmother. 'Roddy,' she used to say, 'the fairies kissed you when you were born. There's a lovely little chap you are.' Then she used to pick me up and squeeze me until my eyes popped. It was an unattractive sight I can tell you."

Elizabeth laughed. "You are being very silly."

"I know. But there, you look lovely with your hair all flying out. Let me take your picture. Now come on, you of all people should know how to pose."

Suddenly Elizabeth felt strangely light of heart as she complied.

"You're a very pretty girl," said Roderick, clicking away. "Will you have dinner with me tonight?"

"What?"

"You heard me." He added something in Welsh which Elizabeth did not understand.

"Am I being given the Roderick Rhys chat-up line, by any chance?"

He could have been annoyed, but instead he laughed. "God, no. All that hell-raiser stuff is rubbish. I'll tell you about myself tonight."

"I'd be honoured," she said, it such an old-fashioned way that he obviously knew she meant it.

"So will I. Are you staying at the Gritti Palace?" She nodded. "I'll call for you there at eight. Good bye, Arianrod."

"The Welsh witch?"

"You know her. I'm glad. By the way, I won't have time to chat when I'm recording but don't think I'm being unfriendly. It's just that I like to concentrate when I'm working. I'll pick you up at eight."

He was gone, and Elizabeth stared after him, hardly believing what had just happened. The Great Man had actually asked her out to dine and in her excitement she had completely forgotten bout Nigel and even about the ghostly twins. With a secret smile, Elizabeth made her way in the direction of her hotel.

As if forgetting him had in some way conjured him up, Nigel telephoned while she was dressing for dinner. She picked up the receiver lightheartedly, expecting it to be one of the film crew or even Roderick himself calling, and so it was a shock when a familiar voice said, "Lizbeth? Is that you, my darling?"

Her stomach tightened and she answered abruptly, "What on earth do you want?"

"You, in one simple word. I love you, and I miss you terribly. All I can think about is you and all the wonderful times we had together. Do you remember–"

Elizabeth replaced the receiver, then she picked it up again and an Italian voice said, "*Si Signora?*"

"If any more calls come for me can you say that I've already left the hotel, please?"

"Certainly, Signora. And also, Signora…"

"Yes?"

"Signor Rhys is in the bar."

"Thank you. I'll be right down."

As she descended the marble staircase, Elizabeth wondered if the stories about Roderick's prodigious drinking had any foundation in truth, but he was sipping a weak looking wine and soda, and appeared perfectly normal.

He read her mind. "No, Elizabeth, it's not true. I'll explain how the story started over dinner. By the way, I've booked a table at the best fish restaurant in the whole world. Mermaids dine there. Or so I'm reliably informed."

She smiled at him, wondering why she felt so loving and gentle. And it seemed the most delicate and yet the most natural thing for him to weave his fingers amongst hers as they sat together in the motor boat crossing the northern lagoon towards the island of Burano, which came into view like a burst of rainbows.

"What a wonderful place," said Elizabeth. "All those tiny houses painted in primary colours."

"It's a place of fishermen and lacemakers, all soup and nets and Venetian point. I hope you like it."

I could fall in love with this man, Elizabeth thought, but I'll bet he's got a wife and a string of girlfriends.

The words were out before she could stop them. "I take it that you're married?"

The green eyes examined her carefully. "If I was, Arianrod, I certainly wouldn't be sitting with you like this. Nor would I have asked you to dinner."

"But you've had a wife?"

"Yes, once. She was very sweet, simple in the best possible sense. But she couldn't bear it when success came for me. Not that she was jealous, she wished me well; it was just that she hated the glitzy side of it all. In the end she ran off with a nice Welsh farmer."

"*She* left *you*?" Elizabeth was astonished.

"Yes, why not? We had grown apart, that's all. She has two lovely children now."

"But what about your affairs? One could hardly look at a gossip column without…"

Roderick smiled. "Well, I have to admit that I did have a few girls after my wife and I divorced. But I never got involved with anyone I might hurt."

She shook her head but further conversation was stopped by the unbelievable fact that their boat was sailing to the very door of a restaurant, tiny and gaudy, and with a mermaid painted on a swaying sign above the door.

"We're here," said Roderick and helped her ashore.

It was an evening of pure enchantment; an evening in which, in his wonderful voice, he told her about himself. But she had almost stopped listening, instead absorbing the atmosphere, and drowning in the feeling of losing her vulnerable and eager heart.

A million times Elizabeth told herself that it was dangerous, and a million times she answered that she didn't care. Nor could she think this was love on the rebound. In the shadow of this great and talented man, Nigel had long since ceased to exist.

As the sun went down they walked beside the church where the nets were hung up to dry, and watched the lacemakers sitting in their doorways, crouching in black, fingers flying and eyes glazed.

"May I take a photograph of you?" said Elizabeth. "I know you're really off duty, but I'd very much like to…"

"I want you to," answered Roderick. "I want you to, Arianrod. Then afterwards it will serve to remind you of tonight."

He jumped onto a low white-washed wall, his back to the sun and his hair transformed into a red halo in its dying light.

"The real Roderick Rhys," she said softly.

"Perhaps I'm still playing a part. Who knows?"

"I hope you're not."

"I'm not," he answered very seriously, and got off the wall and kissed her.

Even if I never see him again at least I can say he kissed me, thought Elizabeth.

"You're cold," he said. "We must get back. We have to film the carnival tonight."

"I know. Only one more day in Venice after that, so my job will soon be over."

"What will you do?"

"Take a short holiday, I think. Try and see some more of Italy."

"In the footsteps of the film company?" he asked.

"No," said Elizabeth, suddenly wary. "I don't think that would be a very good idea."

With his uncanny ability to read her mind, Roderick said, "Don't be cold and clever. I meant no harm. I would love you to come with us, but I understand what you mean. I'd really hate you to be touched by gossip."

But somehow, despite his assurance, she felt that the atmosphere between them had changed and the coolness of the evening swept Elizabeth in every sense. She was glad to get back into her hotel and change into warm clothes for the night's filming that lay ahead.

For the carnival in Venice scene, St Mark's Square had been roped off from the public and was already lit by some powerful lamps, hung high so that they would not appear in the picture. Bright medieval banners wafted everywhere and a flotilla of ancient gondolas had been moored to the posts at the quay beyond the doge's Palace. One magnificent reproduction made of gold-sprayed wood particularly caught Elizabeth's eye, as did the young woman sitting in it. Quite the most beautiful little thing, with a mass of wheaten curls and brilliant violet eyes.

"Who's that?" she whispered to the continuity girl.

"Angelina Cherubino – don't you adore the camp name? She's supposed to be the new sensation."

"Really? And what part will she be playing?"

"Isabella d'Este. Leonardo was supposed to have had a bit of a thing about her – and it looks as if he has in real life as well."

"What do you mean?"

"The Welsh Wonder got her the part. And we can all guess why!"

Elizabeth managed an interested smile and a calm answer. "Nothing ever changes, does it? Well, I must be off to the darkroom. I want to see how the assignment is going."

The continuity girl smiled and said. "You'll have no problem. The camera loves him. Every picture will be a winner, you'll see." Elizabeth nodded and then hurried into the concealing darkness.

A special unit containing a cutting room and a darkroom had been put at the disposal of the film company, and now she made her way there half running, wondering why she wasn't angry.

Perhaps, she thought, as she unloaded her cameras and took the films to the developing table, because I am growing a defensive shell.

She stared moodily into the trays, seeing the images grow ever more distinct. The continuity girl had been right. Every shot of Roderick Rhys was wonderful.

"Damn him," said Elizabeth, laughing at herself. "Why does he have to be so attractive?"

In one of the sinks images of Burano began to appear, the little crazy houses, the baby bridges, the weathered sign of the mermaid, Roderick on the white wall near the church.

"Oh, my God!" said Elizabeth aloud. "It can't be!"

Sitting on the ground at his feet, their heads turned towards him and smiles upon their identical faces, were the twins. As to why this particular photograph should disturb her more than any of the others, Elizabeth never afterwards knew. But she snatched it out of the fluid and tore it to bits before she finally allowed a tear to run down her cheek.

She hardly slept that night, but once Elizabeth thought she heard her phone ring, though she couldn't afterwards be sure that she hadn't dreamt it. But when she next opened her eyes it was daylight and she realised with an extraordinary mix of emotions that the Venetian stint was over. That today the film company would pack up and move on to Florence and she would be left to her own devices.

The continued holiday in Italy suddenly seemed a gloomy prospect and Elizabeth had a mental picture of herself, lonely in hotels and pensions, trailing round with her camera and longing for someone with whom to be enthusiastic. In a mood of despondency she telephoned the airport and booked a flight to Gatwick. Then she parcelled up all the photographs of Roderick Rhys, except for one extra print which, despite her good intentions, she decided to keep.

She knew, even as she said goodbye to them, that the photographs represented some of her most discerning work to date and that Ned Hacker would be pleased. As she left the hotel she gave them to a messenger to deliver and felt, in a strange way, that part of her had been torn away.

The water bus that connected with the coach which, in its turn, went to the airport, was already waiting and Elizabeth and her luggage had just been helped aboard when a noise on the quay made her look round.

"Arianrod!" a voice shouted. "Why didn't you say goodbye?"

"You were otherwise engaged," she shouted back.

"What?"

The actor cupped his hand round his ear while the other passengers stared eagerly and a fat English woman, squeezed into skin-tight jeans, said, "Oh my Gawd, it's Roderick Rhys!"

"Otherwise engaged," roared Elizabeth over the noise of the engine as the boat began to pull away.

Roderick had started to run along the quay to try and catch her words and a detached part of Elizabeth's brain couldn't help but see the funny side. It was like a Fellini film: Roderick sprinting, people flying, somebody tripping over a small evil dog; herself getting hysterical with laughter.

"Out with Angelina" she bellowed.

Roderick increased his speed. "Angel... Oh, you mean Benno's daughter! She's–"

The rest of the sentence was lost as the water bus accelerated, leaving Elizabeth with a vision of the actor staring after her, the droop of his shoulders telling her that he was truly sorry to see her go.

*

She thought about that final glimpse of him every day for the next three weeks; three weeks in which Elizabeth went north without telling anyone she had returned from Italy, and took a series of pictures which were to finally seal her reputation. She photographed the Scottish Isles, the AIDS victims of Edinburgh, the beauty of the border country, the unemployed of Tyneside. She mixed together, in one great cry from the heart, all the glory and pain and ugliness and magnificence of the northern part of Britain in her preparation for an exhibition to be called Watford Gap, based on the silly saying that it was there the North began. Then she returned to her flat.

The answerphone was loaded with calls, most of them from Nigel, but just as she came to the end of the tape her heart lurched as an unmistakeable voice said, "International directory enquiries are not easy, particularly when phoning in a rain storm which has made the River Po burst its banks."

You gorgeous beast, she thought.

"However," the voice went on, "I am still afloat so, Elizabeth, I am ringing to tell you that the beauteous Angelina is not my toy-girl, as gossip would have you believe, but the daughter of my old friend, Benito. I do not refer to Mussolini, but to an Italian who studied with me at RADA, being bilingual because of his English mother. Does this make sense?"

Elizabeth smiled, sitting down amongst her baggage. "Perfect sense," she whispered.

"So, to help an old friend out, I arranged for the sweet little flower of his heart–"

"How good that sounds with a Welsh accent," Elizabeth said to the machine.

"–to have a screen test, and very good she was. So now, having explained that, I am off to find a mermaid in the flood. On my return, you foolish girl, I shall telephone you again and take you, most definitely, into my bosom."

There followed an indecipherable snatch of song and then the message ended. The joy that followed was near delirium. Elizabeth whirled round her flat singing, and even had the courage to look again at the rejected photographs from the Watford Gap collection; the ones that, inevitably, contained the ghostly twins.

They were getting dramatically older, in fact they were now young men, and it seemed to her that perhaps, at last, their mystery had been solved. In the final series of photographs taken in Yorkshire they appeared as pilots, standing side by side, attractive in their helmets and fur-lined jackets.

"The Battle of Britain," she murmured to the print, shining glossily in her hand. "That's how you died, isn't it? Are your bodies hidden in a wood somewhere, never properly laid to rest? Is that why you haunt me? Oh, you funny, sad boys, is that what I have to do? Do I have to find you?"

Elizabeth took the picture over to the cupboard with all the others which she had carried with her, first to Marlborough, then Italy, and finally to Scotland. Then she remembered that the set was incomplete, that the picture of the twins with Roderick Rhys had been torn up. As she once again put the negative into the developing sink and his face formed and became clear, Elizabeth smiled.

"I love you," she said to the picture, adding, "all three of you."

The phone in the studio started to ring and she knew, even before she had picked it up, who it was.

"Hello, you Welsh Wonder," she said, not bothered that her voice was warm with affection, "how's the film doing?"

"In the can, baby, as they say in Hollywood. How about dinner?"

"When do you get back?"

"In about five minutes," he said, and hung up.

Elizabeth ran to the bedroom and examined her face. It was bony, a sure sign that she had been overworking. She dashed colour on to her cheekbones and lengthened her eyes with make-up, then let her hair fall loose.

"At least you look gauntly interesting," she said to her reflection before she turned away.

The doorbell rang and a bottle of champagne surrounded by flowers, a hand on the end of it, appeared. Then followed a face with green eyes and surprisingly curly hair.

"You've had a perm!" said Elizabeth accusingly.

Roderick Rhys looked apologetic. "Sorry, it's for my next part. Petruchio at Stratford," and he took her in his arms.

"You'd better come in," she said, and they both laughed.

What followed, all the love and the tenderness and the beauty, was as natural and as inevitable as if they had been partners for years. It seemed to Elizabeth then, that everything about Roderick was instinctive, and that all that had existed between herself and her ex-lover had been false, mechanical. That all the time, when he made love, Nigel had been mentally awarding himself points, whereas Roderick gave himself quite freely and without inhibition.

Afterwards, as they were standing by the window, looking down on a lilac-coloured Thames, the doorbell rang again and Elizabeth quite cheerfully went to answer it. But, as she turned the knob, her blood ran cold. It was Nigel, very slightly drunk, and in a mood to make trouble.

"You must go," Elizabeth said firmly. "You can't come in."

"Why not?" he answered. "Entertaining?" And with that he pushed her aside and walked into the living room.

Roderick, his back still averted as he contemplated the changing lights in the river, did not move and it was left to Nigel to say aggressively, "And who the devil might you be?"

"Roderick Rhys," said the actor, turning round. "And you?"

"My name's Hart. Nigel Hart. Elizabeth's lover."

"Really? You're not in the least as she described."

Nigel rocked back on his heels very fractionally. "Oh, she's spoken about me then?"

"Indeed. We were discussing one night in Venice all the little threads and knots that go to make up the tapestry of life – if you'll forgive the cliché, Nigel. You, she considered a knot." He grinned comfortably.

"You're bloody cocky, aren't you?" answered Nigel, unpleasantly. "Just because you're hailed as the new Olivier, Burton, whatever, doesn't give you the right to walk all over people."

"People," said Roderick calmly, "I never walk all over. But you, Nigel, I just might."

"Are you threatening me?"

"Not really, it would be pointless. You have a wife and you can't have Elizabeth. There is no need to threaten a loser."

There was a short silence, then Nigel said. "Lizbeth knew I was married all along and made no objection to it at the time."

"There are many objections other than those that are put into words. There are objections of the heart and mind and soul. Knowing Elizabeth as I do, I should imagine she hated every minute of it."

Nigel actually sneered. "Oh, so you think you know her, do you? Why, you've only just met."

"We may have only met recently, but I feel I do know her," answered Roderick slowly. "Well enough to want to marry her, if that answers your question."

There was a stunned silence.

"I'll see you in church," said Roderick, going to the front door and opening it.

"Are you throwing me out?" Nigel's voice was a rasp.

"Yes," answered Elizabeth, losing patience. "We are. Now go."

He turned in the doorway. "God help you with him. He couldn't be faithful if he tried." Then he was gone and the room slowly began to regain its usual calm.

Shyness, an emotion that Elizabeth had not felt for many years, suddenly swept her and she found herself wandering into the kitchen, pretending to be busy.

"Hey," called Roderick, "that's not very friendly, is it? After all, I've just proposed."

"But only to get rid of Nigel," she said under her breath.

"Did you say just to get rid of Nigel?" The actor appeared in the kitchen doorway.

"Well, it was, wasn't it?"

"No, I meant it. Am I taking too much for granted, Arianrod?"

"No, my dear, you're not."

They were married a month later, during the season at Stratford, amidst a hubbub of public attention. Most of the papers gushed about their romantic meeting on a film-set in Venice, went on to describe Roderick's hell-raiser past, and nearly all of them reported that he had been married several times already. However, one of them did track down his ex-wife, who was photographed amongst her husband's sheep, and quoted her as saying, "I wish him luck. He deserves to be happy," which partly set the record straight.

Interviewed just after the wedding, Roderick said, "We won't be going on honeymoon until after the season is over." And to the question as to whether they would raise a family, he answered. "That is entirely up to Elizabeth. But I hope so very much.

And then it was all over and Roderick went back to work playing both Petruchio and Henry V, while Elizabeth busied herself photographing not only the plays in rehearsal, but also various members of the company. The twins and the need to find their bodies were entirely forgotten in the whirlwind activity of the last few weeks.

Then came the day when she was asked to photograph some of the cast of *The Taming Of The Shrew* on stage. As she arrived in the empty theatre, Elizabeth suddenly had the oddest sensation. She almost knew that the boys were going to manifest in one of this series of photographs and it was with bated breath that, the session over, she waited in the darkroom to watch the images form.

At first she could see nothing and then on a photograph of Petruchio and Katharina appeared what looked like a large fault. With her heart thudding, Elizabeth put the print through the enlarging process and took it to the light.

It was the most extraordinary thing she had ever seen, for this time the vague image within the misty outline appeared to be a reproduction of a newspaper photograph. She could vaguely make out the date, *July 25, 20...*, the rest being indecipherable. There was also part of a headline, "*First British Astr...*".

Elizabeth put the photograph down in shock, then picked it up again, studying it through a magnifying glass. The twins were there all right, dressed in air force uniform with some sort of special insignia upon it, and for the first time there was another ghostly figure in the picture. And it was to this figure that Elizabeth's eyes were now drawn in fascinated horror. For there could be no doubt as to who it was; Prince Charles was shaking one of the twins by the hand.

"Dear God," said Elizabeth – because it was not quite Prince Charles. It was surely him as he was yet to be, with a heavy air of responsibility about him.

Elizabeth shook her head in disbelief. She wanted only to lock the print away, terribly afraid of its futuristic quality and not prepared at the moment to try and fathom out its meaning.

A sudden wave of faintness swept over her and Elizabeth sat down abruptly.

"You really must get checked up," she told herself, and picked up the telephone.

The next morning she sat down opposite her doctor. "What can I do for you, Mrs Rhys?" he asked.

"I'm hoping you can confirm that I'm pregnant." He looked rather surprised and Elizabeth added, "I stopped taking the pill at once because Roderick was very anxious to have a family – and I'm getting on a bit."

The doctor looked at her notes and laughed. "Thirty-five isn't considered out of the way these days, my dear. Now hop up on to the couch and we'll see what's happening, shall we?"

Five minutes later she knew that all she and Roderick had wanted was to be theirs.

He drove her to the hospital on the day of her scan, and Elizabeth saw that he was shaking slightly.

"I think you're more nervous than I am."

"I know. It is just that I want you and the baby both to be well."

"We will be."

The ultrasound operator welcomed Elizabeth and grinned widely at Roderick. "I think both your work is marvellous."

"Thank you very much."

"Right, dear. Now this won't hurt. I'll just put some jelly stuff on your bulge, then you rest there and look at the screen. I won't talk to you if you don't mind until it's all over. By the way you can have a photograph of the baby if you like. Though you'll only see a blob and some bones I'm afraid."

"I'd love one. Is there a fee?"

"Yes, just two pounds to the hospital funds."

They settled down and the operator ran an instrument over Elizabeth's abdomen. On the screen shapes began to appear that Elizabeth found impossible to identify. Once the operator went "Um!" and though she was dying to ask some questions, Elizabeth observed the rule of silence.

At last the woman said, "Would you like your picture now?"

"Yes, please."

There was a clunk and then she peeled the paper off the print and handed it to Elizabeth. "Go on, look at it," she smiled.

There was no time left in the universe; there was no beginning and no end to the march of events. Or so Elizabeth thought as she gazed at the picture in her hand, and found herself looking at the first one she had ever taken with her tenth birthday camera. Just for a split second, Elizabeth could not comprehend how this woman had got hold of it.

"But how…?" she said.

"The usual way, my dear. But don't worry. I always think twins are exciting."

Elizabeth looked again at the black blob with the two smaller blobs within its compass and quietly began to cry.

"There's nothing wrong is there?" the operator asked her.

"No," said Elizabeth smiling through her tears. "Nothing at all. I'm not even surprised. Because in a way, you see, I think I have always known."

The Wardrobe

Just for once the estate agent's details, notorious for their fulsome statements and unerring ability to describe a large cupboard as Bedroom Three, did not match up to the splendour of the reality. Standing in the drive, absorbing the size and strength of the house situated at the end of it, Rebecca and Gregory Nicholls gazed in disbelief. "But it's beautiful," she said. "Absolutely beautiful."

"I must admit I hadn't expected anything quite like this," Greg answered, and smiled.

They stood hugging each other, like two excited children, wondering how they could have been lucky enough to find, judging from the outside at least, the place they had always dreamed of. For the house they were looking at was undeniably that.

It stood, large and elegant, a creeper-clad, four-storey pile, built in the style known as Gothic, an architectural form which had reached the height of its popularity in the mid Victorian period. Turrets and towers abounded, and there was both a greenhouse and a flower-filled conservatory. Upstairs there were gables and balconies, and the entire charmingly eccentric effect was crowned by castellated walls.

And it was these walls which gave the house its appeal; originally built in harsh red brick, they had mellowed softly over the years to a rose colour which, combined with its profusion of Virginia creeper, gave the entire place a warm welcoming appearance.

"I want to live here," said Rebecca.

"But the interior could be awful. Not all the conversions of these big old houses are successful, you know."

"This one will be."

But in secret, Rebecca was not so certain, not really believing that the inside could equal the magnificent exterior of The Grange, Dynevor Road, Clapham; the seventh place that she and Greg had looked at in their search for a larger flat.

They had been married almost a year and presently rented what Rebecca thought of as The Dump, a basement flat in Fulham, the area outside which was constantly filled with rubbish blowing in off the streets. Greg had lived there in his bachelor days and not worried over much about its generally dilapidated air, but his new wife felt differently about it and that fact, coupled with the dramatic fall in house prices, had made them decide to raise a mortgage and buy.

"I hope interest rates don't go up yet again," muttered Greg, thinking aloud.

"The building society is offering a special deal for first-time buyers, don't forget," Rebecca said quickly.

"It had better be good," he replied. But she took no notice, knowing he liked The Grange as much as she did and praying yet again that the flat would be as attractive inside as it sounded in the description.

"Listen to this," Rebecca said, reading the details. "The Master Bedroom is both gracious and spacious with distant views of Clapham Common from its charming balcony."

"That probably means you can get a glimpse of a square inch of grass on a clear day."

"Oh don't be such a misery! I wish that estate agent woman would hurry up."

"She'll be here in a minute."

Rebecca said nothing, enraptured by the setting, its green lawns, ancient cedar trees and flowerbeds.

"This house must have been glorious in its heyday," she said, almost to herself. "I wonder who lived here?"

"No idea. Ah! This must be the woman now. Good."

And sure enough a sleek white Toyota was nosing into the drive, its occupant hooting the horn as she caught sight of them.

"Frightfully sorry I'm late," she was shouting. "I got held up in a traffic jam at the Common. Too many cars about these days."

Her next few words were drowned as the Toyota came to a halt with a crunch of tyres, then the driver got out, still speaking.

"You must be Mr and Mrs Nicholls. I'm Veronica Greer-Edwards of Mayhew and King." She stuck out her hand. "Awfully nice to meet you. Do hope you'll like the flat and simply fail to see how you couldn't. The interior designer was Mr Frog. Absolute darling but frightfully extravagant." She rolled her eyes behind a pair of enormous glasses with pink and green frames.

Rebecca smiled politely and waited for her to stop.

"Of course it's an absolute bargain. You simply couldn't get anything decent for that kind of money anywhere else. In fact, in my view it is *hideously* underpriced. Anyway, let's go in, shall we?"

They marched round to the side of the house, Veronica continuing to talk to them over her shoulder.

"This used to be the tradesmen's entrance – those were the days, what? – but now it's the communal way in for the three upper flats. Only the ground floor has the use of the front door, I'm afraid."

"Are all the other flats occupied?" Greg asked as they climbed a flight of stairs obviously put in during the conversion.

"Absolutely not. I mean, the market is utterly *dead*. Only the garden apartment has people in it. He's frightfully smart, in television, directed that series about Art and the Third World. Awfully good, did you see it?"

Rebecca opened her mouth to say "No", but Veronica plunged on without pausing.

"*She's* utterly mousey, boring little creature. But really they're hardly ever there. Got a place in Provence where they spend most of their time. I think one should in this day and age, don't you?"

They had reached the first floor and Veronica turned a labelled key in the lock. "Well, there you are!" she said grandly. "A stunning conversion, in my view. Simply the best."

And it was. With an exclamation of pure delight Rebecca walked through the front door of the place which she knew at once would be her future home to be enveloped by its charm.

An L-shaped hallway, leading to a small passageway, formed the heart of the flat, the doors of the principal rooms all leading off it. To Rebecca's right was the bathroom, beautifully decorated with a blue and white rose print paper, a bath that looked original standing on clawed feet in the middle. In ecstasy, she rushed on, throwing open the next door she came to, to find herself in what was described in the details as the Living Room. This, too, had been converted in Victorian style and, situated at the side of the house as it was, had an excellent view of the gardens below.

"Isn't it great!" said Greg, looking over her shoulder, and once again they hugged each other as they went down the small passageway and opened the door on the left. They stepped into a room which had obviously once been two rooms, that not only adjoined but led into one another, and this plan had been modified to provide a kitchen with dining room leading off. A long room with windows opening onto a balcony at the dining end resulted, a tribute to the architect's skill.

"Only snag, your dinner guests will have to walk through the kitchen first but jolly nice for summer suppers," said Veronica, coming up behind them.

"Yes," they chorused.

"And now the grand finale," Veronica went on. "The Master Bedroom."

Once again she was right. Going back into the hall, the estate agent triumphantly opened a door to the left and there, complete with distant views of the Common, was the most beautiful room Rebecca had ever seen. Mr Frog and his team had gone to enormous lengths to reproduce a Victorian bedroom of quite the most delicious kind.

Perhaps not catering for everyone's tastes, the colour the designer had chosen was crimson, with full length satin curtains draping the elegant windows which led out to the balcony. A crimson carpet, patterned discreetly to make it look genuine, gave the floor a luxurious finish. And above the bed, draped and hung, beautifully ruched, and suspended from the ceiling like something out of the Arabian Nights, was a crimson canopy complete with two matching curtains, at the moment looped back but obviously made to draw round the bed.

"The carpet and fittings are included in the price," Veronica put in carelessly. "Of course, you don't have to have them. It *is* a bit over the top I agree..."

"I love it," Rebecca answered firmly. "I wouldn't change a thing."

And with a contented sigh she looked round again, her eye drawn this time to a large Victorian wardrobe, resplendent with gleaming mahogany and three shining mirrors, one full length, standing against the left-hand wall.

"Is it original?"

"Yes, rather fine too. Now if you want to keep that it would be an advantage because it's been marooned here by the conversion."

"What do you mean?" asked Greg.

"The builders demolished the old central staircase then realised they hadn't got the wardrobe out, and the damn thing's been *in situ* ever since."

"I think it's magnificent," Rebecca said, staring at it in admiration. "And so big. I'm sure all my clothes will fit in there. And probably all Greg's as well."

"Oh good," Veronica answered unenthusiastically. "I mean otherwise one only has two options, hasn't one? Either live with the thing or chop it to pieces."

"We'll live with it."

Veronica tossed a head of straggly blonde hair. "I take it from that comment that you would like to make an offer?"

"We're certainly interested," Greg answered, irritatingly cautious.

"Very!" Rebecca added firmly.

"But one thing puzzles me," he went on.

"What's that?"

"Why is the conversion so new?"

Veronica's face took on an oddly casual expression. "Oh, the house stood empty for years. Some old boy owned the place but never lived in it. It got badly neglected and run down as a result. However, he died and his heirs sold it to a development company. That's the story in a nutshell."

"How interesting," Rebecca said, curious.

"Indeed, indeed," Veronica answered absently. "Now look, why don't you think about it for twenty-four hours and then give me a ring at the office on Monday morning? Here's my card."

Before Greg could utter a word, Rebecca said, "Is there anybody else after the flat?"

Veronica smiled. "There certainly *is*, Johnny Morton Bridges for one. He's Lord Medway's son, you know."

"No, I didn't," answered Rebecca. "Look, we'll be in touch as soon as we can."

If she had had her way she would have made an offer on the spot, regardless of cost. However, she managed to keep quiet until they were in the car, then Rebecca turned to Greg, her eyes wide.

"Well?"

He pulled a face. "It's very expensive. I'm not sure we can really afford it."

"But you're getting a salary increase next year. Oh, Greg."

Her husband's face cracked into a grin. "I'm only teasing, sweetheart. I really love it. Ring Veronica Drear-Bedwards – or whatever her name is – and make another appointment to view, then we'll offer her a thousand less and see what happens."

"But what about Lord Thingy's son?"

"Well Clapham may not be quite his scene," said Greg, and laughed with sheer pleasure that he and Rebecca had seen such a perfect flat at a price they could actually afford.

It seemed a long time till Monday but at last the weekend was over and Rebecca, having arranged a free afternoon, once again found herself climbing the stairs to the first floor flat in The Grange behind a smug looking Veronica.

"I thought you wouldn't be able to resist it," the estate agent was saying over her shoulder. "Johnny Morton Bridges is awfully keen too. He was here this morning."

"Has he made an offer?"

"No, not yet," Veronica answered pointedly. "But I'm expecting him to any time now."

"I see."

But the minute she was through the front door, Rebecca knew that the flat would never belong to Johnny or anyone else, that it was destined to be hers, come what may.

Turning impulsively to the estate agent, she said, "I feel as if it's mine already. The place has such an amazing atmosphere, almost alive. Don't you think so?"

Veronica laughed. "Well, one does come across that sort of thing in the course of one's job. Some houses *are* rather doom laden. But I can't say I've noticed anything about this one."

"Who did you say owned it?" asked Rebecca, walking into the master bedroom and seeing her reflection in the mirrored door of the wardrobe.

"The old chap who died was called Maybury, I believe. But I don't know who lived here before that."

"I think I'll go to the library and look up the street directories," said Rebecca, full of sudden and urgent curiosity.

"Good idea," answered Veronica.

Rebecca put her hand on the other woman's arm. "I really want to have this flat but naturally it has to be a joint decision. I'll get my husband to phone you tomorrow."

"Jolly good!" said Veronica. "Till tomorrow then."

And that was it, the second viewing over. With mixed feelings of excitement and uncertainty, Rebecca made her way through the spring sunshine towards the library, wishing that everything had been signed and sealed and she could truly say Flat One, The Grange, belonged to her already.

The street directories in the library's reference section were comprehensive, going back to the 1850s. Systematically, Rebecca went through each one and was finally rewarded; in 1860 came the first mention of the house, the entry simply saying, "Mr and Mrs Alfred Carthew, The Grange, Clapham."

It was fascinating, like holding a mirror up to the past. Mr and Mrs Carthew had obviously been young and newly married for by the 1880s other names, clearly children, were also added. "Mr George Carthew, Miss Amelia Carthew, Miss Florence Carthew, Miss Anna Carthew."

All those girls and only one boy, Rebecca murmured, and smiled.

The story, as told by the pages of the directories, continued. In 1895 a change came when young George obviously married. There were no more references to Mr and Mrs Alfred Carthew and their daughters, now the entry ran, "Mr and Mrs George Carthew and Miss Ada Claridge."

Rebecca laid the book down. So the parents moved away and let him have the house. In that case, she wondered, who on earth was Miss Ada Claridge?'

Very dimly, right in the back of her mind, a bell rang but with reference to what particular memory, she could not say.

*

They moved in in pouring rain, everybody getting thoroughly soaked as the removal firm humped furniture upstairs to the first floor.

She and Greg had bought a genuine Victorian bedhead made of gleaming brass for the room, reliably informed by the antique dealer that it was called an Arabian. Beneath the crimson drapery it shone superbly, and having pulled the duvet over the sheets, Rebecca flung herself backward onto the bed, loving everything about this most beautiful of rooms. Looking across at the wardrobe, now open to receive her clothes, Rebecca could see herself reflected and she smiled and waved to her own image.

"What are you playing at?" said Greg from the doorway and Rebecca sat up rather guiltily before getting to her feet. Just for a second she saw herself in the mirror again and could have sworn that the bed looked different, covered in white lace, the curtains round it green brocade. She spun round to look – but it was nothing, a trick of the light.

In a relatively short time the flat was sorted out, the furniture and plants arranged to advantage, in fact Rebecca almost immediately felt that The Grange was her home. Yet in many ways the layout puzzled her, particularly the kitchen/dining room which had so obviously once been two rooms, one leading into the other.

"What do you think these were?" she said to Greg, as they carried in their dining table. "I've no idea, though I imagine the living room and bathroom were both bedrooms."

"Yes, I should think so. And this would definitely have been the family floor. The servants always slept at the top of the house in those days."

"Poor things. It couldn't have been much fun struggling about with all those pails of hot water."

"Not to mention the slops."

"Don't please! You'll put me off my supper."

The light airy living room, with its splendid view over the lawns and conservatory, now had their cosy sofa and chairs comfortably installed, the television perched in a corner. And it was here that they sat in the ever-lightening evenings having returned from their jobs, Greg working as a minor accountant with a large City firm, and Rebecca as a junior editor with a group of publishers based in a fashionable London square.

With her thoughts on the beauty of the grounds outside, she would gaze out of the window for hours, while he read a book or watched television. It was all deliciously companionable and Rebecca felt she would never have been happier in her life, were it not for the fact she was sleeping so badly.

They had been in the flat a month, during which time Rebecca found herself getting more and more exhausted, when the first odd thing happened. As usual Greg was reading and she, quite unable to keep her eyes open, had dropped off to sleep in front of a boring television programme, when the sound of his voice, exclaiming loudly, abruptly woke her up.

"What is it?" Rebecca asked.

"Good God, just listen to this," Greg was saying.

"What?"

"This!" And he indicated the old library book in his hand.

"I'm sorry, I've been fast asleep. What about it?"

"It's a long biography of one Edward Marshall Hall, the famous barrister. Do you remember there was a television series about him last year?"

"Yes, I think I do. But what's the connection?"

Greg shook his head. "It's unbelievable," he said, then started to read out aloud. As he did so Rebecca found herself growing stiff and tense, sitting rigid in the chair as his voice filled the room.

"One of Marshall Hall's most famous cases," Greg began, "was what became known as the Carthew Poisoning, the trial for which took place in 1898, late in the reign of Queen Victoria. In many ways similar to the Charles Bravo murder, the Carthew affair has never been solved to this day.

"George Carthew, a rising young barrister of thirty, lived with his family in a spacious residence known as The Grange, situated near Clapham Common, the household consisting of George himself, his wife Charlotte and her spinster sister, Ada..."

"Of course!" breathed Rebecca. "The names in the street directory. I knew I'd heard them before somewhere."

Greg looked at her but after a moment's pause continued to read.

"George became ill, his condition puzzling the many physicians who attended him, none of whom were able to save him. Finally he died after lingering painfully for some weeks, but the autopsy – insisted upon by George's father, a man of great wealth and a respected figure in society – revealed slow arsenical poisoning..."

Rebecca shivered, realising that she had gone completely cold.

". . . There were four suspects, all of whom the police questioned closely. Charlotte, George's twenty-seven-year-old wife; Ada Claridge, her elder sister of forty; Gervais Vere, a man of French extraction who in the past had enjoyed an illicit love affair with Charlotte, the result of which had been an unwanted pregnancy and a back-street abortion – a fact never revealed to George; and Joseph Juggins, a former coachman to the household who had been sacked by Carthew two months before his death. Eventually Juggins was arrested and charged with wilful murder."

Greg stopped reading and exclaimed, "Gracious me!"

"What?" asked Rebecca, feeling unbelievably on edge.

"In one of the most stunning turnabouts in legal history," he continued, "Mr Carthew Senior engaged Marshall Hall to defend the old former servant, the dead man's father making public his belief that he suspected someone else of the crime. It was the appearance of one Alfred Carthew for the defence that gave Counsel the instrument to plant doubt in the minds of the jury and a verdict of Not Guilty was returned."

They stared at each other in amazement. "Then who did do it?" asked Rebecca eventually.

Greg shook his head again. "It says here that no-one else was brought to book for the crime."

"I can't believe it. What an extraordinary story."

"It is rather, isn't it."

*

Newspapers had had a field day with the Carthew Poisoning. Rebecca sat in front of the library microfiche viewer, reading the contemporary newspaper reports.

"Picture the scene", enthused The Bugle, "as Edward Marshall Hall, Queen's Counsel, dark and handsome with spellbinding eyes, rose to announce that he was calling Mr Alfred Carthew, the dead man's father, to appear for the defence. Shocked and amazed, there was no sound in the court as Mr Carthew Senior, tall and stately, made his way to the witness box."

There followed an almost verbatim report of Mr Carthew's words; in which he made it clear that, in his view at least, Joseph Juggins was devoted to George Carthew, had been dismissed on the orders of George's wife, Charlotte, and was quite incapable of murder. Mr Carthew Senior was also quoted as saying, "Another hand lies behind the death of my son, I would stake my own life upon it."

"Phew!" said Rebecca, and fed another microfiche into the machine.

This one was even more riveting, containing as it did sketches of all the principal characters in the drama. She found herself gazing at Alfred Carthew, stern and bewhiskered, an eminent Victorian indeed; beside his portrait, one of his murdered son George, attractive and curly haired, cherubic looking, not at all what Rebecca had imagined. A vision of that face contorted with the agonising effects of poisoning by arsenic flashed into her mind and she gave an involuntary shudder.

Below these two drawings was reproduced an interesting likeness of Charlotte. Rebecca gazed at a pair of limpid light eyes staring through a shade of dark lashes, the expression in them vacant. A great mass of fair hair was drawn up behind their owner's head like a harvest loaf, plaited and curled, and obviously of enormous beauty in reality.

"Lovely, but stupid," commented Rebecca aloud.

But however feckless Charlotte Carthew had been she had obviously not lacked intelligence when it came to choosing a lover, for judging by the sketch of Gervais Vere he was, at least as far as looks were concerned, all that any woman could desire, jet haired and as intensely handsome as George was angelic.

Beside the other portraits, that of Ada Claridge came as something of a shock. Rebecca studied the features of a nondescript female, hair dragged back into a severe bun, eyes obscured by glinting spectacles, and wondered that any two sisters could be so unalike. The final drawing in this collection of "The Principals in the Carthew Affair", as *The Standard* described them, was that of Joseph Juggins, a stolid looking countryman with mutton-chop whiskers.

"Well, well, well," Rebecca said to herself. "Who would have thought this case would turn out to be so fascinating?"

Beneath the series of sketches was reproduced the closing lines of Edward Marshall Hall's summing up to the jury. Reading it and remembering the television series, Rebecca could picture the actor who played the part saying the actual words.

"Imagine if you will, gentlemen of the jury, the scene in the master bedroom of The Grange, with its balcony overlooking beautiful views, the rural peace of Clapham Common, as the ugliness of painful death came to George Carthew. Imagine his weeping family, his distraught father, and imagine the bewilderment of the accused – by then an employee of Lady Stockbridge and removed by many miles from that death of which he was supposed to be the instigator – as he was arrested for a crime which it would have been almost impossible for him to commit and which, indeed, was only brought to his door by the flimsiest web of circumstantial evidence. Gentlemen, you have heard that very evidence for yourselves and there is only one verdict you can find in this case – and that verdict is Not Guilty."

Even after so many years the speech of the man who was to become so famous in legal history, captured Rebecca's imagination and she saw through the medium of his words the scene in the dying man's room, then realised with a horrible lurch of the heart that it must have been *her* bedroom in which George died. That Mr Frog's masterpiece, like the beauty of a poisonous plant, hid something sinister and dark beneath its gilding.

She had left her bedroom door ajar when she had gone out earlier and now, glancing in, Rebecca could see the bed and its beautiful crimson drapery reflected in the wardrobe mirrors. For some awful and inexplicable reason she averted her eyes and instead of going straight in to hang up her coat, went to the living room and turned the television on extra loudly, then banged into the kitchen to make a cup of tea.

"This is terrible" she said aloud, "I am afraid of my own flat, my own bedroom. I can't let this go on."

Eventually, feeling as guilty as if she were an alcoholic, Rebecca had a small tot of brandy to give herself Dutch courage and marched purposefully into the bedroom, a determined expression on her face. It was unnervingly quiet, almost as if the room were listening to the sounds she was making, and Rebecca had to force herself to go to the wardrobe and reach for a hanger.

"This once housed Charlotte's clothes," she thought, and knew a moment of intense cold.

"Oh don't be a fool," she said to herself. "You'll never be happy here again if you go on like this."

And with that she pulled open the section in the middle, complete with its shelves for hats. The drawer she wanted to open was stiff and Rebecca had to use two hands to pull it, leaning against the wardrobe to steady herself and knocking her elbow painfully against a knob as she did so. Instantly, above her head, there was a whirring sound and Rebecca almost fainted in fright as from the back of one of the hat shelves something flew forward.

It took her a moment or two to brace herself and look up. But when she did, surprise and delight took over from panic as she saw that a hidden drawer had been released by the knock and now stood open, ready for her to gaze inside. Like a voice from the past a persistent musky perfume filled the air and, standing on tiptoe, Rebecca found herself looking at a priceless collection of gloves, stockings and hair combs, all perfectly preserved and each one dating from over a hundred years earlier. She reached up with both hands.

She had never seen such elegant gloves, small and narrow, made of the finest kid, they must have fitted a hand almost childlike in its proportions. Picking up a cream pair, Rebecca tried unsuccessfully to pull them on. Yet the very feel of them made her shiver and she went immediately to replace them. As she did so her hand touched something hard at the back of the drawer. With a gasp, Rebecca drew out a bunch of old letters.

A sudden sense of guilt stopped Rebecca from looking further and she put everything back just as it had been to show Greg when he came home from work, dreading the thought that he might be late. But his key sounded in the lock at the usual time and without saying a word, Rebecca took him by the hand and led him to the wardrobe, pressing the knob and watching the drawer fly open.

"Oh my God!" said Greg. "This is amazing. It's a fine collection of Victorian accessories."

"Not only that, there are letters in there as well. Greg, we might just be about to uncover further evidence regarding the old Carthew Case."

They did not bother with any supper, grabbing a bottle of wine and some cheese and taking the snack to the dining room table where they laid out each letter separately. Now it could be seen that there were two distinct hands on the envelopes.

"Love letters from George and Gervais?" asked Rebecca breathlessly. "It can't be, can it?"

"I think so," answered Greg, putting on his gold rimmed reading glasses. "Now we must be systematic. Put

George's in one pile and Gervais's in another, and then get them into date order."

"Is it right that we look?" asked Rebecca, suddenly guilty again. "Should we delve like this?"

"Yes, we must," Greg said, kissing her cheek swiftly "I know how you feel but this is part of history."

The first letter was dated 16th June 1888, and was from Gervais.

"Charlotte would have been seventeen," Greg calculated, "and they had obviously just met. Listen: 'My dear Miss Claridge, it was so delightful to encounter you and your sister on the Brighton promenade. I am with this post writing to Mr William Claridge requesting permission to call. Sincerely your friend, Gervais Vere'."

The story emerged vividly, the fatal attraction becoming too strong and Charlotte giving herself to him physically at some clandestine meeting long ago at Leamington Spa.

Then came the terrible consequences, clearly spelled out in a letter from Gervais. "My darling, you must not do this filthy thing. I implore you not to destroy our child. We can elope and marry despite your father's opposition, which is based solely upon the fact that I am of the Catholic faith. Charlotte, I beg you not to proceed with your plan. It is a sin to take a life".

"Poor things!" whispered Rebecca."

"And it marked the end of their relationship. Listen to this one:

"'My dear Charlotte, I can never forget nor forgive what you have done. Your action has broken my heart. I am returning to my people in France and will not see you again.'

"Well, *she* met George soon after and married him on the rebound. Here's George's proposal: 'My darling Charlotte, The news that you have consented to be my wife has filled me with unbelievable joy. I look forward to a lifetime of happiness with my own dear sweetheart at my side. Ever your loving, George'."

"And all he got for it was death by arsenic poisoning," said Greg.

"Do you think it possible Charlotte heard from Gervais again?"

"She certainly *did*", answered Greg and picked up the last letter in his pile. "It's dated two years after her marriage and says, 'I have been unable to forget you. I am returning soon to England – in two weeks time – and would beg you to meet me in Trafalgar Square on April 15th, at 4.00 pm."

"Do you think she went?"

"I don't know."

"I think they did. I think they sat together and plotted George's murder."

"You're allowing your imagination to run away with you," said Greg and ruffled her hair affectionately. "Come on, it's getting late. Let's get some sleep."

But it took Rebecca hours to lose consciousness, her brain packed with teeming images of love, sex and murder, all festering beneath the genteel surface of the living hypocrisy that had been Victorian society.

*

It gave her quite a shock to hear that Greg was going away for a few days, a shock of which Rebecca, who considered herself a thoroughly liberated young woman, felt somewhat ashamed. She had said nothing to him of her sudden and irrational fear of the flat, and of the bedroom in particular. Nor had she told him that this fear had hardly lessened over the weeks following the discovery that The Grange had once been the scene of a murder. And now she was faced with the prospect of staying there alone while her husband went to Chester to do an audit.

The sensible thing would have been to close the place down and go to stay with someone, but a stubborn streak within Rebecca rebelled at the thought of such weakness. For how could she admit to a soul, let alone a girlfriend, that the thought of the Carthew Poisoning haunted her hourly, simply refusing to go away? Instead, not feeling it to be quite so cowardly, she phoned round to see if anyone would be willing to visit her. But it seemed as if fate was against this idea when friend after friend declined on the grounds that the dates were not convenient.

"Are you sure you don't mind being on your own?" asked Greg on the morning of his departure.

"Of course I don't," lied Rebecca, kissing him an affectionate goodbye.

But she dawdled, leaving the office late that evening, for once being the last to go, putting out the lights on her floor.

"I have got to get over this," Rebecca said to herself again and again as she travelled back on the tube. "It's going to ruin my life if I let this thing take hold."

But still her spine prickled as she went through the front door and she hurried into the living room to put the television on loudly, her old ploy, almost at a run.

She knew it was weak-willed but nonetheless Rebecca took a sleeping pill while watching the late-night film and so got into bed half falling asleep. Because of this she could not tell what time it was when she woke to see the room glittering with moonlight, everything transformed to a shadowy softness, the harshness of daylight all gone away.

The movement of herself sitting up in bed, a hand going to her mouth to cover a yawn, was reflected in the wardrobe's full length mirror and, almost reluctantly, Rebecca looked across the space between it and where she lay. Then she knew that she was either going mad or was dreaming – for Mr Frog's creation had vanished.

A different room was visible in the glass, heavy with opulent furnishings in green brocade patterned with pink flowers; a rose velvet chaise-longue stood at an angle; while the bed was covered in white lace, its elaborate brass frame more costly looking than the one Rebecca had bought. A figure lay slumbering in the bed; Rebecca could only see light-coloured curls on the lace-edge pillows.

She would have screamed then, yelled herself awake, but before she could make a sound her eye was transfixed by another movement in the mirror. In the right-hand wall, directly opposite the wardrobe, she could see a door beginning to open slowly, a door that in reality was no longer there. As if released from a trance, Rebecca threw back her head and started to scream.

*

It was a Saturday evening and still early, but already the restaurant was beginning to get crowded. With a trio of live musicians wildly playing Greek music, and some attractive views of Clapham Common visible through its windows, the proprietors of the Aristophanes could have got away with serving indifferent food, but as it happened their menu was excellent, reminiscent of all the best in Greek cooking, and Rebecca had booked the table for Greg's homecoming meal in advance.

"So you missed me?" he said, as they sat down and the waiter lit the candle on their table.

"Very much so. How about you?"

"Of course."

Rebecca smiled absently, her mind not really on the conversation, wondering yet again when she should broach the subject of her dream. For that was surely what it had been, even though it had seemed so dramatically real at the time.

She had thought, in her sleeping state, that the door reflected in the wardrobe's mirrors had first opened then rapidly but silently closed again when she had started to cry out. And after that, or at least this was how Rebecca remembered it, she had sat upright, leaning against her pillows, watching the wardrobe all night long.

When daylight had come, though, she had woken from a troubled sleep to find herself curled up in bed, the pillows only slightly disarranged and everything apparently back to normal. Yet despite this Rebecca had moved out, had abandoned Mr Frog's delicious master bedroom and slept in the living room, on the sofa bed purchased when they got married for any friends who might stay.

"You're daydreaming," said Greg, cutting through her thoughts. "What's the matter?"

"Nothing."

"Oh yes there is. I know that look of old. Something's upset you while I've been away, hasn't it?"

"I had a peculiar dream while you were gone."

"What about?"

"The wardrobe in our bedroom actually. I dreamt that I woke up and looked across at it and I could see a door opening in the right-hand wall."

"But the wardrobe's on the left."

"That's just the point. I saw the door reflected."

Greg stroked his chin thoughtfully. "How odd! There's nothing there in reality."

"That's the other point," said Rebecca, slightly impatient. "I wondered if I was seeing something from the past, from the time of the Carthew poisoning. Do you think there could have been a door there once, leading into what is now our dining room?"

"I should think it's more likely," answered Greg, "that you've got that damned murder on the brain and it's coming through in dream form."

"Why do you think that?"

"Because I do." Greg took hold of her hand and laced her fingers through his. "Listen, darling, everyone knows that dreams are only extensions of what we've thought or done in daylight hours. You probably wondered what the house used to look like and dreamt of an imaginary door. Anyway, I'm back now. If a ghost comes into our bedroom I'll chase it off, don't you worry."

There didn't seem much point in discussing it further and Rebecca, with an effort, dismissed the whole thing from her mind, instead luxuriating in the good food, the ambience of the restaurant, and most of all the fact that Greg was back.

It was a relief to walk into the softly-lit hall holding her husband's hand, and watch him go into their bedroom, whistling cheerfully as he switched on all the lights. It was at this moment that Rebecca decided she wouldn't admit to not sleeping in there while he was away, that certain things were better left unsaid.

The following day, an unexpected opportunity came to leave the office early and Rebecca accepted it gladly, anxious to get some shopping done. But, almost involuntarily, she found her feet turning in the direction of the library instead of the shops and, looking at her watch, realised she could snatch a precious hour in there before it closed.

"I must be going mad," she thought as she hurried up the stone steps. "Greg's right. I'm getting hooked on the Carthew Case." Yet there was a strange, almost hypnotic, fascination in looking at the old newspapers and their contents, gazing yet again on Charlotte's stunning but vacant beauty and Alfred Carthew's stern unrelenting features.

"Now which one of you did it?" Rebecca muttered, as she came again to the sketches of those involved. But the drawings stared back at her lifelessly, and with a sigh she abandoned that particular microfiche and threaded another into the viewer.

This one was new to her, containing as it did the reports of a different newspaper, *The Recorder*. And though the text revealed no hitherto unknown facts its columns did hold something of enormous interest. Rebecca twisted the magnifying knob as she found herself looking at plans of both the ground and first floors of The Grange. In wonderment at the life style of affluent Victorians, she gazed admiringly at the solid outlines of a drawing room, living room, morning room and library, complete with fernery and conservatory. And then her eye, almost reluctantly, went to the other plan – and everything fell into place.

What was now their bathroom bore the inscription, "Spare Bedroom", while their lovely living room with its splendid views over the garden had once been "Miss Ada Claridge's bedroom". But the most astonishing thing was the explanation of their long thin kitchen and dining room, for the dining end leading onto the balcony had been, "Mrs Carthew's dressing room", and the kitchen, "Mr Carthew's dressing room". The two rooms had led one into the other by means of a communicating door, and while what had once been George Carthew's room opened onto the passageway, as the kitchen still did, Charlotte Carthew's dressing room led straight into the bedroom through a door that was no longer there. So her dream had been right after all! There *had* once been a door in the right-hand wall through which, every night of her life, Charlotte must have walked in order to go to bed.

Supper was strangely silent that evening, but Greg hardly seemed to notice Rebecca's preoccupation, obviously busy with thoughts of his own. In fact as soon as the meal was over he picked up his briefcase and headed in to the living room, saying, "There's just so much work to catch up on after that wretched audit I've had to bring some home. Do you mind, darling? Do you want me to bring the television into the dining room?"

"No thanks," she answered. "I'd rather read."

Greg came late to bed that night forcing her to go before he did, alone in the moonlight, staring into the room's shadowy corners, wishing that they hadn't moved here after all, that she hadn't been so insistent that this was her dream flat and she must own it at all costs.

When Rebecca woke later, the room was much darker, the moon veiled by thin cloud. Beside her, Greg slumbered comfortably, his day's work finally at an end. Sighing, she was just about to close her eyes again when a slight movement in the corner of one of them had every hackle on her body standing on end. In the wardrobe mirror something was stirring. The missing door was once more slowly opening.

To say that she was petrified was to understate her emotions. Rebecca was so afraid that she found herself quite unable to move or even make the smallest cry. All she could do was watch in paralysed horror. Still staring into the mirror she saw that the shadowy figure of a woman stood in the doorway, looking over to where she and Greg lay in bed, regarding them silently for what seemed like a full two or three minutes before she glided into the room. Rebecca crouched against the pillows, frozen and terrified, as the woman came to Greg's side and stood without moving, gazing at him intently.

The darkness at that moment must have been intense, for strain as Rebecca did to see who it was, the face remained featureless, almost void. It was ghastly! She felt forced to watch her husband menaced in this most sinister of ways without being capable of raising a hand to help him. Still looking into the mirrors, Rebecca gasped as the woman suddenly and swiftly leant forward, then turned, hurrying towards the missing door and departing through it as silently as she came.

Rebecca spun round to look at the right hand wall. There was no door and no woman either, yet she knew perfectly well that she was wide awake.

"Help!" she shrieked in panic. "Greg, help me!"

He woke with a start, horribly alarmed yet fighting off sleep. "Whatever's the matter?" he said.

"There was a woman in here," Rebecca cried. "There was Greg, truly. I saw her."

As his arms went round her, Greg could not help an immense yawn. "It's all right, darling. You've had a nightmare."

"But I saw her. I was awake."

"Do you want me to search the flat? I will if it would make you happier."

He said it so wearily that any idea she might have had of saying yes was completely banished.

"No... no. I suppose not."

"Look, darling, it really *was* a nightmare. Let's both get some sleep. I've got a tough day at the office tomorrow."

She must have dozed off she supposed, though it didn't feel as if she had when the radio alarm went off at quarter to seven. Very reluctantly, Rebecca got out of bed and went to have a bath, only to find Greg still sound asleep, his breathing unusually heavy, when she came back again. Feeling rather spiteful, Rebecca leant over and gave him a shake. "Come on, you'll be late for that tough day of yours."

Rather to her surprise, Greg gave a groan. "Sorry, I don't feel well. I really don't."

"Perhaps it will pass if you have a bath and something to eat," Rebecca answered uncaringly, still furious that he had been so disbelieving in the night.

"I hope so." He swung out of bed. "God, I feel terrible."

They had always made it an unwritten rule that they left each other alone in the morning, he in his hurry to get to the City, she to Bloomsbury Square, so Rebecca paid him little attention and it wasn't until she was sitting on the tube that it occurred to her Greg had looked really very unwell indeed. She almost turned back then, but her workload was equally as pressing as his and Rebecca hardened her heart and went on her way.

She knew the moment she went through the front door that evening that her fears had been justified. Her husband's briefcase and the jacket of his suit lay thrown down on a chair, and the bedroom door stood wide open. In a whirl, Rebecca flung herself through the entrance only to be pulled up short. White-faced and almost unconscious, Greg lay on the bed still as a statue, hardly seeming to breathe.

"Darling, what is it?" She had both his hands in hers and was looking anxiously into his face.

He opened his eyes painfully. "I think I've got gastric flu. I was terribly sick at work. I had to come home. Stupid, isn't it?"

"No, it's not," she answered fiercely. "I'll call the doctor."

"Please, wait until tomorrow. It might pass off."

Since they had been married neither of them had been seriously ill until now and Rebecca was torn, longing to get professional help, yet scared to call out an overworked G.P. if it were only an ordinary upset stomach. But by the following morning, looking at Greg's white face and knowing how sick he had been during the night, she hesitated no more. Rebecca went to the phone, rang the surgery and asked one of the doctors to call.

If this was the first time for either of them to be ill it was also the first time she had ever taken time off in order to look after her husband, and it couldn't have come at a worse moment. Rebecca sighed as she thought of the book she was editing that should be finished by now and into production. But there was nothing she could do; the only thing was to wait for the doctor to give his diagnosis.

The mystery stomach complaint, identified as food poisoning, took two days to clear up, but after that Greg seemed absolutely his old self and Rebecca thankfully went back to work and her extremely late book. Yet, despite the fact she should have been going at full speed, she found it difficult to concentrate, persistently nagged by the idea that there was something she ought to realise, to understand, which somehow eluded her. In the end she gave up and took an early lunch hour, deciding on a walk in the sunshine to clear her head.

It was a wonderfully bright day and Rebecca headed off in the direction of Covent Garden, looking into the windows of shops, loving the clothes and hats, and finally finding herself outside her favourite second-hand bookshop. Without hesitating, she went in and started to browse.

She wasn't aware that she had wandered into the crime section until a title leapt out at her from the shelves. In amazement, Rebecca read, *Death At The Grange*, and putting out her hand discovered a book, published some ten years earlier, which purported to be a thorough investigation into the Carthew Poisoning.

It was all she could do to stop reading her new find in the office, and it was only with a great effort that she put off sitting down with the book until after supper. Fortunately, Greg ate lightly then went off to bed, still taking medication and not wanting to push his luck. So, with the house quiet, Rebecca took her purchase into the living room, where once had slept Miss Ada Claridge, and turned the first few pages.

The illustrations were excellent, photographs and well executed drawings of the chief figures in the case. There was also an artist's impression of the murder room, complete with the victim dying in bed, his reflection vaguely shown in the wardrobe mirrors. Rebecca shuddered at the sight of it.

Having started, she went steadily through the book and at about midnight reached the final chapter.

"Though obviously unable to name names publicly," Rebecca read, "Mr Alfred Carthew made it quite clear that he suspected his daughter-in-law of committing the crime.

After the release of Juggins from custody, Mr Carthew paid for his son's ex-employee to retire to Dorset away from the glare of public attention. Here he helped the ex-coachman set up a livery stable and start a completely new life. Then followed Carthew's pursuit of his daughter-in-law, an act quite without mercy.

After badgering the police to take further action – something they were unable to do in view of the lack of fresh evidence – Alfred Carthew dogged the wretched woman's footsteps, going from town to town, regardless of expense or business commitments. Using the alias Mrs Croxley, her mother's maiden name, Charlotte bought herself a modest villa in Worthing, only to be followed there by Carthew, who rented himself a house in the next road. Whenever she took a walk he would follow her, deliberately standing in her path, never speaking, simply glaring silently.

After this sequence of moving house only to be followed by her father-in-law had taken place on three occasions,

Charlotte fled to France. There, she renewed acquaintance with her ex-lover, Gervais Vere, who had started a business in Orléans and whom she had not contacted since the murder.

Now both single, a relationship developed between the couple once more and they even planned to marry. However, one night Gervais Vere most mysteriously walked out of his house, leaving business and Charlotte stranded, and was not heard of again for another twenty years, when he turned up in Australia as an extremely wealthy land owner. There was great speculation at the time that Alfred Carthew had bought him off, but nothing could ever be proved.

In despair, Charlotte went to live in Paris only to find that her father-in-law had picked up her trail, renting an apartment above hers, from which he kept up a continuous barrage of sound twenty-four hours a day. When asked by the landlord to move on, Carthew counter-moved by paying certain Bohemian art students to occupy the premises and drive Charlotte to distraction, making her life a living hell of insults and barracking. Finally, she returned to England where she died alone at the age of thirty-six in a seedy hotel in Half Moon Street."

Rebecca laid the book down open on her lap, seeing again that beautiful silly face with its harvest loaf of hair, the colour of grain, drooping on to the nape of its owner's lovely neck; and the glorious eyes, limpid and light, with not a shred of malice apparent in their depths. So they had closed for ever when their owner had been little more than a young woman. Had she died of grief, Rebecca wondered; grief at losing a child, husband and lover, all three? Or had a guilty conscience sped Charlotte on her way; had she been unable to face the fact that she had murdered George in order to be with Gervais, and ended up with neither of them?

Rebecca picked the book up once more and saw that the next piece consisted of a reproduction of a report in *The Standard* following Charlotte's tragic end.

"The sudden death of Mrs Carthew, whose husband George was poisoned by a person or persons unknown during the summer of 1898, must inevitably bring the notorious Carthew Case once more into the public eye. Readers will remember the *cause célèbre* when Mr Alfred Carthew – father of the deceased – helped the accused man, Joseph Juggins, clear his name by briefing Marshall Hall, QC, to defend him. There were also certain sensational incidents following the trial when Mr Carthew, who died in hospital last year, appeared to pursue his former daughter-in-law from town to town. However, when the lady left for France, in order, or so it was rumoured at the time, to seek out her former lover, Gervais Vere, nothing further was heard of Mr Carthew's strange obsession.

"But now Mrs Carthew is dead at the age of thirty-six, the inquest finding' the immediate cause of death being haemorrhage from the lining of the stomach, produced by alcoholic stimulants'. Poor miserable woman! What sort of life has she been living since leaving these shores? What inner despair drove her to such degraded depths of dipsomania that she died alone and friendless in a small hotel room in Half Moon Street?"

The piece went on, evocatively conjuring up Charlotte's last sad and sordid days, and Rebecca realised that she had reached the final two pages of the book.

". . . and so", she read, "the hunter and the hunted were dead. Alfred Carthew in a hospital for the insane, the entire affair having totally unhinged him; Charlotte in different but equally wretched circumstances.

"Of the only other two survivors of the tragedy, Ada Claridge and Gervais Vere, little further is known. Ada left The Grange shortly after the end of the trial and went to live in Cheltenham, where she was last heard of entering service as a paid companion to Lady Roper. There is no evidence that she and her beloved sister Charlotte ever met again.

As to Vere, perhaps he found happiness at last. He married a Frenchwoman, also settled in Australia, and raised seven children. He never returned to either France or England and died at the age of eighty-three, on his own sheep farm in the outback.

"In conclusion it must be said that the Carthew Poisoning is as baffling today as it was a hundred years ago, for now with all the evidence sifted and sifted again, we are no nearer to solving the crime. The question remains, and probably always will, who killed George Carthew?"

Rebecca closed the book and laid it down realising that a faint noise, shut into the background while she read, had disturbed her. She listened carefully then heard it again; a low moaning sound was coming from the direction of the bedroom. The book fell to the floor as she scrambled to her feet.

Automatically, her eyes turned to the wardrobe but everything was as usual: Mr Frog's design was reflected, not the room with the green and pink brocade which she had seen the night the missing door had first opened. And had also seen, she realised with a start, depicted in her new purchase in that bizarre drawing entitled "The deathbed scene."

Greg's voice brought her back to the present. "Sorry to disturb you, darling. It's been my turn to dream, I'm afraid. Did I make a noise?"

"More of a whimper than a roar, as they say. What happened?"

"Nothing really. I just woke up suddenly, convinced there was somebody leaning over me, staring. It was a dream, of course."

Rebecca felt as if she had frozen to the marrow of her bones. "Was it a woman?"

Greg gave her an unreadable look. "Yes," he said slowly, "as a matter of fact it was."

*

It wasn't until she was on the train and it was actually pulling out of the station, Rebecca realised that as well as the anticipation and excitement of the journey, to say nothing of the job that lay ahead, a large amount of relief was added to her general feeling of well-being. A feeling that put a cheerful song on her lips and had her rushing up to the buffet car like a schoolgirl to buy coffee and scones, despite the fact that she had enjoyed a substantial breakfast. With the excitement, interest, and sense of challenge, Rebecca was looking forward to the coming week.

Some years previously, the diaries and nature notes of an Edwardian country lady had been discovered and had made an enormous hit with readers everywhere, even starting a whole new fashion trend. Now a woman living in Warwickshire had found something similar. Alice Andrews, a writer of children's stories, had come across a mass of her mother's diaries, dating from the twenties and thirties, and all beautifully illustrated. The fact that her mother had been Zara Piotrovich, a White Russian immigrant and a known artist of her day, could do nothing but add to the beauty of the find.

"And I have had the luck to have been chosen as her editor," thought Rebecca, and realised if the venture were successful it could lead to great openings in the publishing world for the person who had steered such a project through.

Little Greys, the village where Alice lived, lay in unspoilt Shakespeare country. As she was driven from the station in Alice's sturdy car, Rebecca could not take her eyes off the voluptuous green of the fields and occasional glimpses of a crystal bright river.

"I envy you living here," she said.

"Not so good in the winter," Alice smiled. "It can get a bit parky. Good thing I've got Russian blood."

Rebecca turned to her enthusiastically. "I can't wait to see your mother's diaries."

Alice nodded. "They really are fascinating. She used to sketch people at social occasions and then go home and make proper drawings and notes. There's some superb stuff on the Duke of Windsor – Prince of Wales as he was then – and Wallis Simpson. And as for the fashions of the day – well, they are out of this world."

And they were! Rebecca sat at Alice's dining table with countless notebooks spread before her, lost in the life of Zara Piotrovich and her contemporaries. For the diaries contained the very best of social comment, recording as they did the toytown tumult of the twenties giving way to the dark thunder of the thirties, and what lay ahead. And all seen through the eyes of a sensitive and beautiful Russian girl, plunged into the social scene by her connection through cousinage with one of the great English aristocratic families.

"Sorry," said Alice, putting her head round the kitchen door. "You'll have to clear those notebooks away now. Dinner is very nearly ready."

Rebecca pulled a face. "I'm sorry to leave them even for a second. They're wonderful."

A smile in which there was something of relief crossed Alice's face. "I hoped you'd think so. There are some quite interesting family photographs as well. I believe one or two of them could be useful."

And, indeed, these were fascinating too. The Thorne family had been a close one, for every Christmas they had invited every living relative, regardless of age, to join them at a big house party.

"That's my English grandmother, Lady Thorne," said Alice, pointing out figures from Christmas, 1932.

Brought into close-up, Lady Thorne's classic English beauty could be clearly seen, in charming contrast to the dark little minx, Zara, who stood in one of the rows grouped behind her mother-in-law. Rebecca looked along the sea of faces, smiling at the characters who were all so much part of another era – and it was then that she suddenly stopped short. Beneath the glass's magnifying lens an elderly but somehow familiar figure had come into view.

"Who on earth's that?" she exclaimed involuntarily.

"Oh, I think that's Ada. May I have the glass? Yes, it is."

"You mean Ada Claridge?" Rebecca simply could not believe her ears.

"No, Ada Croxley."

In Rebecca's mind she saw again the pages of *Death At The Grange*. "Using the alias Mrs Croxley, her mother's maiden name, Charlotte...". So here was the answer to Ada's disappearance after being last heard of entering service in the household of Lady Roper. She had become Ada Croxley and taken on an entirely different identity.

"She was Grannie's companion," Alice was continuing. "Poor old thing, she was as gaga as they come and well in her seventies but Grannie felt sorry for her and kept her on. She originally inherited her from lady Roper I think."

"Yes, she did."

Alice sipped her glass of tawny port, laughing. "We children used to tease Ada terribly, but I think we were a bit frightened of her as well. We always called her The Poisoner."

Rebecca gazed at her in astonishment, quite unable to speak. "Why?"

"There was something very creepy about her. She had eyes like brown pebbles and you could never tell what she was thinking. You could imagine her as the wicked housekeeper in a Victorian melodrama. And actually she did come to rather an awful end."

"What was it?"

"Well, it was all a bit of a mystery. She was found dead one day lying on the path near Grannie's house, with a sliver of glass in her throat. It had severed one of her jugular veins."

"How dreadful!" Rebecca was as astonished as she was amazed.

"Yes, it was. But the odd thing was that none of the windows had broken and no other glass was found anywhere near her body. It was almost as if the shard had come from nowhere."

"What happened?"

"There was an inquest but it didn't shed much light on the affair. The coroner recorded a verdict of Death by Misadventure."

Rebecca shook her head incredulously, holding out her hand for the photograph and the magnifying glass, staring again at the expressionless face, blinkered by those gleaming glasses. "I think this is perhaps an act of fate," she said to Alice slowly. "Let me show you something."

She had brought *Death At The Grange* with her, had glanced at it on the train, her preoccupation with the Carthew poisoning as obsessive as ever, and now she went to fetch it from the guest room, handing the book to her hostess in silence.

"Good heavens!" exclaimed Alice, turning the pages and coming to a photograph of Ada and Charlotte Claridge together. "It *is* Ada."

*

As soon as her key turned in the lock and the front door opened, Rebecca knew at once that the flat was empty. Stepping into the hall she felt the atmosphere rush to meet her, sweeping her up, consuming her with the strange haunting presence of the long-dead Carthews. Nervously putting down her case, she took a few paces forward and saw that the bedroom door stood open, Mr Frog's creation lying beyond in its glory of crimson satin, and nobody there.

"Greg," called Rebecca uneasily.

There was no reply, only the noise of distant traffic breaking the immense quiet.

"Greg," she called again.

Somewhere in the flat a door opened softly and Rebecca rushed in the direction of the sound. But it must have been the wind for the entrance to what had once been Ada Claridge's bedroom hung open revealing an empty room beyond.

"Greg, where are you?" said Rebecca loudly, trying to drown the din of her own frightened heartbeat. Yet again there was no answer.

"Why am I being such a fool?" she thought. "He's popped out to the shops or to the off licence."

But she knew he hadn't, knew that the silence in the flat was not recent, that it had stood empty for quite some while, and that Greg had gone without leaving her a note.

Into the fraught silence, the telephone rang abruptly, startling her so much she could hardly pick up the receiver.

"Greg, is that you?" she blurted out.

"No. This is Dr Lavery speaking. Am I talking to Mrs Nicholls?"

"Yes."

"Oh good, I've been trying to get hold of you all over the place. I'm afraid I've got some rather bad news."

"My husband's not...?"

"No, no, nothing like that. It's just that he collapsed at the office earlier today with severe abdominal pain and he's been admitted to St Mary's. Look, I wonder if you could bring some of his things in with you when you come to visit."

"Yes, of course." Rebecca was so confused she hardly knew what she was saying. "Do you know what's wrong with him?"

"Too early to say, I'm afraid. But they're doing tests on him. Don't worry, Mrs Nicholls, he's in the best place possible."

"I'll be over in half an hour."

It was like a nightmare. Tired with travelling and the week's concentrated work, she was suddenly forced to think clearly about things like pyjamas and shaving brushes. Too tense even to cry, Rebecca packed Greg's bag and set out once more, her own case still in the hall where she had left it.

To say she was shocked by her husband's appearance would not have adequately described her reaction. Greg lay immobile, a drip attached to his right hand, a coronary monitor bleeping beside him, eyes closed in a face the colour of chalk.

"Oh my God, darling," said Rebecca, slumping into the chair by the bed. "How has this happened?"

There was a moment's pause before he looked at her and whispered, "I don't know. One minute I was speaking on the phone, the next I collapsed." There was the merest suggestion of his familiar grin. "It wasn't the drink!"

It tore Rebecca apart to see him joking bravely but she whispered back "That's your story! Now don't speak any more, sweetheart. The doctor explained everything on the phone. I've brought your things, so just be quiet and have a good rest."

Greg nodded and closed his eyes again.

A bell finally rang and the visitors began to file out. Rebecca took a taxi and was driven home through the darkness to the flat, which waited for her, watchful as a beast of prey.

As she went in Rebecca firmly shut the door of the master bedroom, planning to sleep in the living room away from the wardrobe and its terrifying mirrors. But first she went to the kitchen, filling the kettle and putting it on, realising that she had had nothing to eat since a snack lunch with Alice Andrews on the way to Warwick station. Yet she was too tired even to think about making herself anything and, taking a biscuit from the tin, Rebecca sat down.

The tea was hot and soothing, as potent as if it contained a sleeping draught. Unable to stay awake a second longer, Rebecca folded her arms on the table and, cradling her head in them, fell fast asleep.

How long she had stayed like that she could never afterwards tell. All she knew was that somewhere in the dim distance the sound of voices had woken her. Without opening her eyes, Rebecca remained where she was, listening to the faint murmuring.

"It must be a dream," she told herself, "a dream brought on by the stresses of travelling combined with the shock of seeing Greg so seriously and inexplicably ill." Yet for all that it had a horrifying sense of realism.

Beneath Rebecca's fingers the touch of her pine table had been replaced by the feel of cloth, the air held a musty smell, the light – even seen through closed lids – was subdued. And all the time, in the background, droned the sound of voices. Rebecca braced herself and raised her eyelids.

The kitchen had gone, vanished; in its place a small room of identical proportions, this one furnished with a chest of drawers, a cheval glass, a washstand on which stood a serviceable but pretty white bowl and jug decorated with a design of bright blue flowers. In one corner there was a rack containing pair upon pair of men's shoes, all from another era, all elegant, obviously hand made.

Rebecca raised her head from her folded arms to see that she was leaning on what appeared to be a man's dressing table equipped with silver-backed hair and clothes brushes, the mahogany surface covered with a linen runner.

"Oh my God," she whispered. "What is happening to me? Have I gone mad?"

Yet the feeling of reality was so strong that she found herself getting to her feet, longing to see who it was talking so earnestly and in such hushed and anxious tones.

There were two doors leading off the dressing room – for what else could it be? – and going to the one on the right Rebecca saw that another dressing room lay beyond, this one with a long window, presently covered by velvet curtains of a deep plum colour. It was then that she realised she was dreaming of the past, for the shape of the two rooms was undeniably that of her own kitchen and dining room. With greater curiosity than fear, Rebecca turned the handle of the door leading to the passageway and went through.

She was on the first floor of The Grange as it must once have been. A long landing, panelled in mahogany and covered by a cream carpet patterned with rusty red leaves, stretched to what would have been the flat's front door, the space now occupied by a curving staircase, of gleaming wood. Standing on this landing, slightly removed from the door which opened into the master bedroom, were three frock-coated men, one of whom was carrying a leather bag which denoted him as a physician.

Rebecca stared at them dumb-struck, waiting for one to wheel round and question her, but even the man facing her seemed oblivious of her presence and she realised that in this, the most vivid dream she had ever experienced, she was a mere spectator, incapable of either being seen or taking part. It was an extraordinary sensation, to move like a ghost in a house she had read so much about and now was actually able to see. Rebecca crept a little closer, trying to overhear what the whisperers were saying and then the bedroom door flew open dramatically and Charlotte appeared in the opening.

The colourless drawings and photographs of Mrs Carthew had not done the woman justice, for she was more than beautiful; her hair the colour of sunlit wheat, her ice blue eyes rimmed with vivid black, the same colour as the thick long lashes that enhanced her magnolia skin. But now Charlotte was white and breathless, her pretty bosom heaving as she fought for the strength to speak.

The physicians straightened, their conversation abruptly at an end, and it was at this moment that a door behind Rebecca opened wide and Ada rushed past her, gathering Charlotte into her arms before the younger woman could utter a word. Rebecca stared at the tall, bony figure, tin-rimmed spectacles bright in the light that flickered from the gas lamps, large, almost mannish hands, clasping her sister to her meagre breast.

"There, there, angel," Ada was saying soothingly.

"Oh help me, help me," Charlotte sobbed wretchedly, "Georgie's sinking. There's no hope for my darling."

The expressionless face tilted slightly, the spectacles revealing eyes the colour of flint.

She's glad! thought Rebecca. *She's glad he's dying.*

And with a flash of clear insight she could see it all. The elder sister, unmarried and frustrated, bringing up the child whose birth had killed their mother, loving the baby as if it were her own, then finding herself unable to share the girl with anyone.

Ignoring the grief-stricken wife, the physicians hurried into the sick room and Rebecca followed. But even though this was a dream, even though she was moving in a shadow land where nothing could hurt her, she was still not prepared for what she saw.

There, just as she had glimpsed it reflected in the mirrors of the wardrobe, was Charlotte and George's bedroom.

And in the large and magnificent glittering brass bed, George Carthew alone and dying.

Hollow featured, white as wax, he must once have been handsome in a curly haired cherubic way. Now that was all past. The hair lay limp as a sick animal's pelt, the curls dark with sweat, the life gone out of it. Rebecca stifled a cry at what she saw; that any human being could subject another to such torment was beyond understanding. Small wonder that Alfred Carthew had conducted a campaign of hate against the person he had believed to be the murderer.

And as if those thoughts had summoned the man to the room, the door opened again and in strode the victim's father, brushing past Ada and Charlotte who hovered in the doorway, and going straight to kneel beside his dying son. Taking one of George's pale hands in his own he raised it to his lips.

"Oh George, my own dear boy," he said quietly.

The most senior doctor came forward to take his patient's pulse then, looking round at the others, shook his head. It was at that moment that George opened his eyes and spoke his last words. Looking straight at his father, he said. "Oh, Governor," then died without speaking again.

There was absolute silence and everybody froze, before Alfred Carthew rose to his feet, tall and terrifying. Leaning over, he kissed George's icy forehead in farewell, then he said: "If anyone has done this to you my son by God they will pay the penalty in full. Be assured of that."

The dream was now a nightmare. Charlotte, weeping bitterly, rushed past Rebecca, going within an inch of her, her perfume filling the other woman's nostrils, yet Charlotte was unable to see her.

"Oh Georgie, Georgie, speak to me," the frantic girl sobbed, hurling herself towards the bed.

Mr Carthew turned, snarling. "My son has said his last words in this world, Madam, and they were directed to me. Now leave him in peace, he has suffered enough at your hands."

For the first time Ada spoke, and Rebecca was amazed to hear that it was a small mincing voice, not at all like anything she had expected.

"Never mind, dearest. Come downstairs and rest for a while. I'll get Amelia to make some tea."

And with that she led her sister out.

"Come, Sir." The senior physician was addressing Mr Carthew. "There is no need to distress yourself further."

"There is every need," Alfred retorted furiously. "My son has been murdered, do you hear? Murdered! I demand an autopsy."

Another doctor spoke up. "To perform one is our duty, Sir. In these circumstances a death certificate could not possibly be issued. I shall arrange for the deceased's remains to be taken to St Thomas's Hospital tonight."

"Good then," answered Carthew, and brushed at his eyes with his sleeve, suddenly hopeless and forlorn.

"Come along, Sir. You really must rest," put in the senior man, and with that the three doctors led the weeping father out of the room. Rebecca turned to go, having no wish to linger another second, then a slight but unmistakable movement reflected in the wardrobe's mirrors caught her eye, and she froze where she stood. Very slowly and very stealthily, as she had seen it twice before, the dressing room door was opening. A woman's figure stood there, the light from the candle still burning at George's bedside catching her spectacles.

"Ada!" breathed Rebecca. "I should have guessed!"

And now the full horror of the murder consumed Rebecca as Ada, showing no fear of the corpse, walked up to the bed, removed the water beaker and glass from the bedside table, and went back with them to the dressing room. Through the open door Rebecca could see her empty them into the basin, then fill them up again with fresh water from the jug.

"You evil creature!" exclaimed Rebecca and ran into Charlotte's dressing room before Ada could shut the door again; then following as the murderer, armed with jug and basin, hurried through George's dressing room, out on to the landing and down the curving staircase to the entrance hall below. Horrible though the circumstances were, Rebecca could not help but be enraptured at the heady opulence of The Grange at the height of its Gothic splendour.

To the right of the hall an open door revealed a dignified dining room, complete with massive oak sideboard, a table and twelve chairs upholstered in green morocco. Charlotte Carthew obviously entertained in style.

Closely following in Ada's wake, Rebecca came next to the magnificent drawing room, a flower-filled conservatory leading off it.

It was just as they drew level with the door opposite the drawing room, towards the back of the hall, that it opened and one of the doctors came out, standing and looking around him as if waiting for somebody.

Ada paused, the basin containing the poisoned water within a few inches of the doctor's nose, and he stared at her in surprise.

"Oh, Miss Claridge. I thought you were with Mrs Carthew."

The shuttered face turned towards him and the concealing spectacles shone. "I was just clearing up, Dr Bowles. I thought I would get the basins clean in case any of you gentlemen wanted to wash."

Rebecca gasped as the doctor answered, "But surely one of the servants would have done that?"

"I'm making them stay in their quarters, Doctor," answered that demure little voice. "I think it better so."

He pursed his lips. "I see. Well, if you would be good enough to send the footman to the library, Miss Claridge, with a tray of brandy. I have tried the bell but nobody came."

"Certainly, Dr Bowles."

Was there a suggestion of triumph in the smile that played momentarily round the thin lips as Ada swept through the green baize door that separated the kitchen and the butler's pantry from the rest of the house? Rebecca was not certain, for the murderer had temporarily vanished from view. Still curious and without realising what she was doing, Rebecca followed Miss Claridge through.

Ada was already in the scullery, tipping the poison into the large stone sink, but she wheeled round in fright as the door apparently opened and closed on its own.

I'll give her the shock of her miserable life, thought Rebecca, and picking up the jug which Ada had put down on the big wooden table where vegetables were prepared, smashed it on to the stone floor. It broke into uncountable fragments at which Ada stared with growing horror before turning back to the sink, where she wrenched on one of the three brass taps and rapidly rinsed out the last of the evidence.

Rebecca stood watching her, feeling a sense of impotent fury that Ada should so blatantly get away with such foul play. Yet what could she do other than to snatch the bowl from Ada's fingers and smash that to the floor as well, hoping Miss Claridge would think George's avenging spirit was about and stalking its prey.

And, indeed, Ada did let out a muffled scream, then hurried from the room nervously glancing back over her shoulder. Rebecca would have gone quietly upstairs, then, hoping that the dream might end where it had begun, had she not glanced into the room leading off the left hand side of the hall. For there, stretched out on a chaise, asleep amidst her jardinières and whatnots, a sleeping beauty in her boudoir if ever there was one, lay Charlotte. Rebecca took a step inside, enchanted by the girl's delicate beauty, but stopped short, wondering whether it was worth being so lovely if murder and hatred were the products of such physical perfection.

And then Ada Claridge was in the doorway, wringing her hands as she crossed to where Charlotte lay, the material of her sensible dark dress scratching across the carpet as she moved.

The girl woke with a start at the sound then, seeing her sister, said, "What am I going to do? How can I live without him?"

"Hush," Ada answered, sitting down beside her, "everything will be all right soon. I'll look after you. It will be just like the old days again, before that first horrid young man came courting you. Just the two of us."

"How can you say such things?" Charlotte answered sharply, the colour coming up in her delicate skin. "I loved Gervais, you know I did."

"He did you a cruel wrong, angel. He should have been punished for it."

"He *was* punished. He was driven out of England. Poor darling."

Ada's lips drew tightly together. "Well, my dear, if you loved Gervais so much why did you marry George?"

"Because I loved him too," answered her sister.

Ada rallied. "I would have looked after you," she retorted soundly.

"Yes, you would have liked that, wouldn't you?" answered Charlotte bitterly. "You never could bear the fact that I finally grew up."

It was the strangest experience. Rebecca caught herself thinking that she was dreaming this conversation because she had imagined something similar so often. And then events took a turn for which there was no rational explanation.

Very slowly, a strange expression began to cross Charlotte's features and Rebecca watched with a growing sense of horror as the lovely eyes grew hard as glass.

She's guessed! she thought. *She's guessed the truth!*

And, indeed, Charlotte was now shrinking away from Ada's imploring arms, her perfect face wild with emotion.

"It was you, wasn't it?" hissed the widow. "It was *you* who killed George. You did it out of jealousy, didn't you? Get out my sight, you dreadful beast."

It was almost pitiful to see Ada's plain features working with distress, tears pouring down her reddened cheeks.

"Don't, don't," she said chokingly.

Charlotte rose up, glittering with fury. "Don't what? Don't tell what I know? Don't blame you? What do you mean?"

But Ada was incapable of answering, transformed into a sobbing heap of humanity.

"Don't worry," Charlotte went on ruthlessly. "I won't betray you, I owe you that much. But as for blaming you, as for hating you, I will never stop. From this moment forward, Ada Claridge, I never want to see or speak to you again. You are no relation of mine, you murderess."

"Oh no, no!" shrieked Ada and threw herself at Charlotte's feet. But her sister, ice-cold with rage, merely stepped over her and left the room.

That was enough for Rebecca. Turning, she started to run up the stairs, faster and faster, as though she could end the dream if she went quickly enough; and then her foot caught in one of the stair runners and she fell down a great black tunnel into the empty darkness.

Light was the next thing she saw, a great deal of it. Rebecca opened her eyes in terror to find that she was sprawled on the floor, that it was morning and the kitchen clock showed seven. All about her the familiar lines of her own home reassured her that she had been there all the time, that she had done nothing more than have an extraordinarily vivid nightmare, and had fallen off the chair and on to the kitchen floor while she dreamt.

Yet there was just one disturbing fact that gave Rebecca food for thought. No article she had read, no book nor contemporary newspaper, had ever explained why

Charlotte Carthew did not set up home with Ada when all the dust had settled; why the widow had chosen a solitary life of some wretchedness rather than be waited on hand and foot by her doting elder sister.

"Dreams are reflections of what we think or do in daylight hours," said Rebecca to herself, considering. She had been so immersed in the Carthew case, had imagined possible scenes so often, perhaps it had been just a vivid dream. Yet she knew in her heart that she had been privileged to have a glimpse of the past.

*

She had moved out of the flat that day, had borrowed a room in the home of a fellow editor, making the excuse that it was nearer to the hospital and would mean that she could spend more time with Greg during visiting hours. It was partly true but in it was an excuse to leave the scene of that chillingly revealing experience.

For now, another idea was constantly bothering Rebecca; a growing conviction that an event so terrible as the slow poisoning of an innocent man by one of his own relations had left its mark on the very fabric of the building. A certainty that through the medium of the wardrobe, whose mirrors reflected the murder of George Carthew, the past was beginning to recreate itself.

Full of these disturbing fears, it came as a shock to her when Greg, after only a week in hospital, suddenly announced that he was to be discharged on the following day.

"But you don't look well enough," Rebecca protested anxiously.

"Darling, the result of every test is through – and each one of them showed negative."

"But that's not possible."

"Yet it's true! They've come to the conclusion that I must have had a really virulent attack of gastro-enteritis."

"I can hardly credit it."

"I'm sorry, it's a fact. Anyway, they need the bed, I'm being sent home tomorrow morning."

So, once again, Rebecca took a day's leave and collected Greg and his few things, driving him back to their flat in The Grange which had stood empty ever since he had been away. Looking at him where he sat in the car beside her, Rebecca's fears seemed to magnify, for Greg's face was sunken and hollow cheeked, his eyes looked dark and shadowy with prolonged suffering.

Knowing that she was glancing at him, her husband said pathetically, "I promise to take my tablets." She could have wept.

It seemed to her that the flat was quieter than ever and it was almost with a sense of fear that Rebecca saw Greg head towards the bedroom.

"No," she called, her voice urgent.

He stared at her astonished. "But darling, they told me to go straight to bed. I think perhaps I should."

His wife smiled guilessly.

"How about me making up the sofa bed? Then you could watch television and we could chat. I really think that would be much better for you."

"I'd rather get some sleep," Greg answered apologetically.

"You must have had enough of that by now. Come on, darling. I feel in the mood for some conversation."

Even as she spoke Rebecca thought how brittle and uncaring she must sound and only hoped he wouldn't hold it against her. Yet she must keep him where she could see him, afraid to leave Greg within the reflection of that wardrobe where poor Charlotte Carthew's gloves and stockings still lay hidden in a secret drawer.

About three o'clock in the afternoon he finally fell asleep despite a noisy television programme. And it was then, acting on a sudden impulse, that Rebecca decided to visit the library once more. Checking that he was soundly asleep, she slipped on a jacket and quietly made her way out of the flat.

The very first hint of autumn was in the air and Rebecca made her way through the shadow drenched streets, aware that what she was about to do made no sense and yet could hold the key to everything. Without hesitation she went straight to the library's reference section and located a work on poisons. Looking up arsenic in the index, Rebecca turned to the relevant page.

"Arsenic preparations," she read, "belong to the group known as Irritant Poisons. When these substances are given in continued small doses symptoms occur which closely resemble a chronic intestinal infection, and it is this similarity and consequent difficulty in diagnosis which make irritant poisons appealing to poisoners. Slow arsenical poisoning would produce indigestion, vomiting, the passing of blood, wasting and eventual death, similar symptoms to gastro-enteritis."

Rebecca put the book down, trying to remember the night she had seen the reflected figure menacing Greg. The woman had leant over him for a second before creeping away. Had that been the moment when she had dropped something in the mug of water by the bed? Was it possible that the Carthew Poisoning was taking place all over again?

"Whatever the truth, it's time that Ada met her destiny," Rebecca said aloud, and handed the book back to one of the librarians.

Greg was fast asleep when she got back and Rebecca felt positively cruel as she insisted that he get up, try to eat a little, and then bed down for the night in the master bedroom.

"You'll have me in a hammock on the balcony next," he said.

"What a good idea," Rebecca answered smiling, wishing she could tell him but knowing that this was a secret she dared share with no-one.

And yet, while he was taking a warm bath, there was one thing she still had to do before her confrontation with the past. Going to Charlotte's drawer, Rebecca went through each item carefully, eventually taking out two items; a flimsy little wrap that Charlotte presumably had worn round her shoulders when sitting up in bed, and a silver backed hairbrush engraved with the initials C. Putting them on the bedside table, Rebecca got herself ready and prepared for the night.

It was the sudden chill that woke her again and, sitting up, she realised that Charlotte's wrap had slipped to the floor. Putting her arm out of the bed Rebecca leant over to pick it up, draping it round her once more, and it was then that something moving in the wardrobe mirror caught her eye.

Ada was not only in the room but actually bending over Greg, a beaker of water in her hand, a look of such indescribable hatred on her face that Rebecca shuddered.

Just for a moment, watching George Carthew's murderer pour poison into Greg's empty glass, Rebecca felt herself freeze with fear and again experienced the dreadful sensation of being unable to help her sleeping husband. But then a sudden warmth from Charlotte's wrap seemed to release her from her trance and Rebecca wheeled round to look Ada Claridge in the face.

There was nobody there! The room was empty.

Sitting up very straight, Rebecca said quietly, "I know what you are doing, Ada. And now it's my turn."

She watched the mirrored reflection with satisfaction as the woman gave a violent start and looked across to see who had spoken. Rebecca saw her mouth the words "No, Carla no!," her face frantic and blanched.

Stretching her hand out to the bedside table Rebecca closed her fingers round the handle of Charlotte's hairbrush.

"Damn you, Ada," she shouted, then threw the thing against the centre mirror as hard as she could.

There was a deafening crunch followed by the tinkling sound of splintering glass.

"My God," exclaimed Greg, violently awoken by the noise and staring round him. "What was that?"

"I think it must be glass fatigue," Rebecca answered quickly. "The mirror has just cracked in the wardrobe, which will give me a good excuse to get rid of the cumbersome old thing."

"I thought you liked it," he said, reaching out to pick up his water.

"I've changed my mind; a woman's prerogative, I believe. Here, let me get you some more, there might be bits of broken glass in this one."

"Thanks," answered Greg, suddenly wide awake. "Do you know, I really feel miles better. It must be that long sleep I had today."

"Yes", answered Rebecca, kissing him on the forehead. "I think it must."

*

The publishers gave a party on the day that Zara Piotrovich's diaries were published; guests of importance in the publishing, fashion and journalistic worlds cramming into the hotel ball-room which they had hired for the occasion. Alice Andrews, looking very attractive in one of her mother's dresses, made a speech in which she thanked her editor.

"In fact," she said to Rebecca in one of the few quiet moments they had together, "there's a funny twist to Ada's tale," Alice said, "which I only found out the other day."

"And what was that?"

"I discovered amongst her papers a letter of my grandmother's written to my mother at the time of Ada's death."

"Oh yes?"

"You know I told you there was nothing near the body, only a shard of glass embedded in Ada's throat. Well there *was* something, after all."

Even before Alice said any more Rebecca knew what was coming.

"What was it?"

"A silver backed hairbrush bearing the initials C. Do you think it was Charlotte wreaking revenge from beyond the grave?"

Rebecca shook her head. "Who knows?" she said, and slipped her fingers into Greg's warm and comforting hand.

The Anklets

With a suddenness that was momentarily shocking, every light in the room went out, and there was a collective murmur from the audience as their eyes slowly adjusted to the gloom. Outside, it was daylight, brilliant and raw, but within it was mysterious as a cavern, shafts of sunlight spilling through the blinds, picking up whirling motes of dust and casting pools of brightness onto the floor.

"And now, ladies and gentlemen," said the voice of Edgar Pope, "it gives me great pleasure to show you the film of the site, which I hope will fire you with as much enthusiasm for Knidos as I have."

There was subdued and polite clapping from the audience, then the screen of the large television set lit with colour.

"The headland," said Edgar, and relapsed into silence knowing when to be quiet, letting the place speak for itself.

Amazing! thought Alison as she craned forward. For, though she had already seen the video twice, there was something about it that both moved and disturbed her. Even now, as her eyes absorbed the sweep of wild countryside, a scarlet sun falling into the sea beyond, tinting the hills the colour of wine, she felt a strange stir of excitement coupled with another intangible emotion.

"Damn good video," said someone close to her ear. "Did your father film it?"

Alison was about to whisper "Yes" when Edgar answered for her.

"I am rather proud of this and I crave your indulgence that I have dispensed with the customary slides. I took the film myself and am absolutely delighted with the result." He coughed affectedly. "Naturally the thing was idiot proof. Automatic focussing and all that."

"Don't believe it," called someone, but the rest were quiet, looking at an amazing scene – an open-air theatre built into a sheer mountainside, its marble seats suffused with all the shades of the dying day.

"Very difficult to reach," said Edgar, "but obviously of enormous importance to the civilisation, which built it."

"Incredible," exclaimed a voice from the back.

"Incredible, and very fascinating," answered Edgar, "for when Asia Minor fell to Rome, the Romans came to Knidos and also left their mark. Particularly this."

The picture on the screen changed dramatically to a shot of another theatre, this one built at the sea's very edge, its seats seeming to rise up out of the grape blue water itself, so close was it. Even from this invited audience of seasoned archaeologists, there was a low murmur of approval and Alison smiled. Her father had asked this collection of experts to see his film with only one purpose, to persuade them to accompany him on the forthcoming Knidos dig. Now, it seemed from their reaction that he was going to succeed.

The film panned out to show a claw-like promontory of land, a harbour on either side of it.

"The smaller was for galleys only," said Edgar, "but the larger, on the southern side, was a commercial port. Knidos (ancient name Cnidus) was a thriving and important place in its day."

The viewers said nothing, absorbed in what they were seeing; the remains of what had once been a bustling and beautiful city now almost vanished beneath the scrub of the headland, only the harbours and the two incredible theatres left to bear witness.

As the film ended, there was a second's silence and then sustained applause, during which Alison rose to her feet and pulled up the blinds before quietly returning to her seat.

"The plan," said Edgar briskly, before the mood could change, "is to fly to Turkey during next year's Easter vacation and join the dig being carried out by the university, under the direction of Professor Hayati Ilhan. The concept is that this should be a joint effort between English universities and Turkish archaeologists and, as you already know, I have asked you all here to seek your co-operation. In fact, we Oxford people have amongst us today—" Edgar peered round "—several distinguished colleagues whom I am also trying to persuade to join us."

His gaze swept the room again. "Now where is the London contingent?"

"Sorry, Professor, we arrived a bit late," answered an unknown voice and, turning surreptitiously, Alison saw that two newcomers to the meeting hovered in the doorway, obviously waiting for a suitable moment to find a chair.

"Not at all, not at all," said her father, "come and sit down. There are some spare places by my daughter." And with a flowing gesture of his hand, he indicated where Alison was sitting.

She stood up to identify herself and ever afterwards believed that all the strangeness – all the inexplicable, wonderful, frightening things – began there, at that moment in the lecture room of St Nicholas Hall, Oxford, when she first set eyes on Julian Grant.

"I don't want to bore everyone," Edgar was saying, "so I'll give you a very potted history of the site and leave you to look the rest up for yourselves. As you are probably all aware, Cnidus, Halikarnassos, called Bodrum nowadays – together with the islands of Kot and Rhodes – were linked by trade and custom, and belonged to the Dorian division of Ancient Greece. The four of them were an early form of common market really. The Doric games were held in Cnidus every fourth year, in a stadium outside the city walls still to be excavated."

"What religious cults were followed?" asked the man behind Alison.

Edgar smiled in the direction of the newcomers. "One of our eminent visitors here today is Doctor Alan Cosby, whose speciality that is. Doctor Cosby, would you be willing to give us a few words?"

"Certainly," answered one of the strangers, and stood up to go to the front. As he did so, his companion's shoulder brushed against Alison's and she looked up, startled, so familiar was the feel of that touch.

She found herself gazing into a face made extraordinary by slanting eyebrows, dark as the hair that surrounded it was light. Eyes, the vivid blue of harebells, stared into hers. To her horror, Alison felt a blush rise from the soles of her feet to the top of her head. Totally embarrassed, she rather lamely introduced herself.

"I'm Alison Pope, Professor Pope's daughter."

"Grant," he said quietly. "Julian Grant. How do you do?"

She could think of nothing to answer and was only glad that her akwardness was covered by the noise of Alan Cosby clearing his throat before he started to speak.

"Cnidus housed the famous naked statue of Aphrodite sculpted by the celebrated Greek sculptor Praxiteles, which stood in a temple devoted to her worship. However, Athena, Apollo and Demeter also had their shrines, so the beautiful goddess wasn't on her own. The statue, by the way, was considered not only to be the sculptor's finest work – legend has it that the model was his mistress – but the most beautiful in the entire world. People sailed to Cnidus from great distances in order to see it, and King Nikomedes of Bythnia offered to settle the city's considerable debts if he could have the statue in return."

"Dirty old man!" said someone quickly, and the meeting dissolved into laughter.

"Right," answered Alan with a grin. "A pity it's now lost to the world though."

Was that the moment when premonition began, when a sudden lurch of Alison's heart warned her that a chain of events had been set in train which would alter not only her life, but all her thinking?

"What happened to it?" she asked quietly.

"No one knows. Praxiteles's Demeter turned up and is in the British Museum. But as to his masterpiece, who can say?"

"Who indeed?" answered Edgar. "Now, ladies and gentlemen, just before I call this meeting to a close I would like to introduce our other guest, Doctor Julian Grant, whose renowned work in the field of epigraphy I need hardly describe to any of you.

The dark brows slanted up and just for a second the remarkable eyes met Alison's, before Dr Grant got to his feet and acknowledged the applause.

He's too young, she thought. *Too young and too...* She hesitated over the word and could only come up with "attractive", which wasn't quite right somehow... *to be the famous Julian Grant.*

And into her mind's eye came a picture of that saffron-coloured head bent over ancient inscriptions, reading them as if they were books, understanding words from the past where others had failed, joyously translating sentences that had been written thousands of years ago.

Alison's heart leapt with sudden emotion that anybody so clever could yet be so vulnerable. Then wondered in astonishment why she should have thought that when she didn't even know the man.

Edgar's voice broke into her thoughts. "I would ask all those who wish to take part in the dig at Knidos – and I hope that's everyone – to give their names to my daughter before leaving. As you can see it will be an exciting project and I trust the dates will be convenient. Thank you very much indeed for coming this afternoon and have a safe journey home."

"Well?" said Alan Cosby, reappearing beside Julian.

He frowned. "I'm not sure. I had thought of going to France."

Again, it was the sweep of destiny that made Alison, in a most uncharacteristic way, jump up and urgently lay her hand on Julian's arm.

"Oh, please do come, Doctor Grant," she said. "I know that my father is counting on it. There is nobody who can rival you in any way."

He frowned even more deeply and, Alison noticed, almost with a touch of alarm, that the blue eyes had darkened. "Well, I…"

"Think how interesting it will be," she persisted, surprised at herself even as she spoke. "The site has hardly been touched. Heaven knows what we might find."

"Well, I'm joining the expedition." Alan put in, rallying to her side. "The remotest chance of locating the site of Aphrodite's temple is irresistible. Come on, Julian, you can go to France another time."

Still, he hesitated and Alison felt a moment's irritation and turned away, wondering as she did so what it was about Dr Grant that seemed so familiar. But there was no opportunity to work it out, before he spoke.

"What will your role be on the dig, Miss Pope?"

She smiled. "I act as my father's site secretary."

Julian looked serious. "That's a responsible post."

"He appointed me soon after I got my degree," Alison answered defensively. "I always go with him."

Julian gave her an unreadable look. "Then I musn't be a spoilsport."

There was a second's silence, then Alan said, "So you are coming?"

"Yes," Julian answered, and walked away to put his name on the list without saying another word.

*

It bothered Alison all the evening, all the way through a late supper, which she and Edgar ate in the kitchen. Where had she met Julian Grant before?

Surely she must have done sometime, for everything about him had an indefinable air of familiarity.

"Not well?" Her father's voice seemed to come from a long way off.

"What?" Alison focused her eyes and her attention with some difficulty.

"I said, have you got a headache? My dear child, you have spoken no more than two words to me since we got home."

Alison looked at him blankly, wishing that he wasn't there, that she had the privacy to sort out her thoughts in peace, a wish she had had nearly all her adult life.

Often it seemed to her almost as if she were the parent and Edgar the child – and a rather naughty one.

It hadn't been easy to be left motherless at fourteen and suddenly find that one had not only a house to run but a genius to cope with. Yet that had been the way of things. Admittedly, Edgar had engaged housekeepers during the periods when his daughter was studying, but he had always dismissed them again at the first available opportunity.

"Silly women don't go with archaeology," he would say.

That, Alison always thought in hindsight, should have been the moment to tell him she was going as well, that clever women could be silly too. But she had never quite had the heart, and now here she was, fifteen years after her mother's death from cancer, still living at home, and these days working with her father as well.

There were relatively few jobs to be had in Alison's particular field, and on getting her degree, she had been glad to accept a minor research post at the Oxford University college, at which Professor Edgar Pope held the archaeology chair.

"Well, have you?"

"Have I what?" Alison said again.

Edgar exploded. "My dear girl, are you going deaf? I have enquired three times about your health without response. Why are you so quiet?"

"I'm thinking," Alison answered crossly.

"What about?"

"Doctor Grant," she said, and relished the look of blank amazement that came over Edgar's face.

"What about him?"

"I'm wondering where I've met him before."

Edgar stared at her. "I didn't realise that you had."

"Neither did I. But I suppose I must have done because I recognise him from somewhere."

"A conference, I expect," Edgar stated airily. "You've probably both been at one at the same time."

"But surely I'd remember?" Alison spoke slowly. "He's not exactly the forgettable type." On the tip of her tongue came a question and before she could stop herself she had asked it. "Is he married?"

Edgar frowned. "Damned if I can remember. I think so, but I wouldn't swear to it. You'd better look him up." His eyes narrowed. "Why do you ask?"

"Just curiosity," his daughter said casually. "I find him a very interesting man."

"Yes, he's young to have achieved such standing as one of the world's leading authorities on early Latin inscriptions."

"No wonder you wanted him on the dig." Alison smiled as she spoke.

Edgar's face lit up. "Yes, he's coming. His name is on the list. He and Alan Cosby together. What a *coup*!"

Alison resisted the temptation to tell her father that she had helped sway the balance.

But later on, sitting up in bed, she thought of what she had said to Julian Grant and wondered if, in fact, it had made any difference to his decision. With a sigh, Alison picked up the publication that was the equivalent of *Who's Who* in the archaeology world, taken from her father's study.

GRANT, Julian Michael, she read. *Born on 28th April, 1954, in Midhurst, Sussex, Julian Grant was educated at Hurstpiepoint and King's, Cambridge…* These facts were followed by a dazzling list of qualifications and the information that Dr Grant had worked in Italy and Greece for most of his adult life.

Alison read on. *In 1984, Dr Grant married Miss Naomi Christie, daughter of Sir Henry Christie, the Member of Parliament for…*

She put the book down slowly, wondering why she felt such a disheartening sense of loss. Then, painfully but honestly, Alison faced facts.

The truth was that she had found the man stunningly attractive. No, more than that, the feeling of knowing him had brought in its wake an illusion of compatibility which left her yearning to become his friend. *Friend*, was that really the right word? Alison gave a grim smile. She was infatuated with Dr Grant and had been from the moment she saw him, and she might as well admit it.

"If only…" she said aloud, then, with a sigh, switched off the bedside light and lay in the dark, thinking.

She had hoped to drop off to sleep immediately, forgetting Julian and the dig and everything else, but this night unconsciousness would not come. Downstairs, the venerable grandfather clock struck one, then two, and still she lay awake, feeling first too hot, then too cold. Finally, she gave up and, putting on her dressing-gown, made her way downstairs to the kitchen.

A hot drink in her hand, Alison turned to go back to bed and then stopped. It would be better to look at television than lie awake, she thought, and without hesitation made her way quietly into her father's study where they kept the set. Almost at once, the video of Knidos caught her eye, lying on the desk. Rather pleased to have found it, Alison slipped the disc into the machine and switched on, unable to resist the film's heady beauty.

The picture came onto the screen almost at once and Alison relaxed back in the armchair, clasping both hands round her mug of herb tea, feasting her eyes on the towering headland and poppy-red sky.

The scene changed and there was the theatre, perched in the mountains like an eagle's lair, the sea intense and crimson as the sun skimmed its surface. Alison shook her head in wonderment then suddenly leant forward, dazed. This was not the same video. It must be another, very similar, that her father had also taken.

For now, the theatre was packed with people, every marbled row filled, while below, taking place against a backdrop of mountain peaks, a vivid spectacle was being enacted. Alison stared in blank astonishment as she watched acrobats and dancers vying with one another, musicians playing for dear life, and all directed towards what could only be the royal box. In the middle of the central tier, draperies decorated a sectioned-off area in which a solitary figure sat watching the performance.

Alison saw the sunlight gleam on light hair as the man rose to wave his thanks to the artistes.

The scene changed and now Alison found herself gazing at two lovers beneath a tree, both looking up to where the dark leaves glistened with raindrops, though the sun still shone on their naked bodies.

"This *can't* be Father's!" she exclaimed and went to look at the box again. But there was no doubt that it was distinctly marked, "Knidos. Cameraman: Edgar Pope."

Alison stared at the television screen again and saw the couple putting on their clothes, a purple toga for the man, fastened at the shoulder with a sparkling emerald brooch, while the girl dressed herself in a simple white tunic.

"It's a film," said Alison. "I've put one in by mistake."

But even as she thought it, the screen went blank. Going to the machine, Alison clicked the eject button, and out came the disc labelled "Knidos", in Edgar's handwriting.

She sat down heavily in the chair, not knowing what to think, and then sheer tiredness must finally have overcome her because when Alison opened her eyes again, it was daylight and her father was standing in the study doorway, staring at her.

"What on earth are you doing?" he asked.

"I couldn't sleep so I thought I would come down and watch the Knidos video. But, Daddy, it was another one, very like yours but with actors. It was uncanny really because it started off just like your film."

Edgar looked blank. "What do you mean, another one?"

"Well, there *are* two, aren't there? said Alison defensively.

"No, there aren't," Edgar answered, looking at his daughter as if she had taken leave of her senses.

"But I saw it," Alison said uncertainly, and going to the player, pushed in the CD and turned on the television.

On came the picture – Edgar's film just as it had been at the meeting. There were no acrobats and dancers, no lovers beneath the tree. Everything about it was entirely normal.

"You've been dreaming," said Edgar, grinning at her irritatingly. "You were dead to the world when I walked in, Alison, so come along. There's no time for flights of fancy, we have a lot of organising to do."

There was no point in protesting further. In a daze, Alison went to her room to get dressed, staring at herself in the dressing-table mirror, wondering if she looked the type to suffer from delusions. But the same old Alison stared back, inclined to be too thin, her dark hair unruly, her eyes light as fresh water, the cool clear grey of a stream.

"It wasn't a dream," she said to her reflection firmly. "You did see something – but the question is, *what*?"

*

The months between the extraordinary night-time occurrence and leaving for the dig passed rapidly, Alison finding she had no time for strange thoughts, each moment being taken up with improving her knowledge of the site. Added to this, on to her shoulders fell the responsibility of transporting thirty archaeologists and their equipment to Knidos.

Yet, for all that, there was one evening just before Christmas when, her father being out and Alison consequently having time to herself, she found herself drawn, almost against her will, towards the study and the set of videos that were kept there. But try as she would she could find no trace of that double of the Knidos video.

Had it been an illusion? she wondered. Had she really dreamed the entire thing? The experience had been the most uncanny of her entire life. Almost as if she had willed it, the telephone rang and Alison automatically put out her hand and picked it up.

"Hello. Miss Pope?" said a voice she recognized instantly. "It's Julian Grant. I wondered if I might have a word with your father."

Alison sat down rapidly, her heart beating in the most ridiculous way. "I'm afraid he's out, Doctor Grant," she said, amazed that her voice sounded so calm. "Can I help?"

"I'm ringing about the Professor's video of Knidos," came the answer.

"What about it?" said Alison, stiff with sudden apprehension.

Julian gave a laugh. "Don't sound so worried. It's just that I would like to borrow it, if he has no objection. Some of my students are very anxious to have a look at it."

"Oh, I see," Alison said, knowing she must sound rather guarded.

"Do you think he could spare it? I can get it copied once it's here and return it to you almost straight away."

"I'll ask him when he gets back. But I am sure it will be all right. Doctor Grant…" Her voice trailed away as she lost the courage to tell him that she had seen something odd on it.

"Yes?"

"Nothing. Do you want my father to call you back? I'm not expecting him home before eleven but he could ring tomorrow."

"That would be fine." Julian's voice changed. "How very rude of me. I haven't asked how you are."

A wild compulsion to say, "I'm terrible, thanks, and have been ever since I met you because, like the great idiot I am, I've fallen for you hook, line and sinker," was fought off. Instead, in a polite voice, Alison answered, "I'm very well. And you?"

"Bloody busy!" said Julian refreshingly. "Can't wait to get away."

"I know the feeling."

Alison found herself standing very still, listening for wife noises in the background but hearing none.

"Well, thanks for your help. Have a very happy Christmas – and see you at Easter."

"Yes, Happy Christmas to you too."

The receiver clicked at the other end and Alison was left staring at the phone, still clasped in her hand, wondering how she would cope with three weeks in close proximity to him.

Kill or cure, I suppose, she thought.

Disconsolately, she stared at her father's video, abandoned on top of the player. With a gusty sigh, Alison put it into the machine and turned on the television. A rounded coastline appeared, then tier upon tier of stone seats gleaming in the sunshine, built on the very edge of the sea itself.

"Oh no!" said Alison, trembling as she spoke and staring at the screen which, as the picture drew into close-up, revealed that this theatre, too, was full to capacity, pillars supporting a huge awning which shaded the seats, the same light-haired man sitting in a box by himself.

"Be logical," said Alison aloud. "There are no pillars at Knidos, this is another place."

But it wasn't. As the camera angle moved to show the performers, seeming to single out a little dark girl whom Alison vaguely recognised, she could see by the landmarks that it was definitely the site for the dig.

"I can't bear this," shouted Alison, and pressed the off button sharply. The screen went black.

"There's got to be an explanation," she muttered.

Saying it like that gave Alison a sudden rush of courage and, bracing herself for a shock, with a show of great determination, she switched the set back on. All was as usual. This was Edgar's film, unaltered and safe, giving no hint of the extraordinary phenomena she had just witnessed.

"Well, that's it. Out you go," said Alison determinedly, and without hesitation took the disc from the machine, put it in its box, thrust it into a padded envelope and addressed it to Dr Julian Grant in London.

"And jolly good luck," Alison said spitefully. "I hope you and your wife thoroughly enjoy it."

But no amount of bravado could take away the uneasy feeling that seized her like a chill, as she wondered what strange events lay ahead when they finally reached Turkey – and the ancient city of Knidos.

*

Alison's first glimpse of Julian Grant was in the airport departure lounge, where he sat looking rather elegant, reading a paper and quietly ignoring the press of people around him.

Beside Julian, Alan Cosby munched toast, as did two other people – a man and a woman – whom Alison remembered seeing at the meeting but did not know.

"Ah, there's Grant," said Edgar cheerfully and, crossing to the quartet, shook each of them by the hand. More slowly, Alison followed, longing to speak to Julian but suddenly afraid.

The feelings he aroused in her were fierce, uncomfortable, not safe to have about a married man. For even though she hardly knew him, Alison was already highly aware that Julian Grant had the potential for meaning more to her than any of the few lovers she had had before.

Trying to avoid his eye, she nonetheless caught it, wondering if he had looked at her deliberately. His dark brows rose as he said, "Good morning, Miss Pope – or may I call you Alison as we are going to be working together?"

"Of course. Good morning. Did you receive the disc?"

Julian frowned. "Didn't I thank you? How remiss of me. Yes, it arrived safely and has been thoroughly enjoyed by all my students."

"Did you watch it, Doctor Grant?"

"Julian, please. Yes I did, only this time I found it very… unusual."

"Really? Why?"

But his answer never came as just then the flight was called and the party started towards the boarding gate. Had he dropped behind in order to avoid discussing it, Alison wondered. Or was she building up something that had taken place only in her own imagination, that nobody else could have seen?

"Nice day," said Alan Cosby, beside her. "Should be a good flight."

"I'm looking forward to it," Alison answered.

"Then can I change seats and sit next to you? Malcolm Gough – the bearded wonder – loathes flying and shakes throughout. Puts me off."

"Yes, of course." Alison couldn't help laughing. "Is he from London?"

"No, comes from Bristol, but we were at King's together."

"Oh, with Doctor Grant?"

"Yes, same year. Julian and I go back a long way. I was his best man."

Alison physically felt her face freeze as she said, "Oh!" Then some kind fate made her add, "Did his wife drive him to the airport?"

Alan shot her a strange look. "Good God, no. Why should she?"

Surprised, she said. "Isn't it usual to see one's partner off?"

"Not in their case, my dear. they've been divorced eighteen months. She's Naomi Christie, MP. The one that's always going on about healthy eating."

"Oh, *her*!"

Alison could have kissed him. But instead, she simply gave Alan a radiant smile. "I have the feeling this dig is going to be very successful," she said.

"I've got high hopes," he answered. "But just to find the site of Aphrodite's temple would be enough."

*

Alison sat between her father and Alan, occasionally looking to where Julian was seated some rows in front of her. She was full of a strange contentment. It was just before they landed that the aircraft's captain announced watches should be put forward two hours to match local time and Alison realized that they would not arrive in Bodrum until early evening.

"I hope Professor Ilhan is there to meet us," she said to Edgar.

Her father patted her hand. "Dear child, you worry far too much. I spoke to him on the telephone yesterday. He'll be there."

Soon the touch of excitement Alison always felt when arriving in another country shivered along her backbone. She stood at the top of the airplane's steps, relishing the unfamiliar heat, realising that there was sand in the wind that must have come from the desert, and knowing a moment of pure romantic escapism.

"It's always warm and windy at Izmir," said the stewardess, smiling.

"But doesn't it get very hot at this time of year?" said Alison.

"Oh no, just pleasant. Far warmer than an English spring, of course. No, it doesn't really hot up till about June."

"A bit like Greece."

"Very much so. Anyway, I hope everything goes well and thank you for flying with us."

"Thank *you*," said Alison, and went down the steps.

If Gatwick had been packed, Izmir was seething with people, and Alison noticed with a certain amusement that

Julian had been forced to remove his elegant jacket and tie as he struggled through immigration.

Despise her father's reassurances, it was with some relief that she caught sight of Professor Hayati Ilhan from the university, waving to them from beyond the barrier.

"Professor Pope, Edgar, hello," he was shouting, his eyes, bright as topaz and the same colour, shining out of a riverbed of wrinkles, brought on by years of working in the sun.

Edgar waved back enthusiastically as he made his way through the crowd to where Hayati was standing.

"Splendid to see you," he shouted.

He looked like everyone's idea of an English eccentric, thought Alison, smiling, as her father, his long handsome grey hair blowing in the desert wind, led his flock, like Moses, to the waiting coach.

In years after, she often relived that journey from Izmir to Bodrum, seeing again the dusty streets, the poor straggling towns, the sweep of fields and mountains, that was Turkey. Women wearing the traditional baggy trousers, their heads swathed in scarves, looked up with suspicion as the coach roared past, aware that Western money was pouring into their impoverished land through tourism, but they would continue to toil in the fields under the eternal sun.

It was just growing dusk as the coach finally rounded a bend in the coast road and the great curve of the bay could be seen, brilliant with light. They went downhill, through narrow shop-lined streets, and suddenly were in the warmth and glamor of Bodrum Harbour, packed with every kind of sailing and motor vessel.

The evening air was alive with sound, disco music combining with the cries of traders on the waterfront. Alison felt herself to be totally in tune with it all as her eyes were drawn to the sun, plunging redly into the sea.

And then, as the coach came to a halt and the passengers climbed down the steps, Julian Grant was suddenly beside her, obviously sensing, as much as she was, the tangible atmosphere of adventure.

"Like it?" he said.

"Very much," answered Alison eagerly, unaware that her eyes were crystal-bright in the sun's fading radiance, transforming her face. Julian looked away from her to the castle dominating the harbour.

"To think those stones once belonged to one of the Seven Wonders of the World."

"Of course! The Great Tomb of Mausolos was at Bodrum."

"Then called Halikarnassos."

"And Mausolos was its Governor in 300 BC."

They smiled, taken up with their subject, suddenly enjoying each other's company.

"Mausolos married his sister, didn't he?" asked Alison.

Julian grinned. "Yes, that habit was not exclusive to the Pharaohs. Anyway, she gave him a good send off with the tomb. It stood for fifteen hundred years before an earthquake finally brought it down. It was the Knights of St John who vandalised the ruins and used some of the stones in the castle we're looking at now."

Why she said it then she could not imagine, but Alison suddenly blurted out, "What did you think of my father's video?"

Julian gave her a swift glance before he answered, "It was odd but I hadn't remembered it having actors. Did Professor Pope film a theatrical performance of some kind? I know they still do at Epidauros. Use the theatres for modern audiences, I mean."

So he had seen it too! Alison hovered on the brink of confiding.

"I believe so," she answered vaguely, not able to say even to herself why she was being so secretive.

The entire party, having stowed their luggage aboard the two gulets, the graceful tall-masted Turkish sailing ships chartered to take them to Knidos and act as their floating homes while there, went off to dine. The outdoor restaurant lay just a stone's throw from the waterfront and Alison could hardly concentrate on the meal, so taken up was she with her surroundings and the fact that Julian was sitting only two spaces away.

And later, trying to get to sleep in her single cabin, she could do nothing but think of him. The harbour was alive with sound, echoing the strange creaking of the ship as it rode at anchor beside its sister. In fact, it seemed to Alison that she had only just closed her eyes when the high sweet voice of the muezzin called the faithful in to pray at the harbour mosque. With a sigh, Alison gave up any further attempts at sleeping, put on shorts and a T-shirt, and went on deck.

The gulet's Turkish captain said he would sail for Knidos at first light. And now Alison took an unobtrusive position by the ship's rail and watched with interest as the two crewmen heaved up the anchor with a rattle of chains, while the engine burst into life with a roar. There was an answering rumble from their sister vessel, on board which she could see Hayati Ilhan already on deck, and with that the shapely gulets slipped gracefully out to sea.

It was a voyage of almost indescribable beauty, the ships making for the hyacinth blue waters of the strait that lay between Bodrum and the Greek island of Kos.

"Good morning," said an unexpected voice and Alison turned to see Julian, his light hair bright as gilt in the early morning sun.

She was far too unsure of herself to know that these were the conditions which enhanced her looks, the breeze catching her black and lustrous hair, throwing it out like strands of silk, her eyes translucent, reflecting the sea.

"You look wonderful," Julian said quietly. "Did you sleep well?"

"I don't think so," Alison answered breathlessly. "Did you?"

"Alan's snores! I ended up in a blanket on deck."

She laughed. "I can think of worse places."

"So can I. I once slept in a luggage rack when I was a student."

Julian leaned beside her on the rail, conversation dying as the magic of the sea consumed them both. Far out, a shoal of fish leapt one after the other, while in the bays of Kos, now visible through the mist, the water turned to jade.

The ship continued to cleave its way towards the strange claw-shaped peninsula at the end of which lay the ancient city of Knidos. And, suddenly, there was land ahead, and Alison could see crumbling ruins on a savage headland, surely a guardpost for that intriguing civilization which had been both Doric and Roman in its time. Yet even this tantalizing glimpse did not prepare her for what lay in store.

The gulet rounded the promontory and suddenly they were sailing, as had the Greeks and Romans before them, into a breathtaking harbour. The sea was the colour of cornflowers beneath a dazzlingly white Roman theatre which seemed to rise, tier after tier, out of the vivid water. Alison gasped. The last time she had seen this place had been on her father's video – and packed with people.

She stared in fascination, then was suddenly aware that Julian, still standing beside her, was gripping the rail with white-knuckled hands.

She turned to look at him. "What is it? What's the matter?"

"I don't know," he answered. "Alison, I don't know."

She shook her head, not understanding him. "What do you mean? Are you ill?"

He turned on her a look that made her grow suddenly cold. "Oh no, I'm perfectly well. It's just that I feel I know this place, and it frightens me."

"But I thought you said you had never been here," Alison answered.

"That's just the point," said Julian, and Alison saw that every drop of colour had drained from his face. "To the best of my knowledge I have never set eyes on Knidos in my life."

The day was endless. Though it grew dark suddenly, the sun setting with all the drama of a theatrical event, the activity continued relentlessly, seemingly unaffected by the lack of light.

Alison looked round the outdoor restaurant wearily, wishing she could quietly go to bed and not have to socialise with this large group of Turkish archaeologists and students, charming though they all were.

It seemed as if she had now been traveling a full twenty-four hours, the night at Bodrum when she had hardly slept melting into the day the English party sailed to Knidos and saw for the first time the site of what had once been that great and powerful city.

Had it really been only this afternoon when she had stood with her father and Julian, the rest of the group crowding round, and followed the line of Hayati's finger as he pointed out the landmarks of ancient Cnidus? Landmarks now transformed by pegs and strings, for a large area of the headland and its surroundings had been marked out as a grid, a piece sectioned off so that there could be an exact reference should the past begin to reveal its secrets.

Thinking about it, Alison remembered the grim-faced determination with which Julian had marched round the site, seemingly as knowledgeable as Professor Ilhan about the ancient city's probable layout.

"You've certainly done your homework, Julian," Edgar had said in admiration, and over her father's head Julian Grant had caught Alison's eye in a stricken glance.

Since their arrival, he had said nothing further about his strange reaction when he had first sighted Knidos.

Almost, thought Alison, *as if he is embarrassed by it.*

But there could be no mistaking the look he had given her. When Edgar Pope had praised his knowledge of the city, for a moment, Julian had been afraid.

Forcing her tired mind into action, Alison surreptitiously looked round, wondering what Dr Grant was doing and whether he felt as exhausted as she did. Rather to her consternation she saw that while she was dropping with fatigue, he seemed to be thriving on lack of sleep, talking animatedly to a pretty Turkish student.

"Attractive girl," said Alan Cosby, following Alison's glance, and with a start she realised she had been sitting in silence for the last ten minutes.

"The student?"

"Yes. She's very much Julian's type, too," Alan continued, quite unaware that Alison's curving mouth had drawn itself into a line. "The divorce really upset him, you know. These days he only goes out with women he can love and leave."

Was it tiredness that made the crowd of people suddenly seem suffocatingly close, the night air almost unbreathable? With an effort, Alison rose to her feet, aware that Alan was looking at her curiously.

"Please forgive me," she said, with what passed for a smile. "The travelling must have caught up with me. I think I'll go back to the gulet."

Alan stood up. "Do you want me to take you back in the motor boat?"

Alison shook her head. "I can manage, thank you all the same."

She bent to untie the rope attached to one of the small boats carrying an outboard motor, which plied between the gulets and the mainland – and then stopped abruptly. The moon, briefly masked by a single cloud, quite suddenly beamed into a searchlight of silver, lighting the Roman theatre as clearly as if it were day. In her mind's eye, Alison saw again that extraordinary video, the theatre in the mountains – to be visited by the archaeologists next morning – the lovers under the tree, the place she was looking at now, crowded and alive with noise and people. How strange to think that Julian Grant had seen the images too.

All the way back to the gulet, Alison watched the empty theatre, only turning her attention away from it as she drew alongside the sleeping ship and climbed the ladder, which took her on deck. And from there she had one last look across the brilliant water to where every seat shone white in that unrelenting clarity, before she slowly went down to her cabin.

*

Julian had seen her leave and wondered at once if something was wrong, then had been puzzled with himself that he should even notice the comings and goings of Miss Alison Pope, who was, after all, merely a casual acquaintance. Yet, for all that, an acquaintance with whom he had shared the extraordinary experience of seeing Knidos for the first time, and thus someone who had witnessed him suffer a moment of pure anguish.

For that is what it had been. Until that second, Julian had not believed in *déjà vu* – the experience of believing one has been to a place or met a person before. But now it had happened to him. He had looked at Knidos and known it, cherished it at a glance, been both terrified and elated at the beloved familiarity of it all. And Alison Pope, that thin, clever, untouchable girl, had participated in it with him.

Saying goodnight to Farah the pretty student, arranging to have lunch with her next day, he could not get Alison out of his mind. And now, swimming back in his shorts, his shoes and shirt abandoned on the jetty, she haunted him still.

Had she, too, leaning over the ship's rail, black hair riding the breeze and eyes clear as a brook, also seemed familiar? Had the feeling of *déjà vu* spread to people as well?

The night, despite the fact that it was only spring, yet was warm enough for sleeping on deck, Julian, not relishing the prospect of Alan's snores, was only too glad to find a duvet, which had been abandoned on one of the sun loungers, and snuggle beneath it.

Opposite the gulet, the remains of what had once been a cultivated and civilised city stood inexorably staring at him and it was with the enigma of Knidos uppermost in his mind that Julian finally fell asleep.

It had been inevitable that he would dream of the place, with the recent events concerning it so very much on his mind. Yet, strangely, it was not exactly of Knidos itself that Julian dreamed, for in his sleeping state, he stood looking out to sea, realising that he was on an island, an island from which he could see the mainland of Cnidus in the distance.

Julian stared round him, realizing that he was in a typical Roman villa, a courtyard which boasted a fountain in the centre of the square of buildings forming the living quarters. Yet "typical" was not the right word for this place; it was exquisite. Going through an archway, Julian found himself in another, larger court built right on the edge of the cliff, its views unbelievably majestic. From marble pillars surrounding the square, swathes of material, which could be drawn if the sun were too fierce, blew in the wind like sails. It was surely one of the most perfect places in the world.

Looking down, Julian saw that a galley had pulled into the natural sandy harbour below and that a girl had alighted, escorted by male slaves, and was being led up the cliff path. He smiled with pleasure, for Julian knew that he had been awaiting her anxiously.

And suddenly she was there. Julian saw hair dark as a rook's wing, eyes limpid, untroubled as the depths of a sun-warmed stream.

The dancer bowed low before him, shook her long brown legs until the bells she wore on her ankles rang, and began to move. Mosaic tiles were beneath those stamping feet, tiles that showed Triton abducting Amphitrite, both splashing through the waves in splendour. But none so splendid as the creature who swirled just out of his grasp.

"Alissa, Alison, I want you," shouted Julian – and woke to find that he was lying on the hard wooden surface of the deck and he was alone. Nothing was moving but the darkened gulet, which rolled gently on the face of the dark and silent sea.

*

The dream was strange because, to start with, Alison was perfectly aware that she was dreaming. She had gone to the cabin, the one with the small porthole that looked out to the stars, and fallen asleep almost at once, her last thought of Julian Grant and the Turkish student.

Then, or so it had seemed at the time, she had been woken by the sound of knocking against the boat's exterior, and, looking out, seen that a galley had pulled up at the gulet's ladder and shadowy figures were beckoning for her to come.

She had gone willingly, glad to descend into the galley's depths and watch as the shoreline of Knidos – a shoreline strangely covered with buildings, a glorious pillared temple looming on the headland – faded into the distance.

It had been then that Alison had realised this must be a dream, for Knidos – or was she seeing Cnidus? – had nothing but emptiness on its scrubbish heath. Yet it did not seem important, nor did it matter that it was getting lighter and lighter and that the sun was poised over the sea, ready to ascend in an hour or two.

As the galley pulled away from the main land in the direction of Datcha and a distant group of islands, Alison forgot she was dreaming, and lived only for this enormous adventure.

The villa on the top of the cliffs, when they finally pulled into the shallows of the smallest island of all, was so beautiful that Alison exclaimed aloud and clasped her hands in child-like pleasure as she was led up the winding path.

Julian awaited her there of course, tuniced and grand, a sparkling brooch clasping his toga at the shoulder. Alison bent to kiss his ring as she bowed before him, paying it homage as one should the badge of office of the Procurator, who represented the city of Rome itself.

It was after that that she began to dance; stamping her feet on the mosaic tiled floor till the bells on her ankles rang, and tossing her hair till it flew out round her head.

"You're beautiful," said Julian and reached out his hand to touch her. Alison laid her fingers in his, quite calmly considering the crackling atmosphere between them – and it was as if that contact broke the spell.

She woke in her bunk, cold and shivering in the dawning, aware that she had been dreaming but still dazed by the dream's strange message. For where had she seen before the emerald brooch that glistened like green ice on the Procurator's shoulder?

It was not easy to sort fact from fantasy, nor to shake off the influence of the dream. Throughout breakfast, Alison found herself staring at Julian.

Eventually, he must have become aware of her looking for he suddenly returned her glance and equally suddenly looked away again, almost as if he had something to hide, or so Alison thought.

"You slept well, Madame?" It was the delightful captain, mundanely brandishing a large plate of scrambled egg for his guests.

Alison smiled. "Yes and no. I had a really odd dream that there were islands somewhere near here, and I was rowed to the smallest of them."

She looked round almost furtively as she spoke and was relieved to see that Julian was deep in conversation with her father.

"Are there any?" she asked in a lowered tone.

The captain smiled. "There are indeed, Miss Pope. When breakfast is over may I show them to you on my navigation charts?"

"Please," answered Alison, not suspecting that her dream could have been so accurate, until, following the captain's pointing finger she saw that just beyond Datcha, between Turkey and the Greek island of Rhodes, lay a largish island called Simi with a small one lying above it and an even smaller one below. Alison indicated the tiniest.

"What's that one called?"

The captain shrugged. "It belongs to Greece now, of course, though once it was part of the Cnidian empire. But here in Turkey it is known as Roman Island."

Alison's heart skipped a beat. "Why?"

"Because legend has it that during the Roman occupation there was a villa there."

"And are there ruins?"

The captain smiled. "Yes, Madame, there are."

She never knew how she got through that day; an important day, in which the English team visited the mountain theatre, Alan Cosby became immensely cheerful as the search was started for the site of Aphrodite's temple, and Alison set up her office in a large tent in which had been placed a lockable filing cabinet and a safe.

"Two sets of keys for everything," Edgar had said cheerfully. "I'll keep one lot in my cabin, but you can guard the others," and with that he had handed her the master set.

They hadn't been large or heavy and Alison had slipped them on a chain round her neck, knowing that to lose or mislay them would put the whole site in an uproar. For in that safe would be temporarily housed any precious finds that Cnidus might yield up, before they could be taken to Istanbul.

But all the time she had been doing these things, Alison's mind had been on the dream and the strange coincidence of there actually being islands in the very spot she had imagined.

At last it was evening and, rather guiltily, Alison closed her office early, securing the tent flap, and returning to the gulet by way of one of the small motor boats. No one was on board, or so it seemed, and she was just contemplating her next move, determined to see Roman Island before the day was over, when she noticed a dark head making its way towards the ship through the water. Cem – pronounced Gem – the youngest member of the crew of three, was swimming back from the site. He reached the ladder and began to climb out of the water.

"Cem, will you take me…" Alison pointed to herself "…out in the boat?" She indicated the powerful motor vessel, which only the crew manned.

Cem shook his black curls and did a mime of the captain looking angry.

"Pay you," said Alison and drew a note from the wallet, which lay casually on the top of her handbag.

She saw his inner struggle and felt guilty; Cem came from an impoverished nation as she well knew and was obviously tempted to risk the captain's wrath. Very contrite, Alison nonetheless took out another note and held it up. Cem gave her a heartrending look and then admitted defeat. Enacting a mime which this time said, "If the captain is angry will you stick up for me?" he took the money and the deal was struck. Cem and Alison climbed into the motor boat and set off.

The sunset, as always in Turkey, was highly dramatic, the sea like a firebird, red as crimson feathers and somehow menacing. Yet Alison hardly saw it, completely caught up with the similarity between her dreams and the voyage she was now making. So similar, in fact, that Alison found she was searching the clifftops for the villa as the motor boat approached Roman Island.

And, sure enough, as she clambered ashore and then walked up the sandy beach of the uninhabited place, she saw signs of what must once have been a steeply climbing path. Leaving Cem to guard the boat and call to her before it got dark, Alison, with a growing sense of wonderment, began to make her way up, occasionally turning to wave to him to show she was safe. And then, as she reached the summit, she forgot all about her escort, simply staring around in amazement.

To her trained eye, it was obvious that the remains of the courtyard in which she had danced in her dream were still in existence, signs of the pillars from which the swathes of material had swirled distinctly visible. Alison felt convinced that somewhere beneath the rough ground on which she now stood lay Triton lustfully kidnapping Amphitrite, all depicted in mosaic.

Taking a penknife from her bag, she bent down and began to scrape, remembering as she did so that she was on Greek territory and hoping that no motor launch bearing Greek police, suitably sun-glassed and sinister, would come by and see Cem and the boat.

With these thoughts in her mind, it was in fright that Alison realised a shadow had suddenly fallen over hers, and was almost angry when she spun round and saw that Julian Grant stood watching her, an expression of amazement on his face.

"What are you doing here?" she said, realizing even as she spoke that she had sounded snappish and cross.

"I might very well ask the same of you," he retorted briskly.

Alison straightened up. "Sorry. You gave me a fright. I thought it was the police."

He nodded without smiling. "Well, what *are* you doing?"

"The captain told me there were ruins here and I felt I had to come and have a look. These islands originally belonged to Cnidus, you know."

Still Julian did not smile. "Yes, I did know. In fact it's my guess that there was a villa here owned by somebody of considerable importance to the whole Province."

"I'm sure of it,"' Alison answered, losing her nervousness. "Look, there are column remains."

They bent together over the place where great pillars had once stood.

"Obviously an outer court," Julian said softly, "with columns to hold sun blinds."

Alison did not answer, remembering how she had danced, the tossing swathes of material echoing the flow of her hair.

Julian gave her an unreadable look. "I wouldn't be surprised if this island was the exclusive property of the Roman Procurators."

Alison stayed silent, too bemused to think properly and he went on, "I really must come here and have a good look round. Do you think your father would be upset if I took a day or two off from the dig?"

Alison regarded him seriously. "Why don't you simply tell him the truth and bring him with you?"

"Because I don't want to share the secret with anyone except you."

Alison stared at him in astonishment, but Julian continued to speak. "Will you join me here tomorrow evening? When you've finished for the day but before it gets too dark."

"Why me?"

"Because I've got an odd feeling – call it a hunch if you like – that I'm going to find something and that I will need your expert opinion."

So he obviously didn't want the pleasure of her company!

"I'd be delighted," Alison answered with a certain cynicism. "I'll be here between five and half past. Good luck with my father."

During the evening meal, it came to her. With a start Alison remembered where she had seen the Procurator's brooch before. On the mysterious video when she had watched the lovers dress, the man had fastened his toga with an identical clasp.

She must have made some kind of sound because Alan Cosby, sitting opposite, said, "What?"

"I didn't speak," answered Alison contritely, aware that once more she was ignoring the others at her table.

The members of the dig were in the Lively Lobster – the nickname given by the English group to the waterside restaurant because it proudly claimed such a dish on its board. That is, they were all there except for Julian and Farah, the Turkish beauty – a fact which wrung Alison's heart.

"Oh?" Alan looked at her questioningly. "I thought you sighed. There's nothing wrong is there?

"I'm just tired."

"So's Julian. He flaked out early."

"I thought he was with that girl." It was out before Alison could think and now there was a glint of amusement in Alan's eye.

"He might be for all I know! But he told me he was exhausted and wanted an early night. That's his story anyway."

Alison managed a shrug. "He's an adult. What he does is up to him."

Alan grinned widely. "Quite so, quite so. We mustn't begrudge him his few pleasures, must we?"

Oh no, thought Alison, *I'm not rising to that one*. Aloud, she said. "Any ideas about Aphrodite's temple?"

Alan's grin disappeared very rapidly. "No luck so far, I'm afraid."

The dream came back and Alison saw again the shapes of darkened buildings, the great pillared temple on the promontory, as the galley rowed quietly by.

"Try the site on the headland," she said.

Alan stared at her. "Why?"

"Just a hunch," she answered, aware that she was repeating the words spoken by Julian earlier.

Alan smiled tolerantly. "I've nothing to lose. I'll take Hayati up there in the morning."

It was not easy to sleep, with so many disturbing thoughts of lovers, long since turned to dust, who once had dwelt in the city of Cnidus. Yet, disappointingly, when Alison finally slept she did not dream of them and it was almost with a sense of loss that she woke, to remember that this was the day when Julian planned to investigate Roman Island.

Sure enough, he was not at the breakfast table as Alison noticed immediately as she went to kiss her father's cheek by way of daily greeting.

Edgar's lion's-mane head emerged from within a great sheaf of papers. "Good morning, my dear. How are you feeling today?"

"It's a bit early, but I think I'm fine."

"Grant isn't," the Professor continued gloomily.

Alison kept a straight face. "What's the matter with him?'

"Some sort of tummy bug. You'd think he'd be used to different food and hot climates by now, wouldn't you."

"Yes. But one can never tell. Do you remember when you were ill in South America?"

Edgar shuddered delicately, his long hair lifting on the breeze. "Don't, please. I won't eat a mouthful of breakfast if you mention it again."

Alison grinned cheerfully and made a great show of helping herself to black olives and bread as the captain, who also supervised the cooking, appeared with his usual egg dish and surreptitiously slipped a note under Alison's plate. She looked up in surprise and he gave her the merest suggestion of a wink. Guessing where it had come from Alison smiled back at him, suddenly high-spirited and ready to cope with anything.

"I think this dig is going to be a great success," she announced to the world in general, then tucked into her breakfast with relish. And later in the privacy of the site office as she opened Julian's note she felt a glow of unaccustomed happiness.

Dear Alison, she read, *I've told my white lie and will be setting off for the island as soon as everyone has gone to the site. Mustapha is going to take me there and then return to the gulet after shopping in Datcha. Can you meet him on board at five o'clock? Please do try, Julian.*

The hours dragged by after that, even though there was considerable excitement during the afternoon when Alan Cosby identified a fertility symbol adorning a piece broken from a column, a possible clue that the whereabouts of the Temple of Aphrodite had been on the headland.

Alison found herself busy, cross referencing every detail of the discovery. But at last she managed to finish with just five minutes to spare and hurried off to the landing stage to see, alarmingly, that all the small boats had gone.

She didn't hesitate, making headlong for the Roman theatre and climbing up to the middle row of seats, where she turned and shouted "Mustapha" at the top of her voice. The sound carried over the harbour and Alison saw the crewman look up, wave, and climb down the ladder to untie the motorboat. With a small feeling of triumph, she went slowly back down through the rows remembering how, on the video, this theatre had been shown covered by an awning. She was not altogether surprised to see, very much where she had expected, traces of the pillars that had once supported it.

But there was no time to consider the strangeness of everything that was happening. Mustapha in the motorboat was speeding towards the landing stage and, moments later, Alison was off to meet Julian.

The journey there was magical, the powerful craft bouncing over the waves, echoing the ocean's rhythm. The islands were only visible as the boat rose to the crest of each billow and it seemed as if they had entered a place where there was no time. And as she first saw Julian, waiting for her on the deserted beach, how difficult it was to know exactly who stood there, anxiously seeking the arrival of a dark-haired woman.

"I'm glad you've come," he said, then picked her up and carried her through the shallow waters until he could set her down on the sand.

It would have been gauche to protest that she could easily have managed by herself, so instead Alison smiled and said, "Thank you."

"A pleasure," he answered and just for a second held her tight in his arms, before he released her and became serious again. "I think I've found something very important," he added quietly.

"The ruins of the villa?"

"More than that. Something on the beach next to this one. We can get to it by climbing over those rocks. Are you game?"

"I'd rather swim round."

"Then come on," said Julian.

They splashed back into the water, Mustapha gazing in astonishment as both of them threw off their clothes to reveal bathing gear beneath.

Julian laughed. "Do look at his face. I think he imagined he was going to get a free show."

But Alison merely grinned, not wanting to talk, loving the feel of the warm sea next to her skin as they struck off past the rocks.

"There," said Julian, pointing towards the sheer cliff face, as they came dripping out of the surf.

Alison followed the line of his finger and saw a cleft in the rock, somehow suspiciously neat.

"What is it?"

"I'm not absolutely sure but I managed to scramble up a handy boulder and get a closer look. There are some words chipped into the cliff face above it."

"What do they say?"

"In peace."

"Then there must be a funerary urn hidden inside."

Julian gazed at her, his eyes remote. "I shone a torch in. I think there's not only an urn but a pot as well."

Alison stared, excitement mounting in her. "My God! We'd better fetch my father and Hayati."

"Alison, let's do this one ourselves. Please!"

She couldn't resist him, of course; years of training flying away at one smile from him.

"All right. But don't you think we should at least get Mustapha? He's quite hefty."

They called from the rocks to where the Turkish sailor slept in his boat, and felt impatient with the slowness of his response. But at last he woke and understood and brought the motor boat round, helping Julian to climb the boulder, holding him round the knees as the archaeologist delicately began to chip away at the rock.

"It was sealed after the urn was put in, but centuries of weather have worn most of the sealant away."

"Can you get your hand inside?" Alison called, shielding her eyes as she stared up.

"I've got to make more space."

"Right."

Half an hour later, it was done. Julian slid his hand in and drew out an urn, complete with inscription, while Alison, with the greatest care she had ever taken in her life, stood on tiptoe as he passed it down to her. She stared at the words marked on it, not fully understanding them, then laid the precious thing on the sand.

"Ready?" called Julian.

"Yes," she answered and stretched to her full length. But this time Alison's fingers could not quite grasp the obiect and the pot flew past her ear and landed below, hitting the jutting edge of the boulder as it fell.

"Oh no!" she shrieked in anguish, and then stopped in awed silence, staring down almost with a sense of disbelief. Lying on the glittering sand amongst the thousand fragments into which the pot had shattered, were three objects.

Alison stooped to look more closely and knew that she was the first person to set eyes on them for almost two thousand years. With a tentative finger, she reached out and touched a pair of gold anklets hung with minute bells, and a brooch which once must have sparkled green ice as it clasped a man's toga.

The excitement on the dig had been so great that Julian's explanation as to what he was doing on the island, when he was supposed to be lying ill in his cabin, had seemed not to matter. With tears in his eyes, Professor Hayati Ilhan had gazed at the jewellery, unable to speak, while Edgar had declared he had never seen anything quite so fine.

It had been difficult to get the finds away from the other archaeologists but eventually, wearing protective gloves, Hayati had put the anklets and brooch in sealed bags and into the safe, which Alison had ceremoniously locked. Then everyone had gone to the Lively Lobster and celebrated.

As soon as some sort of calm was restored, Hayati had telephoned his University to speak to Professor Bengisu Birgili.

"A wonderful woman," he had told Alison, "one of the world's foremost experts on ancient jewellery."

"Oh yes, I've certainly heard of her," Alison said enthusiastically.

Hayati smiled in delight. "Well, now you're going to meet her; tomorrow she's getting an early flight from Istanbul to Izmir, then she'll be driven to Bodrum where she will stay the night. She'll be here the day after tomorrow in the morning."

Why, Alison wondered, had she a sense of loss that the jewellery was about to become public property; that it would be examined by experts, then go into a museum behind glass and never know the warmth of a human wearer again?

There was no explanation for her extraordinary feelings other than that she had dreamed of dancing to the sound of tiny bells, and that the man in the purple toga had worn an identical brooch to the one they had just found – as indeed had the Procurator! And with that thought, Alison knew for sure that the couple she had seen on the video were the Procurator and the dancer, and that the pair had become lovers.

Suddenly, Alison was overwhelmed by the strangeness of events, uncharacteristically full to the brim with emotion, unable to cope with the noise and crowded atmosphere any longer. Slipping away with a murmured excuse, Alison went to the jetty and started to swim back to the gulet.

It had not occurred to her anyone else might be feeling as she did but as she climbed the ship's ladder, shaking the water from her hair, Alison suddenly realised she was being watched. Looking round she saw that Julian was there.

Alison smiled, wishing that her heart would behave itself.

"Hello," she said.

"Hello," he answered, his voice strangely quiet. "Was I missed in the restaurant?"

Alison turned away. "Alan noticed you weren't there but I believe he thought you were with Farah."

Julian shrugged. "She's pretty enough, but not very interesting. I've actually been sitting here thinking about what was written on the funerary urn."

"Tell me the exact words again."

"Her dust and mine. In the end, one."

Alison shivered, cold to the soul.

"And what is your interpretation?"

"That the ashes of two different people were combined in one urn."

"A devoted husband and wife?"

"Or lovers."

"The Procurator and the dancer," whispered Alison, "it has to be them."

Julian looked up sharply. "What did you say?"

Alison stared out to sea. "Nothing of interest. It's just a dream I had. Now I must go and put on some dry things. Will you excuse me?"

And she was off to her cabin before she could hear Julian exclaim, "You dreamed about them as well! Is it possible?"

*

Quite how Professor Birgili managed it nobody was certain, but on the following day, exactly an hour after sunset, a speed boat from Bodrum arrived at Knidos bearing one of the most engaging women Alison had ever seen. Quite plump, but most attractively so, Madame Birgili had a mass of strawberry coloured hair tied up fashionably in a flowing scarf made of the same material as her designer trousers. Eyes soft, dark and captivating, gleamed with laughter as Hayati said, "Good gracious, Bengisu, did you come by Concorde?"

She smiled. "Well, darling, I did make the driver put his foot down. I was very anxious to get here quickly."

To add to her general charm, Bengisu had a husky voice and spoke English with a Parisian accent.

She slipped her arm through Alison's. "And you must be Miss Pope who made the great discovery. My dear, what a thing you have done for the world. Now please, may we all go to dinner – or at least may I? I am absolutely starving and won't be able to concentrate on a thing until I've eaten."

The warmth of her personality took over and all the principal archaeologists trooped into the Lively Lobster like children.

"Well, my dear," said Bengisu, patting Edgar's hand as she spoke, much to Alison's amusement, "aren't you proud of your daughter?"

"It was Doctor Grant who actually made the find," Alison put in swiftly, and saw Professor Birgili's dark eyes sweep over her in a discerning way.

"Of course! Doctor Grant, I apologise."

Julian bowed from where he sat. "A happy coincidence Madame, that is all.'

Bengisu changed the subject. "Has anything of interest been found on the mainland?"

Alan Cosby spoke for the first time. "It is very early to say, of course, but I think we may have a lead as to the whereabouts of Aphrodite's temple."

Bengisu's eyes glittered. "The home of the great naked statue. Oh, how marvellous!"

"Marvellous but sad," Alan answered ruefully. "To think there are probably traces of the temple left but that its fabulous treasure has vanished forever."

"But Praxiteles's Demeter was found underwater by fishermen was she not? Perhaps Aphrodite suffered the same fate and now lies at the bottom of the ocean."

"I don't suppose we'll ever know."

"No." Bengisu shook her head. "I don't suppose we ever will."

The meal over, Madame Birgili accompanied by Edgar, Hayati and Julian, made her way to the site office where Alison, who had hurried ahead, was busily opening the safe, laying its contents carefully on her desk. It was a gratifying sensation to see one of the world's greatest experts on ancient jewellery shed tears of sheer bliss as, in the flickering light of lamps, she saw for the very first time the property of the long-dead lovers.

Bengisu picked up the anklets and the little bells rang faintly as she did so.

"Oh my dears," she exclaimed, "these are a dancer's anklets, probably used in the theatre. While the brooch..." She picked it up and one of the gems caught the faint light and sparkled vividly, "...belonged to an important man. I hopefully may be able to identify its owner, though that sort of thing is not always easy."

She put the jewellery down again. "You say these two things were hidden with a funerary urn?'

"Concealed in a pot and entombed with it," answered Julian.

"Then we have obviously stumbled across an ancient love affair, and a clandestine one. For the wife of a man of this rank would most certainly not have worked in the theatre."

"The dancer was his mistress," Alison said suddenly.

Everyone stared at her. "How do you know?" asked Bengisu.

"I don't really," she answered awkwardly. "It's just a feeling I have."

Afterwards, Alison never knew how she controlled herself through that next hour – an hour in which she once more locked up the precious finds and chatted politely before she eventually excused herself and went to her cabin. But finally the ordeal was over and she was alone.

She could not sleep, it was hopeless. Alison got up and went on deck, doubting she would be able to close her eyes that night, and stood looking across to the shore opposite the gulet, where the theatre gleamed tantalizingly white in the moonlight.

She had never known until that moment what compulsion really meant, but now it came, strong and urgent. Pausing only to put on an Indian skirt and a bikini top, Alison climbed down the ship's ladder, untied the dinghy that bobbed alongside, and rowed ashore. There was no reality, only a wonderful dream; a dream which led her to the safe; a dream which overrode her professionalism and its thoughts of exposing precious objects to the air; a dream which finally compelled her to take out the anklets and brooch and put on the dancer's adornments. Then, in a state bordering on ecstasy, Alison made her way to the theatre.

It was deserted and bare, the moonshine throwing deep and cavernous shadows but, as Alison began to dance, she heard the cry of the crowd and saw that the stone seats were full that the audience was watching in the moonlight, that the Procurator sat in the royal box and applauded her. Then, unbelievably, the sound of real clapping broke in on her fantasy and, trembling with fright, Alison realised someone was sitting there, a man did indeed applaud her from a central row.

She turned to run, herself again. But before she could even cross the stage area, a pair of hands had grasped hers and she was held fast.

"Where is the brooch?" said a voice, harsh with emotion, which Alison recognised as Julian's.

"There," she answered, awed and frightened, and pointed to where the jewel lay, still in its protective bag.

Without another word, he strode over and pinned the clasp to his shirt, high on the shoulder, just as the Procurator would have worn it. Then he returned to her side and Alison saw that though it was Julian Grant he had changed subtly, his face hard and altered by the silvery light.

"Come with me," he said.

"Where?"

"Don't you know?"

His arm went round her and Alison no longer cared what wildness had come over them both as they started to climb, leaving Knidos behind them, and taking the rough path that led to the mountains.

"Where are we going?"

Julian held her closely. "To the high theatre. Where we always meet."

Reality was slipping away fast. "Yes, of course," answered Alison breathlessly, and let him lead her to where the other auditorium sat perched high, carved into the hill.

Now they were alone beneath the heavens and was it Alison or the dancer who weakened beneath Julian's kisses? Or were they, perhaps, those of the Roman Procurator? Was it she, the respectable, sensible archaeologist who abandoned herself to love, who permitted exquisite intimacies, who gave herself irrevocably to the man she was with? Or did a young girl from the theatre surrender everything, knowing that now she belonged to another until death?

"I love you," said one of the women to her chosen man.

"And I love you too," he answered.

The couple slept then, curled about each other like children, warm and contented, regretting nothing of what they had done. And this sleep was dreamless, blissful, a contrast to all the tensions that had gone before.

But it was with a sense of getting cold that Alison finally awoke, shivering and dew-drenched, the spell cast by the anklets utterly broken. Just for a moment, she forgot where she was then she remembered everything and looked round, a little shy now, for Julian.

He was not there, in fact he was nowhere to be seen. Getting to her feet, Alison began to call out his name. But the only answer came from the echoing mountains, and the only living things beside herself in that desolate place were the wheeling birds, which flew above the remote and ruined theatre in which a dark-haired girl had once danced.

It was nightmarish. Like a lost sheep, Alison picked her way down from the mountains, damaging one of her toes against a rock, while a great tear appeared in her skirt as it caught on a bramble. Yet the physical discomfort she was suffering was nothing compared to her mental anguish. Again and again she thought of Alan Cosby's words, "Julian loves and leaves 'em". And now, surely, it had happened to her. In a moment of wild enchantment, she had let him make love to her, and her future with him was ruined as a result.

Yet how could she deny, even to herself, the adoration she had seen in his eyes, the depth of feeling that had flooded between them. But had that been the longing the Procurator once felt for his dancer, had Julian been acting under the power of some ancient spell? Alison was near to tears.

Surely, she thought, no man could be so callous as to abandon the woman he had just spent the night with in such a strange and dangerous place? Nobody could walk away from their partner without even a word of farewell? Or could they?

Horribly unsure about everything that had happened, Alison wished that Julian would hurry up behind her, apologising, saying he had gone for a walk, anything. But there was no sign of him, and with a heavy heart Alison finally returned to the dig.

Wretched though she was it was not difficult for Alison to see, as she drew nearer the site, that the place was in a state of chaos. Groups of students huddled miserably together, while Professors Hayati Ilhan and Bengisu

Birgili sat side by side outside the restaurant, silent and looking solemn. The only person with any semblance of normality was Alan Cosby and he appeared to be coping with Edgar, who was running about like a man demented. Hoping to hide herself, Alison made stealthily for the site office but not quickly enough to escape her father's eye.

"Where the hell have you been?" he bellowed at her, and Alison had never heard him so angry.

"I went for a stroll and lost the path. I had to wait until daylight to find my way back."

"I thought you were safely in your cabin."

"I couldn't sleep so I came ashore."

"Well, you shouldn't have done. I hold you responsible. If you had been at your post none of this might have happened."

"What *has* happened?" Alison asked desperately, thankful to see that Hayati and Bengisu had left their seats and were coming to join them.

"The safe has been opened during the night, that's what's happened," answered Edgar, white to the lips. "And not only opened but robbed. The anklets and brooch have gone."

Alison fell down a million precipices of guilt and despair as she remembered that not only had she lost Julian in the mountains but that the precious finds had disappeared with him.

"The odd thing is", said Hayati, coming to stand beside her as Alan Cosby strode away, "that it literally was *opened*. There is absolutely no evidence of a break in. Have your keys been stolen?"

Alison's hands flew to the chain round her neck as three pairs of eyes watched her searchingly.

"No, they're still here," she said. "They must have been copied. And anyway I couldn't have been at my post all night long, now could I, Father?"

"But how," thundered Edgar, ignoring her last remark, "were they copied? I keep mine locked in my cabin."

"Perhaps you forgot to close it one day," Alison answered sharply, wishing her cheeks were not so overbright and that the three older people would stop staring at her.

"And there's another thing," Edgar went on. "Julian Grant is missing. His bunk hasn't been slept in and nobody knows where he is."

Even though she was furious with him, Alison's urge to protect the man she loved gained the upper hand.

"He's probably gone to the island to have another look round, and anyway he often sleeps on deck. You ask Alan Cosby."

Bengisu spoke for the first time. "Alison, darling, Mustapha was sent for and says he hasn't taken Doctor Grant out in the boat either this morning or last night and neither has Cem. Julian could not have swum there. It is too far."

There was a horrible logic to it and Alison could only add lamely, "Then there must be a perfectly reasonable explanation. Julian would never do a thing like that."

"It was he who pretended to be ill in order to get to the island in the first place," Edgar answered nastily. "And he who was left alone on board and could have stolen my keys."

The long overdue tears finally erupted. "I think it's terrible to make such accusations behind someone's back,"

Alison sobbed. "I just wish Julian was here to defend himself."

And with that, she stalked into her office and allowed herself the sweet release of passionate weeping.

"Best leave her for a while," said Bengisu, laying a hand on Edgar's arm, as he attempted to follow his daughter. He stared at her in surprise.

"Oh! Do you think so? At home I would have just jollied her out of it."

Bengisu smiled secretively. "I think you have hit Alison on the raw, Professor. Leave her in peace until she calms down."

Edgar's entire manner softened and he suddenly looked younger. "Poor Alison, I suppose I don't really understand her at all."

"Men, men!" said Bengisu, and then she chuckled, a lovely warm golden sound. "Just be very sweet to her when she is better and say how much you appreciate and love her."

"'Love,'" quoted Edgar, "'is a many splendoured thing.' What a pity I have had so little time for it."

"One should always make time for love," answered Bengisu. "I hope Alison will learn that one day."

By some mysterious use of the grapevine, it was round the dig in a matter of fifteen minutes that the site office was temporarily out of bounds. Everyone was saying that Alison Pope was so upset by the loss of the jewellery, particularly as she had been absent at the time, that she was not to be disturbed. Only Alan Cosby, hearing the news where he was working on the headland, raised a sceptical eyebrow at this and, made straight for the tent in which Alison was conducting her own private siege.

She looked up in surprise as he pushed through the closed flap, aware that her face was blotched and her eyes swollen.

Alan sat down opposite her and came straight to the point. "Alison, where's Julian? I know he didn't sleep aboard last night and now everyone is saying he's gone off with the finds. What on earth's happened to him?"

"I don't know," answered Alison, blowing her nose hard. "Your guess is as good as mine. The only thing I'm sure of is that he hasn't taken anything."

Alan regarded her narrowly. "There's more in this than meets the eye, I know it. Listen, I don't know what's happened between you two, but even if you'd had the most monumental row, Julian wouldn't sulk. He'd have come back by now. I believe he's in trouble of some kind."

Alison's face suddenly drained of colour. "What do you mean?"

"I don't know. He could have fallen and hurt himself – anything."

"What shall I do?"

"Go and look for him before the police get here."

"Police," repeated Alison dazedly.

"Yes, Hayati is just on the point of telephoning them. They take a very dim view of losing archaeological treasures over here."

"Oh my God, he mustn't do that."

"Well, he's going to. So get on and search. If you need any help come straight back for me."

"Why don't you come with me now?"

"I wouldn't like," Alan answered smugly, "to intrude. Now get along."

Just for a second after he left the office, Alison hesitated, her wounded pride still telling her not to chase after any man. But then her natural good sense took over.

"If anything's happened," she said aloud, "I'd never forgive myself. He could be injured or even…"

She could not bring herself to say it, only angry now that she had not searched more thoroughly for Julian at the time.

With a feeling of urgency, Alison looked at her watch and saw that it was midday, a good time to get out, for nearly everyone would have left the site for a break. Unnoticed, she quietly left the office, then strolled casually in the direction of the headland before, with gathering speed, she started to retrace her steps of the night before.

How different it had been then, she thought, with the gentle moon transforming the scene and Julian's arm round her. And remembering what had happened between them, whether for good or ill, made Alison's blood race as she climbed the steep hill towards the theatre.

As always, when she finally arrived in that extraordinary basin in the mountains in which the auditorium lay, she was struck afresh by the awesome situation of the place. The actors, performing with their backs to the peaks, would have played against a massive natural backdrop of distant blue crags and wild, uncompromising terrain. While the audience, crammed tightly in the horseshoe shaped and extremely steep rows of stone seats, would have been privileged to see simultaneously both nature's spectacle and mankind's.

Panting and hot in the noonday sun, Alison slowly made her way to the heart of the theatre, the flat circular space known as the orchestra where the chorus once performed, and looked around. Standing like that, her eyes half closed, she thought of the video and the scene which had shown this very place. It had been the dancer she had seen then, of course. And it had been the Procurator who had sat in the box and acknowledged the salutes of the performers. How strange to think that the little dark girl who had made an important official of the mighty Roman Empire fall in love with her, had once danced on this very spot.

Trying to concentrate on the present, Alison raked the auditorium with her eyes, hoping for a sign of Julian, perhaps lying asleep on one of the seats. But there was no stir of life and with a sinking heart, she realised that she would have to search every row, all twenty-five of them, just in case he had slipped down out of sight.

The seats were in six blocks, each block divided by a central aisle that ran from the back of the theatre down to the flat orchestra, and plodding the length of every one was exhausting as the sun was now blazing at its fullest. Occasionally, Alison would stop and call Julian's name but her voice only echoed back to her, as must once the sound of the actors who had stood, masked and unearthly, on a raised stage behind the chorus.

Now Alison wheeled round to look at it, thinking she saw something move, but it was only a bird swooping to catch an insect.

"Julian," she called again, her voice bearing a slightly desperate note. "Where are you? I must find the jewellery – I must find you."

Once more there was a movement, just visible in one of the two doors which stood on either side of the stage and through which the actors had entered. Alison glimpsed something dark, a bird's wing – or hair.

"Who's there?" she called. "Julian, is that you?"

There was no reply but, again, something fluttered and flirted in the crumbling doorway. Alison's mouth went dry with fear. Yet who could say that it was other than a creature, feathered, furred or scaly, that basked in the shade regardless of a human presence? With a determination which was utterly forced, Alison put her elbows flat on the stage and hauled herself up.

Like every Greek theatre, the stage had at one time been pillared, but these columns had now crumbled almost to nothing. Yet the building which had contained the dressing rooms, the stage machinery and props, still had some semblance of how it must have originally looked. Alison stood still, tensely waiting for the thing to move again, but there was nothing. Then she heard it – a faint tinkling like tiny bells.

"The anklets!" Alison shouted. "Oh Julian, where are you?" And she ran through the doorway into the ruins of what had been the backstage area, only to find that there was nothing there, other than crumbling stones.

Alison shook her head, horribly puzzled – and then it was there again. A mane of dark hair tossed in the entrance to the tunnel, through which, the chorus had solemnly filed into the auditorium; a will-o-the-wisp ran ahead of her and little bells jingled in the sudden gloom.

"Who are you?" said Alison, very much afraid, but nothing answered.

Cautiously, she took a few steps forward, hoping the roof was not about to collapse on her head and peering round as best she could without the aid of a torch. To her right another tunnel, in bad repair and strewn with fallen masonry, led away unendingly, while ahead there had obviously been a total collapse of the ceiling at some time, for the way ended abruptly.

Alison stood hesitating, knowing that to proceed alone would be foolhardy to say the least, yet not wanting to go back without making sure that Julian wasn't somewhere inside. Then the decision was made for her as somewhere in the right hand tunnel there was movement.

Alison plunged in, calling, "Julian, is that you?" just in time to see a slight form ahead of her, which vanished as she rushed towards it. The air was full of the sound of the anklets' bells as Alison tripped over a fallen block, fell against a door expertly concealed in the tunnel's wall and, in putting out her hand to save herself, touched a hidden spring so that it slowly slid to one side. Shocked and gasping, Alison stared into the vast and shadowy chamber which lay beyond.

At first, she could make out nothing, but then as she took a few nervous steps into the mighty vault, hewn out of the side of the hill, her eyes grew used to the half dark and Alison found that she could see about her. A vast ceiling of rock reared over her head though the floor bore signs of being man made.

A theatre props room, thought Alison, and then her eyes were drawn to an enormous shape, dominating the chamber's far end.

She walked towards it in the gloom, her gaze widening with disbelief, tears of joy spontaneously springing down her cheeks.

Before Alison stood the statue of a woman, several times greater than life size, her body naked and beautiful, letting her garment glide down onto a bronze hydra in preparation for a bath. Alison gazed at a superb face, the eyes almost human, the expression in them divine. The marble hair that curled about the statute's head could have been living, so lustrously did the locks and tresses fall. For no logical reason, Alison dropped to her knees in a gesture of worship, knowing she had found by chance Praxiteles' Aphrodite, lost to mankind for centuries, sculpted from life, the model the courtesan Phryne, the Greek sculptor's mistress.

How long it was before she realised that someone else was in the room with her Alison could never afterwards tell. Reality had gone again and there was nothing but the statue and herself. So deep was she in this trance-like state that Alison was not frightened when a small movement beside her made her look round, only to see that Julian Grant also knelt before the goddess.

He smiled at her gently. "I was not afraid," he said. "I knew that you would find me."

"I will always come to you," answered Alison, the words forming of their own accord.

"Yes." Julian's voice was distant almost as if he were dreaming. "And I will always be waiting."

He held out his hand to her in exactly the same way that the Procurator had to the dancer, and Alison noticed that Julian still wore the emerald brooch pinned onto his shoulder.

"May I have the anklets?" she said.

"I have kept them safely for you," and taking the anklets carefully out of his pocket, Julian handed them to her.

And it was then that sensible Alison Pope of Oxford felt herself to be possessed by a theatre dancer, wild and dark and beautiful, and did not care at all. Slipping the delicate things onto her ankles, she began to dance in a strange and exotic rhythm, giving her best performance for the man who knelt watching her, the Roman Procurator himself.

The centuries meant nothing; stars were born; Julian and Alison were at one with the other lovers, acting out an ancient destiny, fulfilling promises which had been made two thousand years before, simultaneously lost and found.

Eventually, they must have fallen asleep because the first thing that Alison could recall was waking up and looking with an archaeologist's wonder at the statute of Aphrodite. Then she thought of Julian and stared round in panic. But he was there, sleeping beside her, and she realised that they had been restored to themselves, that they had returned from their strange journey into time.

Almost at that moment, Julian woke, smiled at her, and said, "Hello, remember me?"

Alison smiled back. "I certainly do – and I remember somebody else as well. Do you know who I'm talking about?"

Julian nodded. "The Procurator. Last night I felt that he had taken me over completely."

"But he's gone now?"

"In a sense. But I don't think he will ever leave me permanently."

Alison looked thoughtful and then said quietly, "She's gone too."

He stood up, pulling her to her feet. "But I believe that they are part of us, part of our past, and that they will come back if we let them, if we don't put too much reality in their way."

"Well, I won't," Alison declared.

Julian laughed. "You sweet funny girl. No, neither shall I. But now we must concentrate. Tell me, Miss Alison Pope, archaeologist, whether you noticed this."

And Julian led her by the hand to Aphrodite's statue, pointing to a marble tablet bearing an inscription laid carefully at the goddess's feet.

"Yes, Doctor Grant, epigraphist, I did. But I couldn't translate all the words. What does it say?"

"Brought to this place of safety by order of Procurator Julius Aquila, when Cnidus was under attack from the armies of the Goths, and to be kept here until his order that the goddess may be returned to her temple."

"Hidden in the theatre's props room!" breathed Alison. "The only place big enough to house her."

"And the last place a marauding Goth would think of looking."

"How clever. Does it say when this was?"

"No, we'll have to pinpoint that later. But there's more. It's small wonder the lovers took us over last night. This was one of their meeting places, you see."

Alison looked as Julian pointed to where, long ago, words had been scratched on the far wall, then crossed to touch them, allowing her finger trace the ancient characters. And what do these say?"

"Julius Aquila and Alissa worshipped both the goddess and each other in this place.

Alison stared in amazement. "But their names! They are so like ours."

"I know. The Procurator and the dancer, Julius and Alissa. It can't be simply a coincidence."

Alison shook her head in amazement. "And they still exert their spell."

Julian smiled and held out his hand. "Not for much longer. We must get these precious objects back to the site. God knows how we're going to explain their absence to the others."

In a sudden panic, Alison looked round. "But aren't we locked in?"

"I certainly was," answered Julian, "but for some reason I don't think the door closed behind you. Look…"

And staring into the gloom, Alison saw that he was right, that the sliding panel stood open to let them free.

"They think you might have taken the finds because you didn't come back last night," she said reluctantly. "Hayati was on the point of phoning the police when I came to look for you. And as for Alan, he will have organised a search party by now. It's going to be hell to account for this."

"Then let's go and get it over. There's nothing worse than anticipating trouble and not going to face it." And with that Julian took Alison's hand, wove his fingers round hers, and led her out into the open air.

It had been impossible to tell in that underground chamber what time of day it was, so it was with a sense of relief that they saw the sun beginning its dazzling descent towards the sea, and knew that they would reach the site at dusk when everyone would be getting ready for the evening meal.

"Oh, Julian, what are we going to say?" asked Alison unhappily.

"I shall simply tell the truth. That I thought I saw something moving in the theatre, left you asleep and went to follow it, ended up in what must once have been the properties room and there made a great discovery. The only unfortunate part of the story being that I got shut in and had to wait for you to come and rescue me."

"Is that really the truth?" asked Alison questioningly.

"Yes, why?"

"I just wondered about you seeing something moving. Did you?"

"Yes, I did. What other reason would I have for leaving you?"

"None, I suppose," said Alison with a sudden brilliant smile. "None that I can think of. In fact only one thing worries me. Your story doesn't explain what we were doing with the finds in the first place."

Julian frowned. "No, it doesn't. Listen, I think we'd better have a change of plan. You take the boat back to the gulet and I shall swim. During that time it takes me to get there why don't you have a private word with Madame Birgili? There's something very reassuring about that woman. I think we can trust her."

Alison looked doubtful. "But surely she is the one who must hold the jewellery most dear of all."

"Perhaps," answered Julian thoughtfully, "that is why she should be told. I'm sure she'll understand the rest. She's a woman of the world, old enough to be your mother."

But nobody could have looked less like anybody's mother than Bengisu, dressed for the evening, sipping cocktails with Edgar, Hayati and all the principal archaeologists, aboard the Turkish gulet. Alison could see her from her cabin, the star of the party, and her heart sank.

I can't talk to her in the middle of that crowd, she thought.

At that moment, a burst of Turkish music from the captain's radio drifted into her consciousness, even while she stared hopelessly across the stretch of water separating the two vessels, and with it came a flash of inspiration. Alison, the grime of the last twenty-four hours washed away, wearing a flattering pair of trousers and an evening top, swept into the wheelhouse, gave the captain a brilliant smile, and said, "I need to speak to Professor Birgili. Could you get her on the radio phone please."

He stared in astonishment. "But she is at the party, Madame. And you are on your way there also, I believe?"

Remembering how he had handed her Julian's note, Alison gave the captain the merest suggestion of a wink. "I need to speak to her privately."

He grinned delightedly. "But of course. I understand."

If only you did, thought Alison.

It was much to Bengisu's credit that she asked no questions.

"I would like to talk to you alone, Madame," said Alison over the crackling air waves. "I have something important to return to you."

"They're safe?" said the disembodied voice at the other end.

"Perfectly."

"And you would prefer to see me at once, I take it?"

"Provided you're not with the police," answered Alison, only half joking.

She could hear Bengisu chuckling. "I managed to persuade Hayati to delay his call, and somehow reassured Alan Cosby that you and Julian were having a private disagreement and should be left alone. Was I right in what I said?"

"Yes Professor, you were," answered Alison solemnly.

With what skill she thought, watching, did the older woman disengage herself and charmingly refuse the offer of several gentlemen, including Edgar, to escort her.

"How does she do it? She's got Daddy round her little finger," she said to herself.

And so very pleased was Alison to see Bengisu again that she rushed up to her and gave her an affectionate kiss as the Professor, Yves St Laurent silk trousers clinging to her legs, climbed the ladder and got aboard.

Bengisu smiled. "I feel you have a lot to tell me, my dear. Shall we go starboard where we can't be observed?"

It was as if her mother had returned to her, and warm memories of confidences shared came back to her painfully.

"What I am telling you is in total confidence," Alison began.

"My darling," answered Bengisu with a look of complete understanding. "If it is about you and Doctor Grant please don't be embarrassed. It was obvious to me that you were madly in love with each other."

"It wasn't obvious to either of us."

"It often isn't."

Alison smiled wryly and nodded her head. "You are very wise."

Bengisu smiled back. "I have learned to be. But before you tell me your story, let me tell you mine. I have identified the owner of the brooch, naturally I had taken photographs of it before it vanished so… mysteriously… and today I phoned Istanbul just to confirm my theory. The unusual use of gem stones and the inscription on the urn with which it was found prove it to be the property of

Julius Aquila, Roman Procurator of several districts in southern Asia."

A cold sensation had begun to creep along Alison's spine.

"He was a strange man," Bengisu went on, turning to look out to sea so that all Alison could see was her magnificent profile. "He had been married young but eventually divorced his wife. And though he did not take another, it was rumoured at the time that he had a mistress among one of the theatre dancers of Cnidus."

"My God!" exclaimed Alison.

"The difference in their social status prevented them from marrying, of course, and I would imagine that the affair started out as a purely physical one, on his side at least. But she found her way into his heart and apparently spent most of her time at his private residence."

So everything she had dreamed, everything Alison had experienced when Alissa had taken her over, had already happened in the past.

"But she left him lonely," Bengisu continued dreamily, almost as if she could sense something of what Alison was thinking. "She died young, of a fever, and after that the Procurator became something of a recluse, he was eventually recalled to Rome where he died some twenty years after his mistress. But his principal slave brought his ashes back to Cnidus…"

"I know," whispered Alison.

"…and Julius Aquila had left orders that they were to be mingled in an urn with those of his little dancer, whose anklets you and Julian so dramatically found."

"In the end, one," Alison said, slowly.

"A very great emotion, I think," said Bengisu. "And now, my dear, tell me everything that has happened."

"It's a continuation of the same story really." Alison did not expect to be believed. "Even before we came to Knidos, both Julian and I had seen glimpses of the lovers' past."

And then Alison explained it all to an older woman who took everything in her stride, the strange events, even the extraordinary manifestations on Edgar's video, grateful that not once did Bengisu look disbelieving.

"So you think you and Julian were led to the island by this dream you shared."

"Yes, it's quite incredible. He didn't tell me about his part of the dream until today. But now I believe we were meant to find the jewellery."

"And that is how you came to borrow it? Because it exerted such an extraordinary power over you?"

"Yes. But the finds are perfectly safe. Look—"

And Alison removed from her shoulder bag, the brooch and the anklets. Even through the wrapping, the brooch glittered and shone and as if that were a cue, at that moment Julian appeared on deck.

He kissed Bengisu's hand. "Madame Birgili, I believe I am already in your debt. Alison has explained to you what has happened?"

"Yes, indeed…" Bengisu started, but was interrupted by Alison saying, "I have left out one thing, Julian."

"And what was that?

"I didn't tell Bengisu what we found in the theatre props room. I thought I'd leave that pleasure to you."

"You two!" said Professor Birgili, "I don't think you need the rest of us. You could run a dig all on your own. *What* did you find?"

But even she jumped to her feet when they told her.

"I don't believe it! I simply don't believe it," she repeated several times, laughing and crying, together.

Eventually, she calmed down. "Is it really true? Have you really found the Aphrodite of Praxiteles?"

"Yes," said Julian, "she's there. Now we have to get her out."

Bengisu looked suddenly thoughtful. "I think that tonight we should only tell Alison's father and Hayati. In fact, for security reasons, I wonder if we should tell anyone else anything about it at all."

"We've got to include Alan Cosby," said Julian. "It wouldn't be fair to keep the news from him."

"No, you're right. But please let's wait until later, when the students have gone. For the present I shall rejoin the party. As soon as it's dark I want you two to return to the site and put the jewellery back in the safe."

And with that, Bengisu handed the bag containing the anklets and brooch back to Alison.

"And do I just stroll in to dinner as if nothing's happened? I've been missing twenty-four hours, I've got to say something," Julian put in mildly.

"Leave it to me. I shall whisper in Professor Pope's ear that there has been a major find in the mountain theatre and that you, Julian, stayed there to guard it."

"And the disappearance of the anklets and brooch?"

"What I have already hinted. That some over-enthusiastic but harmless students borrowed them to take photographs but have now returned them to me safely."

"Remarkable!" said Julian, as Bengisu disappeared in the motor launch "That woman is amazing."

"I think my father thinks so too."

"Not before time," answered Julian.

It was wonderful to get into one of the small motorboats, the jewellery safe in its box, a feeling of enormous contentment between the two of them.

"We shall have to say goodbye to the finds forever tonight," said Alison wistfully, the only sad note.

"Yes, so we shall – later on," answered Julian firmly, and Alison realised that he had turned the boat from the mainland and out to sea.

"What are you doing?"

"Saying goodbye to them properly, giving them one last chance to be in their rightful place before we hand them over to the world."

"But what if we are caught?"

"It won't matter, nothing matters, except you and me and our farewell to what once was ours."

"Ours!" echoed Alison, and smiled at old memories.

The sea was calm as a river and dark as death as the boat chugged towards the island. And there was not one breath of wind to ruffle its surface. It seemed as if they were journeying over an endless stretch of water.

The Styx must have been like this thought Alison, and began to dwell on Roman funerary customs, of the putting of a coin into the mouth of the dying so that the ferryman, Charon, could be paid to take the newly dead across the River Styx to the underworld. She wondered if Alissa had died in Julius Aquila's arms, if he had been the one to place the coin on her tongue, if he had wept as he did so.

It was no surprise to her when she thought she saw lights on the island coming from what looked like a Roman villa, and knew that she was looking at something that could not possibly be there. Beside her, she felt Julian suddenly tense.

"Alison—" His voice was low and urgent. "Look! Look up there."

At that moment, the boat was under the cliffs so that she stared straight up the steep escarpment and beyond to where, lit by flickering lamps, the clifftop courtyard was clearly visible.

"My God!" exclaimed Julian, and Alison knew that whatever they were seeing, ghostly vision or hallucination was shared by both of them.

The swathes of material had been drawn shut, like curtains, on every side but the one directly above, making the place like a room. In the centre, on a high couch draped in white, a girl lay sleeping in a cloud of her own dark hair. Yet surely this was the deepest sleep of all, for she did not make the slightest move.

"Alissa," whispered Julian. "She looks like the Sleeping Beauty."

"We are seeing the end of her life," Alison answered, and he said, "I know."

But a sudden movement drew their eyes away from the dead girl. A curtain was thrust aside by a ringed hand and there, resplendent in his purple toga, the emerald brooch glinting on his shoulder, stood the Procurator, Julius Aquila.

Alison could not comprehend the power of her premonition for she saw enacted now what she had been thinking of only five minutes earlier. Julius Aquila leant over the body, kissed the lifeless lips and then, quite obviously, put something into Alissa's mouth, before he wept.

"The coin for Charon," said Julian, enthralled.

But neither of them was prepared for what was to happen next. The Procurator lifted Alissa in his arms, brushing the black hair back from the snowdrop face, kissed the soft mouth once more, then, having laid her down gently, rushed from the courtyard and stood on the cliff's edge, looking down to the dark sea below.

"He's going to jump!" shouted Julian, in panic, and he stood up in the little boat, waving his arms over his head and calling out in a form of Latin. "Stay where you are, my lord Procurator. You must live on."

He heard him, there was no doubt about that. Julius Aquila in his century heard Julian Grant in his. Just for a second, he peered down at them in the dim light, then he started back in fear.

"He's seen us," said Julian quietly. "And he is afraid of what he knows can only be ghosts from the future."

"Go in peace, Julius Aquila," called Alison. "Go in peace."

Before their eyes, the mirage faded and was gone. There were no lights on the island, no villa and no courtyard, only the remains of the crumbling pillars that had seen so much of love and death before finally falling.

*

By next morning, it was all round the dig that Praxiteles' masterpiece, the naked Aphrodite, had been discovered. Any hope that Edgar and Hayati had had of quietly going to the mountain top theatre and letting Dr Grant and the

Professor's daughter lead them to the secret chamber were now thoroughly dashed. As a body, the Turkish students and the other archaeologists appeared wearing sensible footwear, and as Julian and Alison came out of the site office, looking efficient, there was a round of rapturous applause.

"It's no good," said Alan Cosby, grinning like a schoolboy, "they know. We can't keep them away."

So it was a very large crowd that undertook the climb to the Dorian theatre and finally gathered on the orchestra, where Alissa had once danced before a packed auditorium.

"Ladies and gentlemen," said Hayati in Turkish, clambering on to the ruined stage the better to be seen. "I know how excited you are and I promise that if it is at all possible you will all get a chance to see Aphrodite *in situ* but, for the moment, I am going to ask you to be patient. The tunnels are dangerous and could not stand up to a large crowd of people entering them together. Therefore, Doctor Cosby will later today take parties of two or three into the hidden chamber. May I request that you meanwhile wait quietly until your turn comes. Thank you."

"Well," said Alan Cosby, unable to disguise the fact that he was trembling from head to foot, "this is it. Alison, Julian, will you lead the way?"

They passed through the actors' door, all six of them, the three Professors just behind the younger people, and Alison stood quietly in the sudden coolness, remembering all that had happened in this magic place, a place which had once been alive with people; dancers and singers, the masked actors, remote and strange.

"Is it that tunnel there?" asked Alan, his voice echoing a little.

"Yes," answered Julian, "that's the first one, the other, leading to the props room, goes off it on the right."

They strode inside, lamps held high, picking their way with care.

"The chorus would have come through this on their way to the orchestra, so I presume the other one would have originally led to the back of the auditorium."

"Probably," Alan answered Julian. "When do we get to it?"

"You should be able to see it any second now. Or am I getting muddled?" Julian's voice held an enquiring note and Alison raised her lamp to illuminate the right hand wall.

"I should have thought that we would have been there by now."

"What is it?" said Edgar, coming up behind them. "Anything wrong, Alison?"

"Not really. It's just that we seem to have missed the tunnel entrance, though I can't think how."

"You're sure it was here?" asked Alan, with a slight air of anxiety.

"Yes, sure,' answered Julian, sounding puzzled, and going to the wall began to feel his way along.

It was then that Alison knew for certain they weren't going to find her, that by some extraordinary means the entrance to the tunnel leading to the chamber in which Aphrodite lay hidden, had disappeared. But she kept her thoughts to herself and searched with the others, now in a growing state of apprehension.

"Do you think there's been a fall of masonry?" Alan asked anxiously. "Is it possible that by any chance the tunnel could have collapsed?"

"It must have done," said Julian, a shade too quickly. "It's really the only explanation."

"Then we have to drill," he answered. 'We must get the equipment."

"I think we would never manage to get through before it's time for us to leave. It's rock solid," Edgar answered briskly. "I feel you must prepare for a disappointment, old chap."

"If only I could have seen her," Alan said. "Was she *very* beautiful?"

"She was superb, utterly without fault – and somehow not for the eyes of mankind. Oh Alan, don't look so sad. No doubt the Turkish team will get through to her one day."

Alan smiled at Alison bitterly. "I wonder, how I wonder. Well, she's eluded people for over two thousand wears, perhaps she simply doesn't want to be found."

"Perhaps," Alison answered slowly.

All the elation had gone out of the day. The students trooped back miserably, the archaeologists followed looking grim, though one or two stout hearts, spurred on by Alan, decided to stay and continue the search.

"I don't think that Aphrodite will be found," said Bengisu, putting her arm companionably through Edgar's. "After all, she was the goddess of love, the Greek equivalent of Venus. I expect, like all women, she has her whims and moods."

"And very delightful they are too," answered Edgar. "Will you join me in a glass of wine, Madame?

"With pleasure, my dear," she answered. "But first let me put on something glamorous."

"Of course," said Edar. "I'll wait."

"If that had been me,' Alison whispered to Julian. "He would have told me not to be so silly."

"Ah," he answered with a grin, "but you're just a daughter and I think Bengisu could well become something much more important."

"What do you mean?"

"That my father-in-law will have one of the most elegant and accomplished girlfriends in the world."

"Father-in-law?" Alison repeated wonderingly. "So you really would try marriage again?"

"With you it would hardly be a case of again, now would it?"

Alison stared at him, not quite understanding.

"My darling, surely you know as well as I do that this isn't the first time we've been together."

Now everything was clear; the circle was complete, just as winter sees death, so the spring had followed.

Alison stared out on a timeless ocean, an ocean which had flowed for ever, regardless of mortality; an ocean looked upon by Julius Aquila and Alissa when they had stood upon this same headland and pledged a love that would last for eternity…

"I do know it," said Alison.

"And do you also know that the Procurator still protects the statue of Aphrodite, that she will rest hidden in peace until he orders otherwise?"

"I know that too," Alison answered certainly, tremendously aware of all the great forces that lay just beyond the reach of mankind.

"Then I'm content, Alissa," said Julian drawing her into the protection of his arms.

"And so am I," she answered. "So am I – forever."

The Staircase

This evening there seemed a great many people on the staircase, all mingling together, silently rubbing shoulders as they climbed. On the marble steps long skirts swished against high-heeled buckled shoes, while ornamental swords, their handles encrusted with rainbow gems, dipped and rose as their owners made their steady way upwards.

It was dusk, for the magnificent marble pillars and balustrades of the staircase were suffused with the colour of doves, a soft lavender grey that beautified all those strange and silent people in the midst of whom walked Helena, only too miserably aware that she was in her night-clothes, while all the rest were garbed gaudily as a field of butterflies.

As always the mystery of the staircase struck her afresh. For there were those Helena could see going up — or was it down? — and yet never passed. And these people — the ones she could watch but not touch — were different. Faded jeans were plentiful, as if they were a uniform, while shorts and T-shirts abounded. Cameras swung from necks, though none so fine as those carried by a party of Japanese, all dressed formally, grimly enjoying themselves. It was as though two entirely different worlds, people from two disparate times, had come together on the staircase yet could never meet.

The throng with whom Helena reluctantly mingled suddenly began to climb faster, as if they had received a silent signal, and she was forced along with them. And it was then that a girl with the other crowd on the staircase, a tarty-looking girl thrust into skin-tight leggings and stilt-like stilettos, looked across at Helena, shrieked piercingly, then reached out and grabbed her boyfriend's arm.

"Oh, my Gawd, Darryl, I've seen the ghost!" she bellowed as the Japanese turned as one to gaze unsmilingly in Helena's direction.

She stared back, amazed, thinking that her thin nightdress was the culprit, that the girl had mistaken her lacy attire for ghostly veils, but before either woman could look at one another again their varying crowds had swept them apart. Now, for the first time, Helena felt a sensation of fear as she was thrust upwards on a human surge of people, none of whom ever looked at her, yet from whom she could not escape.

"Oh dear," she called hopelessly, "please stop. I must go home."

The throng sped on, hurrying up the broad spiralling curve and drawing level with a stone-flagged landing. Summoning a burst of speed that only a frightened person could achieve, Helena somehow elbowed her way through her companions and managed to get a step ahead, to see that a man stood waiting for her, holding out his hand.

"Quick, little one," he called, "I have come to help you."

She smiled, her heart gaining momentum at the sight of him, as it had done ever since she had been a child. "I'm here at last," she called. Their fingers locked together and then Helena fell, down and down into the drenching darkness, as slowly he vanished from her sight...

Right by her ear the radio alarm burst into life and a disc jockey with a mid-Atlantic accent brightly informed the world that the weather was unsettled and showers could be expected later. With a feeling of desolation, Helena stretched out her hand and switched the radio off, seeing from its illuminated digital face that it was six am, that she had set it too early and was not due to get up for another hour.

So it had happened again! The dream which had recurred ever since childhood had once more returned to haunt her. The staircase with its extraordinary visitors, its shrieking showy girl, its glorious butterflies of another age, had come back, and with it her rescuer, the man who always stood at the top waiting for her. The man whose hair clustered in blue-black curls about his head and whose vivid green eyes had a rim of jade around the iris.

In the silence of her bedroom Helena smiled, partly at her foolish self. Here was she, Miss Helena Holley, aged twenty-six, single by choice, admiring the looks of a dream man, a vision, a creature without substance. And yet he excited her, that dark-haired creature who waited for her at the second landing, his hand extended, his brilliant eyes alight.

Despite the early hour Helena got out of bed and made her way to the kitchen, putting on the kettle and radio simultaneously. Music blared forth reminding her that she was very much in the present and that dream men really had no place in the go-getting world in which she lived. With a sigh she firmly switched off and, enjoying the sudden quiet, sat at the table sipping coffee and thinking about her life.

She supposed that she was what would be described as a small-

town girl, having been born in Stow Wells in Gloucestershire and, other than a year at secretarial school in London — something her father had insisted upon as part of her education — never having left it.

"Being a character's daughter," said Helena to herself, smiling a little wryly, "is not always easy."

She simply couldn't imagine life without her father, just as Stow Wells could not imagine the town without John Holley. Almost from the moment he had been born, fifth son of an impoverished parson with rather more children than he could count, John, with a combination of dazzling charm and ruthless determination, had bent the world to his will.

A place in the local grammar school had led to university and also to meeting the right people.

"And that was where Hal came in," muttered Helena, making her way to the bathroom and stepping under a warm shower.

The richest family in Stow Wells had been the Tymons, the local solicitors, who had made a rule of marrying their sons and daughters well, on occasion even into the aristocracy. At school, Richard Tymon had become a great friend of John Holley, and poor though the parson's son had been, the friendship had continued throughout university and beyond. It had been Richard who had secretly lent his friend the money to buy out an ailing estate agent in the town, and it had been with this first break that John's gifts of charm and drive had finally come to fruition. The business had prospered as never before, John had repaid the money within a year, and within two had bought out his only competitor. Within five he had acquired a chain of estate agencies and was advertising in *Country Life*. The firm of Holley's had arrived.

In a way, Helena would have liked to escape it all, leave the close-knit community and the intimate circle of friends and strike out on her own. But there had been no chance of that. The days of equal opportunity had arrived by then and John, not in the least disappointed that fate had given him only one child and a girl at that, had changed the name of the company to Holley and Daughter. She was trapped, caught, enmeshed. A career as an estate agent had already been chosen for her.

And that, thought Helena reflectively as she dressed, *would not have been so bad. If it had just finished there.*

John Holley, by now a man with prospects, had married a distant cousin of the Tymons; while Richard, in his turn, had married the Honourable Rosalind Owen, daughter of a minor peer. Within a year of the birth of Rosalind's son Harold, known as Hal, Helena had come into the world.

And the marriage was planned at once, she thought. *Hal and Helena. Even the names went well!*

As children they had been inseparable and Helena, an only child, had lived for the company of Hal and his three younger sisters. They had played together, plunged into group scrapes and generally stood up for each other when the adults were cross. But then had come the teens and with them Helena's horrified realisation that what she had considered to be her father's teasing was semi-serious.

"When you marry Hal..." he would say — and then laugh.

"John," Sheila Holley had remonstrated, "Helena will marry whom she likes, when she likes."

"Yes, yes," he would answer, smiling knowingly, "so long as it is Hal."

Nothing could have been guaranteed to put me off more, thought Helena now, biting into toast, *and I'm sure Mummy must have told him so.*

From the age of fifteen onwards she had refused to have anything more to do with Richard Tymon's son, and the remarks about Hal had grown less frequent and finally died out altogether. Whether her mother had intervened or not, Helena was never sure, but something had certainly brought the message home to John. In the end it had been she, after a year away in London, who had first asked after her old childhood friend, and seen her father's face light up.

Meeting Hal again had been strange. In the year in which she had not seen him, though Helena had changed little, merely developing a veneer of sophistication, he had grown out of all recognition. Tall, large and handsome, with thick hair the colour of whisky and very pleasant eyes, grey as a moody sky, or so Helena had thought at the time.

Whether or not he had been programmed by *his* father was impossible to tell — but the result was the same. The twenty-one-year-old Hal, articled clerk in his father's firm and the most eligible bachelor in town, had fallen madly in love with Helena and had never from that day to the present deflected in his wish to marry her.

Six years, thought Helena, making up her eyes with pinks and mauves. *Six whole years. I would have got bored with me ages ago.*

The expression on the face looking back at her from the mirror was just a little smug. In her heart, if she dug deep enough and admitted it, Helena was flattered. It amused her to keep Hal on a string, very occasionally allowing him to stay the night in the flat she had bought to prove her independence to the world. Despite the fact she would one day have to make up her mind about him, one way or the other, an on/off love affair suited Helena Holley very well at this particular stage of her life.

The journey to the estate agency that was in her sole charge was rather too long to walk so Helena took the car, easily finding a space in the car park.

The office when she entered it was dark, unnervingly quiet, and at once the dream came back; the suffocating silence of the staircase, the phantom walkers who strode so relentlessly upward, the tourists who gazed and gazed.

"Tourists!" said Helena aloud, sitting at her desk. "Of course!"

Why had she never thought of it before? What else could those people have been? The camera-loaded Japanese, the shorts and T-shirt brigade. Sightseers swarmed the great staircase along with that multitude of resplendent beings from another age.

Helena found herself shaking at the strangeness of the discovery and it was an effort to go to the lights and switch them on, then make herself another coffee in the little kitchen behind the office. She sat down at her desk again, thinking of the dream and consciously trying to remember the first time she had experienced it.

Had it been the night of her aunt's wedding when she had been a bridesmaid or had it been when she had stayed up late for the first time on Boxing Night? Helena frowned. It had definitely been the wedding because she could remember — distinctly now that she concentrated — dreaming that she wore her bridesmaid's dress as she climbed that vast marble spiral for the very first time. The man at the top had grinned when he had seen it, his brilliant eyes twinkling and his whole face creasing into a spectacular smile.

"Ma petite belle," he had said.

Helena shook her head in bewilderment. She had almost forgotten that occasionally he spoke French on those strange nocturnal visits she made to him. How many times had it been, she wondered. How many times had she seen the staircase in all? Slowly she began to count on her fingers.

There had been that first occasion and then another the following Christmas. Helena remembered now that though there had been snow when she had gone to sleep, the staircase had been bathed in brilliant sunshine. Yet last night it had been dusky, full of shadows. So the time of day could change in the dream.

"How odd," she said aloud.

Sitting like this in the early morning office, with no burbling staff and persistant telephone calls, Helena found herself remembering more vividly than she ever had before the very substance and texture of the dreams. She could almost recollect the feel of the man's hand as his fingers gripped hers, the warmth and strength of him and the faint musky perfume he wore.

Helena smiled. "If only he were real," she said to the desk diary that lay open before her. "I wouldn't have a moment's hesitation. Poor old Hal."

She sighed gustily and, as if she had conjured him up, the telephone rang and Hal's voice spoke.

"Hello, darling, I saw the lights go on and thought you must be there already."

Thinking that having his office building almost opposite hers was a mixed blessing, Helena answered sharply, "You're in early."

"I had some paperwork to catch up with," Hal replied calmly, quite used to her little barbs. "I thought I'd make a start before the phones begin to ring."

"Me too."

"Well, as we're being so enthusiastic about work. I think we owe it to ourselves to have a pleasant lunch, don't you?"

"When did you have in mind?" asked Helena guardedly.

"Today, of course. Are you free?"

She hesitated. "Well..."

"Oh please," said Hal. "There's something I want to ask you."

Helena's heart sank. There had been no proposal of marriage since last Christmas and she supposed that he was working his way up to the next one.

As though he had read her mind, Hal went on, "It's nothing serious. Just a nice surprise."

Relenting, Helena said, "All right then. What time and where?"

"The wine bar at twelve-thirty. I've booked a table."

"Sure of me, eh?" Helena laughed and rang off.

The Purple Grapes, as their meeting place was called, was already filling up when Helena walked through the door. Country town equivalents of yuppies made a lot of noise saying nothing while, somewhat out of place in the midst of them, looking splendidly leonine in a biscuit coloured suit, was Hal.

"You look nice," said Helena, hurrying over and planting a peck on his cheek.

"So do you," he replied, and smiled in such a way that she wished she really could fall in love with him.

She busied herself with choosing her lunch.

"Not a bad selection," murmured Hal, almost to himself. "But then of course one can never beat French cooking."

Helena looked up, and said in surprise, "We're in a wine bar in Stow Wells, Hal. We're hardly likely to be offered haute cuisine."

"*I'm* offering it," he said, still in an undertone.

"What are you on about?" asked Helena, putting the menu down and staring at him.

Hal did likewise. "I'm on about you coming to Paris with me for a few days. It's my birthday soon – though I suppose you've forgotten – and I thought it would be nice to go away and celebrate."

"I haven't forgotten actually. I've been saving for weeks."

She had always been able to do that, make Hal smile when he was getting serious. But now, though his grin flashed at her, he persisted, saying "Helena, don't wriggle. I know very well you've never been to Paris and that you're longing to. Remember what you said to me once? You felt like a social failure because you had never walked up the Champs Elysées."

"I was joking."

"Well the joke is over. I want to take you."

Helena sat looking at Hal thinking that in many ways she was a fool not to marry him. After all he was good looking, getting more so with maturity, and his one concern in life seemed to be to please her.

Impetuously she said, "Hal, I know that I've been a bitch to you sometimes but it was just reaction to family pressure. I'm sorry."

He laid his hand over hers. "I understand. Anyone would think arranged marriages were still in fashion going by our fathers."

Helena withdrew her hand and laughed lightly. "Perhaps it would be a good thing if they were. It might stop people making mistakes." Seeing the expression on his face, she went on, "I don't really mean that."

Hal smiled wryly. "Sometimes I think you don't know what you mean at all."

"Meaning?" asked Helena, and they both giggled wildly.

The lunch was a success and it was in lighthearted mood that they left the wine bar and Hal walked back with Helena to her office.

"It's been lovely," she said, kissing him on the cheek.

"France would be lovelier," Hal answered, then took both her hands in his. "Listen, Helena, I want you to come with me to Paris for a reason you don't know yet."

"What?"

"I've been offered a job with a firm of American lawyers in Washington. It would only be for about two years but nonetheless it would be the end of us. If there is an us, that is. And that's what I want to find out."

"Oh, Hal, be plain. Are you asking me to go with you to America?"

"No," he answered fiercely, "no, I'm not. I'm asking you to come to France as the final attempt to make our relationship work. If you decide you don't want to marry me after the delights of Paris then I'm leaving your life for ever. But if you do, then we can stay here, go to the States, do whatever you like." He caught her close. "Helena, I love you so much that you must give me this last chance. I swear that if it doesn't work I won't bother you again."

He was embarrassingly earnest and Helena looked away. "I don't know what to say."

"Then I'll say it for you. We'll go to France for five days and celebrate my birthday. When we come back I will give you twenty-four hours to make up your mind and that is all. Then it's marriage or goodbye. After all," he added wearily, "you've been messing me around for twenty-five years. A few days isn't much more to ask."

"No it isn't," she said impulsively, "of course I'll come. I've been unsure too long. It is high time I had an ultimatum."

"Well," said Hal, kissing her swiftly, "you've finally got one."

*

The staircase was packed, hot, stifling, and tonight the silent walkers, pressed so closely together, had a sinister air about them as they ascended the marble sweep. From the moment Helena set foot on the bottom step she felt a thrill of fearful excitement, terrified at being amongst them, yet longing to reach the top and see the man standing there, waiting for her.

Yet on this occasion she was to be disappointed for as Helena mounted to the second landing she realised that the face she expected to see, the handsome face surmounted by that blue-black nimbus of curls, had been replaced by another.

A woman stood there — a woman with dark, secretive features and brown eyes that, as she turned to look at

Helena, seemed to glow black. Behind her hovered a man, a tall cloaked figure, and as Helena approached they whispered together. She strained to hear their conversation and as the press of people took her nearer, she managed to pick out the words.

"You've summoned her?" said the woman.

"There's the proof, Madam," replied the man, pointing at Helena.

"And will she do my bidding?"

"That remains to be seen."

The woman smiled at Helena, said, "Come, little one," and put out her hand, just as if she were the man whose place she had usurped.

"No," shrieked Helena, "I don't want you," and then she fell again, down and down into a sweating wakefulness, gasping and panting herself conscious.

It was daybreak and the radio alarm showed ten minutes past five. For a moment Helena lay quite still, her night terror still with her, and then she gradually returned to reality.

It was Thursday, the day that she and Hal were leaving for France and rather than having woken too early she was late. They were to be gone by six if they were to catch the midday hovercraft from Dover to Boulogne.

An enormous and inexplicable excitement swept over Helena. "In September when the grapes are purple, Margarita drinking wine with me," she sang as she jumped out of bed and headed for the shower.

And she was still humming when at six o'clock sharp Hal pressed the door bell and they bundled into the car, heading for Dover before the traffic built up.

"Hey, this is going to be good," she said as they clicked into their seatbelts. "I'll buy you a bottle of champagne."

Hal winked. "I love being indulged. Get me a crate."

And with that he turned the ignition and they were off, singing as the sun came up, and chattering all the way to France.

Helena thought, as they drove off at Boulogne and followed the signs to Paris, that she had not felt so at ease with him since they were children and then, for no reason at all, she remembered the dream and sighed.

"What is it?" asked Hal, finely attuned to her swings of mood.

Helena hesitated. "Nothing really. I had rather a bad night."

"Me too. I was terrified I would miss the alarm!"

Helena nodded sympathetically but said nothing and Hal looked at her sharply. "What happened? Did you have a nightmare?"

"Not really. More a recurring dream."

"Oh? You've never mentioned it before."

"Concentrate on the road," said Helena as they swerved. "Remember we're on the wrong side."

Hal grinned. "Your job is to map read, remember? What do you dream?"

"About a staircase."

"A what?" Hal asked, amazed.

"I know that it sounds ridiculous, but it's always the same. I dream that I'm climbing a great marble staircase with two different lots of people. One group wear old-fashioned clothes and the others seem to be sightseers." Her voice trailed away. "Pathetic, isn't it?"

"Not at all," said Hal. "I think it sounds fascinating. Is it a staircase you know?"

"No, it's nowhere I've ever been. The weird thing is that I dream about it in differing conditions. Sometimes it's sunny, sometimes cold. It's never the same twice."

"It's probably something you've seen as a child and forgotten about. At a conscious level I mean."

Helena shook her head. "I don't think so somehow." She realised then that she had omitted to tell Hal of the man who waited for her at the second landing and at the same moment decided that she would rather not.

"But why?" she murmured to herself — and could come up with no logical explanation.

Helena was not disappointed by her first sight of Paris. The great city rose like a pearl in the early evening sunshine, the mighty Seine alive with light and sparkle, the *bateaux-mouches* chugging up and down its surface full of tourists, the gothic outline of Notre-Dame looming majestically in the distance, the Eiffel Tower huge yet somehow not quite believable.

"Oh, how marvellous!" breathed Helena, and Hal smiled.

He had booked them into a small hotel near the Place de la Republique, a family run establishment with no lift, which left them breathless as they panted up to a room at the top of the building. From the window Helena could see a view of eaves and roofs, washing and crooked chimneys.

"It's like a theatre set," she said, turning to Hal and laughing.

"I could have taken you somewhere better," he answered, "but I wanted you to see the *real* Paris on your first visit. So hurry up and get ready, I formally invite you out to dinner."

In the bathroom mirror a puzzled face looked back at Helena.

"Why this sense of elation?" it seemed to ask. "What are you so cheerful about when Hal has given you an ultimatum?"

A curious sensation gripped her: a sensation that whatever she did, whatever she said, a destiny lay in wait that she could not escape.

"What's going to happen?" she wondered. Then knew she must have spoken aloud as Hal called, "What?" from the bedroom.

With a last look in the mirror, Helena crossed to where he sat in front of the old-fashioned dressing table, rather uselessly running a comb through the lion's mane hair. Standing behind him she put her hands on his shoulders.

"I said I wonder what is going to happen."

He turned round to look at her and asked "You mean about us?"

"Partly. But there's something else."

"What?"

"I don't know. I can't really explain. I just have a momentous feeling. Here somewhere." She pointed vaguely in the direction of her stomach.

"It's hunger," answered Hal firmly. "Come on, I've starved you long enough." And so saying he resolutely took her by the hand and led her out to explore.

They dined in a small intimate restaurant where the Muscadet was chilled to perfection and nobody else spoke English. They ate *fruits de mere* followed by dream-like soufflé, and afterwards wandered in the darkness down an exciting avenue where all the shops were open and people swarmed and chattered as they would have done at midday in England. Helena bought exotic earrings that hung to her shoulders and Hal insisted on giving her a pair shaped like glittering fish. Then, both exhausted, they returned through quiet streets to their hotel room where Helena threw back the shutters to look at the roofs of Paris lit by stars.

"Hal," she said into the dusk.

"Yes?"

"I will make up my mind more easily about the future if we don't force things this weekend."

"I suppose that's your way of saying that you want me to sleep in the chair."

Helena turned to him, large-eyed with seriousness. "Of course it isn't. It's just that I don't want you to take me for granted."

Hal held her at arm's length. "I don't, my darling. Nobody could do so less. In fact sometimes I think I'm *too* patient. So be assured, I won't force myself upon you."

Whenever he spoke like that Helena felt guilty and now she hid her face from him, snuggling against his chest.

"I *do* love you, Hal," she muttered, "but for some reason I can't sort myself out."

"You've got till the end of next week," he answered firmly and put her away from him.

Although it was September, Paris nights were warm and at first Helena found it difficult to sleep, though Hal breathed steadily beside her. Then the walls of the room slowly began to recede further and further away. There was a buzzing sound which grew intolerably loud and as Helena clapped her hands over her ears to protect them, she felt other fingers close over her own.

"I'm waiting, little one," said a familiar voice. "You must come to me soon."

With a scream Helena woke up, sitting bolt upright in the darkness and immediately Hal woke too, his arms going round her protectively. "Was it the dream again?"

"Yes. Oh, Hal…"

It was easy, then, to let him love her as he wanted, gently at first and then with restraint forgotten, and afterwards, when he slept again, Helena stared at the sloping ceiling and wondered whether it was solely family pressure that had driven her away from him or whether the feeling she had of a destiny unfulfilled also played its part.

They both woke early the next morning to see a Paris bathed in sunshine, the streets still wet from the cleansing carts, the waiters sweeping the pavements outside the cafes and setting out the chairs.

Open mouthed at the sheer excitement and beauty of the city, Helena walked like one entranced up the Champs Elysées, past the elegant shops and cafés, outside which Parisians sat reading their papers and sipping coffee in the morning sunlight, to where the Arc de Triomphe reared into the sky.

"I wish we'd come for a month," she exclaimed without thinking. And when Hal answered, "So do I," his meaning obvious, realised that she would have to watch what she said if she were to be fair to him.

They lunched outside a smart restaurant overlooking the Paris Opéra and then, at Helena's insistence, walked across the Pont d'Abcole to the Ile de la Cité, the island in the Seine which had been the ancient birthplace of modern Pars. But it was not just for its early connections that Helena had wanted to go there; the island housed the

Conciergerie, the prison to which Marie Antoinette had been brought seven months after her royal husband had gone bravely to meet his death, and from which she herself had left for the guillotine.

Joining the tour and smiling very slightly at an earnest English woman and her companion, obviously ardent supporters of the ill-fated French Queen, Hal and Helena bought their tickets and entered the prison.

In a strange manner none of the Revolution seemed quite real to Helena, not even the original guillotine blade in the prison chapel. In fact nothing registered until they left the Conciergerie and began to walk, following the route of the condemned from the prison to oblivion. Crossing the bridge again they made their way down the rue St Honoré, past the Palais Royal towards the Place de la Concorde, where once had stood the dreadful guillotine.

They turned sharp left into Concorde and Helena drew breath at what she saw. She had always imagined that the square in which Louis XVI and his glamorous wife and so many others had met their ends, would be small. But now Helena gazed on a vast traffic-filled concourse as large if not even larger than Trafalgar Square.

"How terrible!" she exclaimed.

"What?" said Hal.

"That the place is so huge. As they turned the corner and saw all those thousands of people staring at them, the condemned must have been terrified."

"Even worse," answered Hal thoughtfully, "for those coming in alone, like the King and Queen."

"Oh don't." Helena shivered.

"French history wasn't always so grim," he said, changing the mood. "They must have had a wonderful time earlier, when Diane de Poitiers was mistress to both the King and Dauphin, and Francois I said that a court without women was like a spring without roses."

"But roses don't bloom in the spring," objected Helena.

"Perhaps that's what the old fox meant!" answered Hal, and once again they were laughing.

They were sipping lemon tea in a pavement cafe, when it suddenly started to rain and everyone hastily moved inside.

"Well," said Hal, "there's only one thing for it. The Louvre."

"Indeed."

Hal and Helena rushed through the Tuileries Gardens in the showers, then the Carousel Gardens to where the museum, once a palace of the French Kings, rose enormously before them.

"It's literally miles long," said Hal as they bought their tickets. "It's best to concentrate on one thing and then come back another day. So what shall it be?"

"The Mona Lisa," answered Helena without hesitation. "Let's look at that famous smile."

But Leonardo da Vinci's masterpiece was difficult to see, smaller than she had thought and surrounded by tourists. When they did get close enough, though, the enigma of the Florentine woman's expression struck her afresh.

"Have you ever heard the theory," Helena asked, "that that is actually a self-portrait? That Leonardo painted himself in drag?"

"No," answered Hal, "I haven't. And I don't believe it."

But he was chuckling as he turned away to look at da Vinci's sketches for aeroplanes, parachutes, tanks; over forty machines of the future visualised by a fifteenth century artist.

"Do you think he was a time lord?" said Helena coming to stand by Hal and gazing in wonderment.

"They don't exist outside fiction," he answered slowly. "But none the less it does make you think."

He left Helena gazing and wandered off on his own and she had almost forgotten his presence, so that it was a shock when she suddenly heard him exclaim, "Good God!"

Looking over her shoulder, Helena saw that Hal had stopped before one of the sketches and was staring at it in awed astonishment.

"What is it?" she said, and crossed over to him.

It was herself, of course, Helena could see that at a glance, wearing what appeared to be one of her more flimsy nightdresses. The room span as the full impact of what she was looking at came to her and Helena put her hand to her forehead, though Hal didn't even look up, so absorbed in the drawing that, for once, he had not noticed her.

"I don't believe it," she whispered.

He stared at her, his eyes bright with consternation. "It's just like you. I would swear it *is* you."

"Of course it can't be," she said, her voice unnaturally light. "Look in the catalogue and see who it really is."

Hal thumbed through and Helena could not help but notice that his hands were shaking. "Number three hundred and forty," he repeated several times, then gave a sigh of relief as he found the reference.

"What does it say," she asked.

"Mystery," he read aloud. "This drawing by Leonardo, known as Mystery, is supposedly a sketch for a portrait that he never executed. It is from the late period and can be dated circa 1518, the time when the artist was living in France under the protection of the French King, Francois I."

"Does it give the model's name?"

"No, that's all it says."

Helena drew nearer and stared closely at the sketch. It was the most extraordinary coincidence she had ever seen, for a pattern of rosebuds round the neck, sleeves and hem of the garment worn by Leonardo's sitter were identical to those on a nightdress of Helena's.

Over her shoulder, Hal said, "They say that everyone has a double and this woman certainly was yours."

Helena turned to him, a strange expression on her face. "Hal, I know it's foolish but I've simply got to find out who she was."

His eyes lit up. "That's fine by me. I'll help you in any way I can." His voice changed. "Helena, you're not being silly, are you?"

"What do you mean?"

"You're not going to let this upset you. I mean, it's just a strange co-incidence."

"It doesn't upset me," Helena answered slowly, "that isn't the right word."

"Then what is?"

"Intrigue. That woman from the past intrigues me. I won't rest until I've found out all about her." Helena turned back to the picture.

"Watch out, little one, I'm coming to get you", she said, then froze in horror at the words that had just come from her lips.

The two women working in the tourist office were a contrast in types: one pure Parisienne, dark haired, brown eyed, very chic; the other a sultry international blonde, pretty and pouting. Both wore smart uniforms reminiscent of air hostesses and one was as helpful as the other was offhand.

"You want to trace the origin of one of da Vinci's sketches?" said the blonde in perfect English, every syllable affirming that she considered Hal's request quite the most idiotic thing it had ever been her misfortune to hear.

"Yes," he said, his neck colouring very slightly. "It really caught our attention and we wondered if there was any way of finding out who the model was."

The blonde looked down her nose. "You have consulted the Louvre, I suppose."

Hal looked uncomfortable. "Yes, they were very helpful. They spent several hours looking things up, but could throw no light on the matter, I'm afraid."

"Then how can we?" said the blonde, and spread her hands.

The Parisienne came over to where Hal and Helena stood by the counter. "Leonardo's home at Clos-Luce is my speciality," she said. "What exactly is it you want?"

Helena spoke for the first time, saying, "I know it sounds silly, but I have become really fascinated by one of his sketches because the girl in it looks very like me. We thought we would extend our holiday in France for a few days and track down the name of the original sitter."

The girl smiled. "If the Louvre were unable to help, then I really would recommend that you go to Clos-Luce. It was where Leonardo spent the last four years of his life. He died there, you know."

Hal brightened up. "Where is it exactly?"

"In the Loire Valley, near Amboise. He lived there under the protection of King François. The house has an exhibition of models based on da Vinci's sketches. He invented the aeroplane, the helicopter..."

Her voice went on, but Helena was no longer listening; instead, she was looking at the poster on the wall of the tourist office to which the girl had pointed. It showed a small Renaissance manor house with the words Clos-Luce beneath, but it was to the photograph next to it that Helena's eyes were drawn, almost against her will.

In the foreground of the picture she saw a grassy drive, flanked on either side by tree-filled banks; in the distance a chateau, its roof like a dream from the Arabian Nights, full of towers, cupolas and minarets. Standing there in the tourist office in Paris, on an ordinary business-like day, Helena found herself suddenly drenched in a cold sweat.

A memory had come, a memory half grasped at, a memory that brought a suffocating sense of fear in its wake. When had she stood on that very spot, looking to where the chateau, partially hidden by trees, gleamed so white? When had she run lightly down the drive, through the arched entrance, across the courtyard and into the chateau itself? When had she passed, silent and unseen, through the palace's open doors and into the building's very heart, to see, winding and omnipresent, the staircase?

"Oh God," said Helena aloud, as the world spun about her.

"Are you all right, madame?"

The Parisienne was suddenly at her side, bringing a chair for Helena to sit on and producing a glass of water almost simultaneously. Hal's outline blurred and then became clear again.

"Helena, darling! What's the matter?" he asked.

"Nothing, I'm all right. Did I faint?"

"Not quite. I caught you on the way down," he answered tenderly.

"Oh, how awful. I am so sorry."

Her gaze took in the French girl who said, "It is no problem, madame. It is the travelling. It is more tiring than one imagines."

Helena smiled. "You've been very kind. Thank you."

The girl, whose lapel badge identified her as Marie-Laure Rolin, became business-like. "So, may I help you with road maps? You *are* travelling by car, are you not?"

"I don't know," said Hal uncertainly, "perhaps we ought not..."

Helena stole a lightning look sideways, seeing what she had failed to notice at first. The chateau which so fascinated yet terrified her had a name beneath.

"The Chateau de Chambord," she read aloud, "royal residence of the Loire Valley." Helena stood up. "Hal, I really do want to go. I can't wait to see the Loire and all its marvellous chateaux. Please don't let a moment's faintness spoil everything."

"Are you sure you're up to it?

"Positive," she answered as Marie-Laure smiled, and the blonde, after a cool appraising stare, muttered, "These English," under her breath, before turning all her charm onto a middle-aged but wealthy-looking American.

*

Leaving Paris, Hal took one of France's beautiful D roads which ambled along through pleasant villages, at one of which Hal and Helena stopped for lunch. It was only then, sitting beneath a striped awning in a narrow but picturesque one-way street, that Hal said, "Was it really tiredness that made you faint?"

"What do you mean?" asked Helena innocently.

"Because, my darling, you were staring so fixedly at that poster of the chateau I wondered if it had anything to do with it."

"How could it?" Helena eyed Hal narrowly, surprised at his unexpected perception.

"That I don't know."

She hesitated, on the brink of confession, and then drew back. How could she share with Hal the details of that claustrophobic dream? She had already told him more than she meant to, but not for anything would she discuss the feel of the man's hand on hers, the touch of those long cool fingers before she fell away from him.

"You're mistaken," said Helena firmly, hoping he believed her. "I just happened to be looking at it, that's all." She deliberately turned the conversation away. "Do you think we will find anywhere to stay in Amboise? And what on earth shall we tell the parents?"

"That we're getting on better than we hoped. That will shut them up." Hal looked just a little wistful. "You haven't forgotten my birthday, have you?"

Helena leaned forward, wondering at herself for wanting to kiss him so much. "Of course not. It's on Sunday, and I'm taking you out to dinner."

"Don't forget," said Hal, and gave her such a smile that she felt quite stricken.

They reached Amboise just as the light began to fade, having followed the course of the river Loire west of the town of la Chapelle, past Blois and on to Amboise, once seeing a sign post marked Chambord, at which Helena had craned her neck.

"Want to stop?" Hal had asked but she had refused.

"I'd rather see what Clos-Lucé has to tell us first."

"But you do want to visit Chambord while we're here?" asked Hal, his face expressionless.

"Oh yes," answered Helena, trying hard to sound casual.

Both of them had seemed to find conversation difficult from then on and it had not been until they had found a delightful hotel outside the town, once the home of an Amboise banking family, that they had settled again to chatting easily.

Sitting together on the terrace, a sea of geraniums, all spilling out of earthenware pots, they comfortably watched the sun go down, and everything suddenly seemed to be more than right between them.

"I love you, Helena," said Hal, staring steadily into the middle distance not glancing in her direction.

"I know," she answered quietly.

"And you?"

"Still that wretched hang up about marriage. Hal, I've got the oddest feeling that this visit will decide everything, one way or another."

He frowned. "But that's why you came, remember? To make your mind up."

"It's not a question of that," Helena answered slowly. "I somehow think that all the answers will come, here in France."

Hal looked at her quizzically. "You've lost me."

"I believe we will get more than we bargained for."

"It's because of that picture, isn't it?" Hal drained his gin and tonic and called to the young girl at the bar who brought him another.

"I don't know."

"How is it possible," Hal went on, almost as if she hadn't spoken, "that a woman was alive four centuries ago who looked exactly like you?"

"Perhaps she wasn't," Helena answered thoughtfully. "Perhaps she was just a figment of Leonardo's imagination."

"Somehow I don't think so. He mostly worked from life, with the exception of his inventions."

"Then I don't suppose we'll ever know."

"Helena," said Hal grimly, "don't bluff. I know that look. You won't rest until you've combed the poor man's life right through. You'll find the name of his model if it is the last thing you do."

She shivered. "I hope it isn't."

Suddenly solemn, Hal answered, "So do I."

Next morning they went to Clos-Luce early, seeing it before the house became too crowded. The rooms, lovingly adorned with furniture contemporary with Leonardo, were full of atmosphere, while the collection of models, made from the great man's sketches, was astounding. Helena found herself looking at a tank, a swinging bridge, a parachute, even an aeroplane and automobile. It was almost unbelievable and in a way unnerving, too much to take in at once. But there was nothing that gave any clues as to the origins of the sketch, *Mystery*. Yet, after reading her guide book, Helena realised with a slight sense of shock that there was a connection between Leonardo da Vinci and the Chateau of Chambord.

"The great painter spent the last four years of his life in the service of King François," it said. "Some say that it was on da Vinci's designs that the Chateau of Chambord was based. For it was in 1517 that Leonardo signed a project for a huge castle at Romorantin, proving that he was already at work as an architect. However he did not live to see his grand design come to fruition, dying as he did in 1519 in the arms of the King himself."

"So," she said to Hal, as they walked through the Renaissance rose garden, "we are no further forward."

"Perhaps we will be after you have seen that chateau that so attracts you."

"But Leonardo could never have gone there."

"It seems to me that he could visualise something without actually seeing it. Look at that exhibition. It was mind blowing. I'm almost beginning to believe he *could* time travel."

"Perhaps he did and saw me," said Helena, and was surprised when Hal didn't laugh.

By mutual agreement they went on to Chambord early that afternoon, the car turning into the vast walled forest land through a pair of magnificent gates, beneath the full glare of the sun at its highest point.

Hal looked at her out of the corner of his eye and Helena was only too pitifully aware that she had started to shake, that for some perverse reason she could not control her body, was having to fight to keep still.

She drew breath in wonderment as into view came a huge dome adorned at the top by a stone crown, the fleur-de-lys carved triumphantly above. Then she glimpsed towers and roofs and skylights, and the most glorious selection of decorative chimney stacks she had ever seen. The top storey of the chateau was so fantastic as to be almost a city in its own right, each blue-slated dome an imaginary dwelling place.

"Pure fantasia," said Hal, shaking his head.

Helena nodded automatically, then felt utterly bereft as the car went round a bend and the chateau was lost to view.

Why am I feeling so odd? she thought wretchedly, *what is it that both draws and repels me?*

And then realisation came as they rounded another bend and Chambord was once more in their sight. It was so familiar to her that if she had not known for sure that this was the very first time she had set eyes on it, Helena would have sworn she had visited the chateau before. The memory half recalled in the tourist office had become a reality. She would have staked her life on the fact that the staircase lay within the chateau.

"You're very quiet," said Hal, so suddenly that Helena jumped. "Is there something wrong?"

"What could there be?" she answered defensively.

Hal skimmed into the car park and pulled up rather fast. "Listen," he said, "you seem to forget that I've known you since you were born. You can't deceive me, Helena. This place scares you, doesn't it? Now why?"

Helena lowered her eyes, feeling near to tears. "I've never been here, but it's part of my recurring dream," she said eventually.

Hal sat back in his seat. "You realise that there's probably a perfectly logical explanation. Everything that one ever sees or hears, ever, is registered somewhere in the subconscious. You probably saw a book about Chambord when you were a child, maybe even before you could read. Then you stored it away and began to dream about it."

Helena nodded doubtfully and Hal went on, "I presume that this is the dream about the staircase?"

"Yes."

"Well then, it's probably here. Shall we go in?"

She had never known a feeling like it; half of her wanting to run into Chambord and absorb it, to become part of its very fabric; the other half cringing with fear and foreboding.

"Darling," said Hal gently, "it's no good sitting there shaking. You must slay your dragon, whatever it is. Remember that I'm right here beside you."

They got out of the car and walked through the car park, packed with coaches and other vehicles despite the fact that it was late in the season. Tourists were everywhere, thronging the tree-lined street where every shop sold postcards and souvenirs of the chateau. With every step Helena and Hal took the amazing place grew nearer and more huge: comparable in both size and grandeur with a palace.

They were approaching the building from the side and could see from this angle that the chateau was built in a square courtyard, protected by a single storey wall culminating at both ends in two round pill boxes, like towers with their tops sliced off. Helena felt at once that they shouldn't have been there, that the chateau had at one time been fully moated. But the only evidence of this was some neat canals going two-thirds of the way round, looking dull and turgid in the brilliant afternoon light.

The path which she and Hal now took, along with a throng of others, turned left and Helena found herself approaching a door in the outer wall which gave admittance to the chateau. Despite the blazing sun she shivered, wishing she could walk away.

To the right of the entrance was a huge vaulted room, now given over entirely to the selling of tickets and souvenirs. Hal bore down on a series of tape recorded tour guides. The one he hired had two ear pieces coming from a central player and having made sure that Helena could hear from hers, he led her out into the glaring brilliance of the courtyard. Before her the chateau reared like a place of legend, full of soaring arches and windows.

"All right?" said Hal as they crossed the square.

"Fine," answered Helena, and desperately wished it were true.

The tape player which had been running silently now burst into sudden life.

"Welcome to the Chateau of Chambord," it said. "You will see two doors ahead of you. Enter through either and then look around you at the breathtaking spectacle. Stare and wonder at the hunting lodge of the hunter King, François I."

Hal laughed out loud. "Some hunting lodge!"

And as if it had heard him, the voice of the commentator chuckled. "Yes, that is how François liked to describe it. But as you will see for yourselves Chambord is no lodge but an enormous palace with 440 rooms, 14 great staircases and 70 secondary staircases and a chimney for every day of the year. 365 in all!"

Hal and Helena exchanged a smiling glance but said nothing.

"The Chateau is designed in the shape of the Greek cross at the centre of which is the great staircase," the commentary continued and Helena felt her blood run cold. "At the corners of the cross are four towers — the François I Tower, the Dieudonné, the Bell or Henri IV, and the Caroline de Berry. Please make your way to the King's Hunting Party room by the de Berry tower and switch the tape on again when you get there."

Hal hesitated and Helena suddenly knew that he was nervous, but desperately trying to conceal the fact.

"Do you want to go there, or do you want to see the staircase straight away?" he asked.

"I'd rather do the tour properly," she answered, afraid to proceed too fast.

He nodded and they obediently made their way to the tower, gazing in silent admiration at the wonderfully carved stone ceilings, alternate squares revealing the letter F and the King's personal emblem, the salamander.

"What a place." breathed Hal but before Helena was able to answer they were surrounded by a party of Americans, twenty strong, all carrying the taped tour and following it to the letter. In fact the group even watched their leader, a short stubby man bristling with self-importance, for the signal to switch on.

"Right, everybody," he was calling, waving his arms to attract attention. "We are now at the Caroline de Berry tower — and boy, oh boy, do we know that she was no lady! Mistress to the King and all."

Someone argued, "Wasn't that du Barry?" and got a withering look for their pains.

"As I said we are now at the tower so we'll all step into the King's Hunting Party room."

He stumped off to the left but lost his way and had to come back. Meanwhile, several members of his party had used their initiative and found the right place. The little man swelled with indignation.

"*Please*, everybody. We really must stick together. Who knows who might go missing!"

At any other time Helena would have been giggling uncontrollably, but now a finger of fear once again laid itself on her spine as she turned the tape back on.

"In this room you will see the only known portrait of a ghost."

Helena and Hal stared at one another soundlessly. "Yes, the great staircase is supposedly haunted and, so it is said, several members of François's court actually saw the phantom. In fact there is a legend that the ghost was the basis of a sketch by Leonardo da Vinci who, so it is said, designed both chateau and staircase. Be that as it may, in the sixteenth century the Vicomte de Fleurmont claimed that he saw the spectre and painted her likeness in oils. There are several paintings on the walls, but hers is on the far left."

The tape ran on but Helena was no longer listening. It was as if every morsel of terror had suddenly become focussed. Without a word she scrambled through the Americans who were now laughing uproariously.

"Gee, think of that! A real live ghost."

"Did you hear yourself? A *real live* ghost."

"I said that? Oh my!"

Right behind her she could hear Hal apologising and pushing his way through the crowd but she did not even turn to look at him. For Helena had stopped short before a painting which could only be a portrait of herself, her hair loose about her shoulders, a strangely wistful smile on her lips, and wearing the satin nightgown her mother had given her last Christmas.

"Oh my God!" she said, her voice rising in panic. "I don't believe it!"

"It's a coincidence." Hal was saying over her shoulder.

On the breath of hysteria, Helena answered, "But she's wearing my clothes. Look Hal, look! You can even see the label."

It was true. Both of them could make out the shadow where the artist had painted in a suggestion of the maker's label adorning the much-prized nightdress.

Just for once Hal was silent, his great good sense defeated.

"It's me, Hal. You must admit it. It's a portrait of me."

The sound coming from Helena's lips was high-pitched, frenzied, drowning out all others. With horror she realised that every other voice had hushed, that every eye had turned to look at her, and that somebody somewhere with a cry like hers was calling out.

"Quiet, Helena, quiet," shouted Hal, shaking her violently.

But it was too late. With a sound of anguish she escaped from him and plunged headlong through the chateau's great expanse, running as if her life depended on it towards the staircase. It was crowded, packed with people, their presence suffocatingly close to her. Almost without moving, Helena found herself being borne upwards and was strangely comforted.

She had never noticed before how open the staircase was, how much one could observe through the beautiful marble balustrade. Glancing towards the central column which supported the spiral, Helena could see that it contained windows, or rather observation bays so that one could watch all the other people climbing – or was it descending. The inevitable party of Japanese were there and a flashy girl, encased in tight leggings. She was staring straight at Helena.

"Oh my Gawd, Darryl," the girl screamed, "I've seen the ghost."

"I'm not a ghost," Helena cried, but the screamer had already gone.

She was being tightly pressed now, long skirts swishing against Helena's legs, and male feet in buckled shoes touching hers. She looked round and saw that she was amongst them, that strange press of silent people who resolutely climbed together, yet who never glanced at her, nor ever spoke.

"Oh Hal," she wept, "is this a dream? What's happening to me?"

And then the hand came out to help her and Helena took it. Grasped the long fingers and felt their touch, electric and exciting against her own. It was the man of course. Staring up, Helena saw the sheen of blueish curls and the dark green eyes, rimmed with jade, as he pulled her towards him.

She was so close that she could smell his perfume but, more than that, as he held her against him she could actually feel the rhythm of his heart. So he was alive; somewhere, somehow, the creature of her dreams had substance.

He spoke French, an archaic form, but strangely she understood his words. "You've come at last, and you are full grown!" he said. "You see I had this terrible fear that you might still be a child."

"You knew me as a child?" Helena shook her head in disbelief.

"You don't remember? When you crawled up the staircase?"

"I *crawled* up. What are you talking about?"

"My darling, you were only a year old."

Nothing made sense any more, there was no reality, only the beating of his living heart.

"Am I dead?" gasped Helena. "Am I a ghost?"

"A ghost only of what is to come," he said.

She fell then, down and down into a sickening, frightening darkness, to wake with a sharp smell beneath her nose and to see a ring of shocked faces all staring at her.

"It's okay, honey," said an American voice. "I'm a nurse. You fainted, that's all. You're going to be fine."

"Hal?" said Helena wearily, and then realised that the arms which held her were his.

"Darling," he said thankfully, "thank God you're all right."

*

Lying in the car afterwards, skimming through the early evening and thankful that it was cooler, Helena finally spoke.

"Hal, what happened? Did I really faint?"

"Yes. Do you remember running away and up the staircase?"

"Of course I do."

"Well, I followed you. I saw you step off at the landing and then, after standing there a moment or two, you collapsed."

"*You saw me?*" repeated Helena disbelievingly. "You actually saw me there?"

"Yes. Why?"

Immediately a warning bell went off in her brain. "No reason really. Was I on my own?"

"There were tourists about but you were by yourself, yes. Helena, you didn't 'see things', did you?"

She looked at him very directly. "What a funny question. Why should I 'see things'?"

"Because this business of the portraits, not to mention that recurring dream of yours, is obviously getting you down. You know I had a second look at that ghost picture. What you took for your nightdress label could have been anything. A fold in the material. Anything."

"So you still think it is all a coincidence?"

"Yes," answered Hal stoutly, "I certainly do."

It wasn't, of course, Helena knew that. But how could she tell him that she had touched another flesh-and-blood being, that she had been held so close to another man's heart that she had heard its beat?

Hal's voice broke in on her thoughts. "After all you've endured I don't suppose you will ever want to set eyes on Chambord again."

"On the contrary," she answered lightly, "I won't rest till I've been back and seen every stick and stone of the place."

She was rewarded with a startled look and rather a grim silence which did not disappear until they sat on the geranium terrace after their evening meal, watching the sun go down in ribbons of red.

Then Hal said, "I suppose it *was* the staircase. The one you ran up, I presume it was the one you dream about."

She smiled a small, secret smile, remembering a pair of spectacular eyes and the hardness of the body against which, for one glorious moment, she had been held.

"Yes, it's the same," she answered. "But I've lost my fear of it. I really want to go back and see the place properly. I think fainting must have cured me."

"And what about the portrait? Has that been exorcised as well?"

"Now I just feel a healthy curiosity," Helena insisted.

Hal's face was unreadable and at any other time Helena would have wondered what was going on behind his eyes, which seemed curiously shuttered and expressionless. But tonight she had no time to think of anything except the problem which absorbed her. If the man was alive somewhere, how could she find him again? Yet the "if" troubled her. Suppose that this had been just a more than usually vivid dream; that he was, in truth, nothing but a figment conjured up by herself.

Her thoughts were interrupted abruptly by Hal asking, "Have you rung home?"

Rather crossly Helena answered. "Not yet. Why?"

"I spoke to my father this morning while you were in the bath. He seemed to think that congratulations were in order because we were staying on. So you had probably better disillusion them all before they open the champagne."

His voice held a bitter note, unusual for him, and Helena looked at him sadly.

"Hal, I'll tell Daddy the truth. That you've told me to make up my mind and I'm doing just that."

"So you won't say we're really on a ghost hunt?"

"What do you mean?"

"Tracking down Leonardo's model, researching dream world staircases, to name a few supernatural items."

"No," she said, feeling a stir of anger, and without saying more went into the hotel to phone.

Her father's voice spoke as clearly as if he was in the next room. "Helena, how lovely! Are you having a good time?"

"Yes, marvellous," she answered guardedly.

"We had dinner with Rosalind and Richard last night. They told us that you and Hal are staying on in France."

He had that familiar note in his voice, the one Helena disliked so much. It meant he was once more looking on them as a viable couple. Determinedly, Helena spoke up.

"Daddy, please don't raise your hopes. It's true that I have come here to make up my mind finally about Hal, but at the moment I am no nearer a solution than when I started."

With the acuteness which made him such a daunting adversary in business, John Holley said, "Is there someone else?"

Caught completely off guard, Helena found herself saying, "In a way, yes."

"Anyone I know?"

"It's someone even I don't know, not well that is. And yet I can't stop thinking about him."

John Holley again changed tack so fast that Helena was left gasping. "Then get to know him, my dear. Don't waste time mooning. Seek him out and then make up your mind.

Otherwise it's not fair on you, Hal, or this other chap. Whoever he might be."

"But I don't quite know how to reach him," said Helena, half wishing she could tell her father everything.

There was a muffled snort and then John answered, "Well, make it your business to find out. Of all the feeble excuses..."

Helena laughed. "I love you. Daddy, and on this occasion you are probably right. The way will be fraught with difficulties but I'll give it a whirl."

"Good girl," he said cheerily, and hung up.

Helena was smiling as she went to rejoin Hal on the shadowy terrace, and still, though faintly, as she lay sleepless beside him, staring at the moonlight and wishing she was back in Chambord.

Up to that moment everything had seemed impossible, longing for a man who probably had no substance, then suddenly, almost as if she was receiving guidance, Helena knew what to do. Rising from the bed soundlessly, she took her clothes and dressed in the bathroom. Then, making sure that Hal still slept, she crept from the bedroom and out of the sleeping hotel.

Once outside, Helena looked round. She had picked up the keys of Hal's car from the dressing table and now she could see it, bathed in moonlight. It took only a second to open the door and turn the ignition, and the engine roared into life.

Helena had a mental picture of Hal waking instantly, rushing to the window, then hurling downstairs to pursue her. But as she drove away, looking behind apprehensively, she saw that the hotel slept peacefully and there was no furious figure standing in the doorway shouting at her to come back.

It seemed to Helena that she drove through a deserted land. The river Loire, whose course she was following, stretched supple and silver as it slithered past the towns and villages that slept dreamily on its banks.

Helena drove on. Through Chaumont, to whose chateau, perched unbelievably high on a cliff above the river, Diane de Poitiers had been exiled by Catherine de Medici. Then on, through the outskirts of Blois, where Anne of Brittany had once held court, and the same Medici queen had hatched many of her most merciless plots. Then, as she drove away from the town, the road forked right and suddenly she was heading for Chambord.

Now that she could actually see the name on the signpost, Helena for the first time began to question her actions. What could a professional woman be thinking of, flitting round France in the moonlight in pursuit of a man who did not even exist? And the more she thought about it the more Helena was sure that she had dreamt everything.

She stopped the engine and sat quite still, trying to decide the best course of action. Ought she to turn round and quietly drive back to Amboise, pretending to Hal, should he be awake, that she had gone for a solitary drive because she could not sleep? Or, if he still slumbered, clamber in quietly beside him, shamefaced as a schoolgirl breaking the rules? Or should she continue to seek the answer to the mystery, one way or another? Almost as if she could not help herself, Helena switched the engine back on and drove fast towards the chateau.

She had half feared the gates to the estate might be closed against the night. But then she remembered that people lived in the village, that there was an hotel overlooking the chateau. Obviously the entrances would remain open. Nevertheless, Helena heaved a sigh of relief as the car turned into the forest of Chambord.

Looking above the trees she saw that the moon had picked out towers and turrets, while the blue roofs of the chateau glimmered darkly, deep as an uncut sapphire. All the way along the road Helena kept staring until the bend came and Chambord was lost to view. But then, as she turned into the now deserted car park, it reappeared, looming magnificent and powerful.

"Oh please be in there," said Helena beneath her breath as, imitating a late returning hotel guest, she strolled nonchalantly up the tree-lined street, the souvenir shops now shuttered and dark.

As with all great and stately houses, the chateau was securely protected against intruders. A wire fence, which Helena suspected might well be electrified, bounded the estate up to the point where the canal that had once been a moat protected the building. And it was to this canal that she now turned her attention. Knowing it was the only possible way in, Helena did not hesitate. She kicked off her shoes and dived, realising as she did so that she was probably committing the greatest folly of her whole life.

The water, heated by the sun all day, was reasonably warm and Helena, a strong swimmer, struck out in the direction of the chateau, passing beneath the arches of a bridge which echoed the splash and swirl of the river as she broke its calm surface. Looking round her, Helena saw that she had entered the grounds of Chambord.

One thing she hadn't bargained for was the steepness of the canal's sides, entirely unscaleable if it had not been for some white paled railings beside the canal wall. With an enormous heave, Helena managed to clutch a post and drag herself up. Then stood, dripping in the moonlight, staring at the main façade of the chateau which once would have been approached by that great driveway through the forest, a bridge of stone crossing the moat.

Helena shivered, in a state between elation and pure terror wondering, now that she had got this far, what her next move should be. The main door to the chateau, approached by a short flight of steps, looked well secured but the wing to Helena's left had an exterior stone staircase, situated in a small tower. Without further thought she made for it, wondering what she would find at the top.

She climbed a flight, then another, and to her astonishment found herself in an open gallery that ran along the outside of the wing's apartments. Helena peered through one of the windows, aware that she was looking into a furnished room, though the outlines of the furniture were mere looming shadows beneath the three paths of light thrown by the three windows. In the centre path something was shining in the moonlight. Narrowing her eyes Helena saw that it was a diamond ring, large as an egg, lying on the floor.

Even as she watched, a hand in a purple laced sleeve snatched it up and for a moment Helena stood on the point of shouting a warning. Someone else had broken into Chambord that night and she was alone with an intruder. But then the owner of the sleeve stepped forward into the light and she saw him distinctly. It was the man, and yet in a way it was not, for everything about him was grey. Helena gazed on a shadow, a creature without reality.

As she watched he came towards the window and saw her, a smile lighting up his grey features. He pressed his face to the glass.

"Little one," he said, with joy in his voice, "you have come!"

"You're a ghost," Helena found herself saying, "you're not really here at all."

He smiled at her, a sweet heart-stopping smile. "Funny little phantom," he said and opened the window for her. "Come to me."

Very vaguely, as if from a million miles away, Helena realised that as she stepped through the floor-length casement a burglar alarm had started to ring somewhere in the chateau's heart.

"I've set the bell off," she said slowly.

"What bell?" he answered, looking puzzled. "There is no bell."

He stretched his hand out to her, as he had done so many times in her dreams, and Helena took it. Just for a moment it seemed cold to her touch and then she felt the life blood pound through it and that magical electricity that there was between them, that incredible sensation that she knew must be raw attraction between two lovers, shot through her.

Without any further hesitation Helena stepped into the room and saw that the greyness which enveloped him had gone, that it had merely been a trick of the moonlight. His hair gleamed blue-black, his sensational eyes were the clear bright green of stained glass, his teeth as he smiled at her were strong and white.

"Who are you?" she breathed as he bent to kiss her.

"Etienne de Fleurmont, my love," he said softly.

She held him away one second longer, knowing that she had heard that name recently.

"But..."

"No buts, little one, for at last you have come to Chambord to be with me."

And with the kiss he gave her, wilder and more beautiful than anything Helena had ever known, she thought that indeed she had.

The room in which she found herself now revealed itself in all its glory. Candles flamed in candelabra suspended from the ceiling by gold chains, while a blazing log fire threw more illumination from the grate. On the largest walls hung fine tapestries, all depicting Diana as goddess of the hunt, while the floor was covered with a red Turkish carpet, which was echoed in the bed which had a canopy above, an elaborately woven back of considerable height, and a stiff, formal embroidered bedcover.

"What is this place?" said Helena, still held closely in Etienne de Fleurmont's arms.

"The bedroom in my apartment at Chambord," he answered.

Helena struggled loose. "Please tell me where I really am."

The expression on Etienne's face changed dramatically and he turned away from her, the colour mounting in his thin-boned cheeks.

"Please," Helena persisted.

"Before I do so, be assured of one thing," he said without meeting her eyes. "I love you, have loved you ever since you were a child; that is what made me do what I did."

Helena stared at him blankly, longing to comfort him but somehow afraid. "What *have* you done?"

"I summoned you here," Etienne said softly. "Or rather, I asked another to do so on my behalf."

Helena's legs felt suddenly weak and she shivered, remembering that she was wet through from her recent spell in the river. Etienne rushed to her, pulling her close to him and leading her to the fire.

"First let me get you some dry clothes. Then I will tell you everything that I know."

Giving a small bow he left the room and Helena was alone, instantly gripped by panic, knowing that she should run away, yet held fast by the attraction that this extraordinary man had for her. She stood by the fire, arms clutched round herself, wondering what to do next, then crossed to the window and stared out, face pressed against the glass, to see more clearly.

Outside it was as light as day, and in this amazing clarity every detail of the grounds round the chateau could be seen distinctly. For the first time, Helena realised that something was seriously amiss, that she was either suffering a terrifying hallucination or an event beyond her comprehension had occurred.

Gone were the canals and the formal, shaped green lawns; now a carpet of grass ran down to a crescent of water that shimmered like a brooch in the moonlight. Helena's hand clutched her throat and she closed her eyes. But when she opened them again the image had not changed. Chambord was fully moated once more.

A sound from the doorway had her wheeling round, eyes staring, but it was only the return of Etienne de Fleurmont, who stood smiling at her, holding out a gown so elaborate that Helena could only think it had come from a film set.

"For you," he said, and shocked as she was, Helena could not help but admire the beauty of the richly-embellished underskirt and the mulberry velvet of the jewel encrusted bodice.

She walked right up to him, putting her face close to his and trying hard to be angry. "Monsieur, what is all this? What is going on? Is this some enormous prank?"

"What do you mean, little one?"

"Everything would suggest that I am still dreaming, but I know that can't be true. My hair wouldn't be wet if I were dreaming." She picked up a lock of dripping hair and twirled it round her fingers. "You said earlier that you had me summoned here. Could you tell me exactly what that means?"

Etienne did not answer at first, instead silently leading her to where the fire consumed a log the size of a branch, urging her to sit on a low wooden chair with a tapestry back and seat, near to the stone hearth.

"The very first time I saw you," he said, sitting down opposite her, "was when you crawled up the staircase towards me. You were like a rose, so pink and round that I could have plucked you to my heart. But when I came down to catch you, you were on the other flight and were gone. I thought then that I was hallucinating but when, a month later, a beautiful little girl, proud as a *grande dame* in her long swirling frock, came towards me I realised that something strange was taking place. That my daydream was being filled with a child who appeared to be growing up."

"But Etienne," Helena answered softly, "*I* dreamed of *you*."

"Perhaps, then, it is true," he said, "that time is continuous."

She stole a glance at his face and saw that he was staring into the fire, remembering.

"For a year I watched you," he said, "always growing, becoming beautiful, your eyes consuming my soul whenever you came to me. I even painted your portrait looking at me like that. I was in love with you, Helena, by the time you were fourteen."

"And you," she asked in wonder, "you did not age while I grew up?"

"Only by one year."

She hid her face in her hands. "Am I going mad? Is any of this possible?"

At once he was beside her, his arms going round her and holding her tightly against his heart. Yet again Helena felt his irresistible attraction.

"My darling, forgive me. In the end I consulted Ruggieri and begged him to bring you to me by whatever means he chose. Yesterday he almost succeeded. You were within my grasp, and then something pulled you away."

"It was yesterday for me too," said Helena. "But why did you say then that you were glad I was a woman not a child?"

"He warned me that magic sometimes has a sting in its tail."

"Magic?" said Helena, feeling yet again that none of this could be real, that she was truly in bed, sleeping beside Hal, and dreaming the most vivid dream of all.

Etienne looked at her curiously. "But of course. You have heard of Ruggieri surely?"

"No, I'm afraid not. Who is he?"

"Madame la Dauphine's personal astrologer."

Helena stared at him. "Etienne, for God's sake tell me the truth. Where am I?"

"In Chambord..."

"I know that," she interrupted fiercely, "but *when*?"

He took both her hands to steady her. "In my world, little one, and in your dream too, it is the year 1541."

Helena got to her feet feeling physically sick. "You are lying, I know it. It isn't possible."

"It is, *ma cherie*. You have come here at last, as we both wanted."

"We?" she repeated dazedly.

"Yes," said a voice from the doorway and Helena spun round.

A tall, gaunt figure in a black cloak was moving slowly towards her, and on seeing him a memory came back. A memory in which a dark-eyed woman and a tall thin man stood in Etienne's place and called to her to come. Helena went cold with fear though the man smiled and continued to advance.

"Greetings, my dear. I am Ruggieri," he said.

She stared at him blankly and as if he could read her thoughts the man went on, "I can see that you are disturbed. Yet to those who study the stars and true nature, there is no such thing as time. You must understand that it is perfectly possible to leave one's body behind when one dreams, and in that state to visit other times, other places. You dreamed of Etienne while you were a child, he saw you in his visions. You were close to one another even though centuries held you apart."

"Are you are asking me to accept that I am here, in the year 1541?"

Ruggieri smiled and spread his hands. "Whether you accept it or not, it is a fact."

"But what of my own time? Have I died?"

"I think you are in suspended animation, perhaps asleep."

"And can I go back?"

"If you wish it, if Etienne wishes it, possibly you can."

Helena stood quite still, trying to cope with the violent beating of her heart and with all the thoughts that were teeming in her brain. If this had really happened to her, if she was having some kind of incredible psychic experience, then what could she do? Only by persuading this gaunt astrologer — who was now regarding her with an amused and cynical smile upon his face — could she ever hope to return to her own life and to Hal.

Instantly Etienne was beside her. "Do you forgive me?" he whispered anxiously.

Helena looked up at him. "Of course I do."

When she had said the words she understood that she half meant them. That it was almost worth all the fear and torment just to be close to him.

"Then will you stay with me tonight?" he went on, too softly for Ruggieri to hear.

Helena laughed, shaking her head. "I see that men are the same whatever the century."

He looked stricken. "But I summoned you here so that I could marry you."

She stared at him, amazed, but was rescued from further conversation by a knock on the door. Instantly Ruggieri rose from his seat by the fire and melted like a shadow behind the drape of the floor-length bed curtain. Helena looked round frantically, terrified of being seen and subjected to questioning, but too late. The door opened imperiously and a gorgeously dressed vision swept into the room before Helena could make a move.

She found herself gazing on a vivid creature whom she instantly recognised as the woman who had waited for her on the staircase. She was dressed from head to toe in shimmering gold, the overskirt threaded with red and decorated with pearls. A gold net collar brushed against lustrous ebony hair pulled back into a chignon, from which one solitary and glistening lock escaped, while her figure was slender, that of a woman in her twenties.

"Well," said the newcomer, casting her dark eyes round the room, "I thought I heard voices and could have sworn my astrologer was with you. What do you have to say, Monsieur le Vicomte?"

Helena stood motionless, digesting two pieces of information simultaneously. Etienne had a title, and this striking girl had referred to the astrologer as hers, and therefore could be none other than Catherine de Medici. Helena stared in frank amazement.

Catherine whirled round the room searching, and Helena, who had taken the precaution of crouching behind a chair, was able to study her more closely. Feature by feature the Dauphine was not really attractive, her Italian blood making her somewhat olive skinned and Roman nosed. But the Medici strain had also given her beautiful hair and eyes, coupled with a powerful personality, so that she was in her way quite stunning.

Catherine's inspection of the room continued as she peered beneath the bed and amongst its massive drapes before attacking the very spot where Ruggieri had vanished. To Helena's astonishment the astrologer was not there, obviously having slipped silently away. Then she cowered as Catherine crossed over to the chair where she hid and looked behind it.

There was no doubt that she saw her, for Helena watched as the Dauphine's hand flew to her mouth in fright and the glittering eyes widened to twice their size. But her control was amazing, impeccable. The two women exchanged a measured glance and then, with a small smile of triumph about her mouth, Catherine turned away.

"Well, Etienne," she said, lightly tapping him under the chin with her ostrich feather fan, "I see that I misjudged you. There is nobody here."

He bowed and kissed her hand. "As you say, I am alone, Madame."

"And will be all night?" she asked and laughed softly.

Etienne bowed, and the door quietly closed behind her.

Helena stood up. "Who was that...?"

He nodded. "That was Catherine, future Queen of France."

The dreamlike quality of the events unfolding swept Helena again and in a way she found this comforting. The situation was so unlikely that she expected to wake and see Hal at any second. But thinking about him filled her with unexpected anxiety. She crossed to Etienne's side and put her hands on his arm.

"Monsieur le Vicomte, if this is really happening, how shall I ever return?"

Etienne frowned. "Why do you say that? Do you want to leave me?" Helena hesitated and he went on, "I hope that is not so because, Madame, I am formally asking you to marry me. I brought you here to make you the Vicomtesse de Fleurmont."

"You know that is not possible."

"Why?" said Etienne, and gathered her into his arms. And then everything was indeed possible as Helena allowed him to carry her to that great and beautiful bed, to slowly take off his garments and then remove hers. Then take her slowly but exquisitely to heights which she had never before known existed.

*

She woke the next morning not sure whether she would find Hal sleeping beside her. If the ecstatic night before had been nothing but a glorious dream. But a sound brought her attention back to the present for the door swept open to reveal Etienne and a scuttling little servant who carried a tray loaded with delicacies.

"Put it over there," he said, "I will send for you later."

The servant bobbed her way out as Etienne crossed to kiss Helena good morning.

"Etienne..." she began, but then stopped, remembering his words on the previous night. It was Ruggieri and he alone who could return her to the twenty-first century.

"When you have breakfasted and dressed, my darling," said the Vicomte, "I shall show you the wonders of Chambord, both the chateau and the estate."

Despite everything Helena glowed with excitement. To see the palace of Francois I, fully furnished and populated by that strange race of people who so claustrophobically packed the staircase, would be a magical experience indeed.

"There are clothes for you in the cupboard," Etienne said, then smiled. "I hope you can manage to put them on."

"I thought everyone was dressed by a maid," Helena answered.

"They are, my darling, but in this case a servant would find it rather difficult."

"Why?"

"Because, little ghost, nobody other than Ruggieri and myself can see you."

She stared at him aghast. "What?" she exclaimed.

Etienne smiled disarmingly, his splendid eyes warm. "Sweetheart, the mysterious path that you and I have chosen was not meant to be shared with others. We have achieved our impossible wish, but no one else may know the secret."

Helena sat in the midst of the enormous bed, hugging her knees to her chin. Was she truly invisible as Etienne said? And if so, why had the Dauphine apparently recognised her last night? *Had* she come to Etienne of her own free will? Had she wished to be with him as much as he had wanted her? She remembered how she had driven through the night and swum a dark river to get to Chambord. Had that been Ruggieri's doing or her own?

"You are very quiet," he said.

"I was just thinking things through. Etienne..." she went on, suddenly practical, "I think *you* had better help me into these clothes."

It was like dressing for a play. First came the underskirt heavily embroidered and made of brocade, then the bodice and crimson overskirt, the sleeves slashed and tied with gold cords. Onto her head Helena manoeuvred a headdress trimmed with pearls, a floating veil hanging from it, and finally she adorned herself with jewels — a gold chain belt from which hung a gem-covered pomander case, chains of gold and ruby, heavy with pendants, then finally rings and earrings, glistening and glittering as she turned this way and that.

"Come my dearest beauty," said Etienne, giving her his hand, "let me show you the place that has brought the two of us together."

And with that he led her into the corridor, and towards the staircase.

"I want you to learn its secret," he said and laughed. "Close your eyes for a second."

Helena obediently did so only to find that Etienne had gone when she opened them again. She stood still for a moment then decided to descend, only to see through one of the observation windows in the central column that Etienne was climbing up. Helena turned to join him but when she reached the landing found he was not there. Puzzled, she took to the stairs once more to discover that he was running down behind her.

"How did you manage that?" she said, nonplussed.

"My darling," he answered teasingly, "haven't you guessed?"

"No." Helena shook her head. "It's obviously some trick. I can't work it out."

"There are *two* staircases, both spiral, one above the other. In that way you can walk round and talk in private, still seeing everything that goes on."

Helena gazed at him, then rushed to look for herself. Going as near to the hollow central pillar of the staircase as she could, she stared down. Everything went blurred for a moment, then she distinctly saw Hal, kneeling on the ground and bending over something which Helena could not distinguish.

"Hal," she called out. "I'm up here. Look."

He gazed round, and she watched as he obviously tried to locate the sound but could not do so. In the dim distance she realised that a bell was going off.

"Here," she shouted again. "I'm here."

He gazed upwards and just for a second Helena could have sworn that he stared straight at her, then he turned away and once more gave his attention to the object on the ground. Poor Hal, part of her still wanted to be with him. Then she saw with a wild mix of emotions, that Etienne had joined her.

"What is it?" he said. "You look distressed."

She took a deep breath. "It's a long way down."

"But you are all right?" Etienne's eyes stared into hers anxiously.

"Perfectly. I love the staircase. Please can we go to the bottom and look up."

"Of course. It's a fantastic concept, isn't it?" said Etienne, taking Helena's arm and walking beside her. "Master da Vinci designed it, but did not live to see it built. He originally wanted four spirals for an ultimate optical illusion."

"Do you think he could travel into the future?" asked Helena. "Could he have seen me there?"

"Who knows who he saw or met when he practised his arts," Etienne told her. He did not seem happy to pursue the subject.

He opened a door beneath the staircase and Helena found herself standing within the hollow central column, looking up to where a great lantern dome towered above it.

"What a work of art," she said.

A sudden noise from outside broke the stillness within the hollow and Etienne said hastily, "The King is returning from his morning stroll."

Passing through the door again, Helena found herself in the entrance hallway which, only yesterday, had been packed with tourists, but now teemed with a horde of preening exquisites. In the midst of his pretty courtiers, François I had returned to his chateau.

Heavily jewelled men vied for glory with the host of beautiful females who surrounded the King, himself tall and elegant, his dark good looks marred only by a very long nose. However, his bright blue eyes twinkled and it was obvious from the press of women that they did not consider François's one ugly feature of any significance.

"Who are they all?" whispered Helena.

"The least attractive is the Queen, Eleanor. She is his second wife but he prefers to be in the arms of that little fair one."

Helena looked to where a dazzling blonde flirted in the centre of a crowd of admirers.

"She's Anne d'Heuilly, la Duchesse d'Etampes."

"And who is that giving her black and white looks?"

"His other lady, Françoise de Chateaubriant."

"Well, well!" said Helena smiling and shaking her head. Then her eye was suddenly caught by the most beautiful woman of all, standing alone, starkly clad in black, a white veil hanging from her headdress, yet with a presence that outshone every other woman in the room.

"Who's that?" she murmured.

Etienne laughed gently. "*La plus bel de belles*. She is Diane de Poitiers, widow of the Senechal of Normandy."

Helena gazed in wonderment at a legend, the woman who, though twenty-one years his senior, held the Dauphin of France totally within her thrall.

"How old is she?"

"Over forty."

"No!" breathed Helena, looking at smooth milky skin, glorious eyes, blue as sea deeps, and a body on which there was not one ounce of superfluous flesh.

"And here comes Diane's lover together with her bitterest enemy," said Etienne quietly and Helena saw Catherine de Medici coming into the hall with her husband the Dauphin, who also wore black and white with a large crescent moon brooch pinned high on his shoulder.

"It is the emblem of the goddess Diana and he wears it to please his mistress," Etienne whispered but could say no more as the royal gathering began to move to where he stood.

"Fleurmont," the King was calling. "Where have you been? Did you lie long abed after a riotous night?"

There was laughter as Etienne bowed low and said, "Indeed I did, Sir."

They all drew nearer and it was then that it became utterly clear to Helena that Etienne was right, none of them could see her at all. It was the weirdest sensation and yet in a way intriguing.

And yet Helena had the strongest feeling that someone was looking at her. Glancing up suddenly, she saw the Dauphine staring straight at her, just as she had done last night. Helena dropped a curtsy and saw the faintest of smiles play around Catherine's lips.

As the procession moved on, taking Catherine right past her, she heard the woman whisper, "This afternoon. In the

Pavilion de la Chaussée. The astrologer will bring you to me."

Then she was gone and so was the Vicomte, and Helena was left alone to explore the chateau and forlornly search for Hal.

It was afternoon when Helena wandered out into the gardens, lifting her face up to the sun, only to feel a pair of arms circle her waist from behind and a kiss being planted on her hair.

"I've caught you at last, little rogue," said Etienne. "I think you've been hiding."

Helena thought long afterwards that that was one of the best moments in her experience, to stand in the beautiful gardens of Chambord, in the warmth of the summer sun, exchanging kisses with Etienne de Fleurmont until, arms still entwined around each other, he finally took her in silence back inside the chateau and to the tower opposite that in which lay the King's apartments. Still in silence Etienne opened two wooden doors and Helena found that she was in a chapel, very plain and stark and not in the least imposing, as she had thought Chambord's place of worship would be.

"My darling," he said simply. "I have come here to pledge my undying love for you."

It was said so sincerely that Helena found all the million and one protests that should have been on her lips suddenly stilled as Etienne led her to the altar and knelt on the mosaic floor before it. Feeling in a mood of total harmony with him, Helena did the same.

"This ring," he said, producing the diamond she had seen lying on his bedroom floor, "has always belonged to the Vicomtesses de Fleurmont. I want you to wear it."

Before Helena could say a word he had slipped it on her left hand.

"In my eyes and also, I humbly believe, in God's," Etienne said softly, "we are now man and wife."

Helena did not know what to say. How could she at such a moment tell such a truly splendid person that she had suddenly discovered, even in the last few hours, that Hal was, despite everything, the man who dominated her other existence.

Instead, with equal sincerity she answered, "As long as I am here, in your century, know that I do love you."

At that they joined hands and without saying more rose from the altar and turned to go. In the doorway a gaunt, instantly recognisable figure waited for them and as they approached bowed low.

"I greet the new Vicomtesse with much joy, but alas I must speak with her privately," said Ruggieri.

Etienne put a protective arm round Helena. "What do you want with my wife?"

"That I cannot reveal, Sir."

"You must," said the Vicomte, his hand flying to the hilt of his sword.

"Please," Helena put in, "don't quarrel." She turned to Etienne. "My dear, Madame la Dauphine knows of my presence here. She has asked me to meet her in the Pavilion de la Chaussée.

His face paled. "Why did you not tell me of this before?"

"There has been no time."

Over Helena's head, Etienne stared at the astrologer. "What is this about? What does the Dauphine want with my wife?"

Ruggieri smiled his cynical smile and spread his hands. "How would I know that, Sir? Madame does not confide all her secrets to me."

"You lying dog," said Etienne, grabbing him by the collar. "Tell me the truth."

"Let him go," said Helena, suddenly afraid, "there is no need to make an enemy of him."

Etienne released his hold and looked at her sadly. "Because only he can help you to return? Is that why you defend him?"

"It's as well," said Ruggieri, brushing at his collar, "that no injury befell me. If it had done you would have left me no choice but to inform Madame."

"That will not be necessary," answered Helena determinedly. "I am coming with you now."

And as Etienne moved forward to stop her, she sidestepped. "It is no use. I am determined to go."

Ruggieri bowed. "You are a wise woman, my dear. Nonetheless, let me give you my personal assurance that you are in absolutely no danger." He shot Etienne a dark, unreadable look.

"Pretty words, but I shall accompany my wife as far as the pavilion," said the Vicomte.

"You will do no such thing," answered the astrologer briskly. "Keep to your own quarters, Monsieur, and I will return your little ghost to you within two hours."

And with that he took Helena firmly by the elbow and propelled her out of the chapel, leaving Etienne staring anxiously after them.

Once outside the astrologer moved quickly and Helena found herself hurrying up the drive which led through the forest and away from Chambord. It seemed to her that they had gone at least a mile, in fact the walls of the estate were visible in the distance, before Ruggieri swiftly bore left in the direction of a collonaded pavilion.

"I will leave you at the steps," he said. "Madame's conversation with you is to be entirely private."

"What does she want with me?" asked Helena, striving to keep up. "And how is it that she alone of those at Court can see me?"

"Madame has long been interested in things that are beyond the narrow confines of the known," Ruggieri answered tersely.

"You mean magic?" asked Helena, but he would say no more.

The light in the pavilion was dim after the brightness of the day and it took Helena several minutes, straining to adjust her vision, to realise that Catherine stood in the shadows, silently watching her. Yet again a chill of foreboding made her shiver as the Dauphine softly spoke.

"So we have succeeded. A triumph, don't you think?"

"What do you mean, Madame?"

"I think it remarkable that between us Ruggieri and I brought you here."

"But I thought Etienne..."

Catherine gave a contemptuous laugh and stepped forward, the light from the windows falling on her face in stripes from the closed shutters.

"Etienne? He was used. I have studied magic since I was a girl and it was *I* who called you to me, assisted by my astrologer."

"Then please," said Helena firmly, "send me back again."

The Dauphine looked genuinely astonished. "But I thought you loved the Vicomte?"

"I do," Helena answered. "But I have another life to live as well."

Catherine's dark eyes had pools of fire in their depths which flickered as she leaned close to Helena's ear.

"In that case it will not be as difficult to persuade you as I thought."

Helena recoiled. "To do what?"

Catherine laughed, a chill and bitter sound. "I wonder how much you know of real love, if you have ever suffered the torment of adoring yet being spurned in return. I was fourteen when I married the Dauphin and I was in love with him then. But he had eyes for only one woman, the widow Diane, and I hate her more than words can say."

She paused, thinking her own private thoughts and Helena tensed, almost guessing what was coming next.

"So that is where you come in, my dear. In return for special services Ruggieri and I will have you away from here tonight."

"And what must I do?"

Catherine smiled wickedly. "Did you know that this evening the King has ordered a masked ball?" Helena shook her head and the Dauphine went on, "The masks will be elaborate, disguising, but it is always easy to recognise the Widow. She wears black to show up the cream of her skin and white near her face to enhance its perfection." Catherine ground her teeth. "And have you noticed that Monsieur le Dauphin dresses in the same sober colours simply to please his lady?"

Helena nodded mutely, the feeling of horror deepening.

"So little ghost, I have a simple task for you. Tonight you must kill Diane."

Helena froze where she stood. "But I can't do that."

Catherine's face transformed. "You *will* do it, exactly as I say. Otherwise you can stay here forever. A ghost without substance, marooned in time."

Helena stood stock still, thinking of the prospect that lay before her. "What do you want me to do?" she said eventually.

Catherine de Medici laughed soundlessly. "Why, turn your invisibility to good use, of course. At the height of the festivities when all have drunk too much I want you to push the Widow to her death."

It was on the tip of Helena's tongue to say, "But Diane de Poitiers was never murdered", then she thought better of it.

"And what guarantee have I that you will send me back to my own time if I do this for you?"

"You have the word of a Medici," said Catherine icily. "The word of a Dauphine of France."

"It seems to me I have little choice," answered Helena slowly.

"My dear, you have none. Now, will you do it?"

"Yes," said Helena, "I promise that before midnight tonight, Diane de Poitiers will be dead."

She turned, running from the pavilion so fast that she actually seemed to glide above the earth, part of her mind back in the Paris Tourist Office, seeing the poster of Chambord and remembering the vision in which she had hastened down this very drive and entered the chateau.

Had that been a premonition of this moment rather than a memory, Helena wondered now. But there was no time to dwell on anything so abstract. Her principal concern must be to escape both from the palace and Catherine de Medici's scheme. And yet what hope was there? Her dream seemed to have become a reality. How could she turn it into fantasy once more?

Helena ran on blindly, unaware that she had left the forest behind and had entered the furthest of the beautiful gardens, until the sound of voices caught her attention and she slowed her pace.

There was no one immediately in sight though the murmuring continued and instinctively Helena froze behind a tree. A second later she was glad she had done so for two of the three people to whom she was visible came into view. Etienne walked right past her with none other than Ruggieri himself. Helena's eyes widened in amazement to see a couple who had so recently quarrelled deep in conversation.

". . . she wants to leave, astrologer. My love is not enough for her. Will you help me keep Helena here?" Etienne was saying.

"Monsieur le Vicomte, I am in difficulties. Today Madame struck some kind of bargain with her to which even I was not privy, though I believe it may concern Helena's return to her own time."

"But surely you..." Etienne interrupted.

"Surely, nothing," Ruggieri answered swiftly. "You must believe that Madame had more than a little to do with your wife's strange arrival at Chambord."

"You mean that her influence is greater than mine... or yours?"

Ruggieri nodded gravely. "I fear so, Monsieur. Madame is a mistress of the hidden arts. If she has promised to send Helena home, then beware."

Their voices were lost as they went on down the path, still in earnest debate.

Slowly Helena stepped out of her hiding place, her mind now in a turmoil. If Ruggieri had a foot in both camps, as it would appear he obviously had, what hope had she of persuading him to help her? It seemed that she had come up against a blank wall, for she most certainly could never kill the widow Diane de Poitiers to earn her escape. The very thought was so horrifying that Helena put it straight from her mind.

Wretchedly she entered the chateau, not quite sure in which direction to go, but vaguely heading for Etienne's apartments. Then an idea struck her. Perhaps it had been the bridge under which she had swum, the bridge which had echoed and re-echoed with the sound of cleaving water, that might hold the key.

Could it be that, if Helena retraced her steps exactly, the reverse process would take place and she would find herself standing by the river bank, the chateau closed and dark, the last hotel guests having a late-night drink on the terrace?

With sudden purpose she entered the Vicomte's rooms silently and went to the cupboard where her clothes had been put after they had dried.

With a beating heart Helena opened the door to find that her luck had held, they were still there. Now came the difficult business of wrestling with laces and buttons but with maximum concentration she finally managed to divest herself of the heavy garments and put on the trousers and tee shirt in which she had arrived. They seemed slight and superficial after the richness of the others and Helena caught herself wishing that modern clothes were more romantic, more sumptuous, as she turned from the mirror to go.

She had actually put her hand out to unlock the door when it suddenly flew open and there was Etienne, standing staring at her aghast, his smile dying on his lips as he took in how she was dressed.

"My sweet .." Helena began, but he would not let her finish, instead slamming the door behind him and leaning on it to bar the way out.

"Where are you going?" he asked angrily.

"I have to leave — or try to," Helena answered desperately. "If I stay here I will be forced to commit a crime." She flew into his arms. "Etienne, I *must* go. Please help me, oh please."

"Is this to do with Madame?" he asked tersely.

"Of course it is. She wants me to push Diane de Poitiers to her death."

"Tonight at the ball?"

"Yes," she said simply.

Helena felt the whole of Etienne's body tense as the impact of what she had just said dawned on him. Finally he held her at arm's length to look at her.

"You are telling me the truth?" he asked.

"Of course I am. Etienne," Helena went on impulsively, "I heard you try to persuade the astrologer to keep me here, but if you succeed you realise the cost to me. I am visible to Catherine de Medici who will give me no peace until I obey her wishes."

"Then there is no hope," said the Vicomte wretchedly, "you must leave here, and quickly."

Words came onto Helena's lips over which she seemed to have no control. "If you help me, I promise that one day, somehow, I'll come back. It would be unbearable never to see you again."

"My little wife, I will wait for you for ever, you know that," Etienne said with feeling.

They kissed swiftly but deeply, then Helena said, "As soon as it is dark I plan to retrace my steps from the night I arrived. If you will let me out through your balcony window, just exactly as you let me in, I intend to swim from the moat to the river and see if I can reverse the chain of events which led to me being here."

Etienne frowned. "But it is the staircase that originally brought us together. Surely that would be the way to go."

"I don't know. I simply don't know."

"Neither do I, unless..."

"What?" asked Helena, torn between hope and fear.

"If Master Leonardo could really travel through time as you believe, then somewhere in his journals or notebooks he must have referred to it. If we could see those..."

"But surely they are locked away at Clos-Luce?" said Helena despairingly.

"No, they are here. After da Vinci's death, the King brought everything to Chambord. He has them now, under lock and key."

"Then how do we get to see them?"

"Very simply," said Etienne, his face slanting a smile at her. "I will ask His Grace if I may examine the Master's papers. Francois does not wish them to be secret, merely secure."

"It's worth a try, my darling," Helena said eagerly.

Etienne smiled his spectacular smile and said gently, "Think of me as your darling always, Helena. Then I shall be happy until you return to me."

And with that the Vicomte left the room and she was alone.

Suddenly nervous, Helena went toward the great bed with the thought of trying to rest for an hour, but the door opened once more and the astrologer put his head round it.

"You are to come at once, Helena," he said. "Madame has a gift for you."

With one sweep of his eyes Ruggieri took in the fact that she had changed her clothes to those in which she had arrived.

"Cooler for you, no doubt," he said but made no other comment as he bowed low, letting her pass in front of him.

The palace seemed amazingly quiet and Helena guessed that the peacock King and his butterfly court must be at rest before the night's festivities.

"The Dauphine does not sleep?" she asked tentatively, only to see the astrologer smile wryly.

"Madame will never rest until her purpose is done," he answered, the double meaning obvious.

But Catherine at least had removed her heavy skirts and put a loose robe over her many petticoats, even if she had not taken to her bed.

"The Widow sleeps till noon every day, did you know that?" she asked inconsequentially as Helena was ushered in. "But yet she rises at dawn, bathes in cold water winter and summer alike, then goes for a long ride, before sleeping again. All this to preserve her legendary beauty. But she won't be so beautiful tomorrow, will she, little ghost?"

Catherine's dark eyes lingered on Helena, absorbing every detail. "I see you are wearing the strange things you wore when you came here last night. You are not thinking of leaving us before the ball surely?"

"No," countered Helena, "I am already dressed for what I must do. Then you promised to return me, Madame."

"So I did," said Catherine with a half-smile. "And so I shall, when you have done your part. But meanwhile your dress offends me. I suggest that I lend you some more fitting clothes and that you stay with me until the ball begins so that I may help you prepare."

"But I must see Etienne, Madame. I haven't yet said goodbye to him."

"Plenty of time for that," answered Catherine soothingly, "I promise you that you will be alone with him before this evening is over."

She crossed to a small wooden chest and took from it a jewelled pomander case on a heavy gold chain. "This is for you, Helena. I want you to wear it and think of me. It is scented, you know. One sniffs it to keep away the smell of the common people," she explained.

Helena took it silently, lifting the precious thing to her nose. The scent coming from it was heavy, almost sleep-inducing, and it was with a certain reluctance that she put it down again.

"Now," said Catherine softly, "why don't you rest here a while? I will take care of you, Helena. I will keep you safe from harm until the time comes for you to do what I tell you. Sleep now, deep sleep."

And with that Helena closed her eyes, the lids suddenly too weighty to stay open, and was instantly unconscious.

*

That evening there seemed to be a great many people on the staircase all mingling together, silently rubbing shoulders as they climbed. On the marble steps skirts swished against high-heeled buckled shoes while ornamental swords, their handles encrusted with rainbow gems dipped and rose as their owners made their steady way upwards.

It was the dream, only this night, this suffocating, fragrance-filled night when every courtier at Chambord graced the King's masked ball, it was difficult to know dream from reality.

From the pomander case hanging at Helena's waist rose a heavy musky smell like incense which made her senses dance and reasoning power slow. But, despite that, she knew, however real some of the people and events might seem, it was in truth the most vivid dream of all.

Pressed in the midst of a crowd, none of whom knew she was there, Helena could have panicked had not the scent from the pomander calmed and soothed her so that nothing seemed threatening. Not even climbing the staircase to the spot where stood that frozen beauty, that superb being who never smiled or showed emotion, the most beautiful of the beautiful, the Seneschal's widow, Diane de Poitiers.

Helena knew that all she had to do this evening to please her dear friend Catherine was simply to push the Widow through one of the observation bays in the staircase's hollow central column and watch from above as Diane crunched onto the distant floor below.

Then... Helena blinked hard as for a moment she saw clearly before the sensation passed. Then... she would stay and serve the Dauphine always, living with Etienne, but really being her friend Catherine's invisible servant, though everything would still be a dream.

The throng with whom Helena mingled suddenly began to climb faster, as if they had together received a silent signal, but straining her ears she realised what it was. The musicians on the first floor, seated between the window and the staircase, had struck up. Laughing to herself at the strange merry sound, Helena hurried with them.

It was then that through the pillars of the balustrade, she saw Diane, talking to he who loved her so much that he would publicly insult his wife. The Dauphin, dressed in black and white, his large eyes brimming with adoration, was just about to lead his lady out in the dance.

Helena's eyes swept the crowd for Catherine but there was no sign of her, nor of Etienne. She had been left quite alone to do the Dauphine's bidding, though the wonderful vapour which issued from the pomander was comforting, giving her courage. As she reached the first floor and joined the throng of dancers, Helena raised it to her nose.

She had not noticed the Vicomte ascend the other staircase, the one that spiralled above that which she had climbed, so that when he surreptitiously came up to her and murmured, "Follow me to the roof terrace, my dear," Helena felt quite startled.

"Must I?" she answered distantly, and was surprised when he wheeled quickly round to look at her more closely.

"What has she done to you?" he snapped, and sent the pomander flying from her hand. "Oh my dear heart, you've let yourself be drugged. Come into the fresh air."

Helena would far rather have stayed where she was, listening to the music and watching the ladies and their gallants.

"This is only a dream, Etienne," she said slowly. "You don't exist. Only Hal exists, but Madame says I would be happier staying with her than going back to him."

Her arm was almost wrenched from its socket as Etienne grabbed her hand at once and pulled her roughly towards the staircase, pushing his way unceremoniously through his fellow courtiers and dragging Helena behind him to where both the spirals came to the end of their secret joke. With his hand in the small of her back Helena felt herself propelled out onto the roof of the Chateau de Chambord.

She gazed on a different world, full of avenues and towers, the lantern dome huge as a church, the narrow walls looking out over magnificent vistas of forestland.

"Listen," said Etienne urgently, "the Medicis are known for their use of poisons and potions to achieve their ends. Whatever Catherine has told you is false. You must leave Chambord now, at once."

"But how?" she answered, not really caring.

"With me. We will go to my estates at Fleurmont. There you can be safe from the world."

"But does it matter when none of this is real?"

"The power of Catherine de Medici is always real."

Helena's brain cleared slightly and she remembered something. "But what about Leonardo's papers. Have you learned his secrets?" she asked.

"No," said Etienne briefly, "at least not yet. There are boxes and boxes of diaries and notes. I only skimmed the surface."

"Then what am I to do?" Now reality was coming back.

"Stay here and watch. When you see me come round from the stables with two horses run down the staircase and join me." He pulled her close to him. "If we should miss one another, come to Fleurmont. I shall wait for you there."

"I will come," said Helena, kissing him goodbye. "I promise you that."

Then he was gone and she was alone in the moonlight, staring down at the moat and the gardens, watching for the first sign of a rider. A dark shadow detached itself from behind a chimney stack decorated with a monumental salamander, emblem of King Francois.

"Come, little one," said Ruggieri, "it is time."

It turned from dream into nightmare as he took her by the arm, his fingers digging into her flesh, strong as wire, and led her down to the second floor where Catherine de Medici awaited him. Without a word they pushed Helena forward and she saw that two lovers stood on the staircase, locked in a deep embrace. She knew from the dark velvet of the woman's gown and the white lace that trimmed it, that she was looking at the incomparable Diane and her lover, so enamoured with her that he could not keep from touching his mistress, even though others observed them together.

Catherine smiled her dark secret smile and lifted the pomander so that the blue haze wafted into Helena's face.

"Remember this is only a dream, little one. Now do as I command," she said softly.

Hearing something, Diane de Poitiers looked up and Helena stared straight into that amazing face, quite chilling in its flawless splendour.

"It's cold," said the Widow. "I think the ghost of the staircase must be near by."

Henri laughed. "You don't believe that old story, do you. Come, my darling, would you like to dance again? As long as I am close to you I am happy whatever you decide."

In agony Helena looked as the couple kissed again, quite unaware that death stalked one of them in the shape of a girl who had yet to be born. Right behind her, hidden in shadow, she sensed rather than heard Catherine de Medici draw breath. So this was to be the moment, there could be no escape for her.

Taking off Etienne's diamond ring and closing her eyes, Helena rushed past the lovers and hurled herself bodily through the bay, plunging down and down into darkness, as somewhere in the dimmest of distances, a shrill bell began to ring.

*

A hand was reaching out towards her, a hand that Helena took so very gratefully and pressed against her cheek. She lay quite still then, feeling the comfort of the hand, and wishing that she did not have to open her eyes.

"Helena," said a familiar voice, "Helena, my darling, are you all right?"

"Yes," she whispered, though it was barely audible, "yes, I think I am."

"Then look at me."

Almost with reluctance, Helena raised her lids. She lay within the cramped confines of the staircase's central column; above her, at a distance that looked enormous, was the rearing vastness of the lantern dome. Between the dome and herself was Hal, leaning over her, holding her gently in his arms, and gazing at her with both concern and love.

"The Widow?" she murmured anxiously. "Did she fall too?"

"She's concussed," said a voice beside her other ear. "A doctor has been sent for."

Helena peered round and saw that men in uniforms, men who could only be security guards, stood in the doorway leading from the hall, shining torches onto where she lay.

"Can't you turn that alarm bell off," said Hal, but nobody made a move.

"Oh, my God," said Helena, frantically trying to sit up. "Please tell me what has happened and why you are here."

"Helena," said Hal, "don't move. You've had a nasty fall and you must keep still until a doctor's had a look at you."

"I didn't fall — I jumped. It was the only way out."

"Try to be quiet," Hal said soothingly. "The doctor will be coming any minute."

Helena rolled desperate eyes at him. "The date, Hal please."

"28th September, and it's two o'clock in the morning."

"2018?"

"Yes, of course."

Helena lay back, exhausted. "But if it's that time on the 28th it means I've been here only an hour."

Hal looked at her in bewilderment. "At the most. You see, I've been behind you throughout."

Helena stared at him bleakly. "You followed me?"

"Yes, I heard the car start up and watched you go from the bedroom window. I knew you had headed for Chambord."

"What did you do?"

"I hired a taxi, middle of the night though it was. I lost you when we got to the chateau but then I heard the alarm ringing."

As if Hal had put a spell on it, at that moment the bell stopped. "Apparently the guards found a window open, which had triggered off the mechanism, then they searched the chateau and discovered you here, unconscious."

"You mean that I broke into Chambord, wandered about for a while and then fell through the staircase?" She sounded amazed. "That's all that happened?"

"Yes, I'm afraid so. But you're alive and in one piece, or so I should imagine from the way you're moving. We might even get to celebrate my birthday today, if we're lucky."

"Oh, Hal," answered Helena, bursting into tears. "A very happy birthday, my dear."

They left France the next day, Helena having been pronounced fit, though somewhat bruised, and the officials at Chambord deciding to forget the whole affair. Leaving the Loire behind, Hal went west, making for the coast, but it was as they entered the Forest of Chandelais that Helena, who had scarcely spoken since her fall, saw a signpost marked Fleurmont.

"Hal," she said urgently, "please. I must go there. Bear with me just a little longer."

"You know I'll bear with you whatever, so long as you don't forget your promise."

"What promise?" she answered vaguely.

"To tell me before this holiday is over whether or not you are going to marry me."

"Has it occurred to you," asked Helena very primly, "that there might be something odd about me? Do you really want to marry someone who goes round breaking into chateaux and falling downstairs in the dark of night?"

"Yes, please," answered Hal, and they both laughed.

The village of Fleurmont was charming, centred round a village square full of flowers, as befitted its name. On the hill above sat the chateau, small compared to Chambord, yet large enough to be an imposing sight.

"If I buy the lunch," said Helena, "can we go there?"

"There's no need to bribe me," Hal answered. "We'll go if you feel up to it."

Helena would have liked to have been honest with him then, to have told him that the name meant a great deal to her; that in the dream she had experienced in Chambord, the owner of that particular castle had gone through a form of marriage with her. But common sense prevailed.

So it was with her secret held closely to her that Helena walked through the entrance and bought the English version guide book, finding herself in a long and beautiful hall round which hung family portraits. Almost as if it had spoken to her, Helena went immediately to the portrait of

Etienne which she identified in her guide as number sixty-four.

"This portrait painted in 1550," she read, "is of Etienne Charles, eleventh and last of the direct line of Vicomtes de Fleurmont. From a lively and handsome young man, as he is depicted here, Etienne – a friend and courtier of Francois I — became lonely and reclusive in middle age and the subject of rumour and gossip.

"Although there is no record of the Vicomte ever having married he always maintained that he had a wife who, for mysterious reasons which he would never divulge, left him for long periods at a time. Even when she was supposedly in residence, according to contemporary records, the Vicomtesse was never seen or heard and the servants conjectured that Etienne was mad and had no wife at all.

"According to his physician Dr Le Blond, however, the Vicomte was perfectly sane and he once glimpsed the Vicomtesse 'wearing outlandish clothes that did show both her legs'. A strange tale that brings a note of mystery to the lovely Chateau de Fleurmont. Whatever the solution, Etienne died childless in 1575, at the age of sixty-five, leaving no heirs but his cousins whose descendants are the present Viscomtes de Fleurmont."

As Helena's eyes filled with tears she suddenly realised that Hal was standing behind her.

"Darling," she said, without turning round, "would you mind if I did the rest of this tour alone? I just want to be private when I look round this particular chateau."

He smiled at her wryly, a lock of his hair falling forward as he shook his head.

"I'll go the other way. Meet you in the hall in half an hour."

In a daze Helena set off, seeing the table at which Etienne had eaten, the desk at which he had sat to write letters, then the beauty of his bedroom. Opposite the bed, which was as grand and formal as the one in Chambord, hung a painting in oils of Etienne and herself in very elaborate and elegant formal dress. She was wearing the Fleurmont diamond on her finger.

"Number seventy," Helena read, "is a portrait of the Vicomte and Vicomtesse de Fleurmont on the occasion of their anniversary. As this picture was painted by the Vicomte himself and as there is absolutely no evidence that the Vicomtesse ever existed, it is treated with suspicion by historians and is generally considered to be a work of imagination."

"A work of imagination," said Helena to herself with a slight smile. "I wonder."

It was almost a relief to leave behind the coolness of the chateau and step into the warmth of the sunshine, Hal's long body casting a shadow that consumed them both.

"What did you think of the place?" he asked, just a shade too casually.

"Wonderful. A pretty home in which to live."

"Did you see your portrait?"

Helena looked at him blankly. "My what?"

"The picture of you opposite the bed, painted by the eleventh Vicomte."

Helena pealed with laughter. "Now who's getting carried away! It was nothing like me."

"I thought it was, very."

"Well, I didn't."

They got into the car and Hal opened the sun roof, then bent to kiss her. "The Vicomte may have dreamed of you,

Helena, but I have the reality here beside me. I don't know whose wife you were, when, but will you be mine now?"

"Yes," she said, "I really will, Hal. For all of my waking life."

"That's an odd way of saying yes, but who cares. Here's to the future Mrs Tymon."

And with that Hal accelerated into the sunshine smiling more happily than Helena could ever remember.

*

The engagement party was held in John Holley's beautiful Georgian house five miles from Stow Wells, and was packed with friends and relations of both families. John Holley, his face a permanent grin, served champagne throughout the evening and there was a discotheque in a marquee erected near the lake.

"Never thought she'd do it," Helena could hear him confiding to his closest friends.

"And she most certainly wouldn't if you'd been given your head," retorted her mother. "Talk about over-kill!"

"As a matter of fact," answered John, pretending to be pompous, "I do believe that if it hadn't been for certain advice I gave Helena recently, she would still be dithering."

"Oh, and what advice was that?" said Sheila.

John laid a finger to his lips. "Top secret, my dear, top secret."

Dawn was coming up over the lake as the last guest departed and Helena said goodbye to Hal, sensibly going home in a taxi.

"See you tomorrow?" he asked.

"You can be sure of it."

She turned, then, to go into the house but out of the corner of her eye spotted her father, a bottle of champagne in one hand and two glasses in the other.

"Helena," he called, "come and have one last drink with your proud father."

They sat side by side on the seat set at the lake's edge, giving a perfect view of the dawn deepening scarlet over the parkland.

"Well, my girl," said John with a laugh, "there is something I really have to ask you."

"What's that?"

"Do you remember when you telephoned from France and told me you had met somebody else but didn't know how to contact him?"

"Yes."

"Well, did you take my advice? Did you seek him out?"

Helena looked at him over the rim of her champagne glass. "Yes, as a matter of fact I did."

John smiled knowingly. "And when you saw him again you found he didn't match up to Hal?"

"No, Daddy, not quite. As a matter of fact he and Hal are so different that one simply can't compare them. They come from two different worlds."

"But you've finished with him now?"

Helena gave a slow, secretive smile. "In a way."

Her father frowned deeply. "What is that supposed to mean?"

Helena stood up, her face glowing in the dawning.

"It means, dearest Daddy, that from now on I shall see him only in my dreams."

John's face cleared. "Thank goodness for that," he said, and finished the champagne as Helena went slowly towards the house.

The Mermaid's Kiss

After it was over, after all the sadness, the magic, after all the laughter and tears had gone, the island was left to itself once more. The house at first grew silent then, eventually, the wind and the weather took control and seeped into the fabric of the building so that it stood on the cliff tops, a sad sentinel of what it once had been. Round the Mermaid's Pool the planks of the wooden decking, the laying of which had been so carefully supervised by the house's builder, rotted and twisted into ugly shapes like misplaced teeth, and the skeleton of an old deckchair, its canvas long-since torn and shredded, flapped miserably in the breeze blowing from the ocean. And that was all that was left, all that remained to bear witness to the fact that once people had dwelled on the island, had made their home on a place that, perhaps, belonged to the sea itself. The sea which had, eventually, claimed it back.

Two girls who should have known better once walked across the clinging sand as the tide went out, their object to take hallucinatory drugs. They had climbed up the wooden steps, barely visible through the forest of weeds that had grown across them, and made it into the echoing spaces of the big house that sat on the cliffs. And there they had, giggling, injected the substance and sat down side-by-side on the remnants of a great Victorian sofa. And that was how they were found, a week later, by a coastguard who was out looking for them. He never forgot the expression on their young corrupting faces; a kind of ecstatic horror, a deadly awful bliss. After that, nobody went near the place and then, one night when a violent storm blew up, the old house had given up the ghost and collapsed into the churning waters at the bottom of the cliff. And that had been the end of it – or so it seemed. But from the end to the beginning, which means a step back in time.

On a fine spring morning in the year 1892, when the sea was the colour of hyacinths and there was that smell in the air, blown from the red Devon earth, which stirred the blood and filled one with the vague discontent that only an April day could bring, a bright green dinghy rowed into a small beach on an uninhabited island and moored up. Two men got out and looked around them. One was small and wiry, dark, slightly close-together eyes, a regular little compact fellow, the sort you would want to have by your side if a fight should break out. The other was entirely different. Tall, a military man, with a bright blue gaze and a neat brown moustache. His rank was major, though he was no longer on active service, having been invalided out of the army after a serious leg wound, obtained during the Boer War, a war that was finally grinding to a thankful halt.

Major Hugh Delamare was forty-two years old and quite an attractive man, though his success with women was pitiful. In their company he was reduced to a state of such overpowering shyness that, as a result, he had retained his virgin status into the present day, a fact unknown to anyone else, and only guessed at by some of his fellow soldiers. Hugh covered his unhappy tracks, joining in with somewhat naughty banter in the officers' mess, though one or two of the more seasoned campaigners had guessed at his guilt-free secret and smiled a little behind his back. But his batman, Jock Lennie, who had also been wounded at the battle of Talana Hill and who had returned to civilian life to become the major's valet, kept as silent as the grave if anyone should question him about it. Now, though, Hugh looked up at the cliff which rose above them.

"I say, Lennie, what a remarkable place. How do you feel about a climb?"

"It's alright by me, sir. Seems to have some sort of track going up."

The major nodded. "Probably an animal path. Come on."

They clambered up the hill as best they could, the Major's limping leg slowing their progress a little. Finally, though, they reached the top and stood gazing about them at the glory of sea and sky which spread before their eyes. It seemed as if they were joined, as if the whole of the ocean and the heavens became one, with only the thinnest of dividing lines. Revolving slowly, like two marionettes, the Major and his servant, could see on the far side of the island the lovely dip and curve of the Devon coast, a small town nestling the cliff top and then descending gently to the sea below.

Hugh turned to Jock. "The tide goes right out, doesn't it?"

"Yes, indeed. You can walk here at certain times of day."

"That would definitely be handy."

"What do you mean by that, sir?"

"Because I intend to buy the place." The Major gave a jolly laugh at the expression on his valet's face. "It's up for sale, my dear fellow. I went into the estate agent's office in Exmouth this morning. I have the particulars here in my pocket. See." And he thrust them under Jock's nose.

The valet took a few minutes to digest the facts, then said, "I take it you intend to build a house here?"

"In time. But first I want to walk right round and get the feel of the place."

They set off, following another faintly outlined path which led up a hill. Standing on the summit was a primitive brick building with a large square space in the wall which overlooked the ocean.

"What was this for?" the Major asked, puzzled.

"It's a pilchard hut, Sir. The wives of the fishermen used to go to it at daybreak and stand there until they saw a shoal at sea. Then they would shout and wave at their menfolk and direct them to the catch."

"Seems a bit unfair on the pilchards."

Jock shrugged. "No more unfair than the battles of war, sir."

But the Major wasn't listening, staring out to sea, where the blue deeps turned indigo and the ocean looked dark and disturbing.

"Bit remote this place."

"That's why I asked if it could be reached by land. I think a woman might feel too cut off from the shops and meeting her friends otherwise."

Jock looked up sharply. "Have you a particular woman in mind, sir?"

Hugh sighed, then smiled. "You would be the first to know, my dear Lennie. Alas there is no-one."

"That's a pity. Now, shall we continue our tour, Major?"

Half an hour later and they had completed the circular route and come back to the spot on the cliffs overlooking the cove where their little boat was rocked by frisky waves. There was a slight breeze coming up.

"Here's the place for my house, Lennie. Back where we started."

"It's a fine view, looking out to sea like that."

"And on the west side I shall have windows put in so that we don't lose sight of land."

"A good idea, sir." There was a pause. "Do you intend to live here alone?"

The Major gave a chuckle which was meant to be jovial but rang with the sadness of years.

"An old bachelor like me? Well, I'll just have to make the best of it, eh."

They clambered back down the steep path to where their boat was moored and stood momentarily, drawn to look at the ocean once more. Beyond the natural pool that was formed, the sea crashed over two rocks, blowing up a vast spume of frothing white. Gazing at them, Hugh suddenly tensed.

"Who's that swimming out there?"

Jock Lennie shielded his eyes with his hand. "Where, sir?"

"Between those two crags, where the sea is thundering white."

Jock peered. "I can't see anyone. Besides, it looks lethal water. I can't imagine bathing in it."

Hugh narrowed his eyes. "I wish I'd brought my binoculars. Meant to do so. Must have been an optical illusion but I could have sworn that I saw a great pair of arms threshing through the wave."

Jock smiled neatly. "It would have to have been Neptune himself, sir."

"You're right. Sound chap as always. Let's get back to the guest house, shall we."

They rowed back through a calm sea. Hugh was silent, wondering whether to put a bid in for Mermaid Island or whether he was just being fanciful. The fact was that for the first time in his life he actually had the funds to do so. His mother – who had turned into a vengeful old beast, mad and malicious – had recently died. In a way Hugh had been thankful, glad that the raging old hag who had taken his kind, gentle mother over, had gone for good. He had wept, in private of course, wouldn't do to show emotion publicly. But then had come his new-found wealth, inherited from his grandfather. It seemed that his mother's father had been a tea planter in India and as the sole heir, his mother had been left the entire profits from the sale of the business.

She had never said anything at the time, her dementia already giving her hidden enemies, but now for the first time in his life, Hugh felt comfortably off. His grandfather had been a wealthy man. It had put a slight saunter into his limping step.

He met Jock Lennie in the hallway of *Tide Ways*, the rather up-market guest house in Exmouth in which they were staying, taking advantage of Hugh's increase in funds.

"D'you know, Lennie. I've almost decided to buy that island. Do you think you could bear living there? I mean could you get around?"

"Why, yes, sir. The tide goes out twice a day and if we could invest in a small rowing boat, that would be ideal."

"But do you think a woman would like it?"

"That would depend on her, sir."

Yet despite the fact that there was no female remotely on the horizon, Hugh had architects draw up plans and rented a small villa in Maybury-on-Sea, the little coastal town to which Mermaid Island was attached. That is to say twice a day at low tide, regular as clockwork.

Though he often spent hours on the island, watching, with satisfaction, the building of his dream house, Hugh had never spent a night in the place. Yet once, when the tide was in full flood and there was no sign of Jock Lennie's reliable rowing boat, Hugh had found himself sitting on the clifftop, watching as the sun sank. The sky had slowly turned the colour of ripening plums and a little breeze had come up. A breeze that had whistled round the rocks and sounded like a voice singing, an unearthly voice, pitched somewhere between mankind and the stars. It had sent a shiver down Hugh's unimaginative spine and he had been glad to see his manservant pull into the inlet below him.

They had not spoken much on the journey back, both preoccupied with thoughts. The Major eventually said, "Can you hear the wind, Lennie? Sounds just like singing, doesn't it?"

His valet cocked an ear. "Can't say that it does, sir. What makes you think that?"

"Oh, it's just my old fanciful nature, I suppose. While I was waiting for you it was if something was chanting aloud. It quite startled me."

"The wind can play funny tricks. Sometimes it sounds quite human."

"Yes, you're right. It does. But it was an odd illusion though."

"Think no more about it, Major. We're nearly back now."

And looking over his shoulder, Hugh could see the welcoming – and somehow comforting – lights of Maybury-on-Sea drawing ever closer.

Major Hugh Delamare had spent some of his recently acquired money on renting a small bright beach hut in which he changed into his bathing costume for his daily dip in the sea. This was usually done in the late afternoon when the tide went out and he could walk back from Mermaid's Island, then on to his hut. Yet, one day, whistling and cheerful, he had decided to change his routine and go for a morning swim instead. He had entered the cosy confines of the beach hut and carefully locked the door – or so he thought. But somewhere, somehow, fate deemed otherwise. At the precise moment that he had stripped off every item of clothing and was standing stark naked, facing the entrance, the door flew open and he was left standing, horror struck and embarrassed, in full view of the passing parade.

Two women who were out having a morning stroll turned their heads at the sound of the door opening. One, the younger, a little delicate thing with a sweet high neck and a pair of large dark eyes, gazed in frank astonishment. Hugh, with a muffled cry, put his hand over his penis, but other than for that stood rooted to the spot.

The girl continued to stare, not lasciviously, but with large-eyed wonderment and Hugh knew at that moment that she had never seen a naked man before. That she was an only child with a somewhat overbearing mother. Sure enough the girl's companion said, "Millicent, don't look."

But those soft and gentle eyes were still regarding the web of reddish hair that covered the Major's chest and groin. And then he saw the delicate skin of the neck deepen in colour and rise up to the creamy cheeks before the girl finally tore her look away.

Her guardian stepped forward and slammed the door in his face, saying "Pervert," quite distinctly.

Hugh stood aghast, momentarily frozen, before he locked the door tightly, then climbed into his two-piece bathing costume, knee length drawers and a shirt, making sure that as little of him was visible as was possible. Then, timorously, he opened the door and peeped out. There was nobody about so he seized the moment and literally raced down the beach and into the sea. He was a good swimmer and struck out boldly, doing an impeccable crawl. But thoughts of that delicate girl kept penetrating his consciousness.

He saw again the curve of the fragile neck, the dark hair, tendrils of which had escaped the confines of her hat and tumbled down in little tiny ringlets, the sincerity of that wide child-like gaze. And as he remembered her Hugh felt stirrings in the lower part of his body and enjoyed a few moments of guilty pleasure. Then as his mind dwelled on the girl, at that precise second, as if by a miracle, he saw her again, walking with her companion – Mama presumably – right at the end of the promenade. He knew then, however difficult it was going to be, that he must see her and try to explain those few disastrous moments that she, nonetheless, had seemed to have found compulsive.

As luck would have it Hugh was out to take afternoon tea at the Esplanade Tea Rooms, sitting solitary and letting his eyes roam over a mouth-watering collection of edibles, when he was aware that someone had come in and was standing at his side. Looking up, his gaze widened and he jumped to his feet with a broad smile.

"Archie, old chap. What a pleasure. I haven't seen you since Africa. How did you know I was here?"

The new arrival, bald as a coot, gleaming blue eyes, large hay-coloured moustache, ginger tweeds, said, "I didn't, dear boy. Sheer coincidence. Got an old aunt who lives hereabouts. But tell me, how's life treating you since you retired from the army?"

"Well, very well. But please join me. Have you got a spare thirty minutes?"

"Absolutely. The old girl – going a bit gaga now, alas – is having her afternoon snooze so I'm just wandering about, killing time as if were. I'd be delighted."

Over the tea cups the two men discussed their various fortunes, Captain Archibald Arbuthnot – known to his friends and family as Archie – bemoaning the fact that he had married a rather silly girl.

"She was the sister of old Teddy Dalrymple, you know. Anyway, she ran off with a park keeper and left me on my own-y-oh. Had to divorce her – awful palaver that – and now here I am, footloose and fancy free. What about you, old fellow?"

For some reason, perhaps because he had been longing to talk to someone about the terrible incident in the beach hut, Hugh found himself confiding in Archie, describing his profound shock as the door had swung open to reveal him as nature intended. He did not, however, describe the expression on the girl's face as she had taken in the detail of his naked body, nor the profound innocent wonderment in those arresting amber-coloured eyes.

"But now the problem is, Archie, however do I explain it all to them? The old mother called me a pervert."

Hugh's friend chortled, inadvertently losing a little of his egg sandwich. "No problem, my friend. I shall leave it all to my auntie. She may be gaga but she knows everyone around – and that includes the visitors. She will give a small soiree and invite both the old dragon and her beautiful daughter. And you, of course."

Hugh went red with pleasure. "If you can do that for me you will have earned my deepest thanks."

"Think nothing of it, old chap. I shall enjoy myself immensely, watching who will win the contest, you or the elderly Mama."

"So you think I might lose?"

"If Mrs. whatever-her-name-is truly believes that you are a man who fiddles beneath a dirty raincoat, yes."

Hugh's honest face fell. "But it would be so untrue, Archie. It just wouldn't be fair."

"What in life is, dear boy? Think of all the dying and the dead we saw during that beastly Boer war. Was it fair on any one of them to meet their end as bitterly as they did? So, I'm afraid old thing that you'll just have to take your chance."

Hugh nodded glumly. "Yes," he sighed. "If I'm prepared for the worst it won't seem quite so bad."

But inside he knew that a certain spark would wither away and never return if he could not become better acquainted with all the innocent loveliness that was Millicent. Thoughts of falling in love at first sight came to him then, and he wondered if that was what he had experienced. Had he been pierced by Cupid's dart? It was just such a jubilant thought, so romantic and silly, that a broad grin spread over his features and he found himself humming about the house.

Two days later Archie's Aunt Effie went into action, sending out little invitation cards. And as she was the Honourable Mrs. Frederick Etherington she did not get one single refusal. It seemed that all her neighbours were most keen to join her for a Soiree Musicale.

She had employed two local amateurs to provide the musical services. One was a glum looking boy, suffering from a terrible attack of acne, his hair, gingerish and wiry, reusing to yield to a mountain of hair cream and sticking up like a brush. The other was an eager woman in her early thirties with a terribly weak soprano voice, who smiled constantly and fluttered a large piece of chiffon which was attached to a minute elastic encircling her finger.

Aunt Effie, who had been tipped off by Archie as to the importance of his friend the Major being introduced to all comers, did so in a very loud boom.

"Mrs. George Dwyer and Miss Millicent Dwyer," proclaimed the butler from the door.

"Ah, my dear Mrs. Dwyer. So nice of you to call. May I introduce my nephew, Captain Archibald Arbuthnot," Aunt Effie said, narrowing her gaze and adding meaningfully, "And his friend Major Hugh Delamare."

The smile which Mrs. Dwyer had pasted on her lips in preparation dropped as she cast eyes on Hugh. But before she could say a word, Archie came in.

"Dear lady, I see you look askance and I can only presume from that that poor Hugh's twin brother Cyril has shocked you in some way." Without pausing for breath he continued. "Poor Cyril was badly wounded in the head during the recent war and I'm afraid that it left the poor soul with the terrible habit of removing his clothes in public. Things finally came to a head when the King went to visit the wounded in hospital and Cyril, stark naked, bent to kiss the Queen's hand. After that he lived in seclusion with his alienist. But dear Hugh has given the poor man – I refer to the doctor, of course – a short holiday and is currently entertaining Cyril at home."

During this monologue Mrs. Dwyer's eyebrows had shot up and down with breath taking rapidity while poor little Millie went pale.

"Was that the man we saw in the bathing hut?" she whispered.

"If he was naked, then the answer is yes. Poor Cyril. He is to be greatly pitied."

"And poor Major Delamare for having such a thing happen to a member of his family," the girl answered.

"Indeed, indeed," said Archie, looking at Hugh with very bright eyes. "Well, if you'll excuse me, ladies, I must return to my aunt's side. I shall leave you with the Major."

Mrs. Dwyer raised her lorgnette and stared at him with a rather fanatical gaze. "And what have you done with your brother tonight?"

Hugh, who had had no idea of what yarn Archie had been about to pitch, gazed at her blankly and then gathered his wits. "He is being cared for," he answered slowly. "I have left him in good hands."

Millie spoke up. "It's such a sad story, Major Delamare. Think of losing all your faculties whilst serving your country."

"Better than being killed," Hugh answered, a note of cheeriness entering his voice.

"I suppose so."

"And you suppose right, Miss Dwyer."

"This conversation is far too serious for young people like yourselves," put in Mrs. Dwyer. "Come Millicent. You are not to bother the Major with your childish chatter."

Hugh spoke up. "May I say that I think your daughter's views are most interesting, Madam. But you are right, of course. It is not the occasion for serious conversation. Now, may I get you ladies some refreshment?"

And so the evening wore on. The glum boy looked even glummer as he produced a series of wrong notes on the pianoforte, the quavering soprano launched herself into all four of the Indian Love Lyrics with mixed results. Mrs. Dwyer applauded frostily while Archie stamped on the floor and shouted 'Bravo' several times. Hugh got slightly tipsy and couldn't take his eyes off Millie, who grew in beauty the more he looked at her. Strangely, despite the paucity of performance, he had felt moved by the words and music of the Love Lyrics and decided that their composer, Amy Woodforde-Finden, must have been quite an exotic person.

"What did you think?" he whispered to Millie as the thin applause died away.

"I found the songs... disturbing."

"So did I," he answered, wondering how he was going to contrive another meeting. But in that there was a surprise in store. As the soiree ended and Mrs. Dwyer clutched her furs and Millicent to her noble bosom before departing, she turned to Hugh who was hovering in the doorway.

"Do you have to stay with your brother all day?"

Archie piped up, a fantasist to the last. "He's going home tomorrow, isn't he Hugh."

The Major nodded dumbly, too full of turbulent thoughts to speak.

"In that case, Major Delamare and Captain Arbuthnot, I invite you both to dine with Millicent and myself. Shall we say the day after tomorrow? Would that be in order?"

Hugh spoke up at last. "I do apologise for any distress I might have caused you and your daughter, Mrs. Dwyer."

She looked at him with narrowed eyes. "It *was* Cyril in the beach hut, was it not?"

"Of course it was," Archie responded cheerily.

After they had gone Hugh looked at him, shaking his head from side to side.

"That was the most appalling yarn you've ever spun, you know."

"Saved your bacon though, didn't it."

"Yes, I'm in your debt, old friend."

"Well, in future, whenever you're caught doing something bad you can blame it on your brother Cyril."

Having taken their leave, they stepped outside and both men shivered slightly. The night was as clear as glass and the sea was singing its relentless eternal canticle of waves tumbling onto the shore. Hugh's gaze automatically turned towards his island – and then he froze, standing stock still, peering into the brilliant light thrown by the million stars that glinted in the vivid night.

"Look," he said hoarsely, grabbing Archie's arm, pointing out to sea.

"What?"

"There. On the island. Can't you see a light?"

"Where?"

"On the headland, where the house is being built. In fact it looks as if someone is inside the very foundations."

"Yes, you're right. I can see a lantern bobbing about."

"I must go there at once. They might be vandals."

Archie laid a restraining hand on his friend's arm. "My dear Hugh, be sensible. The tide's in and you can't possibly take a boat out in the darkness. Go there in the morning."

"But there's somebody on the island."

"Well, whoever it is has gone now. The light's disappeared."

But despite Archie's best efforts Hugh would not be quietened. He walked briskly to his guest house and there he paced the floor for a while and eventually woke Jock Lennie.

"Sorry to disturb you, Lennie, but there's something amiss on the island. Saw a light out there, bobbing about. Captain Arbuthnot saw it as well. My plan is to walk over as soon as the tide goes out and catch them at it."

"At what, sir?"

"At whatever they think they're playing at."

It was a seashell dawning. The sky, pink as coral in the east, majestic as the dark deep depths in the west, slowly succumbed to the relentless arrival of day. The sea was sighing as it rolled back the water. In its voice one could hear the constant pull of stones and shells, murmuring and growling. A chill and numbing wind blew over the waves as the two men walked across the wet sand towards the island.

They were completely alone. Not a mortal thing passed them. It was as if they were the only two beings in the dawning of a new world. Jock broke the immense silence.

"We've seen no-one so whatever you noticed is still on the island, sir."

"Unless they swam for it."

"Now that is a bit fanciful if you don't mind my saying so. It would have to be an Olympic champion."

"Lennie, I know you're mocking me but I can assure you that Captain Arbuthnot saw the light as well. We're not on a fool's errand."

"Very good, Major."

But though they searched the entire length and breadth of Mermaid Island, nothing was there. Hugh had made straight for the house's foundations but there was no sign that anyone had been present. It was as if the light must have been a trick of the eye, an hallucination.

"Do you know what I think it was, sir?"

"No, tell me."

"I believe that a fishing boat was moored out at sea and what you saw was the reflection of its lamp moving with the swell."

Hugh frowned. "I suppose it could have been. But that didn't occur to me at the time."

"Well what other explanation could there be, sir? I mean we've searched the island; we didn't pass anyone walking over the sand. It speaks for itself."

"Yes, I suppose you're right."

But still the Major was doubtful, his belief that someone – or something – had been on his property never quite leaving him.

The dinner with Mrs. Dwyer was relatively successful, though Hugh had not much to say for himself, too busy staring at Millie and knowing that he was hopelessly, helplessly, drawn to her. That she – sweet innocent soul that she was – was the woman that he wanted to marry and spend the rest of his days on earth with.

Archie did most of the talking and after the ladies had withdrawn briefly, leant across the table and said sternly, "Listen, old boy, you're going to have to speak up. It's no good gazing at Millicent as if she's the first woman you ever saw. You'll have to ask her out to a tea dance or something."

Hugh looked at him helplessly. "Archie, I'm not used to this kind of thing."

"Obviously. Why not ask her mother if you may pay your addresses to her daughter?"

"But what happens if she says I can't?"

"Don't be ridiculous. You're a good catch. A retired major with a small fortune. It's what every widowed mother with girls to marry off prays for."

"Then I shall engage her in private conversation."

As they were leaving, Archie gave Hugh a surreptitious nudge and drew Millicent's attention to a small discreet brooch she was wearing, saying how much he admired it and how similar it was to something his sister possessed. Hugh, realising that his moment had come, bowed solemnly before Mrs. Dwyer.

"Madam," he said, his voice suddenly gruff, "would it be acceptable if I were to call formally upon Miss Dwyer."

She stared at him for a moment, then dropped her eyes.

"I take it, Major Delamare, that you have no other attachments."

"None, Madam, let me hasten to assure you."

"You are somewhat older than is customary for a gentleman caller."

"That is because I have been an army man all my life. To be perfectly frank with you, Millicent is the first young lady that I have ever felt drawn to."

Her head was bent, her face unreadable. Then she finally looked up and smiled graciously.

"Then you have my permission to leave your card. But do not rush her, mind. She is a thoroughly respectable young lady."

Hugh was so grateful that he felt a moment's dizziness. Then he collected himself and bowed once more.

"Then I will, if I may, take Miss Millicent out to coffee tomorrow morning."

"Of course. I shall sit at another table in order to keep an eye on you both."

And in that way the somewhat laboured courtship began. After the first dozen or thereabouts assignations, however, Mrs. Dwyer left them to their own devices and so it was that at a military reunion, with Hugh looking handsome in army regalia and Millie enchanting in pink tulle, they exchanged their first kiss.

Hugh had kissed a dozen or so young ladies in his time but this experience was quite new to him. He felt a wave of passion that rocked him to the core. Almost involuntarily his tongue came out and pushed against her tightly compressed little mouth. She drew back sharply.

"Why are you doing that Hugh?"

"Don't you want me to?"

"I don't know. I don't think so."

"Oh let me try. Please Millie darling."

"Oh very well."

"I'll stop if you really don't like it."

But she did like it, eventually opening her lips beneath his and returning his ardent caress. Hugh was in heaven as Millie fell back breathlessly in his arms.

"Oh Hugh, I feel so strange. I can't explain it."

"But did you enjoy it, Millie?"

"Oh yes, very much."

"Then shall we try again?"

"It wouldn't be proper, Hugh. I could not look Mama in the face if I did."

"But, dearest little girl, I want to marry you. I love you with all my heart. I knew it when I first saw you."

"I don't know about marriage," she answered, not coyly but thoughtfully. "There are several years between us."

"Is that your way of saying I am too old for you?" he had asked, hurt beyond words.

"No," she said, then again, "no. I love you Hugh. It's just that I have a feeling we are not meant to be together."

"Whatever do you mean? What are you saying?"

"I don't know. It's just a thought I've always had. That I cannot bring happiness to a man."

"But that's rubbish. You have made me terribly happy, deliriously so. And you could make me the happiest man that ever lived if you would just say yes to me."

Millie frowned. "Are you sure of that? Certain?"

"Of course I am, dearest girl."

She was silent for a moment or two and then said in rather a sad little voice, "Then you will have to ask Mama."

And Hugh did so, the very next day. After only a few minutes hesitation Mrs. Dwyer, dark-eyed, agreed and Millicent was called in from the other room, where she had been sitting patiently trying to read a book. Wasting no time, Hugh and she set off in a carriage to Exmouth to buy a ring, deciding on a sparkling aquamarine, the colour of the sea which ringed the island.

Realising that in his intense courtship of Millie, Hugh had left the overseeing of the building work on Mermaid's Island under Jock's ultra-reliable guidance, he now hurried to put this matter right. The day after the announcement of his forthcoming marriage to Millicent appeared in The Times, he personally rowed his fiancée across from Maybury-on-Sea to the place where they were going to live. The first stop was at the little bay that Hugh intended to convert into a swimming pool.

"I thought we could surround it with planking on which we can place garden furniture, deck chairs, you know the kind of thing."

Millie's beautiful eyes had turned on him a sweet, sad look. "I can't swim, Hugh dearest. I shall feel such a ninny just watching everyone else."

"But I shall teach you, my sweet. You will soon learn I promise you."

Unexpectedly, Millie gave a deep shiver.

"What's the matter, darling?"

"I don't know. Sometimes I feel terribly afraid."

"Of what?"

"Nothing, everything. Oh Hugh, don't question me so."

She turned away, her dear little face so miserable that Hugh felt a sudden guilt, as if he had committed some terrible sin. But even as he was asking himself what, Millie turned and buried her tearful self against his chest.

"Oh, don't be cross with me, Hugh. I know it is childish but I really can't help it. I've always been the same."

"But what *is* it that scares you, Millicent? If I knew perhaps I would be able to help you."

"As I said, I'm not sure what it is. Perhaps it is the sea itself."

"Then, darling, this would be the wrong place for you to live. I shall have to sell the island and look for somewhere inland."

She pulled away from him and stared up into his face.

"No, Hugh, no. That would be an awful thing to do. I shall live here with you and be incredibly happy. Besides, you told me that twice a day we are joined to the mainland. I shall happily walk across and take tea with friends and go shopping and... and..." She burst into a full-blown fit of weeping and the Major, puzzled and out of his depth, took her into his arms and made silly little useless 'there, there' noises.

Jock, watching them from the top of the path, felt saddened and worried for them both, but he merely smiled and nodded as they gained the summit, and said, "I hope you'll be pleased by what you see, Miss Millicent."

And she was. Her face changed to one of joy and she clapped her hands together in delight.

"Oh, Hugh, it's wonderful, like a beautiful pearl. I wasn't expecting anything like this."

The exterior of the house was complete. It stood three storeys high, the bare windows overlooking the sea as if they were challenging it, daring it to be rough or unpleasing. And Hugh, staring at his dream house, thought that the team of builders had done him proud and erected a place of beauty and grace that he would be delighted to call his own. But the transformation in Millicent was patent. She ran through the empty front door space and looked about her with wonderment.

"Oh Hugh, it's so beautiful," she exclaimed. "I never pictured anything quite like this. I love the house. I am sure it will protect me."

Her odd choice of word was neither noticed nor remarked on. Hugh simply put a fatherly arm round her and said, "I'm so glad, dear girl."

But Millicent was not looking at him, craning her neck upwards. "How many bedrooms will there be?"

"Five, not including our dressing rooms of course. The servants will sleep at the very top."

She clapped her hands together, like a child in anticipation of a sweet. "How big a staff are we going to have?"

"I thought of three or four maids – including a lady's maid for yourself, sweetheart – and a footman to help out Jock Lennie, who will act as butler. And a cook. We can't forget her, can we. And, perhaps, a gardener and boy. But they can live on the mainland. Would this be agreeable to you?"

And Millicent, who was as soft as a kitten and could be equally as charming, said, "Whatever you think best, Hugh," and snuggled close to him.

It was a pretty wedding, held in the ancient church of St. Mary's at Winterbourne Abbas, the village being the bridal home. Hugh's old regiment had rallied to his side and he and Millie stepped out beneath an arch of drawn swords, before making their way in a carriage trimmed with white to the reception at nearby Church View House, owned by friends of the family who had kindly loaned their home for the occasion.

Hugh had wanted something larger in which to have his wedding breakfast but in the end sense had prevailed and the old house had echoed with the clink of glasses and the merry peal of bells, still ringing as the couple stepped from their chaise and were showered with rose petals by the village children. At the end of the day Millie had changed into an adorable outfit, a far too sophisticated travelling dress topped with a tiny feathered hat which made her look like a little girl dressing in her mother's clothes. Hugh's heart was bursting with new-found joy as he escorted her into the landau that was to carry them to Weymouth and their honeymoon.

The wedding night was something that he preferred not to think about however. He had fumbled inexpertly, had reached the climax too quickly, and when he had sought Millie's privy parts with his hand – as he had been advised to do by Archie Arbuthnot – she had shrunk away in horror. It had not been a happy experience for either of them. The next night had been no better. Millie had lain beneath him, rigid and uncomplaining, as Hugh had repeated the previous performance. For him there had been a moment of intense pleasure, for her nothing at all but soreness and pain.

Other than for that they were happy. Millie was thoroughly taken up with choosing wallpapers and furniture for the new home, and though she and Hugh were still living in the rented villa in Maybury, she plunged merrily into overseeing cascades of curtaining and ordering everything that could possibly be thought of to set up a house. Hugh, meanwhile, was puzzling over how the heavier items of furniture could be transported to the new dwelling, which now stood complete, visible from all directions, a gallant building on the headland of that beautiful, lonely island.

It was Jock Lennie who finally worked it out.

"A tractor could get through the water when the tide was low, sir."

"Yes, I realise that. But how could one get a large dining table – or come to that, a sofa – onto a tractor?"

"Suppose that one built a sizeable cabin on top. Wouldn't that be enough?"

"Yes, by Jove, I think it would. If I draw it out perhaps we could arrange with a local chap to put it into practice."

"Good idea, Major. Perhaps it could be adapted to contain some seats."

"Now that *is* a splendid plan. Millie could go into town whenever she felt like it with that sort of machinery."

"Not quite, sir. Everything would depend on the tide."

"Of course. Just for a moment I had forgotten that the ocean rules us all."

But in that way the idea of a sea-going tractor had been born and Hugh and Jock spent many happy hours with a local mechanic deciding how exactly it would work. Millie, utterly preoccupied with damask and chintz, was too busy to notice their absence, though she was always welcoming to her husband when they finally met up at seven-thirty for the evening meal. It was only afterwards, in the privacy of their bedchamber, that she grew distant, often going to the window to stare out at the moon shining on the water below. Hugh was almost afraid of her when she stared like that. Curtains drawn back, she would sit motionless on the window sill and gaze out at the relentless rise and fall of the sea.

"Come little Millie, let me give you a goodnight kiss."

She would sigh then and reluctantly turn away, shutting the drapery behind her.

"Don't you want to kiss me, my darling?"

"Yes, I do. It's just that I am rather tired."

For once Hugh felt marginally irritated. "Really? Or is that just an excuse?"

"You're horrible to say such things to me," Millie answered, and looked so childish and pathetic that all the bluster went out of Hugh immediately.

He took her into his arms and, as always, standing so close to her had its habitual effect. Her dressing gown fell open at the front and the contours of her boyish body seemed to melt into his. Hugh gave her one of the deep kisses that she seemed to have enjoyed before and though she returned it, it was not with any genuine enthusiasm. Deep inside him, he sighed. He faced the prospect that he had married a cold fish and the rest of his days were going to be spent without the bliss of ever enjoying a full-blooded sexual relationship. He would just have to concentrate on other things, he thought.

Over the next two weeks he and Millicent were frantically busy organising things for the move to Mermaid Island, while a team of decorators, who had walked over in a body when the tide was out, had camped there for the whole of the time. Hugh had passed one of them coming back for provisions as he had made his way to inspect their progress.

"Hello Dave, how are you enjoying your stay?"

"It's all right, sir. That is apart from the singing."

"Singing?" Hugh exclaimed. "What singing?"

"Every night, just as the sun is going down there used to come this singing in a weird voice. We all heard it but Bert said it was the wind. But it didn't sound like no wind to me."

"Oh yes. I know what you're talking about. I heard it once when I was on the island late. Like a low chanting.

But I can assure you that it was the wind. I mean what other explanation could there be?"

Dave had put his head on one side thoughtfully. "Could be the Mer people."

Hugh stared. "Mer people. But there are no such things, my friend. Nobody's ever seen a mermaid, have they?"

"My Da did. Told me of it when I was just a little chap. Pulled her up in his nets when he was out in the deeps."

"And what did he do with this fantastical creature? Fall in love with her?" Hugh chuckled, though deep inside him he grew grave cold.

"Nothing he could do, Major, she be dead, d'you see."

Hugh was slightly stunned though he let none of this show on his face.

"So what happened? Did he throw her back in?"

"Yes, sir. He thought that was the Christian thing to do. To throw her back to her own people. But not before he'd cut a little bit off her hair. Kept it forever, he did. In a little leather pouch."

"And did you see it?"

"Indeed I did. He got it out for me to look at just once. It was bright as guinea gold."

To have made scoffing noises would have been insulting. Dave clearly was telling the truth as he saw it. So Hugh merely tipped his hat and went on his way to the island. Yet the man's words rung in his head. How easily, he thought, could that evening wind be mistaken for an unearthly song. And the Mermaid's hair. Bright as guinea gold! Why he could almost visualise it. But then he was in the West Country and legends of Mer folk and little people abounded in Devon and Cornwall.

The decorators had done a splendid job on his house. They may have been a gang of superstitious locals but Hugh's future home was rigged out to perfection. A spacious hallway, with a drawing room, a dining room and a morning room leading off it, achieved final splendour in a conservatory, inside which Millie could order plants both rare and domestic, assisted by a gardener of course. She ran through the rooms clasping her hands in pleasure, exclaiming aloud as Hugh lit one of the gas lamps – a pipe supplying gas had been installed under the sea – and it glowed brightly. Chandeliers glinted everywhere, their diamond facets reflecting that glorious sea light and dancing on the walls as they were moved by a little breeze. Hugh watched her and then took her to a smaller room, the door of which he opened with a little chuckle.

"This is going to be my den, darling. The place where I shall withdraw to read the papers in the morning while you will be organising things in the house."

She frowned. "Are we able to get newspapers here?"

"Of course, I shall walk across as soon as the tide goes out and fetch our mail and anything else we might need. It will be my constitutional."

"Will you be gone long?"

"Of course not. I shall be back before the sand vanishes again. Why do you ask?"

She turned to him. "Because I like having you close by."

"Not at night though," Hugh muttered under his breath.

"What did you say?"

"Nothing, my darling. Come, let me show you the next floor."

They walked, hand-in-hand, up the beautiful baroque staircase which curved elegantly to the rooms above. The master bedroom was glorious, with windows overlooking three sides, giving the impression that it was painted blue. But it was an optical illusion created by the reflection of the sea. Millicent rushed to the front and leaned forward, her hands on the low sill, kneeling on the window seat which was yet to receive its cushion and where – or so Hugh had thought when he had ordered it built – one could sit for hours, gazing outwards, indulging in a sea dream.

"I know what we must call this house," she said, without turning to look at him.

"What name are you thinking of, dearest?"

"It shall be called *Sea Tryst*. Do you like that?"

"Very much," he answered, coming up behind her and putting his arms round her waist.

"It's not too fanciful?"

"No I don't think so."

But Millie was no longer listening to him, instead craning forward and peering at something. "Who's that swimming down there?" she asked.

Hugh followed her pointing finger and had a momentary fancy that he saw a powerful male torso tumbling and turning in the mighty white wave that ceaselessly pounded between the two rocks that formed the far end of what Hugh already thought of as the Mermaid's Pool.

"Do you know I thought I saw something swimming there when I first came to the island. Obviously I was wrong."

"But there was somebody, Hugh. I saw him and I know I was not mistaken."

"But, darling, you must be. No-one could bathe there. They'd be dashed to pieces on the boulders. Truly."

She turned and looked at him, childlike in her innocence. "Perhaps it was a seal."

Hugh felt his love for her well up and possess him utterly. "You're right, my dear. That explains it, of course. It was a seal."

The next few weeks were busy ones for Millie. She had finally moved in, riding over in the sea tractor amidst a motley collection of new furniture – a satinwood suite, a piano made by John Broadwood, crimson hangings for the master bedroom, blue draperies for the drawing room, a vast collection of whatnots, clocks and candelabra. To crown all an exotic Arabian bedstead. Then had followed the wonderful task of getting everything into its rightful place.

Hugh, meanwhile, had started work on the conversion of the Mermaid's Pool into a suitable area for swimming. The rough path leading down to the place was turned into a smart wooden staircase with handrail, decking had been laid round two-thirds of the area, and then Millie had been given the onerous task of choosing items of garden furniture, together with thoroughly modern canvas seats and deckchairs from the Army and Navy catalogue. She had been like a child with a bowl of luscious sweets. Hugh had never seen her happier than in this period of their life together and he patted her dark head whenever he passed by her chair, where she sat poring over the things on offer. Eventually, though, the swimming pool – together with a small diving board – was ready and waiting. Millie put in her order and in due course the faithful sea tractor chugged across bearing the many goods she had decided upon.

"Time you learned to swim, my dear. There's no need to be afraid. I promise to hold you tightly."

Millie looked at him, slightly nervously despite the fact that she was smiling.

"I'd better buy a costume then."

Jock took her across to Maybury-on-Sea in the little motor boat that the Major had acquired and which he often used to go ashore. Hugh, resolutely keeping away from women's shopping, decided to go with her and retire with his papers to one of the little tea rooms where he could read for half an hour in peace. But his wish was not to be granted. A hand darkened with age spots rattled the papers under his very nose and a woman's voice said, "Mind if I join you?" It was the Honourable Effie Etherington, elderly aunt of Archie Arbuthnot.

Reluctantly Hugh rose to his feet. "No, dear lady, it would be my pleasure. Please sit down and tell me how you are."

She lowered herself into the seat opposite his and the smell of ancient lavender and cracking face powder wafted in his direction.

"I'll have tea," Effie told the hovering waitress. "You know how I like it – strong and immensely hot. And a toasted tea cake with plenty of butter." She turned her attention back to Hugh. "Tell me how is your brother Cyril?"

Momentarily, the Major was puzzled. Then the memory of his naked form in the beach hut and the look on the faces of the passers-by made him colour to his ears. He swallowed hard, trying to think of something to say but Effie spoke for him.

"Dead is he? I guessed as much by your expression. Ah well, better out of it with his nasty affliction. Harsh to say but hearing the truth is not easy."

Hugh nodded agreement, very ill at ease.

Effie continued. "And how's that little wife of yours. Archie told me all about the wedding. Good girl, is she? Too cowed to be anything else I should think with that ghastly mother. But then, I mustn't speak ill of your relatives."

The Major was dumfounded. He knew that Archibald's aunt was highly eccentric but her blunt speech was bordering on downright rudeness. Nevertheless, she was elderly and one must take that into account, he supposed.

Effie was ploughing on. "Of course, one can't blame the poor child for being so under the thumb. After all, Mrs. Dwyer has been very good to her. Adopting her like that."

Hugh found his voice. "Like what? What are you saying, Mrs. Etherington?"

"But surely you knew that Millie was adopted by that old bore calling herself her mother?"

Suddenly realising that if he denied it Aunt Effie would be silenced, Hugh nodded his head in affirmation.

"Yes, I know the rough details. But please continue."

"Well, I heard from a cousin of theirs who knew the family well that there were two sisters, Ada and Lettice – damn silly names in my opinion. Anyway the elder one – being our Mrs. Dwyer – managed to take the younger one's boyfriend away. One can't imagine how – or, there again, perhaps one can. Anyway Lettice was broken hearted and accepted a governess's job with a Dutch family in Rotterdam. There she fell into the Rhine – attempted suicide I ask myself – but was fished out again and sent home to England. Only to discover, my dear, that she was pregnant. Apparently she wouldn't – or couldn't –

say anything other than repeating the same sentence over and over again."

"Which was?"

"He pulled me in, he pulled me in. Poor thing. Lost her wits entirely."

Hugh gazed at her, feelings of sheer amazement filling him. Could Effie possibly be completely senile or was what she was speaking by chance the truth.

"I see you look startled, Major Delamare, but surely you know the story. How Ada must have been overcome by conscience that she had stolen poor Lettice's sweetheart away. So she nursed her sister as best she could."

"No I... I don't... not completely. Did Lettice die then? What happened?"

"She had gone off her head and had to be committed to an asylum, gave birth to Millicent in the wretched place. Succumbed a few days later to puerperal fever. Ada came and took the baby and brought it up as her own. Never told Millie apparently. But there, I've said too much. Yet secrets have a way of coming out, you know, however hard you try and sit on them."

To say that Hugh was dumbstruck was to understate the case. He just sat in horrified silence, quite unable to make any comment, gazing at Effie Etherington as if she had just delivered the death sentence. And in a way she had. To think that some poor pale creature, of whose very existence he had not had so much as a glimmer until a few minutes ago, was the birth mother of his beloved Millicent. And this gave rise to ghastly thoughts of who her father had been. Some drunken sailor wandering round the port looking for his next victim, rape on his mind and a hardness within his trousers. It did not bear considering. Rather abruptly, Hugh stood up.

"I have another appointment. Forgive me, Mrs. Etherington. Allow me to pay for your refreshments."

That said, he put some money down on the table and blundered out.

He must have wandered down to the harbour because Jock Lennie was there talking to some of the local men tending their boats. One look at his master and old fighting companion's face and his servant knew that something was badly wrong.

"Sit down, sir. Here, on this little wall. In a while can you speak to me about what's happened?"

Suddenly Hugh could. It was a relief just to talk, to tell someone else the truth about Millie's mother, knowing that Lennie would rather die than pass on a word. He sat in silence, gazing at the ground, not so much as asking a single question, listening as the Major repeated the story he had just been told. In the end, when there was total quiet, he spoke.

"What makes you think the poor woman was raped by a low-life dock prowler?"

"It's obvious surely."

"Not at all, sir. I should think it was the son of the house that is to blame."

"What do you mean exactly?"

"You have only to look at Mrs. Delamare to see that she comes from good stock. Believe me, I've seen some rough craft in my time and they leave their stamp, I know it. From what I can gather Miss Lettice – disappointed in love – is offered a job as governess to the children of a prosperous Amsterdam merchant. But supposing the family has an elder son, a university student say, or perhaps a young officer?"

Hugh's face brightened a little.

"Suppose that he and Lettice fall in love at first sight but that the Mijnheer refuses to hear of it, says that he planned on his son marrying the daughter of another wealthy merchant. But the couple have already consummated their love. The young man is sent away and Lettice is given notice. She tries to kill herself but her life is saved. She comes back to England like a whipped dog and then discovers she is pregnant. That is the more likely scenario, sir."

"And that is what sent her mad?"

"Undoubtedly. One sorrow upon another. Enough to rock anyone of a strong constitution, let alone a frail one."

The Major nodded silently. "Not a whisper of this, Lennie, to anyone. Particularly not Mrs. Delamare. She must continue to believe that Mrs. Dwyer is her actual Mama."

"You have my word on it, sir."

"But what of Mrs. Etherington? Supposing that Millie should run into her in a tea room. She is quite capable of blabbing the whole story."

"I would simply say that the poor woman is deluded. That the senility of old age is upon her."

Somewhat relieved, though not entirely certain that Jock's yarn was the truth of the matter, Hugh got to his feet. And for the rest of that day felt a sense of unease whenever he remembered his encounter in the tea room. But later Millie returned from her shopping trip in triumph, two brand new swimming costumes, each wrapped in delicate tissue, side-by-side in an expensive ribboned box.

"Are you going to give me a fashion show?" Hugh asked, trying to be merry but thinking all the time of the green glass waters of the Rhine closing over the head of a desperate girl.

"Of course I will, dearest. But shall I meet you down at the Mermaid's Pool?"

"A splendid idea. And I can give you your first swimming lesson."

Millie nodded, somewhat reluctantly, and Hugh hurried down the newly-built staircase and there discreetly changed into a striped bathing dress. He was followed some fifteen minutes later by his wife, self-consciously walking down the staircase, looking highly desirable in a sailor-suit knee-touching dress, a pair of knickers which came to mid-calf, black stockings and black pumps rounding off the effect. Hugh gazed at her lovingly, wishing that she would return his great passion of which, as she had demonstrated just once at the officers reunion dinner, she was extremely capable.

"Ready for your lesson, my dear?" he called jovially.

"Yes, I think so," she answered nervously.

"Remember I'm going to hold you and won't let go, I promise you. By the way, you look very beautiful in your bathing clothes."

"I thought you were going to say bathing suit," she answered cheekily, gasping as she went down the ladder and the cool waters of the swimming pool engulfed her.

"We could always swim in the altogether," Hugh responded, "on a warm summer's night when nobody could see us."

She looked at him seriously. "I think it would be too cold for me, dear. I find the water quite chilly."

Even his mildest of naughty suggestions were turned down flat or just not understood. Inwardly Hugh sighed to his heart.

Millicent was not a natural swimmer. She tensed in his firm hold and her legs kicked wildly, not coordinating with her arm movements at all. She also swallowed a great deal of water and ended the lesson by bursting into tears and shrieking when a great wave broke between the two rocks that stood where the sea came into the Pool.

Hugh tried to be gentle with her. "That will be enough for today. You did very well, Millie."

"I didn't," she answered wretchedly, climbing out, sitting down on one of the many chairs and shivering violently. "I hate swimming."

"There, there, darling. We'll try again tomorrow. Go on up to the house and change into some warm clothes. I'll just do a few lengths and join you."

He was glad to see her leave and feel free to push out towards the sea. Hugh was a strong swimmer and liked nothing better than to do a brisk crawl, keeping his face below the surface of the water, only raising it to snatch a breath. In this way, he came near to the rocks and suddenly felt himself drawn into the current of churning water that flowed between them. And it was at precisely that moment, just as he was kicking hard to turn and swim away, that he felt his leg touch something. It was not painful, no subaquatic jarring, but something that instead was cold and slithery. Hugh could not account for what he did next. He took a deep breath and plunged his head below the surface. Just for a second he thought he saw a glint of glittering scales and a large fish's tail but then he was knocked sideways by the fierceness of the current and had to fight to get control and himself out of the broiling ocean. Finally, he did so, and was never more glad than when he reached the rungs of the small flat entry ladder he had had put in on both sides of the Pool. Hugh climbed out and collapsed into a deck chair, somewhat shocked by his recent experience.

An hour later, warmly clad and much revived by a large whisky and soda, he was sitting in front of a fire, for the evening had grown nippingly cold in the way of late summer nights. Millicent sat opposite him, looking particularly lovely, her profile etched against the rose red curtains which were half drawn so that there was a glimpse of the spectacular sea, bonfire scarlet as the sun gasped its last.

"Did you enjoy your swim?" she asked quietly.

Hugh lied. "Very much indeed. But you're right. The water was a bit chilly. I'm afraid that autumn is approaching fast. Are you sure you're going to like it here when the weather gets rough."

"I can still walk across when the tide is out."

"But if there's a fierce wind blowing it might be rather unpleasant."

"I could always go and stay with friends for a few days."

"Yes, I suppose so," Hugh answered sadly, then before he could control his words asked, "You do still love me, don't you?"

Millicent put down her embroidery and looked at him. "What a strange question."

"Not really. I suppose you must think me a dull old stick sometimes. It's not as if you have a child to keep you occupied."

The second the words were out he regretted them for Millie blushed an unbecoming red and turned her head away.

"Oh, dearest, don't. I didn't mean that as a criticism."

She wept bitterly and soundlessly, a fact that moved him to the heart. In a second he was on his knees beside her, holding her tightly, feeling her sad little body racked with sobs even though no sound was coming out.

"I'm sorry," she gasped eventually.

"Oh darling, it is I who should be apologising to you. It's not your fault. I'm certain of it. I shall go and have a word with my doctor, an army man. He'll tell me straight."

But of course the medical man couldn't. When Hugh left his consulting room he did so with a downhearted tread.

"There's no way of knowing, Major Delamare. I suppose one could reckon that with the passing of the years the chances of siring a child might lessen. But then one hears of old fellows becoming fathers in their seventies. Keep trying, my dear chap. Just keep trying."

And he gave Hugh a hearty wink which hadn't cheered him up in the least. Nor did the change in the weather. Autumn was golden, looking around him through his pair of binoculars, the Major could see all the glorious colours subtly changing, the sea turning to deep shades of indigo. But then, inexorably, winter followed with savage gusty blasts. The landscape became grey and the sea like iron. The smart new house, built so daringly on the headland of an island, shook like a baby's rattle in the rages of the savage wind.

One day a storm, hideously severe, blasted Mermaid's Island so cruelly that the inhabitants of the house did not dare leave it for fear of being blown off the cliffs and onto the rocks below. For the first time ever, Hugh suffered from claustrophobia and poor Millie was forced to lie down, crippled by a severe headache. Outside the rain hissed out of an ashen sky and the sea was lashed into a vast, frenetic, frothing beast. Within the house the servants crept round, hardly daring to raise their voices. Only Jock Lennie sat unperturbed, reading a newspaper, glasses half way down his nose.

Dinner was served at 7.30 to where Hugh sat solitary in the dining room.

"Is Mrs. Delamare not coming down?"

"I don't know, Major. I'll make enquiries."

The footman disappeared but came back a few minutes later. "I've asked her maid, sir, but madam is not in her room."

Hugh looked mildly surprised. "Oh. When she returns tell her maid to enquire if she would like something sent up."

He started on his soup, fearing that it might grow cold, but by the time he had finished it had become slightly impatient.

"Would you make further enquiries as to my wife's wishes."

This time the footman returned with a flustered Mary Ann, Millicent's personal maid.

"Oh sir. I don't know where Mrs. Delamare is. I thought she must be in the water closet but I tried the door and it opened. I've been up to the servants quarters and searched there. I can't think where she can have got to."

Hugh shot to his feet. "Well, she must be in the house somewhere. I'll organise a search."

As usual it was Jock Lennie who took charge and deputed himself, the Major and all the available servants to search a floor thoroughly, the gardener and boy – stranded on the island because of the deplorable weather – taking on the conservatory and the greenhouse. Half an hour later they all met in the library. Millie was not in the house.

Despite the terrible weather, despite the fact that the wind was dangerous and the rain of the sort that would soak you to the skin in five minutes, all the men set out, wearing waterproofs and wellingtons. The boy, only thirteen years old, was told to search the gardens then go indoors. Meanwhile the women huddled and the cook prepared steaming broth.

Jock had sent the Major and Dawkins, the footman, off to look in the Pilchard Hut area. He had chosen the lower coastal area. He searched the Mermaid's Pool first of all, hearing the ocean thundering furiously against the far rocks. Flashing his torch round the furniture, glad that he had had the foresight to collapse all the deckchairs and parasols, he could see that the seats were empty. Not a sign of life. Yet, an hour later, when he was drenched to the skin, his hands white and raw with clawing his way round the cliffs, something made him go down the treacherously wet wooden steps once more.

She was sitting there, quite still. Her hair soaking and clinging round her shoulders, her breasts like two marble spheres in the light of his torch. For Mrs. Delamare was stark naked, not a stitch of clothing on her, motionless as a statue where she sat in one of the garden chairs.

Jock called out. "Madam, are you all right? We've been looking for you for hours."

Millie did not speak, did not even turn her head, sitting still as death, white and blanched in the flickering flashlight. Gingerly, Jock descended the last few steps, clinging to the hand rail. She did not even turn her head in his direction as he approached, staring out to sea, her expression totally blank.

"Come on, madam. You can't sit there like that. You'll catch your death."

Millie made no reply, as if something had touched her and she had turned to ice. Just for a second Jock wondered if she were dead but the rise and fall of her chest reassured him. He put out his hand and gently took hold of hers.

"Here, put this on." And he took off his soaking waterproof and covered her nakedness. Then, step by faltering step, he led her up the stairs toward the house.

The women were still huddled in the kitchen but Mary Ann came running into the hall when she heard the sound of footsteps. She took one look at Millie and her hand flew to her mouth.

"Oh madam," she gasped. "What has happened to you?"

Millicent turned her glacial stare in the girl's direction but did not utter a word. Jock handed her into the maid's care.

"Get her warmed up and put the poor creature to bed. Is the Major still out?"

"Yes, no-one's back accept the boy. Where's she been?" she added in a whisper.

Jock shrugged. "Just wandering I imagine. I'll go and find him."

He set off once more, without any protection against the rain, his shivering waterproof still draped round Millie's naked shoulders. Meanwhile Mary Ann coaxed her employer up the stairs, talking to her sweetly, almost as if she were a child, then into the master bedroom. There she stripped off the waterproof and felt the icy chill which inhabited the poor woman's frame.

"Oh, madam, you're so cold. Stand there, in front of the fire. I'll send for some hot water and give you a wash down. Try to warm you up a bit."

Whether Millie was grateful or not, whether she felt any emotion at all, was not clear to the servant, who hurried about her tasks with an air of quiet desperation. Right in the back of her mind Mary Ann wondered if Millie had lost her senses, whether her ordeal in the cold and the wet had actually unhinged her. She stood implacable and mute while her maid washed her in warm water and tucked her into a thick nightgown before snuggling her into a bed heated by as many hot bottles as the house could muster. When Millie was finally settled, Mary Ann turned to her.

"Can I get you something to eat or drink, Madam? Is there anything you would like?"

But Millie was neither looking at nor listening to her, her eyes fixed firmly on the ceiling with a blind, sightless gaze. A commotion in the hall downstairs heralded the return of Hugh, who came charging up the staircase and into the bedroom, where he knelt down beside the bed and lifted Millicent into his arms.

"Oh, my little darling," he said, his voice muffled to hide the fact that he was on the verge of tears, "thank God, thank God, you've been found."

She lay impassively in his embrace, her gaze still on the ceiling, and to Mary Ann, quietly slipping out of the door, the thought returned that her mistress had gone out of her mind.

"She's gone barmy," she whispered to Cook, in the silence of the kitchen.

"What d'you mean?"

"Well, she doesn't seem to know anyone, not even the Major. Something awful must have happened to her outside, though I can't think what."

Cook shivered. "I reckon this island is haunted. I think it's an eerie place."

"Oh go on! It's lovely in the summer. Beautiful really."

"You've got your opinion and I have mine," Cook answered emphatically. "There's something odd about this spot and that's all there is to it."

The storm blew itself out at about midnight and Hugh, who was sitting in the library, drinking brandy and worrying himself silly about Millie's wretched apathy, thought that he should finally go to bed. Jock Lennie had retired over an hour ago, worn out by the night of searching. But Hugh had lingered, not wanting to disturb that pale, silent figure – looking so small and so still in the great marital bed. Eventually, though, he climbed the staircase quietly and undressed in his dressing room. Then he opened the interconnecting door and tiptoed into the bedroom.

Millie was still awake, or at least her eyes were open. Her hair, dried out now, spread over the pillow like a net, giving the fragile face within a sad but somehow exotic look. Quietly Hugh blew out the candle and plunged the room into darkness.

A hand reached out under the sheet – it could only have been Millicent's – and reached for his private part, which she began to agitate until Hugh, gasping, felt it grow large and hard. Then she was upon him, riding him, stripping off her night gown and bending her mouth to his, sucking kiss after kiss out of him. At last, he thought wildly, at last she has become passionate, her tongue seeking his, the thrust of her small body that of a vastly experienced woman.

"Oh God, Millie," he shouted out in ecstasy, then he rolled her onto her back and took control of every move, lunging into her without a care, plunging deep into her until at last a great feeling, a sensation like one he had never experienced before, swept over him and he bellowed a great cry of pleasure as he discharged mightily and magnificently. But she was shrieking too. Giving out a cry of satisfaction as they remained locked together, until Hugh, overcome by an immensely pleasurable fatigue, finally fell asleep.

In the morning he awoke, glowing with pleasure, but Millie had resumed her posture of the night before and was so deeply asleep that only a cad would have disturbed her. The sole evidence of the hectic lovemaking was her nightgown, which lay on the floor like an abandoned flower. Hugh's penis stirred at the very sight of her and he had to plunge into a cold bath to cool off – a bathroom had been installed in his new home, a modern idea indeed.

But his jaunty happiness came tumbling down when he went to thank Jock for rescuing Millie on the previous night.

"I'm so grateful to you, Lennie. You truly are a miracle worker."

"That's all right, Major. I was glad to be of help. How is the lady this morning?"

"Still asleep when I left the house."

"Has she spoken yet?"

Hugh cast his mind back, recalling that at the end of that fantastic lovemaking Millie had let out a throaty scream of ecstasy, but that she had not actually said a word.

"No. No I don't think she has. Why do you ask?"

Jock looked Hugh straight in the eye. "It occurred to me quite forcibly that Mrs. Delamare was in deep shock and as a consequence had lost her voice. If I were you, sir, I would get a doctor to look her over."

"She didn't say a word to you?"

"Not a solitary one. Neither did she turn to look at me. She seemed to be frozen, just staring out to sea."

Hugh shuffled his feet. "When she wakes up I'll go and have a word with her."

"You'll be lucky to get one, sir."

And with that dry comment the Major had to be content. But things turned out very much as his former batman had predicted. Millie neither smiled nor wept, laughed nor cried. In short, her facial expression did not change from one hour to the next. She was, in behaviour, exactly as she had been when Jock had found her, totally frigid. And nothing could shake her out of it. She allowed Mary Ann to dress her, she let her husband put her in a chair by the fire, and though he gave her a book she would not read it nor even look at it. Millie just stared into space for hour after hour and though Hugh longed for the return of that passionate girl who had, just once, driven him to the heights of abandonment, she never came back.

A doctor had been sent for and then a specialist from Harley Street. They had both looked grave.

"I've never seen such deep post shock withdrawal," the Harley Street man had said. "It confounds belief. I would suggest hypnosis as a treatment if you would be willing, Major Delamare."

In despair Hugh had agreed. But Millie had made a low guttural sound in her throat on seeing the hypnotist and had averted her eyes from him. It was the greatest reaction that anyone had managed to bring about but for all that the man left the island without success.

Then one day when Hugh sat in the library, reading yesterday's newspaper, there had come a polite knock on the door.

"Come in," he called.

It was Mary Ann. She curtseyed. "Sorry to trouble you, sir."

"Not at all. Come in and close the door."

"It's about Mrs. Delamare, sir."

Immediately, Hugh was filled with alarm. "What's happened? Is she ill?"

"Not exactly. No."

"Then what is it?"

Mary Ann hesitated, but she was a country girl and had seen nature in the raw on her father's farm.

"It's about her courses, sir," she said firmly.

"Her what?"

"Her monthlies. The condition women have every four weeks," she added as Hugh continued to look blank.

"What about them?"

"They've stopped. There's been no sign of them for two months. As God is my judge, sir, unless it's something else that's wrong, I'll swear that Mrs. Delamare is in the family way."

Mary Ann paused, wondering if she had spoken too bluntly. But the expression on Hugh's face set her mind at rest. It was one of pure, unimaginable joy. His whole sad expression changed to one of ecstatic elation.

"Are you sure?"

"As sure as I can be, sir. I'm not a doctor."

The local man had been sent for and came across from Maybury-on-Sea in the sea tractor. Millie had been impassive when he examined her, her eyes fixed firmly on the windows. She had not even looked at him when he had said, "You're going to have a baby, Mrs. Delamare. Aren't you delighted?"

Just for a minute she had turned her gaze on him and the doctor had thought it was like looking into the eyes of a child, completely guileless, innocent of all the wickedness in the world. Downstairs, Hugh was greeting the announcement with another kind of childlike happiness.

"My dear Doctor Ellsworth, this is wonderful news indeed. It is probably the best thing I could possibly hear." The Major's face had fallen. "But how will this affect Millie? I mean, she's no longer quite – normal – is she? Mary Ann copes very well but do you think in the circumstances I should get a live-in nurse?"

Dr. Ellsworth stroked his small pointed beard, looking serious. "I would answer, when Mrs. Delamare begins to grow in size, I think it would be a splendid notion."

Hugh regarded him with earnest eyes. "Has she any idea of what's going on?"

The doctor looked at him straight forwardly. "I am not an alienist, Major, so I really can't say. But if you want my opinion, it is that your wife has reverted to childhood and has no conception – if you will forgive the pun – that she is carrying a child. I do not envy you, sir."

"But what will happen when she goes into labour?"

Dr. Ellsworth looked grey. "We will just have to cope as best we can, sir."

The trouble lay in the fact that Millie's face never changed its expression. Her features showed no emotion whatsoever, she opened her mouth to eat, closed her eyes when she went to sleep. The doctor's likening of her to a child was only true in one regard. Children smile, cry and are animated, Millie's appearance never changed whatever the circumstances.

Every day Mary Ann got her out of bed, took her by the hand to the water closet, then washed and dressed her. She would sit in front of the dressing table mirror and stare blankly at herself while Mary Ann arranged her hair. Then she would walk downstairs for breakfast. After that her routine was always the same. In the finer weather Millicent would sit in the garden, a book at which she would never look, on a small table beside her. She would stare at the ocean for hour upon hour, and once – just once – gave a great cry and rose to her feet as if something had attracted her attention. Mary Ann had rushed to her side saying, "What is it, Mam? What has startled you?" But, as usual, there was no reply, no clue, everything seeming as normal other than for the fact that the ocean had broken a bit wildly at the entrance to the Mermaid's Pool.

In this way the spring passed tranquilly enough. The Major, consumed with guilt, sometimes felt so full of raw desire that he had mounted Millie in the darkness of their bedroom and pushed into her, thus achieving a kind of satisfaction. She had lain beneath him, utterly unresponsive, and afterwards he had usually crept off to his dressing room where a single bed lay waiting. Once he had wept but had taken himself to task for being a sissy fellow.

A month before the expected confinement, a resident midwife had come to live on Mermaid's Island and the doctor – complete with a young man who had just qualified and was being shown the ropes – came over daily on the sea tractor. In the final week, by Dr. Ellsworth's calculations, the junior, Dr. Nixson had offered to stay in the house. An offer that Hugh eagerly took up as the younger doctor was extremely good with Millicent, chatting to her for hours on end even though he never got a reply.

It finally began in the middle of the night. Hugh was woken by a firm rap on the dressing room door. Jock Lennie stood there.

"I'm sorry to bother you, sir, but we thought you should know. Mrs. Delamare has gone into labour."

Like a true soldier, the Major leapt out of bed.

"How is she Jock?"

"She's got the young doctor and the midwife at her side so there's nothing to be alarmed about."

"But how is *she?* Is she suffering much?"

"I don't know, Major. I am not admitted into the delivery room," Jock answered primly.

And when Hugh knocked discreetly on Millie's bedroom door he was faced by the midwife who said, "Your place is downstairs, sir."

"I was just enquiring...".

But he stopped short as he heard an unearthly sound. It was Millie's voice, not screaming or shrieking, but letting forth a hollow noise, like someone calling into a shell. It unnerved Hugh horribly, the very notes like the distant tolling of a sunken bell. Then from within the room came the voice of Dr. Nixson.

"Good, good. Now ride the waves, my little Ondine."

Startled, Hugh turned to Jock. "What is he talking about?"

"He's just trying to soothe her. Now come on, sir. Don't fret. Mrs. Delamare is in the best of hands."

Hugh went downstairs, somewhat unwillingly, wishing that he had been allowed one glimpse of his child wife, as he thought of her these days. But Jock's generous measures of whisky eventually calmed him down, enough to have him dozing as the sun rose in full glory, dying the sea crimson as it raised its scintillating head above the horizon. The birth of the sun was echoed by another birth upstairs. As the pink fingers of daytime crept into the Major's study, so there was the distant mewling of a newborn babe.

Hugh woke up in a haze of whisky to hear the distant but distinct sound. He took the stairs two steps at a time but still was discreet enough to knock on the bedroom door. Once admitted, he did not know where to look first. The baby was lying in a cot, well wrapped up but making little noises which proved that it was alive and well. The sight of Millie, however, brought a great sob of emotion from his throat.

She was lying on the bed, dressed in a clean, fresh nightdress. Her dark hair was spread round her as if it had been brushed out, her eyes were closed. The midwife stood in a respectful silence, Dr. Nixson was drying his hands on a towel, somewhere in the background came the sound of muffled weeping. Hugh knew then, without even having to ask, that it had been too much for his Millie. That she had left him, stepped out of life and gone who knows where? Crossing slowly to the bed, the Major knelt, and taking one of her pale hands in his, silently shed desolate tears.

After a while, he did not know how long, he felt Jock's touch on his shoulder.

"Are you not coming to look at your son, sir?"

Hugh stood up. "A boy? You say it's a boy?"

Dr. Nixson stepped forward. "A healthy child, Major Delamare. But let me offer you my sincerest condolences on the loss of your wife. She was, alas, too unaware to take part."

Hugh gazed at him. "What do you mean exactly?"

"The strains of labour were too great for her. It was if it was happening to a child. She couldn't understand what was taking place and she just – shut it out."

"Do you mean she died deliberately?"

"In a way, yes I do. Now, do you want to see your son?"

And Hugh felt his arm being seized, gently but firmly, as he was led towards the cradle.

Its occupant looked up at him in quite an extraordinary way, though Hugh – knowing little of babies – did not remark it. The infant's eyes were not the dark colour of the newborn but instead were a highly individual and sparkling shade of radiant sapphire. Large, startlingly so, and amazingly vivid for one so new to the world. Hugh gazed at him and his chest heaved in a muffled sob, partly because poor sad Millie was no longer there and mostly because she had left behind this wonderful little creature to be what he had always wanted, a son and heir.

Dr. Nixson came over to the cradle. "There is just one thing you ought to know, Major Delamare."

Hugh looked up at him. "And that is?"

"The boy was born with a fine membrane over his legs. But it is nothing to worry about. I shall remove it immediately. It is not a case of sirenomelia let me hasten to assure you."

Hugh stared at him blankly.

"That is a when babies are born with their two legs fused together. This is not so in the case of your son. Do you wish to see?"

"Best to take a glance, sir," Jock whispered behind him. "After all, the operation cannot proceed without your agreement."

Hugh nodded, his heart beating too fast to allow him to speak. The doctor pulled aside the blanket covering the baby's body.

Hugh had seen some sights during the Boer War, had torn his eyes from horrendous deaths and had even delivered the *coup de grace* to some begging for their suffering to end. But nothing prepared him for the sight that awaited him.

The bottom half of the baby's body – from the genitalia downwards – was covered with a tissue thin skein, so thin that one could see through it. Both legs were there, perfectly formed, and as Hugh looked on in a mixture of horror and wonderment, they gave a little kick outwards as if they were trying to free themselves. Dr. Nixson spoke.

"You can see for yourself, Major. It is merely a transparent membrane. Do I have your permission to proceed?"

Hugh nodded, too overcome by a million differing emotions to utter a word.

"Then I would ask you to leave the room."

Somehow the Major shuffled out and stood on the landing, lit by a large window overlooking the sea.

"There's a rough ocean going today," said Jock quietly.

Hugh broke down. "She's gone, Lennie. My poor little Millicent. She died having my child."

"She wouldn't have minded, sir. Bless her heart but I don't think she got much out of being alive. Not after the storm. But think what she's left you. A beautiful son. What are you going to call him?"

But Hugh did not answer, listening intently to hear his child cry out when the membrane was incised away. But there was no sound, only the muted voices of the doctor and the midwife talking together. After a while, the door opened and the nurse put her head out.

"You can come in now, Major. Baby is ready."

Hugh walked up to the cradle but even before he could look at the child's legs, the little creature gave him another brilliant glance from those incredible eyes. A glance that seemed to announce he was here and was looking forward to life and all that it had to offer. The midwife approached.

"The operation's all done, sir. Do you want to see?"

"Of course," Hugh answered. "But first tell me. Was it a complete success?"

"Totally."

And it was true. The bowed baby legs were already kicking outwards as if to make clear that their encasing shroud had gone. The Major looked round for the medical man.

"Where is Dr. Nixson? I owe him my sincere thanks."

"He must have passed you on the stairs, sir. He noticed that the tide was out and he's walking back to Maybury. He told me to tell you that you should call the child Benedict."

Hugh looked at her, slightly askance. "Benedict. Good gracious. I wouldn't have thought of that. I was thinking of something more formal. But indeed I do like it. It means 'blessed', you know."

"And you have indeed been blessed, sir. For a bonnier newborn infant I have never seen," put in the midwife.

The Major turned back to the cradle. "Hello, Benedict, my son."

And the infant kicked its tiny legs and listened, yes listened, to the relentless pounding of the waves against the rugged shores of Mermaid Island and, though no-one could see it, smiled a little smile.

It was as if the sun shone on the Major from that day forward. Nothing could lower his spirits, not even the funeral of poor Millicent at the country church in which she had been married. Sad though the occasion was, all he could think of was getting home to his infant son. And so the golden years began to unfold, with Benedict laughing his way through childhood and making Hugh happier than he had ever been in his entire life.

The boy grew up handsome, with a mass of hair, a bright rich red, the vivid shade of autumn fire. This, together with his wonderful eyes and easy-going temperament, ensured that everyone who met him, loved him. He just had that way with him, he was quite naturally and without affectation, charming.

Because the Major could not bear to be parted from him for any length of time, Benedict (in full; never Ben) was not sent to boarding school. Instead, excellent tutors arrived to stay on Mermaid Island, finding their pupil ferociously intelligent and eager to please. As far as anyone could see, the child only had one fault. And that was his addiction to the Mermaid's Pool.

When Benedict had been barely two years old he and his father, accompanied by Jock Lennie, had walked down the wooden steps to the swimming pool and stood on the side, looking to where the sea foamed and broiled round the distant rocks which guarded the entrance. Benedict, held tightly in the Major's arms, had suddenly given an eel-like wriggle and had plunged into the water below before anything could be done to stop him.

Hugh had gone white and made to dive in to rescue the child but had paused on the decking edge, open-mouthed. For Benedict, fully clothed as he was, was swimming like a fish, his small arms and legs cutting through the water with a strength that his father would not have thought possible if he had not seen it with his own eyes. In the end it was the resourceful Jock who had fished the child out, calling him by name and watching as the boy steered himself to the side. The Major did not know whether to laugh or cry and ended up doing both simultaneously.

"Oh Benedict, Benedict! That was a very naughty thing to do."

"Now don't be too cross with him, sir. The child's a water baby. He has a natural gift. He'll probably end up swimming the Channel."

"But, Lennie, my boy could have drowned."

"But he didn't did he, Major. If he were mine I'd teach him to swim properly. And quickly at that."

And having learned over the years that Jock Lennie's advice was always well heeded, that is what Hugh did. Soon Benedict's swimming was legendary. Trophies were won and placed in prominent positions throughout the house and some years later – a great prank – he swam from Mermaid Island to Maybury-on-Sea on a particularly rough day. The dressing down in Hugh's study was inevitable.

"Benedict, whatever were you thinking of? I mean to say, that journey is perilous. I really must forbid you to attempt such a thing in the future."

Inwardly Benedict sighed. He was now twenty years old and had virtually no friends or social life to speak of, other than for one roguish fellow he had saved from drowning. Holiday maker Jonathan Oates – known to everyone as Titus – had got caught in a treacherous current quite far out and was starting to sink beneath the ocean's waves. Benedict had realised Titus was drowning and had swum down deep so that he had come up underneath him, lifting the inert body high above the water. Where his strength had come from, Benedict never queried. He had always known that his power lay in the sea. In there he was king, on land he was just an ordinary bloke, devoted to his dear old dad, educated beyond belief, and desperately lonely.

Now he spoke. "But Father I can manage that kind of swim. You know I can. It's in my blood."

"I can't think why," Hugh answered irritably.

Even as he said the words a vision came into his head. He saw a lonely girl walking by herself, absently staring into the tranquil mirror of the flowing river, gazing down into its unfathomable green, when a pair of arms slowly – oh so slowly – rose up out of the depths and pulled her beneath the surface. Had this been what had really happened to Millicent's mother?

But Benedict was speaking. "Would you mind, Father, if I went to stay in London for a few days. Titus has invited me and I would very much like to accept."

The Major dragged himself back to the present day. "When would this be, this trip?"

"Next week. You liked Titus, didn't you? He came to stay here in the spring and offers this visit by way of thanks. I should so enjoy going."

"He has a house in Belgravia, you say."

"Yes, frightfully swish. His father is something high up in the Foreign Office. You would approve, sir, truly you would."

Benedict knew he was pleading but didn't care. Titus had written to him that he was going to give a party and was hiring a jazz band to play. And all this because his parents were in Scotland shooting innocent birds. After all, it was 1925 and sons of the house – and daughters – were revelling in the freedom of the Jazz Age. And Benedict secretly wanted to be one of them. Something that dear old Hugh intuitively guessed.

"My dear child, we were discussing your swim to Maybury not a visit to London. But of course you can go – and with my blessing. You say it is next week?"

"Yes, it's this coming Friday. Thanks, Papa, you are so big hearted."

And with one of his impulsive moves, Benedict gave his father a resounding kiss on the cheek, his brilliant blue eyes grateful yet sparkling with mischief.

Now we must leave Hugh for a while, to read the papers and sit in the sun. The tale for the moment must change to the adventures of Benedict.

It was the first time that he had travelled any great distance from home, Jock Lennie driving him in the car that the Major kept at Maybury-on-Sea to Ivybridge station, where Benedict – looking smart as paint in a brand new fashionable outfit, of which Hugh did not approve – mounted a train to London.

Entering a first-class compartment, he saw that several occupants were already within. A small sad-looking man, with an equally dull wife, wearing a hat shaped like a cowpat on one side of her iron locks, were glaring uneasily at a third passenger who sat nonchalantly, one leg crossed over the other, reading a newspaper and utterly ignoring them. He was dark, obviously of foreign extraction, a slouch black fedora hat with a white band, which he wore well pulled down, giving him a slightly raffish air. He was smoking a cigarette in a holder. The fourth person was a heavily made-up blonde, painted lips parted in an ingenuous smile which deceived no-one, sitting in a corner.

Benedict, well brought up by Hugh, bowed and said, "Is this seat engaged?" pointing to the one opposite hers.

"No, do take it," she answered and gazed at him appraisingly. The elderly couple glared, obviously hoping for someone more their type to occupy the empty space. Disappointed, they dived into a bag the same colour as the woman's chapeau and fished out a pack of sandwiches which they solemnly started to eat.

The man in the fedora hat lowered his paper, said, "How do you do," to Benedict in an accent foreign and thrilling, then the whistle blew on the platform, and the chug and stir of the mighty wheels told the young man that he was off on his great adventure. Attempting to look nonchalant, he opened a copy of Punch and pretended to read.

After a while, the foreign man rose and made his way in the direction of the dining car. Benedict, thinking this to be a good plan, followed him and the girl, giving Benedict a crimson-lipped smile, said, "Do you mind if I join you?"

"Not at all," he answered, and stood aside to let her lead the way, his nostrils assailed by a great whiff of *Soir de Paris* as she passed him. He heard the cowpat woman saying, "She wears Soirdee, that one," as if it were some form of indictment.

The dining car was quarter-full, the main bulk of passengers getting on the train at Plymouth. The foreigner rose to his feet and bowed as Benedict entered with the blonde, who was pouting prettily.

"Please do join me," he said,

"It would be my pleasure," answered the girl immediately, her hoity-toity pronunciation shrill on Benedict's ears. She held out a hand with short, stubby vermillion nails. "I'm Boo Leighton. May I know your name?"

He bowed again. "I am Alexei Nikoschenkin. I have been in Sidmouth visiting my aunt Helena." He turned to Benedict. "And you are?"

Benedict raised his hat, wishing it was as smart as the other man's, and said, "Benedict Delamare. I take it you are of Russian origin, sir?"

"That is correct. My parents left everything behind when the revolution broke out. We just walked out of St. Petersburg. I can remember it vividly. I was seventeen and I was holding my two sisters by their hands. My mother pushed the pram in which was my younger brother. My father had on an old coat, my mother had got herself up like a cleaning woman, and I had to abandon my cadet's uniform and wear something resembling a sack. It was, in its way, quite amusing."

Boo looked at him, limpid-eyed. "But weren't you horribly frightened?" She had a very slight lisp.

"Yes. But in a way triumphant. My mother and my sisters had stitched all the family jewels into their corsets and nobody checked them. So we walked out quite wealthy, as it were."

"Tho exciting."

Benedict said, "I say, isn't Helena of Sidmouth a Grand Duchess?"

"Quite right. She is."

"But if she's your aunt, you must be..."

"Yes, my family is related to the late Tsar."

"Are you a prince?" asked Boo, eyes little circles of wonderment.

"Yes," Alexei answered carelessly. "Now what would you like to drink?"

It became obvious to Benedict that Boo was making a serious play for the Russian aristocrat, who remained polite but sublimely indifferent. Undeterred, she gazed at him constantly, fluttered her lashes, and laughed at everything remotely amusing that he said. But when the train pulled in at Plymouth and a set of five friends, clearly Londoners who had been enjoying a weekend jolly in Devon got in, she was clearly put into the shade.

There were three girls, two of them exquisite, with short sleek haircuts, fabulous clothes and the very latest in smart talk. The third was more withdrawn, a cloche hat pulled tightly round her face, which was small and vulnerable, dominated by an enormous pair of dark gentian-coloured eyes. With the three girls were two young men, dressed to the inch, superbly elegant but somewhat loud of voice and manner. One, dark and handsome with an elegant thin moustache, looked like an actor in the movies. The other, blonder and blander, was clearly the heir to some enormous estate or a title – or perhaps both.

Prince Alexei, never backward in such matters, rose to his feet and introduced himself with a great deal of Russian courtesy and charm. Benedict found himself having to change places as the smart crowd swarmed to join their new acquaintance. He ended up once more sitting next to Boo, who had changed her mind and tactics, and was now flirting voraciously with the man with the moustache, who turned out to be the Hon. Simon Cassell-Heggs, an actor in repertory theatre. Opposite Benedict at the dining car table was the girl with the cloche hat, who did not join the conversation but gazed out of the window at the rolling Devon countryside.

Benedict cleared his throat. "Would you like something to drink, Miss er...?"

She looked at him and he was consumed by her great eyes.

"Are you going to have one?"

"Yes, why not." He suddenly felt young and carefree and somehow – and this feeling he could not explain – powerful. "What would you like?"

"A Mermaid's Kiss – but I don't suppose they'll have the ingredients on the train."

He grinned. "Are you psychic?"

"I don't think so. Why?"

"Because that's where I come from. Mermaid Island."

"You don't mean that place near Maybury-on-Sea?" Benedict nodded. "I lived in Devon when I was a small girl. My parents used to take me on the beach nearby. I used to stare across at the island and think how remote it was; a mysterious and lonely situation."

"Yes, it is in its way. But it was glorious growing up there. Trouble was my father had me educated at home so I'm not terrible good at the social necessities."

"I think you're very good," answered the girl, smiling at him and giving him her remarkable look. She held out her hand. "I'm Sybella Grey. And I could not possible accept a drink from someone I do not know."

But she was teasing him, laughing silently up at him. Benedict imitated Alexei and bowed low. "Benedict Delamare," he said.

And so the journey to London, a place that Benedict had visited only twice before, passed very pleasantly. Then came the excitement of arriving beneath the great arched roof of Paddington Station, the smoke from the incoming train caught beneath its struts and billowing along the platform, shrouding the passengers in a tantalising mist.

The new crowd of friends were busy shouting at one another and exchanging cards. Cries of, "We must meet again soon," and "It's been so lovely chatting, Prince

Alexei," rose above the general melee, while Benedict, somewhat sadly, found a porter and handed Miss Sybella Grey into a taxi.

"I'm in London for a week or so. I would really like to see you again. Could you spare the time, do you think?"

"Yes I will," said Miss Grey. She leant forward and pressed a card into Benedict's hand. He glanced at it and saw to his surprise that it was from The Lady magazine.

"Are you the editor?" he asked, impressed.

She laughed gently. "Nothing so grand. I work in the Fashion department."

The taxi driver coughed meaningfully and Benedict said, "I'm staying with a friend, Titus Oates. He lives in Belgravia. But if you like I could come to your offices and take you out to dinner."

Sybella leant forward. "Ring me." Then she smiled and was gone into the night.

Alexei approached. "Did I hear you say you were staying with a friend in Belgravia? Because I'm going there myself to visit Nikki von Frankenburg. Shall we share a cab?"

Benedict nodded and felt that already he had come a long way from Mermaid Island, not just in distance but in experience as well. To arrive in London with a Russian prince, particularly one who was related to the late Tsar, was making an entrance indeed. He was certain that at long last he was beginning to taste life.

Three days later he had tasted it indeed. He had got drunk, boozed out of his brain with a selection of various incredibly named cocktails, among which had been the exotic Mermaid's Kiss. He had spent an entire night with a madly modern miss, name of Bunny, who had taught him everything she knew – and that was plenty – about sexual intercourse. He had at long last lost his hated virginity, smoked vast quantities of cigarettes and gone down to breakfast stark naked except for a silk dressing gown.

None of these sinful pastimes would have been possible had it not been for the fact that Titus's parents were away killing innocent birds. As most of the staff had gone with them this left behind a skeleton crew who were quite willing to turn a blind eye to the goings-on in exchange for an expensive tip from the outrageous guests.

And what a bunch they were. A sprinkling of young men who appeared to be sharply divided between the athletic and the aesthetic. Thin little girls with drooping shoulders, upper-class voices and long cigarette holders. Other bolder, brighter females who seemed determined to keep up with the boys and who slept with all the men who wanted them, in turn. A good time was being had by all except perhaps Benedict who, in his more sober moments, missed the quiet of Mermaid Island and the lovely feeling of oneness that he had when swimming in the Mermaid's Pool.

After a few days of debauchery, Titus suddenly got bored, as was common with most vapid young people of the era, always looking for a new sensation in times of frenetic excitement and frantic fun.

"Let's motor down to my people's country place. It's near Ascot. We can take along that girl you rather liked," he announced one breakfast time.

"Who do you mean?" asked Benedict casually, just a shade too nonchalantly to deceive his friend's sharp ears.

"The girl you met on the train. One of Cynthia Podmore's sharp set."

"Oh you mean Sybella Grey. She's not in the set really. She works."

"So we'll go at the weekend. When she's free. Go on, ring her up."

And he handed Benedict the telephone receiver.

Sybella sounded pleased to hear from him and agreed quite happily to be ready on the steps of Montague Mansions in Kensington at 10 o'clock.

"Not a bad address," said Cynthia Podmore, the dark girl who had joined the party on the train at Plymouth and who was currently sitting in the back of the Peugeot 175 Torpedo Sport that Titus drove like a maniac.

"And she's quite a looker," answered Titus, surveying the elegantly dressed young woman who stood waiting for them, wearing quite the latest line in hats.

Benedict didn't say anything but he felt the steady rhythm of his heart increase and his palms grow unattractively moist. From nowhere came a brief vision of himself and Sybella swimming together, united in a beautiful sea – and then it faded. But not before Benedict had seen another being in the day dream, dim and distant, watching them, something surreal. It had scared him rather and he came back to reality breathing rapidly.

"Hello again," said Sybella, climbing into the back. "Are you all right? You look a bit pale."

"No, absolutely fine, thanks. How have you been?"

"Working hard. Really looking forward to this weekend."

Cynthia gave her a long cool stare. "How on earth do you manage to fit work in? I'm just so busy with my social engagements I simply wouldn't have the time."

Sitting in the front seat, trying not to think too much about Titus's driving, Benedict felt himself getting irritated on Sybella's behalf.

"I very much admire women with aim and ambition. Much better than wandering from party to party in my opinion."

"Do *you* work at anything, Benedict?" Cynthia asked pointedly.

He was just about to answer when Titus shouted, "I say, there go Alexei and Nikki von Frankenberg in a Mercedes sports. I'll bet that was bought in Berlin." He honked the klaxon furiously. "Want a race?" he bellowed at the other car. Frankenberg, in goggles and leather cap, stuck his thumb up and accelerated.

"Oh God," said Cynthia, and clutched Sybella for support.

Despite the breakneck speed in which the journey was accomplished the country home of the Hon. Gerald Oates and Lady Freda Oates, born the daughter of some obscure Earl or other, was spectacular indeed. An imposing Queen Anne mansion, with a quarter of a mile drive and impressive trees, also had a glorious lake behind it, which immediately caught Benedict's eye as he stood for a moment, regaining his breath.

"Wonderful," said Sybella's voice beside him.

He turned to her. "You mean the house or the lake?"

"Both really. But the lake is very beautiful. I'd like to swim it."

Benedict looked at Sybella in surprise. "I didn't realise you swam."

She laughed. "Everybody can swim – well, most people anyway. But I'm a member of a swimming club for young ladies. Have been since I left school. As for you – you're famous."

"Am I?" he asked, genuinely surprised.

"Yes. That little incident you were involved in recently. The one when you swam from Mermaid Island to the mainland. It was picked up by the local paper, you know."

"I didn't realise."

"My grandfather sent me a cutting. He knew how interested I was as a child. I always thought the place was so mysterious. I used to ask him about it when I stayed with them."

Benedict laughed. "You must come and visit us. My father would love to meet you. And I can show you round and we can swim in the Mermaid's Pool."

Sybella regarded him, round-eyed. "What a lovely name. What is it exactly?"

"Well, it's a natural inlet of the sea but my father, years ago, converted it into a swimming pool. The entrance to it is guarded by two large rocks and the sea comes in between them – quite violently sometimes."

"Do you really mean that I can come and see you? Or are you just being polite?"

"Sybella, I would like you to visit the island more than anything else in the world." Thinking that that sounded a bit intense, Benedict added, "It would be absolutely spiffing."

"Top hole," Sybella replied. Was there just the faintest hint of mockery in her voice?

Titus was the most generous of hosts and the party filled up. Zuzu Laney, current star of *Moonlit Autumn*, the smash hit West End musical, arrived accompanied by Joshua Mandalay, a black jazz singer. Benedict thought this frightfully outre but was glad to be included with such a fast set. The gathering was completed by Freya Darke, an ageless woman who travelled extensively and then wrote books about it. She was quite the most exotic creature that Benedict had ever set eyes on.

Despite the heavy drinking of the night before and the sniffing of cocaine – a pastime in which certain guests indulged but which Benedict declined – he was up early the next morning and headed purposefully for the lake, only to see that somebody was there before him. A small figure splashed and played in the shallows which, on drawing nearer, Benedict recognised as that of Sybella Grey.

"I was waiting for you," she called out as he approached.

Benedict suddenly felt very conscious of the fact that his new bathing costume – complete with top and shoulder straps, very like the female equivalent – showed off his body parts. Before, in the all-male household on Mermaid Island, the thought had not occurred to him. But now with Sybella, treading water and smiling at him, he suddenly became conscious of it. To cover his confusion, he sprinted forward and ran into the chilly shallows. Sybella's smile deepened.

"Race you to the island," she said.

Benedict stared at her. "But that's a long way out."

It was. The island – little more than a mound rising from the water, a couple of sparse trees growing upon it – was a fair swim away, the lake itself being vast, a sheet of placid water with scarcely a ripple upon its surface. Sybella laughed.

"I told you I was a good swimmer," she said, and set off immediately with an absolutely splendid crawl.

As soon as the water got deeper Benedict did the same. His great affinity with the ocean and his lithe, muscular body carried him through the tranquil lake at speed and he reached the eyot and hauled himself out, waiting for Sybella to catch him up.

Leaning over, he gazed into the translucent shallows and then had the oddest optical illusion. It seemed to him that something was staring back at him, something that lived under the surface and was reaching up its arms to pull him in. Benedict bent forward, so real was the image, and then Sybella's arrival broke the surface and the vision was shattered.

"It's not fair," she said, but smiling as she spoke. "Wherever did you learn to swim like that? You went off like a rocket."

"I've won a few cups at home," he said, helping her out of the water.

She sat down beside him, her face lit by the sun, her hair tucked neatly inside her bathing cap. Benedict, overtaken by an irresistible urge, seized her, quite roughly, into his arms and gave her a full-blooded kiss, which she returned with an obvious delight.

"Sorry," he said, releasing her but still holding her close. "I've been wanting to do that for rather a long time. Ever since I first met you, in fact."

"Have you indeed? I would never have guessed."

"I am good at concealing my feelings."

Sybella laughed uproariously. "Benedict Delamare, you are a simply rotten liar. You've been giving me the glad eye – as they say – ever since we first met. Now tell me the truth."

"Do you really want me to?"

"Yes."

"Then I fancied you – to use common parlance – when I first saw you on the train. It was those wonderful eyes of yours that stole my heart away."

Sybella snuggled closer to him. "You've a lovely way with words, young fellow."

"Not so much of that. I'm twenty."

"Is that all?"

"How old are you?"

"Now that would be telling."

Benedict kissed her again, then said, "I want to make love to you. Properly, I mean."

"I've never heard of proper lovemaking. I thought it was very improper."

"Oh Sybella, stop playing games with me."

She withdrew from him slightly and gave him a look from her unusual eyes. "Benedict, I do not think you are very experienced in these matters. So can we leave that part out until we know one another a little better."

"Of course we can. But promise me something."

"What's that?"

"That you won't let anyone else love you like I do."

She gave him a slow and gorgeous smile. "Oh no. I think we were born for one another."

And with that she slid down the bank and into the water, and swam away. Benedict followed her, his heart beating fast, but as he entered the lake he felt something pull at his legs. He looked down but could see nothing, yet there was something there, tugging at him, not wanting to let go. Whatever it was, he gave it an impatient kick and broke free, then swam so fast that he passed Sybella in midstream and stood waiting for her return, towelling down on the shore and grinning at her arrival, out of breath and beautiful.

But somewhat later, relaxing in a hot bath and thinking about her, his pleasant mood was broken by a loud knock on the bathroom door and Titus's voice calling urgently, "Benedict, are you in there? There's someone on the phone for you."

"I'm in the bath. Who is it, do you know?"

"It's someone called Lennie. He's asking for you."

Suddenly there was a cold stone in Benedict's stomach and he shouted, "Can you tell him I'll be down in a minute."

He heard Titus's retreating footsteps as he got out, reached for a towel and then thrust on a dressing gown. Clad only in that, Benedict descended the stairs on the double.

"Hello, is that you Jock? What's the trouble? It's not Papa is it?"

"Yes, sir, it is. The master had a stroke yesterday and today he's not any better. He's asking for you, sir."

Benedict gulped, hardly able to get his voice out. "Tell him I'm coming. I'll get the next train. I'll phone when I've checked the time table. Can you meet me at Plymouth in the car?"

"Of course I can. Now don't you worry, Mater B. Everything is going to be all right."

But all the way in the train from Aylesbury to Marylebone Benedict felt as if a leaden weight was sitting in his brain. Then during the taxi ride to Paddington and the frantic running to catch the Plymouth Express with two minutes to spare, it never left him. By the greatest good fortune he managed to get a window seat and then decided to go to the dining car to try to drown the wretched unhappiness which had invaded his entire system. Yet even three gins and tonic and half a bottle of wine could not bring about relaxation. Instead, Benedict found himself thinking about his life on the island and his closeted existence with Hugh. Yet, even though he had known little of childhood friends and the general companionship that boys have with others, he didn't regret a second of it.

His father had been the greatest companion he could have wished for. As for the island, it had been a constant source of amazement and beauty, even when the weather had been foul and the wind a veritable tempest. And there had been something else that was special about the place – the song it sang to him every night just when the sun was going down. What a sweet, wild sound; almost like a human voice, comforting him and loving him and calling to him. Sometimes the feelings it aroused in Benedict had been so strong that he had been almost tempted to jump off the cliffs and into the sea that rolled in a constant wave below. But Hugh had been in the house with hot tea and freshly cut sandwiches and homemade cake, and he had always resisted the urge and gone indoors.

Now, as the train finally steamed into Portsmouth station, Benedict grabbed his luggage, crammed on his hat, and descended, making his way out via the booking hall. There was no sign of Jock but he spotted the car and saw that it was being driven by Soames, the gardener.

"Hello Soames. Where's Lennie?" Then a thought occurred and he added, "Is my father...?"

"He's as well as can be expected, Master Benedict. There's been no change."

"What did the doctor say?"

"That he might recover, slowly and in time."

"Oh dear God. My poor Papa. Drive as quickly as you can, Soames, there's a good chap."

They went as fast as the old motor and the even older driver would allow, but when they got to Maybury-on-Sea it was to discover that there was no sign of the sea tractor.

"Where the hell is it?" Benedict asked, fuming.

"I don't know, sir. I asked it to stand by."

"Well, it hasn't. Soames, when it comes take my luggage on board. I'm going to swim for it."

"But you can't, sir. You know how cross the Master was last time you did so."

"Well I won't tell him so he'll never know. And I know you'll be discreet."

And with that, despite the fact there were several people remaining on the beach in the early evening sunshine, Benedict stripped off to his underpants and plunged into the ocean.

He didn't realise how much he had missed it until he felt its cold caress upon his body. The lake water had been pallid in comparison. What Benedict adored above all else was the burr of salt upon his skin, the feeling of being at one with the sea. As he swam towards the island, he saw the ocean go pink, reflecting the final sunburst, and heard – all around him – that strange sweet melancholy song which always arose at this time of day. Benedict had the fanciful idea that the sea was welcoming him home.

He arrived at the small sandy beach beneath the steep path leading up to the house. Hugh had had proper wooden steps and a handrail put in when Millie had joined the household, and now Benedict shot up them, dripping as he went. But first, before he saw his father, he went into th kitchen and towelled himself dry and sent a servant to collect some clothes from his bedroom. Only then did he go into the library to see Hugh. Jock was with him.

"He ought really to be in bed, you know. But he knew you were coming and insisted that he be brought down here."

"How did you know that? He couldn't have told you."

"He just made a lot of noise and I guessed."

Benedict shook his head. "When did the stroke happen?"

"One night there was another bad storm, the sea was really rough and the spray from the waves was beating on the windows, so you can imagine the size of the swell. Anyway, I was asleep in my quarters but I was woken by the sound of a terrible scream. I knew it was the Master so I bolted downstairs. He was sitting up in bed pointing at the window, a look of sheer terror on his face. He managed to say a word or two and then he had a stroke."

"What frightened him, do you know?"

"I looked out but there was nothing there. I can only presume that a monstrous wave broke against the cliffs and must have hit the window with a smack. Your father probably woke up and thought somebody was trying to get in."

Benedict nodded but was not assured because, frankly, he did not believe the story. Hugh was an old soldier and members of that breed did not take fright easily. And what human being could have climbed up to a first-floor window on a remote island to give the Major such a stroke-inducing shock? Or, indeed, be thrown high on the crest of a wave? It did not ring true to him at all. But what other explanation could there possibly be? Yet it was a puzzle he could not work out and in the prevailing circumstances he decided was best to overlook.

But, that aside, Benedict could not have been a better son or companion in the days that lay ahead. He spent every waking hour at Hugh's side, talking to him, reading aloud, doing a crossword and pretending that his father had given him most of the answers. He even held the chamber pot when the Major had to relieve himself. His devotion was second to none. Only once did he leave the invalid's side and go to Maybury-on-Sea and that was to see the doctor and discuss the prognosis.

Much to his surprise the old medic was still in practice, though these days with very few patients. So after only a few minutes wait, Benedict was called through. Dr. Ellsworth rose from his chair and held out his hand.

"My dear boy, how very nice to see you."

"And you, sir. But in rather tragic circumstances I fear."

"Terrible indeed. Poor old Hugh. What a damn shame."

"Is there any hope of him making a recovery?"

"It is not unknown, of course. But at the Major's age I should think the chances are pretty remote. Though there will be some improvement as long as he has stimulation and company."

"I can assure you that I will do my absolute best regarding that, sir."

"I know, my boy. You are the sort of son that every father wants. But anyway, how are you? How are your legs these days?"

Benedict looked at him in some surprise. "They're absolutely fine. Why do you ask?"

"Because of the little problem you had when you were born."

"Oh that. I'd absolutely forgotten about it. They were joined together in some sort of skin, weren't they?"

"Yes. A type of transparent membrane."

"Did you remove it Dr. Ellsworth?"

"No, I had a young junior working with me at the time. A Dr. Nixson. He was a very competent young man – but very strange."

"Oh? In what way?"

"Well, it was obvious that I needed an assistant but I hadn't got around to advertising the fact. I was on the point of doing so when one evening Dr. Nixson turned up and said he was newly qualified and was looking for a post. To cut the story short, I took him on and it was he who offered to move into your house and deliver the baby."

"Why was that? Was my mother in a frail condition?"

Dr. Ellsworth realised at that moment that Benedict had been told nothing of his mother's dementia and was asking in complete ignorance.

"Somewhat frail, yes," he answered. "Anyway, Dr Nixson delivered you and did the operation on your legs. All beautifully as it worked out. But now comes the mystery."

"Yes?"

"He never came back here. He just disappeared. To make it even odder, he wasn't even seen leaving Mermaid Island. Mary Ann, who was your mother's maid servant, watched the sand appear and waited for him to walk across. But he never did apparently. Or so she told me when we happened to meet one day in Maybury. I think she had a bit of a crush on him and that was why she stood at the window for so long. A strange twist to the story don't you reckon?"

Benedict was silent for a few moments, then said, "But you don't believe he drowned, do you?"

"I don't see how that would have been possible. After all, it was daylight and there was the gardener and boy around."

"Perhaps he swam."

"Now we're entering the realms of fantasy," Dr Ellsworth replied, chuckling.

"Indeed," Benedict answered, and smiled a secretive smile.

Nevertheless, the story of the doctor who vanished stuck in his mind, so much so that when he got home he consulted a book of surnames. This didn't get him very far but an Encyclopaedia did. Though what to make of it bewildered him utterly.

Nix is the name given in High German to a water sprite. Its roots are unknown because it probably originated amongst the tales delivered orally. The plural is Nixie. In Norwegian folklore the Nix is represented as a man performing on a violin whom, it is said, was a particularly good dancer. The Nix are regarded as malevolent, luring people to their death by singing and playing music to their victims. But they were also capable of taking human form and marrying mortals.

Benedict smiled. To think that the disappearing doctor had been the son of a Nix was plainly ridiculous – and yet. But his mind was taken off such amusing pleasantries by rapid deterioration in Hugh's condition.

During the night the Major suffered another stroke and the household was woken by the nurse who was constantly at his side throughout the hours of darkness. Benedict rushed in in his pyjamas and helped her cope with all the nasty little necessities that looking after a helpless man involved. After that, he and Jock Lennie, propped the old veteran up and Benedict, leaving him just for a moment, threw on some trousers and a sweater then hurried back to Hugh's side. He knew, just from the look – or rather lack of it – on his father's face, that this was his final night. Benedict also knew that whatever happened he must not shed a tear until the Major had left this life. That he must be the strength, the living force, to which the dying man could cling until he breathed his final sigh.

Dawn came up in the east and the sea, at one with the scene being played out behind the great curved windows, was flat as an ice rink, suffused with the shade of glorious anemones. Jock drew back the curtains and stood motionless, gazing out on that tremendous vista. Benedict saw nothing of it, his arms round the shadow man who had taken his father's place, thinking only of the vastness of that mighty expanse of water, flowing on and on, unpitying and unloving and quite regardless of the sufferings of mankind, obeying only the orders of its mistress, the Moon. Nobody spoke and the silence was almost audible and then, quite strangely, there rose up from outside that strange song the wind made, which Benedict had heard so many times before.

"The island is singing his requiem," said Jock quietly.

And as his manservant uttered those words Hugh turned his eyes to look at his son, gave a crooked smile and let out a final breath. Benedict became aware of something leaving his father's body. It was an odd sensation because there was really nothing to see but for all that he knew that Hugh had departed from them. With a soul-raking shudder Benedict laid his father back on the bed, then he turned to Jock and went to stand beside him, weeping silently, listening to the call of the sea.

Benedict had wanted to bury Hugh on the island but Jock had persuaded him otherwise.

"What happens if you leave the place and there's nobody left to tend the grave? Surely the Major should be laid to rest where people can visit. I have a fancy that he would like to be put down beside your mother, Benedict."

So, despite the many assurances that he would never quit Mermaid Island, the undertakers – black hatted and grim faced – came across on the sea tractor and left again with the coffin, while Benedict arranged for cards to be sent to the regiment and relatives telling them that the funeral would take place in St. Mary's Church, Winterbourne Abbas, in the county of Dorset.

A week later and the solemn business was over. Yet it had not been as depressing as he had feared. In spite of Benedict's concern about the distance, several of those still alive came from the old army brigade and, surprisingly, the sons of those who had died, out of respect for his late father. And it was pleasant to see his mother's grave again and to be able to lay flowers on it. But there was one small mystery that no-one, including Jock, had any explanation for. Carved on her headstone, by whom or when nobody knew, was a small figure of a merman. It was quite distinct, showing a handsome bare-chested man – with long hair and a beard – having human genitalia beneath which grew a long curving fish's tail. Benedict stared at it

He could not remember on his somewhat infrequent visits to his mother's grave, ever having seen it before.

"Jock, do you remember ever seeing that small carved figure before?" Benedict knelt down and pointed to it.

Lennie peered. "No, I don't. Who could have done that? Surely not your father."

"It must have been. I wonder why."

But Jock, thinking back to all that he had heard and seen, the story of Millie's mother being pulled into the Rhine, and the way in which he had found Millie on the night of the great storm, sitting so pale and so naked, in a place which he had already searched, and struck so very, very dumb. Facts which must be kept from Benedict at all costs, said, "It's probably part of her coat of arms."

"I didn't know she had one."

"No, neither did I. But your father must have known and probably added it to the stone. Don't worry your head about it anymore."

"No, I won't," Benedict answered – but he did.

He was now, under the terms of Hugh's will, master of Mermaid Island and owner of the house and its entire contents. Yet the fact brought him no particular joy. Without a career, without anything to occupy his time, Benedict felt bored to distraction. He took to going to the mainland on pleasure trips but they brought him little satisfaction. Just to add to his general lassitude, he missed Hugh's company like a cut from a knife, realising, perhaps for the first time, just how deep had been there love for one another. It was Jock, coming to see Benedict, as the young man climbed out of the Mermiad's Pool, dripping water, who made the suggestion that was to change everything for ever more.

"Why don't you go and see your friend Titus, Benedict? A trip to London would do you the world of good. You're moping down here and I know that the Major would not approve of that."

"You're right, my old friend. I *am* pretty fed up. This has become a house of shadows lately."

"Then leave it awhile. Go to town and see what's going on. Mix with people your own age."

So that night Benedict phoned Sybella Grey, followed by another call to Titus. He had been in touch with them both since Hugh's death, keeping them up-to-date with his somewhat miserable self. And though they had expressed their sorrow and been polite, neither of them had offered to come and see him, which had depressed Benedict a great deal, particularly in the case of Sybella. Now, though, Titus was full of beans.

"Benedict, my dear fellow. How are you? Not still in the doldrums I trust. We've missed you, by Jove we have. Why don't you get the night train and come straight away?"

"Titus, I can't. But I can get a train tomorrow and be with you tomorrow night if that would be all right?"

"I'll say it would. The crowd are all off to Binky Folkestone's for a grand ball. Pack your tails."

"I haven't got any."

"Don't worry. You can wear my spare pair. See you tomorrow evening then. Bye the way, how's Sybella Grey?"

"I don't know. I haven't seen her."

"Oh pity. I'll ask her to join us if you like."

"Yes, I like very much."

"Jolly good. Bye."

And that was that. Everything had to be arranged at the last minute. Benedict realised as he packed that the sea had certainly offered up one of its greatest gifts on the day he had saved Titus Oates's young life. A belief echoed by Jock Lennie who drove Benedict to the station next day. Though his master was strangely quiet during the drive.

"What's the matter, sir? You seem lost in thought."

"Sorry."

"Now this is not like you. You're off to London and going to a grand ball. You should be feeling on top of the world."

"I'm remembering the dream I had last night. It's hanging over me rather."

"What was it?"

"Well, I was swimming in the Mermaid's Pool and heading out towards the rocks when suddenly my legs were gripped by something. And then there rose up out of the water this man. Swimming in front of me. A big handsome fellow with red hair on his head and chest. He was huge, Jock, twice my size. Anyway, he held his arms open for me and, d'you know, I wanted to go to him and be embraced. He looked – kindly."

"What happened?"

"I swam away from him. I rejected him. But I turned and watched him depart and I saw a huge tail, threshing in the water. And I knew he was angry with me. I should have gone with him."

"Come now, Benedict. It was only a dream. Don't upset yourself over it."

"But it was so real, Jock. I wonder if it was a premonition."

"That you're going to be eaten by a sea monster? Get away with you! You're twenty now and next year will be the big birthday. Get a hold on yourself, lad."

But secretly Jock felt worried. He was a Scot and knew the mysteries of the lochs and glens and things that go bump in the night. But his face remained impassive. What use would there be in telling Benedict the truth about his grandmother being pulled into the river and rescued some while later by fisherfolk? By the fact that he had found Millie stark naked on the night of the big storm, almost as if every stitch of clothing had been removed from her. No, the craggy-faced Jock Lennie would keep his thoughts – and fears – to himself, until the time came when he could leave this accursed little island behind him.

Benedict had shaken off the lingering effects of the dream by the time the train, issuing clouds of steam, pulled into the cavernous dome of Paddington Station. And he felt his spirits rising as he hailed a taxi and made his way towards Titus's splendid home. There he found his friend somewhat subdued.

"The Mater and Pater are here," he said in a lowered voice. "They've invited some girl they want to hitch me to. She's come for dinner."

Benedict pulled a face. "What is she like?"

"Bovine in the extreme. I thought you could deal with her."

"Thanks a lot! Are you sure I'm invited?"

"Positive. Mater was rather impressed when I said you owned an island."

Benedict pulled his rumpled dinner jacket from his luggage too late to have it pressed so decided that an air of nonchalance would have to be the order of the evening. He tied his bow tie somewhat crookedly and strolled down the stairs to meet Titus's formidable mother. She was not at all what he had expected. A tiny little creature with a warm smile greeted him and thanked him profusely for having saved her son's life all those years ago.

The would-be girlfriend, however, was as terrible as Titus had warned him. Plump, with projecting teeth that looked as if they could eat a bun at half a mile, she wore an awfully short skirt displaying somewhat large white thighs. Benedict felt terribly sorry for her and paid her quite a lot of dutiful attention, for which she was clearly grateful. On hearing that he owned Mermaid Island she went into raptures.

"Daddy told me the most incredible story about an island off the coast of Devon. Apparently he and a friend rowed out to it because they thought they could see a girl stranded there. She was standing on the top near some kind of hut..."

Benedict felt a shiver run down his spine as he wondered whether she could be referring to his home.

". . . and waving like mad. Anyway, they were drawing close when the sea turned horribly rough and something rose out of the water and frightened them off."

"What do you mean exactly?"

"Well Papa said it was a merman, though his friend said it was just someone swimming with no clothes on." She blushed violently.

"Did the man have a tail?"

"Pa thought so but his friend didn't see it."

"Gracious," said Lady Freda, Titus's far from formidable mother. "What happened?"

"They rowed away fast."

"But what about the stranded girl?"

"They told the coastguard but he said that there wasn't anyone on the island. The guards searched it once after a lot of people reported seeing her and there was nobody there at all. That it was an optical illusion."

"Sounds like your place, Benedict," said Titus.

"No, I don't think so," he answered. But inside he had a dreadful feeling that it was.

Binky Folkestone's grand ball – or rather that given by Earl and Countess Folkestone – turned out to be very grand indeed, made all the more so by the presence of Miss Sybella Grey. Benedict thought she looked enchanting, wearing a beautiful floaty dress in shades of lilac and sea green accompanied by a matching turban which became her enormously.

"Hello again," she said. "I was hoping that you might be here."

"I very nearly wasn't," Benedict answered. "In fact I wouldn't be but for a phone call I made to Titus."

"I know about that," she said mysteriously. "Shall we dance? It's the Tango."

"I can't think of anything I'd enjoy more."

And it was a thrill to take her into his arms and smell the wonderful perfume that seemed to exude from her entire being. Gazing into her enchanting eyes, Benedict felt that he was in heaven. The rhythm of the tango enhanced his mood and he relaxed into a sensual dream from which he awoke abruptly as the music came to an end.

The evening's entertainment was provided by Zuzu Laney, who had finished her run in the musical and was these days hanging round the film studios. There was no sign of her erstwhile boyfriend – the black Joshua

Mandalay – and she now had a vacuous-looking young man in tow. On further enquiries Benedict learned that he was a marquis and the heir to some enormous dukedom. Having had one dance with Zuzu, the Turkey Trot – which he gamely struggled through – Benedict decided that this was an entirely different world to the one in which he had been brought up. Yet even at the height of his enormous pleasure in the glittering company, part of him could not forget the splendid solitude of Mermaid Island.

The idea of giving a party came to him as he held Sybella in a loving embrace while they danced the last waltz. It was four o'clock in the morning, the Earl and Countess had retired, and breakfast was to be served at five.

"You are so beautiful," he said as they finally drew apart.

She held him at arm's length. "I'm too old for you."

"How old is that?"

"Did I not tell you? Two or three hundred years. I've forgotten actually."

"Oh Sybella, don't mess around. I'm serious."

"So am I," she said, then she laughed her delicious laugh and Benedict knew that one day he would be with her for ever.

Invitations for the Island Party – as he named it – were sent off in due course. And acceptances came in by the shoal. It seemed that everyone wanted the experience of partying on a privately owned island off the coast of Devon, particularly one that could only be reached by sea tractor. Indeed, so many people replied in the affirmative that Benedict was forced to take every bedroom in The Grand Hotel, Maybury-on-Sea, to accommodate them all.

He also arranged to give up his bedroom to Sybella and sleep in the smaller guest room opposite – and perhaps creep across in the darkness of night and ask if he could make love to her.

Of course entertaining on such a level meant taking on extra catering staff, plus waiters and general dogsbodies. The sea tractor went back and forth and Benedict was exceedingly grateful that the sea remained calm enough for it to travel like a shuttle service. Finally came the afternoon when the guests poured off the train, lighting up the station with their expensive clothes, their risqué behaviour and their cultivated speech. And later, after being checked in at The Grand Hotel, arrayed in their svelte dresses, feathered headbands, wafting great delicious perfumes into the evening air, accompanied by louche extravagant males and idle, wilting youths, the company – thirty in number – took their turn in being ferried to the mysterious island.

There they found Benedict, nervous and feeling somewhat overpowered but rising gallantly to the occasion, waiting to meet them, impeccably dressed and determined to play the role of host to its maximum. He was never more relieved than when Sybella, gorgeous in drifting chiffon, stepped down the white stairs, and plonked a kiss on his cheek.

"Hello, my dear," she said, and gave him the most wonderful smile.

Benedict gazed at her, thinking that her lovely eyes looked almost purple in the afternoon light. But she was whisked away by Binky Folkestone who seemed to have taken an enormous fancy to her and Benedict was left to be charming and splendid to everyone else and explain that the dancing would be tomorrow and tonight would just be drinks and, perhaps, a swim for those who fancied it.

"But dahling," said Zuzu Laney, who had put aside the film studios – where she had been given a small part in *Bulldog Drummond's Third Round*, starring Jack Buchanan – for the weekend, "we haven't got swimming costumes."

"No," said the forgettable young man she was with, "but we could bathe in the altogether. Hahaha." And he brayed like a donkey.

"I've taken the liberty," announced Benedict, "of sending for some swimming gear from Selfridges. I hope you'll accept it as a present from me."

There was a loud cheer and then the party mood got into full swing and the guests, spilling out onto the lawn, admired the island and the view and the house, and life in general. It was about two hours later that the first of them made their way – some with more difficulty than others – down the steep wooden staircase to the Mermaid's Pool. Then there were shouts of laughter as some discreetly changed into bathing costumes while others – particularly those whose naked selves revealed intriguing glamour – did it all in public, laughing and quipping all the while.

Benedict, who had changed in the house, went down the steps in the midst of a group of laughing people, terribly aware that close behind him came Sybella on the arm of Titus Oates. Zuzu, who looked positively ravishing in the nude, insisted on swimming stark naked, shouting out loudly that the water was cold. At this, several young men dived in and tried to catch her, and there were squeals of sexually heightened horseplay. Other guests, both male and female, pretended not to notice and lounged round in the many deckchairs, while several of the girls sat on the decking edge and dangled their feet in the water.

Sybella, in Benedict's view the most ravishing woman present, turned to look at him and gave him a cheeky grin. He could not help but notice that her eyes were enormous, deep purple in colour, dominating her face. She gave him a wink and said, "Do you remember the lake?"

"Of course I do. How could I forget?"

"What's all this?" asked Titus.

"We had a swimming race in your lake, early one morning."

"And who won?"

"I did," said Benedict, giving Sybella a sheepish smile.

"Yes, he won. But now I'm going to challenge you again, my dear friend. First to reach the far rocks shall be the ultimate victor."

And with that she raced down the remainder of the steps, sprinted towards the Pool and dived in, causing Zuzu to give a shriek of alarm.

"Go on Benedict. You're not going to take that lying down, are you?"

"No, I'm not." And jumping the remaining stairs, he dived in after her.

Sybella was swimming strongly with a powerful crawl, her strength quite amazing for a slip of a girl. Benedict followed her at great speed, watching the top of her head with its purple cap, stark against the azure of the ocean. And then it vanished. Quite suddenly. One minute she was there, the next she was not.

"Oh my God," he exclaimed, and doubled his stroke.

And then a white arm shot up from the middle of the wave that crashed between the two rocks.

"Sybella," he shouted, and swam towards it.

The current was upon him, he could feel it swirling round his legs, pulling him under. Then he saw her, floating and still, coming down in the midst of that great white froth. She was so limp that he knew she was dead. Another mighty wave was forming and Benedict braced himself to go with it. And then he realised that he was not alone.

A man was riding the crest, sitting on it, and singing the same weird song that Benedict had heard so many times before. A big, muscular fellow he was, with hair exactly the same shade as Benedict's and vast eyes the colour of vivid sapphires. His barrel chest was covered with red hair, his genitalia swung low and heavy, oh so heavy, in the sea, and beneath them he had a tail like a huge fish that flashed a million points of light.

Benedict gazed at him awestruck. His brain telling him that the merman was a figment of his imagination, his eyes telling him that he was not. The mighty creature came sliding down the wave and at that moment the body of Sybella floated into Benedict's arms. She was very pale but he saw that her lovely delicate lips were quivering.

Benedict stared back at his effete group of friends. One or two were swimming in his direction but he knew quite certainly that they would never reach him. Zuzu was standing on the side of the pool, her naked body reflecting the last rays of the dying sun. He felt that she seemed cheap and tawdry.

The merman was diving but as he went he cast a long deep look at Benedict, and in that moment the young man knew that those brilliant jewel eyes and his own were identical, that he was at last with his fellow creatures.

And then he felt a slight stir in his arms and heard Sybella's faint voice.

"Come to us, my darling."

He looked down at her and saw that her huge purple eyes had opened.

"But if I do I shall drown."

She gave a faint smile. "You will never drown, sweetheart. Just let me kiss you and you will be beyond all that."

Benedict gave one last look at the distant figures round the pool. They had given up searching for him and were climbing out to join the chattering crowd. They had turned their backs on him.

He bent his head and Sybella gave him a long deep kiss. And then they were plunging down into the emerald green depths lit by a zillion little diamonds which danced and flew around their heads when the wave crashed over the rocks at the far end of the Mermaid's Pool.

It was left to Jock Lennie to see the fast crowd leave for their various destinations, to dismiss the servants and spend one last night alone in the great house before he turned the final key in the lock and left it unattended until, at last, it crashed into the sea where it was lapped by the waters and vanished.

But still, or so they say in stories told by the folk who know those parts of Devon well, there come nights when a strange singing comes from the island and when the water is crystal clear you can see two figures – which many people have mistaken for dolphins – racing one another at the bows of a ship. The creepiest thing of all, perhaps happened to Julian Oates grandson of Benedict's friend who made a million pounds on the Stock Exchange and to whom he bore a stunning resemblance. He was having a late-night cigarette, sitting on his moored ocean-going yacht – a present from Grandpa – when a man suddenly climbed out of the sea and held on to the rails.

"Titus?" he said. "Is that you?"

Julian leapt from his seat, thinking the man must be drowning, but the next minute he had disappeared under the waves. And peering down into the moonlit water he saw that a girl had joined him and was beckoning him away. He watched them swim to an island, not far from which he had moored, and there they climbed onto the beach and lay sunning themselves in the moonlight. They stayed there until the sun tipped the horizon when they vanished from mortal sight. And in this way was the legend of Mermaid Island born, for so few people were left who knew the whole true story.

About the Author

Deryn Lake started to write stories at the age of five then graduated to novels but destroyed all her early work because, she says, it was hopeless. A chance meeting with one of the Getty family took her to Sutton Place and her first serious novel was born. Deryn was married to a journalist and writer, the late L. F. (Bill) Lampitt, has two grown-up children and four grandchildren, three boys and a girl. She has written thirty plus novels to date and now lives near the famous battlefield of 1066. She has one large cat and a life that is full of surprises.

Printed by Amazon Italia Logistica S.r.l.
Torrazza Piemonte (TO), Italy